The Accidentals

ALSO BY MINROSE GWIN

Promise

The Queen of Palmyra

Wishing for Snow

The Accidentals

A Novel

Minrose Gwin

An Imprint of HarperCollins*Publishers*

HarperCollins books may be purchased for educational, business, or sales promotional use. For information, please e-mail the Special Markets Department at SPsales@harpercollins.com.

FIRST HARPERLUXE EDITION

ISBN: 978-0-06-291235-0

HarperLuxe™ is a trademark of HarperCollins Publishers.

Library of Congress Cataloging-in-Publication Data is available upon request.

19 20 21 22 23 LSC 10 9 8 7 6 5 4 3 2 1

For Ruth

Accidental:

Adjective:
Happening by chance, undesignedly or unexpectedly; produced by accident: fortuitous
Present by chance: nonessential
—Oxford English Dictionary

Noun:
A bird found outside its normal geographic range, migration route, or season: vagrant
—Merriam-Webster Dictionary

Accidentals are the rarest of the rarities.
—A Field Guide to the Birds: Giving Field Marks of All Species Found East of the Rockies

The Accidentals

1

Olivia

Listen hard now, and you can tell what they're saying. This morning, the cardinal. *Sweetheart, sweetheart, sweetheart, sweet.* Then, two houses down, a mockingbird. *Redemption, redemption.*

The *sweetheart,* that's easy enough. Even now, in November, birds love sex and reproduction; it's all they think about. But *redemption?* What can redemption possibly mean to a bird? A stocked feeder in this cold drizzle? Some suet? You tell me.

Now, the shushes and tiptoes coming down the hall. The click of the front door when Holly takes the girls. Long after everyone's out of the house, the voices. Someone calling out. A child replying, *Stay, let me stay.* A dog barks, high-pitched, angry.

Cheer, cheer, cheer. I'm all ears, little wren.

When I open my eyes, they burn and sting. It's barely dawn outside, my head a full pitcher, the taste of burnt toast on my tongue. Why the hell can't Holly get any decent liquor in this house?

I don't want to be sick when I do it.

So I lie here flat on my back, waiting out Holly's rot-gut cherry bounce, my feet torn loose from the tangled sheet. *Whoopee, whoopee,* somebody sings. *Cheat, cheat, cheat.* The cardinal again. I don't have to ask him what he means.

Tick tock. Now the wren perches on my head, scratches, makes a nest in my hair. Wrens will make a nest just about anywhere. I quake like a leaf in a freezing wind, then burn down to ash, my nightgown, the last one left in the drawer, soaked through. Why so hot? It's November, for god's sake. Somebody needs to do the wash, open a window.

Who? Who?

When I wake up the second time, the headache is gone. It's just the nausea now, not the hangover. I'm used to the queasiness, have had it for weeks. I know the drill. Ginger ale and saltines in bed. Throw them up and brush teeth. More ginger ale and saltines, more upchucking, more brushing. Then I can have my tea, whoopee.

After that I can do it. After that I *will* do it.

When I went to the bank on Thursday and asked to cash out the savings, the manager came out with pursed lips and wanted to know where my husband, Holly McAlister Jr., was, why he hadn't come too. I didn't bat an eye. "Why, my poor husband's lying half dead in University Hospital up in Jackson," I sang out, quick as a chickadee. "He sent me to cash out the savings to pay for his treatments. My name's on the account too," I chirped. "I have every right."

I tried to keep the desperation out of my voice. My plan had taken weeks to hatch, and I was growing edgy. Time was of the essence. Just that morning, I'd gotten up from the bathtub to meet the dark circles around the nipples, the thickness at the middle. I was cutting it close.

I knew I could get by with the lie. Opelika was a little scrub-pine town where everybody knew everybody else's comings and goings; that's what I hated most about it. But Holly and I had come in under the radar when he got the job as bookkeeper with the lumber mill. We didn't fit. Not into the mill workers' world of shotgun houses with their paper-thin walls and slag-eyed children or in the rarified social circles of the doctors and lawyers who lived in brick houses with fake columns and ate Sunday buffet at the Best Western in Gulfport. Even when the girls came, first Grace, then June, the four of us stayed to ourselves. They didn't bring home schoolmates, probably because of me, and I didn't go out unless absolutely necessary. Holly must have had his friends at the mill, but he never talked about them.

Sometimes I drove through the Negro side of town just to feel at home. I loved the women's late summer marigolds and fall mums, the sheets flapping like great white egrets on the lines. At dusk, after the supper dishes were done, the women perched on front porch steps, laughing and telling stories. I wanted to stop the car and sit down with them and talk about the old days of the war, how in the City we worked side by side deep into the hot summer nights, black and white shoulder to shoulder, building the landing boats that would bring our boys home, how at break time the older ones would speak of their children and the younger ones their boyfriends, and color was a detail not a world.

Back then, I was running the main office at Higgins Boat Yard, handling everything like a drill sergeant, writing the checks, saying you come and you go, making it all work. I'd talked Mr. Higgins into hiring women and Negroes and even the old and crippled to work the assembly lines. Everybody, black and white, men and girls, old and young, got paid the same for the same work (I'd talked Higgins into that too). There were twenty-five thousand of us, spread across seven plants, the first in New Orleans to cross the color line. We worked around the clock to turn out the landing boats that would end up winning the war. Louisiana swamp boats. On the grounds where they were stored, the upside-down hulls stretched out in row upon row. At night under the stars and moon, they shone, like large animals asleep together, gathering strength for the task ahead.

But now it was the fall of 1957. The war seemed like a dream. And here I was, blown off course and plunked down in this shoe box of a house, two kids and a husband who sashayed out the front door every morning and back in it every night, day in and day out, like the world was their oyster.

When I drove by, the marigold women lowered their eyes, probably taking one look at me and seeing Trouble with a capital T, maybe thinking of that boy up in Money, shackled to a wagon wheel, beaten to a pulp just a couple of years ago for something silly he said to a woman who looked like me. Sometimes in my dreams I saw his face, more like a rotted pumpkin than an impish little boy with kestrel eyes.

I had no idea there was so much in the bank account. Apparently Holly had been squirreling it away while we pinched pennies, and for what? I ask you. We could have had ourselves some fun, maybe sent me up to Hattiesburg to finish out my degree at Southern or set us up in the Monteleone Hotel for Mardi Gras. How he'd saved $638.76 out of his paycheck I had no earthly idea. For a moment I thought maybe I'd misjudged him, maybe he was more interesting than I'd realized. Maybe he had a secret life, a mistress he bought perfumes and silk hose for. Oddly, the thought thrilled me.

On Friday morning, right after Holly left for work and the girls set out for school, I went out and sat down on the top step of our front porch to wait. I had packed a paper sack with everything they'd told me to pack, some pads and a belt, a change of clothes, the roll of cash that felt as warm and alive as a small animal in my palm. I crouched like a cat under the hummingbird feeder, keeping my head low, watching the street out of the corner of my eye. The birds were swooping in, fighting for the syrup, filling up for the long migration to a warmer place. Some had already left; their numbers dwindled every day.

After a while, a rusty pickup clattered up and stopped. The driver, a gaunt woman in a man's sweater, rolled down the window and looked hard at me. I came down the sidewalk and climbed in.

"Hello," I said.

She looked at me strangely as if I'd said something completely unexpected. The vertical lines in her face called to mind the veins of a large sycamore leaf. The truck coughed and sputtered and died. She cranked it back up and gunned it, smoke billowing from the rear end.

"You got the money?"

"Yes." I lifted the paper sack.

"I'll take it now."

I pulled out the roll of bills and handed it to her. She sat there slowly counting out the twenties, then put the roll between her legs and let out on the clutch.

We rode along in silence. The truck's engine was running ragged and the cab reeked of exhaust. After a few blocks, I began to shiver and quake. It started in my bottom, from the vibration, then traveled down to my knees, which began to knock together. I considered telling the woman to turn around, to take me home, but something about the way her hands clinched the steering wheel, the forward tilt of her head, kept me quiet.

We took a dirt road off Highway 90, turning inland, and continued on for what seemed like five or so miles, the truck pitching wildly when the tires caught a rut.

"I'll be home by three, you say?" I needed to be there before the girls got home. Then I could lie down and tell them I didn't feel well. That, at least, they were used to.

The woman took another turn onto a narrower road. "Before three."

The sugar maples that overlapped the road were orange and red. It was as if I were being driven through a tunnel of fire. My legs had taken on a life of their own, jumping about like oversized crickets. I felt a burning deep inside, low in my belly. Perhaps *it* was untangling itself, as eager to be gone as I was to let it go.

The woman glanced at my lively legs. "It ain't that bad," she said.

She took one last turn onto a dirt drive and through a stand of dark pines. Underneath them, the house, colorless as air, looked like a child's playhouse. With the window shades pulled all the way down, the filthy panes stared blindly. Taped in one of the front windows: "Chiro Treatments. Pane Free."

When I got out of the truck, my legs buckled. The ground felt rubbery.

The woman came around and took my elbow. "Don't go wasting folks' own good time now." She led me up through the waist-high weeds to the front door and we went in. I was expecting a waiting room, a neatly dressed receptionist behind a desk; but there was only a dark, dusty corridor with closed doors up and down. As we walked down the hall with its peeling wallpaper and filthy linoleum floor, I heard murmurs, then an exclamation of surprise. There was a stink of rancid bacon grease. I began to gag.

The woman opened the door to the third room on the right. I had imagined an examining table with stirrups but instead there was a regular bed and over it a contraption hanging from the ceiling, a stained piece of canvas with some belts. It looked jerry-rigged and oddly sexual. The unexpectedness of the device, its foreignness, sucked the breath from my chest. I'd left earth for another planet, never to return to the dear familiar. These people would kill me and steal my money. I would be buried out in the woods, under the pine needles, never to be found. Holly and the girls would think I'd just taken off, left them for another kind of life. I turned around, intent on heading out the door, when the woman told me to take off my underwear and lie down. She handed me a frayed sheet to put over my legs and said the doctor would be with me shortly.

After she left the room, I collapsed on the bed and put my head between my legs to keep from fainting. Should I run? I willed myself to think straight. I thought of real work, work you could see: those Louisiana swamp boats stretching out into the night, landing on the coast of Normandy, saving us all. The girls were growing up, now was my time to build something new. I picked up the sheet. Its ordinariness calmed me.

The canvas went around my legs and neck. The woman came back and got me situated. She tightened the contraption and it lifted me until I dangled like a fish caught in a net, my legs splayed.

Then a fat man in a stained white jacket came into the room. He gave me two pills that looked like aspirin, told me to think about something pleasant. So I imagined my future. Soon the girls would be able to take care of themselves. I'd go back and get my degree. Maybe I'd teach biology, spending weeks and weeks on birds. I'd explain lift and thrust—the mechanics of how a bird takes the air. We'd build nest boxes, study exotic species. In the summer, I'd take the girls to Paris, France. At the picture show I'd seen a woman in the French Resistance wearing a beret low over one eye as she ran down one dark street after another, carrying secret documents through the rain. I'd get myself one of those berets. I'd smoke long thin cigarettes from a mother-of-pearl holder.

The man pried me apart with something that looked like a pair of tongs for canning; then he brought out a rubber tube, impossibly long, and began to insert it. He turned it around and around as he pushed it in, higher and higher up. A grenade of pain gathered deep inside, then exploded. I screamed for him to stop and, finally, he did. Then he produced what appeared to be a bread knife and sawed away the rest of the tube and pushed it up too. He told me to get dressed, go home, and wait. On Sunday, he said, I must pull out the tube. Then, in a few hours, it would all be over. Prepare for bleeding, he said.

I had thought he would finish it, I thought by now it would be over. I started to cry. I said, "You mean I have to keep this thing inside me until *Sunday*?" By then he was out the door.

I bent double when the woman lowered me back down to the bed and took me out of the contraption. I checked my watch. It was 1:30. The woman rummaged around in my sack, came out with the pad and belt, hooked up the pad, and handed them to me along with my underwear.

On the way home my hips ached and my stomach lurched when we hit the ruts in the road. I bent over and banged my head on the dashboard. I was bleeding and cramping something terrible.

But there was a lifting too, as if I had suddenly grown feathers. I thought of myself as a hummingbird hatchling. Hummingbird babies are unlike other birds. They don't hop about on the ground when they leave the nest; they pitch themselves from the edge as if their nest is on fire, and take flight.

Last night, Saturday, I floated on air, hovering above myself in the bed. When Holly came in to see about me and saw the blood, I told him what I'd done. He began to cry. "It would have been a boy," he said. "I could have shown him things. I could have taught him to *do* things."

I told him he had two perfectly good children who followed him around like puppies. He could teach them whatever he wanted.

"They're girls," he said. "It's not the same." Then he walked over to me and grabbed both of my arms hard. How he wanted to hit me! "Is it done? What if you went to a real doctor instead of a slimy butcher? Can it be fixed?"

I fingered the knobs on the bedpost. "You can't put the rain back in the sky."

"Where'd you get the money?"

"Your secret savings," I said, "the one you've been hiding."

He squeezed my arms until I cried out, then dropped them and strode out of the room. I heard him go down into the basement and bring up the cherry bounce and put it on the kitchen counter. I heard him pull the cork. A chill swept through me. I began to shake, then pour sweat. The bed felt oily. There were rose blossoms on the sheets.

He brought the jar of cherry bounce into the bedroom and set it on the dresser. He'd already opened it and was carrying a half-empty glass. He downed it, poured another, downed it too. "Would you like to know what that money was for?" His voice had a different tone than I'd ever heard. Soft, with menace behind it, the purr of the cat before it pounces.

Then he told me about Paris, how he wanted it to be a nice trip with all the extras. "We would have gone in May," he said, "when everything is in bloom and the cafés set up their tables outside." He'd wanted to show me the street the French and American battalions had come down after they'd liberated the city and the Parisians had kissed their liberators, men on the cheeks, girls on the lips. The Champs-Élysées. Then he went to the closet and rummaged around and pulled out the beret. It was bright blue, not a color I'd have chosen. "I hope you enjoy wearing it in Opelika," he said. He threw it to the floor and ground it under his heel.

He wanted me to cry, he wanted me to say I was sorry. But I couldn't and I wasn't.

What's done is done. Now, finally, it's time to finish it. The man said just to give the tube a yank, like it was the cord to the closet light. There'd be cramps, he said, then the expulsion. I've been bleeding and cramping more than I'd thought possible, but all that will stop when I get rid of it.

I will feel my way. I will be a river opening to the sea, inevitable and sure.

Once, when I was a girl, my mother took me on a Greyhound bus to the ocean. Late that afternoon we stood out on the beach watching the sun go down. A dog ran in and out of the surf, a stick in its mouth. Pelicans skimmed the waves in perfect formation. My mother's hair blew up against her cheek, a piece snagged on her eyelash. She said, "There's a whole world out there, Olivia. There are places where people sit at tables in the street and eat and drink all day long. They sit under trees and the blossoms fall in their hair." She turned to me, her hair now blown back from her face, and I saw she was crying.

Whose? Whose? Whose? That's the dove.

Peace, peace, peace. That's my song.

2
June

The year my mother went and did what she did, I was ten and my sister, Grace McAlister, was twelve. We lived in a little clunker of a town in south Mississippi called Opelika, where my father, Holly McAlister, worked as an accountant at the local lumber mill.

I fault myself. I should have seen it, the disaster that was about to befall us. I can make excuses, I can say I was just a girl. But I should have been able to stop it. I should have tried to stop it. Over the course of my short life, I'd become a finely tuned gauge of my mother's many and varied moods. I could tell by the way she crunched her Rice Krispies in the morning what kind of day lay ahead. A toss of her head could make my heart leap in my throat. So that night at the traveling rendition of *Madame Butterfly,* when she flinched at the peculiar way the cherry blossoms fell, I knew that trouble lay coiled in the wings, ready to strike.

The blossoms were hard plastic so they came down hard, as if descending from some terrible calamity at a great height, hitting the gym floor with a splat and a clatter rather than gently troubling the air the way real cherry blossoms would have. When they started to fall, in clumps, not individually as they ought to have, my mother began to cry.

I should have comforted her, patted her hand. I should have told her to listen to the music and not worry about the stupid blossoms.

Instead, I told her to buck up. Just what kind of performance was she expecting from a flea-bag opera company that set up shop in a high school gym stinking of wet sneakers? And why in heaven's name had she dragged a defenseless ten-year-old with a tendency toward bronchitis out in a bone-chilling February rain to witness this shambles of a show, this disaster?

All of which made her cry harder.

I knew the answer to the second question. I was the last port in my mother's stormy life. Olivia LaMonde McAlister had no friends whatsoever. It's 1957, mind you, and here's a woman who doesn't go to sewing circles or potluck suppers. She doesn't belong to the DAR, Junior League, or Ladies' Hospital Auxiliary. She doesn't play bridge or shop for recreational pleasure or wear a girdle or eat egg and olive salad with her girl-friends at K & T Drugstore. She doesn't even take Christmas hams to the poor. She thinks women who engage in such activities are brainless nincompoops. "Idiots, every one of them!" she tells my father when he tries to get her out and about, tells her she's stuck up. She says birds have more brains.

But the number one reason she and I are crouched on a bleacher watching fake cherry blossoms being catapulted to the gym floor is that my mother loves the sound of sound. When I was younger, I found this mildly entertaining, the way she lost herself in Glenn Miller and bird calls and the whistle of the teakettle, the way she glued herself to sound, composed her life across its chords and cadences. As the years went by, though, and she began to twitter and coo and sing full-throatedly, I became deeply afraid. I came to fear that she'd never find her way out of the maze of sound and return to the world of seeing and clarity, of you come and you go, a world I had chosen without a second thought from day one.

In and of itself, there was nothing earth-shattering about my mother's crying. She was what people in those days called tenderhearted, which meant she had the annoying tendency of bursting into tears at the drop of a hat. That night at the opera, I could see she was revving up when she opened her mouth and started to pant. She once told me this was her way of trying *not* to cry in public. To this end, she'd open her eyes as wide as they would go and pant like a winded dog, which made her look like she was watching a murder in progress. While engaging in these episodes of bug-eyed staring and breathing in fits and starts, she'd count any available objects within her line of vision, tilting her head back and gazing heavenward, which kept the tears from cascading down her cheeks and becoming noticeable. In this prayerful pose, counting under her breath—tiles, beams, clouds, stars, you name it—she'd pause to tell me to wipe that worried look off my face; some people were just sad, period. It was their nature.

Worst were the mishaps to her birds. Summer before last it had been the mother bluebird, who'd been messily dispatched by a house sparrow in the nest box Mama had prepared. After slaughtering the mother, whose offspring had just emerged from their eggs, the sparrow had pecked the nestlings to death too. It had then built its own sloppy home atop their bloodied bodies. When Mama came home from grocery shopping that afternoon, she spotted its dark sparrow head sticking out of the birdhouse as if it owned the place, as if it had lived there a million years. She shooed it out and unhinged the front of the nest box, only to be met with the scene of bloody mayhem.

Her shriek jolted Grace and me out of my multiplication tables, which Grace was drilling me on since I hadn't done especially well in arithmetic over the past school year. We threw down the cards she'd made for me and ran outside and planted ourselves on either side of our sobbing mother, who stood on tiptoe, steadying herself by placing her hands on our small sturdy shoulders and peering into the box. Then, still sobbing, she lifted each of us up to survey the carnage, as though she couldn't bear the burden of having witnessed it alone. The bluebird mother had defended her offspring to the death. She'd been pecked so badly that she appeared to have been decapitated, her rose breast flecked in blood. On the bottom of the nest, the mutilated bodies of the four little ones were sprawled about, wings and necks twisted at unnatural angles. Featherless, bony, and raw. Bits of twigs and pine needles piled atop their corpses.

Mama poked at what was left of the mother bluebird and sobbed on. She prized her bluebirds for their way of flying—their lightning flutter, the shocking flash of blue—but she especially thrilled to the male's spring mating call, which she thought sounded like *where, where, where are you,* which she said made perfect sense. She kept the nest box in full view of the bay window next to the kitchen table and waited for the birds to arrive each spring, first the male scouting the nest. She'd murmur indignantly that he should know by now that she kept a good clean box. Tight too, and on a pole nothing on earth could climb. Still, he would flit in and out, peering into the hole, weighing his alternatives, making up his mind. "Why's he dithering so?" she'd say. "He couldn't ask for a better home."

The night of the massacre, her face red and swollen from crying, she read up on house sparrows. They were an imported menace that pecked others of their species to death, the bird book said, and stole what the industrious first comers, the songbirds, had so carefully built. Left unchecked, they would decimate the North American bluebird population; euthanasia was required.

Euthanasia. A pretty-sounding word. I raised my eyebrows at Grace to signal I didn't know what it meant. She scowled at me and made a slicing motion across her throat.

Mama pored over the bird book a good long time. Grace and I read over her shoulder, wanting her to feel our concern. She reached behind her and touched our forearms, and we drew close. (Our mother loved us, really she did!) Judging by the way she read and reread one page, we discerned that she had decided on the book's second method of euthanasia, to trap the sparrow in a mesh bag and then whap it up against some hard surface. The book said it might be necessary to do this two or three times to achieve the desired results. The bird would expire with little or no blood. (There was also the method of cervical dislocation, which involved breaking the bird's neck.) We were instructed by the book that the bird's death should be arrived at humanely, though *humane*, the book said, is a somewhat subjective term.

It was August, and this had been the bluebirds' third set of babies, a record for our mother's nest box. The last of the blossoms on the gnarled mimosa in the backyard cloaked the tree in a pink fur. The heat had wilted everything else in the yard. The next morning Mama walked out and down the street, heading for Lafitte's Market. A while later she returned home carrying a mesh bag. It sat on the kitchen counter for several more days. Finally, on the fourth night, our father put it away in a drawer before he went to bed. "It's nature, you can't change nature, survival of the fittest and all that." He spoke in what he must have imagined to be a soothing tone. Our mother was sitting at the kitchen table, having just finished filling a salt shaker from the

Morton's salt box when he made this pronouncement. She carefully opened the spigot on the salt box and began pouring salt on the floor. The box was almost full, so it piled up in little white ant hills around her chair. "I guess that's what you'd say if you came home and found us all hacked to pieces by barbarians," she said. "I guess that'd just be nature too. I guess that'd just be hunky-dory." Then she got up and headed back to her room and slammed the door, leaving our father standing in the middle of the kitchen rubbing his mouth and Grace running for the broom.

Meanwhile, the house sparrow and its mate busied themselves fixing up the bluebird box, bringing in bits of leaves and more pine needles. The next morning, a Saturday, our mother, her eyes ringed in red, planted herself at the kitchen table, pulled out her binoculars, and began to keep watch over the murderers.

Then, after our father had taken off to get a tune-up for his Nash Rambler and Grace and I were just finishing our Rice Krispies, Mama put down the binoculars, tucked in her lips, rummaged through the drawer, and pulled out the mesh bag. She headed out the back door, walked around to the back of the nest box, and began to move stealthily toward it, the mesh bag held open with both hands. One of the house sparrows was at home, savoring the morning air, its dark head thrust from the box's entry hole. Settled and placid, pleased as punch with its new home.

Grace and I watched from the kitchen window. I reached for her hand. "Do you think she's really going to do it?" I asked my sister. Neither of us could imagine our mother killing a bird. Just as she closed in, the sparrow saw her and disappeared into the depths of the box. Coming around from behind, Mama moved like a thief in the night, slowly sliding the mesh bag over the box's hole. She held the bag in place with one hand and then whapped the back of the box with the other so that the startled sparrow, trying to escape, bolted from the box directly into the bag.

The sparrow was larger than expected. It fought hard, flapping and pecking, furious and brave. I found myself rooting for it. Holding the bag at arm's length, Mama began to tighten the drawstring while the panicked bird worked itself into a frenzy of wings and beak. Then a quick jerk of the string and she had it.

The arm is swung in a wide circular, windmill motion, one or two revolutions, then rapidly swung into a concrete step/brick wall/tree trunk/flat rock. Despite these explicit instructions, Mama's face went blank, as if she couldn't think where she might find such hard surfaces, even though she was standing next to the sturdy trunk of the old mimosa, the blossoms fanning around her so that she herself appeared to have grown feathers and a crest.

In the bag, the sparrow seemed more uncertain. It quieted, its black eyes flashing gold in the morning light, breast heaving, feet curved around the mesh of the bag, shifting its weight from side to side to keep from turning upside down. Mama looked down at it; then her eyes met ours through the window. She made a shooing motion at us.

I abandoned my post at the window, threw back the sliding glass door, and ran out into the yard, waving my hands. "Don't do it!"

Grace was right behind me. "Don't you dare go killing that bird!" Of the two of us, Grace was the more easily upset by our mother's shenanigans; that Mama would actually murder a helpless bird was beyond the pale.

"Let's take it somewhere in the car. Let's *relocate* it." I had read in the book that relocation was an option, though not a recommended one.

A lock of our mother's hair had fallen over one eye. "It'll just come back."

"Let's at least try it," I said.

Just then our father drove up into the carport.

"Look, Mama, Dad's home," I said. "We can take it out in the country, let it loose. I'll hold it while you drive. We'll take it so far it'll never come back."

"It will reproduce," Mama said. "There will be more of them and they'll kill all the bluebirds. It's the right thing to do, the only thing to do." Her tone was calm, but when she shook her hair off her face, her gray eyes, dull as old blacktop on the road, bulged alarmingly. She looked flat-out crazy.

As if sensing our support, the bird began to struggle again, throw itself this way and that.

Grace began to shriek and I began to sob. We were unaccustomed to murder and mayhem. We didn't want to be the daughters of a bug-eyed woman who killed birds, no matter what kind. We demanded a sane solution, one that didn't involve blood or brokenness.

Our father rounded the corner of the backyard and took one look at Mama and the sparrow, which was now hanging on one side of the mesh bag, its mouth open wide as if silently screaming.

"Olivia, what the hell are you doing with that bird?" He came toward her, his hand outstretched. "Give me that thing."

For a long moment, Mama looked at him and us and the sparrow. "We're *relocating* this horrid bird," she said finally, with a nasty look in my direction. "Holly, you drive."

So here we went, the four of us. Grace got in the back seat and commenced chewing her nails. Our mother tied up the bag and put it on the floorboard between her feet. Dad drove to the outskirts of town and turned onto Highway 90. When we got outside of Waveland into the tree farms, he slowed the car and began to pull over on the shoulder.

"Drive farther," Mama commanded.

I looked over at my sister, who was staring out the window and chewing ferociously on her left thumbnail. Every so often the sparrow fluttered and flailed about, but mostly it was quiet. We continued on for several more miles, through old farmland, the second crop of cotton coming along, green and hopeful, the crepe myrtles and calla lilies splashing the yards of dilapidated homesteads with pink and red. There'd been some weather, and the road was wet. Someone had mowed down a field of corn stalks, which poked up at odd angles from the upturned ground.

We crossed a one-lane bridge over the swamp, then another. When Dad pulled to the side of the road a second time, we were surrounded by marsh grass. Grace and I got out with our mother. The sparrow had become a trembling mass of brown feathers, its head tucked under, but not in a natural way. A part of one of its wings stuck out from the bag at an odd angle, reminding me of a feather pasted atop a lady's hat.

When our mother opened the sack, the bird hesitated, as if fearful of being further entrapped. Then, after a moment, it shuddered and lifted off, a brown whir of motion over the marsh, soon gone.

Grace and I cheered. Mama watched it fly away, something in her face laid bare.

On the way home, Dad turned on the radio and lit a cigarette. The news was about North and South, the Gulf of Tonkin, the Red Tide of Communism sweeping through Asia. They'd just pulled a boy from Chicago, a black boy, out of the Tallahatchie River up near Money. He was all torn up, as dead as dead could be. He'd been tied to a wheel.

Mama slammed her hand down onto the dash, then covered her face. "Damn those peckerwoods in sheets," she said. "Damn them to hell." Dad sighed and changed the channel to baseball.

When we pulled into the carport, Mama got out and headed for the backyard. Grace and I trooped after her. She opened the nest box, picked up a stick, and scraped out the nest, dead bluebirds and all. The sparrow had laid eggs; Mama scooped them out and stomped them on the ground. Then she went to the shed in the carport and got some electric tape and taped the box's hole shut. She wept as she went about her tasks, but later on she fixed us grilled cheese sandwiches and put a roast in the oven for supper before going to her room and turning on the radio.

Grace, meanwhile, decided the bluebird mother and hatchlings deserved a decent burial. She dug a hole, then ordered me to gather mimosa puffs to cover the grave. "They died a terrible death," she said. "They need something pretty." It was dusk by that time. The heat pressed down like a hot hand. When I reached up for the mimosa leaves, they shrank from my touch. In my hands, the blossoms seemed to come alive like tiny creatures, sticky and willing. I pushed the stems into the ground around the edges of the grave my sister had made.

We stood together, my sister and I, looking down at the upturned dirt. Grace waved her hand over the grave. "Nothing goes away forever," she murmured. "Everything comes back. Amen."

All this time the sparrow's mate sat on a high outer branch of the mimosa, eyeing us. Then it began to make its way down, branch by branch, toward the box. I went inside to go to the bathroom and when I came back out, Mama's tape was fraying and had holes in it. The sparrow sat on top of the box grooming itself, its feathers splayed. Dad was trimming his hedges in the front yard, the steady chop of his clippers playing backup to the evening song of a thrush. We ran to tell him about the sparrow's mate.

He threw down his clippers. "What next?"

He stormed over to the shed where he kept his lawn mower and came out with a couple of boards and a hammer. He'd stuck some nails in his mouth. Grace and I held the boards while he nailed them over the nest box hole. The sparrow's mate had retreated to the top of the mimosa, but then it made another end run for the nest box, dive-bombing us, chittering and flapping its wings. Grace screamed, I ducked, and Dad swatted at it.

"Damn thing," Dad said.

"It's after its eggs, poor thing," said my sister.

Dad slapped at the bird and it retreated again. Then night came on and it melted into the dark.

While Dad put up his yard tools, I gathered more mimosa blooms and took them into the house. I floated them in a glass bowl and put them on the kitchen table, hoping to cheer Mama up. By the time she came out of her room, they'd begun to turn at the edges and stain the water reddish brown. Their scent, though, filled the house, over even the smell of the roast. She sat down at the table and picked one up and twirled it under her nose. Then she got up and opened the sliding glass door and called out to Grace, who was putting the final touches on the bluebirds' grave, and to our father, gathering the last of his things. She called out, *Supper's ready,* and her voice rinsed the air like rain.

I'd been dreading *Madame Butterfly* since Christmas. It was a year and a half after the sparrow episode, a miserable night, the driving rain falling sideways in sheets. To make matters worse, I did not care for opera. When Mama played it on the record player, the songs took me by surprise, the high notes sounding like screaming, which heaven knows we had enough of around the house, given our parents' long-echoing, high-decibel arguments.

Our parents fought about living in Opelika. Mama wanted to move back to New Orleans, where she'd grown up, where there were places to go and sights to see, juke joints and oyster bars, picture shows and parades and river boats, the Monteleone Hotel where a lady could go midafternoons and perch on a stool at the revolving bar and treat herself to a Sazerac: a city where she could find a real job like she'd had at Higgins during the war. Our father, who had grown up in Opelika, worried about getting comparable work in New Orleans. He had a good solid job at the lumber mill, an office job managing payroll. It would be irresponsible to just take off, throw caution to the wind at our mother's whim. He studied the ads in the *Times-Picayune* and even made a few trips over to the City when he had a day off, but he never found the kind of work he'd come to expect as his rightful due. He'd be damned if he was going to collect garbage just so our mother could guzzle Sazeracs on weekday afternoons.

Meanwhile, Mama went on crying jags. Here she was, dying a dreary, boring death in this rattrap of a town in the middle of the swamps. How much more of this life could she bear?

It was not that my mother didn't have her moments. One afternoon in September Grace and I arrived home from school to find her in the backyard singing like a bird. She was stretched out on her chaise lounge on the little back patio, her eyes closed, her full lips in the shape of an inner tube, chirping and twittering and cooing for all she was worth. In her sunglasses with the bright yellow frames and a turquoise scarf, she looked like a giant parakeet. There was a convention of birds in the trees, even a few squirrels, watching and listening, their heads cocked quizzically. Occasionally one of the birds, notably the male cardinal, would sing back to her, like she was a mate he was trying to attract.

After observing our mother for only the briefest of moments, Grace headed down the hall to her room and slammed the door. Mama jumped like she'd heard a gunshot, sat straight up in her lounge chair, and peered through the screen of the sliding glass door.

"Is that you, girls?" she called out.

I slid the screen door open and poked out my head. "We're home."

"Good. There's lemonade in the icebox." She lay back on the chaise and lit a cig, turning her shoulders against the breeze to shield the Zippo.

That night Grace slipped into my room and told me we were going to have to face the music: our mother was a fruitcake, all we could do was try to avert disaster until we were eighteen and could get out of there. Grace would go first. Then, when she'd found a job and a place to live, she'd come back for me. She'd tap on my window three times. I should have my bag packed. Meanwhile, we would both begin stealing our parents' spare change so that when the moment arrived, she'd have some cash to make her getaway.

Over time, I'd begun to observe my sister's face, how it turned in on itself, even her full mouth; how the lines on her face were already being drawn, like the thinnest of hairs, between the brows, from the sides of her nose running south to the corners of her mouth, then down to the edge of her jaw.

On our mother's long-awaited opera night, I trooped out of the bedroom in last year's Easter dress, a thin dotted swiss. Grace lay curled up like a cat on the living room sofa. Outside, the rain had settled in for the long haul. I was already shivering in my skimpy getup, which was both too tight and too short, but, unlike my sister, I'd become so unnerved by my mother's unhappiness I would have endured just about anything to put even a whisper of a smile on her face. Even now, years after that night, even after my mother went and did what she did, her unhappiness still hovers in its long lazy circles, always watchful for that loosed moment when my guard is down. I turn a corner and see dark hair on a woman or a snag of color in a tree, and it plunges.

Mama swept out of her room like a queen. She had on her best outfit, the dusty pink suit with its matching blouse she'd worn when she and Dad got married. She'd ratted her hair so it stood high on her head, then smoothed it into a French twist with two jeweled picks poked through it. Her lips were Fire Engine Red and, over that lipstick shade, which she used only on special occasions, she'd slathered Vaseline.

Dad whistled. "Well now. It's Madame Butterfly herself."

She ignored him, turned to me. "Do you think the picks are too much?"

Personally, I did find the picks a bit much. Between the two of them, covered in rhinestones and antennae-like, and the dizzying height of her hairdo, she looked a bit like a praying mantis. In that moment I glanced at my father, who raised his eyebrows at me, reminding me of my job, which was to calm the waters of my mother's stormy soul. "No ma'am," I said, "I absolutely do not think they're too much. In fact, they are just right for the occasion, just perfect."

So here I am, shivering beside my mother on a bench in the drafty school gymnasium, watching as the Japanese lady in the cheesy kimono frets on the gym floor with her little boy. She waits endlessly for her man to come back to her when everybody with a brain in their head knows he never will, jerk that he is. Meanwhile my mother hums to the music and stares up into the rafters, tears galloping down her cheeks, counting under her breath for dear life. She's at one hundred twelve of whatever it is she's counting. Her powder is streaked and clotted, the left pick in her updo sagging alarmingly.

What I'm not prepared for will come at the end, when the Japanese lady, her eyes drawn to slits (is she *really* Japanese? I wonder), gives, *gives*, her little boy to that wastrel of a father and his new wife like the poor kid's a dress she's outgrown. Then, lo and behold, just to top things off, she takes a monster knife to herself, hara-kiri style. This, in my opinion, is an overreaction of massive proportion, an unnatural thing for a mother to do. You don't just fly off and leave your little child like that.

Mama taught me that the overture to an opera establishes the elements of the score to follow, its tensions and passions and grandeur. She would play the overture to *Madame Butterfly* for illustration and say, "Now listen, here's where it sneaks in like a thief in the night: *there*, can you hear it?"

Later that night, I will crawl into my sister's bed and warm myself against her back. Across the hall, I will hear something prophetic in my mother's voice as she tells my father about the way the blossoms came down wrong.

Now she will begin her song: she will say to my father she hates this place, there is nothing here for her. Here, she will say, she is an alien species, a foreigner. Underneath her words, I listen for the thief, the intruder in the nest, the one who will lay us all low.

My father, for his part, will murmur a reply I can't make out, a flutter of wings.

3

Grace

We might have saved her if we hadn't been late that afternoon, if I hadn't insisted on those two extra hours at the zoo. When you think about it, I'm really the one to blame. I should have been content with the giraffes, not asked for more.

It started like a regular Sunday in the City, nothing more or less. When we were girls together, June and I, our father would take us to watch the giraffes dance. It was an hour's drive to New Orleans, first through Mississippi scrub pine, then the still swamps where egrets waded on their stick legs. When we turned onto Highway 90, red clay gave way to long fingers of alligator-still water and marsh grasses flat and bristly as our dad's crew cut. It was as if we were at the center of the world with a million paths to choose from.

Out on the open road Dad would turn on the radio. Usually he played hillbilly, white trash music our mother called it, though she never made these trips with us. He'd tap the underside of the steering wheel. Sometimes he'd hum a few lines under his breath, then whistle along. June and I would be in the back seat, playing tic-tac-toe on a little notebook we kept handy, the backs of our sweaty thighs sticking to the vinyl upholstery, our hair blowing in the wind. We'd twitch and squirm and make fun of Dad's ears, which stuck out like flaps on a box and exploded at the edges in curly brown hairs.

We traveled over three rickety one-lane bridges and then the drawbridge over the sparkling Rigolets, where the Gulf and fresh water mingled. Finally we turned south onto Highway 47, which just plunged us deeper into swampland so that the road seemed like the thinnest of ribbons threaded through the murky water. When 47 became Good Children Street with stoplights and scraggly clusters of juke joints and Laundromats and fried fish shacks, it was as if we were entering the mouth of a huge exotic flower. "What happens when children are good?" Dad would call out when we hit Good Children, and my sister and I would answer in unison, "They get a street named after them!"

On the trip over, the chance we'd be disappointed

loomed large. Sometimes the giraffes felt the urge to dance and sometimes they didn't. When they didn't, they behaved just like ordinary giraffes, nibbling the tops of the already bare trees in their enclosure or walking in wide circles like trained horses in a circus ring. Sometimes they didn't even show up at all, in which case our father would shrug and say, *Oh well, you can't win 'em all,* and take us to Morning Call in the Quarter for café au lait and beignets. The coffee's heat would seal the sugar from the beignets to the roofs of our mouths like tar, the only thing standing between us and utter despair.

But it was the chanciness of it that we adored; our hearts did somersaults over giraffes. We imagined thundering herds of them galloping across the savannahs. Reticulated giraffes were our specialty. We thought we knew everything about them, how their kick could kill a lion on the Somalian plains, how they were cousins to camels and could go weeks without water, how their patternings were unique to each and every one, how they had four stomachs. That year, our science teacher, Miss Whiteside, had accused poor June of copying my giraffe report from two years back, which was a joke since June had done nothing but eat and sleep giraffes the whole month before the report was due.

We made the trip on Sundays. On Saturdays our father busied himself mowing the grass and trimming his bushes, or in the fall, raking his leaves (he called them "his leaves") from one side of our small fenced backyard to the other. After Sunday dinner, we left our mother to clean roasting pans with black lines of hardened grease, bowls of congealed mashed potatoes, pots of gumbo and field peas. When she looked at all the mess, Mama made a noise in her throat that sounded like a cross between a chuckle and a snarl. Sometimes, when she thought Dad wasn't watching, she slid whole casserole dishes into the garbage can.

We're going to get out of your hair, Olivia, head on over to the City, Dad would say, cool as a cucumber. While we changed from our Sunday clothes, our mother went outside and walked along the inside edge of the backyard, tracing the fence line like a restless dog. Her pacing had worn a path through Dad's grass. He asked her why she wouldn't go out and take a walk on the sidewalk like normal people. She said she detested normal people and didn't want to run into any.

While he waited for us, our father would go outside and lean against the Rambler's hood and have a smoke. June and I would troop out in single file, quietly, as if ashamed. No goodbye or have a good time or even be careful on the road from Mama, though if she were back in the kitchen, we could feel her eyes burning holes in our backs as we walked out the door and down the front sidewalk.

The place we went was not the zoo, but its outer east side, where an extension of the giraffe enclosure backed up to a grove of massive live oaks, limbs resting on the ground as if they'd been severed and sculpted in place. We knew not to ask to go to the actual zoo. There wasn't much money and Dad was tight with a dollar, had to be, he said. He simply parked the Rambler on Annunciation Street, and we set off walking.

We entered down a small path between houses. He would lead us safari style through the brush, holding back the branches of small trees so they didn't smack me in the face. I would in turn hold them for June. As he parted the way for us, we admired the heft of our father's shoulders, the ropiness of his arms, the way highways crisscrossed on the back of his neck.

He said the enclosure was a secret place no one else knew about. The giraffes needed a special place, a private place, to dance and do the other natural things they were meant to do. Otherwise, he said, they would be miserable and live unfulfilled and therefore short lives. The longevity of animals, he told us, is directly related to their happiness.

We hardscrabbled our way through the brambles and, in summer, smoky clusters of mosquitoes. June, poor thing, suffered from their bites, which turned her legs into a pulp of bloody welts. If the giraffes were there, all we could see of them as we approached were the tops of their heads and about halfway down their necks. Usually there were two, never more than three. They would gaze at us politely but vaguely as though we were distant cousins passing through town, sometimes unrolling their snakelike tongues to lick our scent from the air.

Their enclosure was bordered by a penitentiary-style fence with exposed twists at the top. The fence had metal slats woven in and out of the links. My sister and I took turns peering at the giraffes through the gaps in the slats while Dad stood around and smoked. In the distance we could hear the monkeys cry out *nobody nobody.* Every so often a lion would groan. Our father never rushed us. Sometimes he took a peek, but mostly he seemed satisfied to watch us watching the giraffes. We stayed a good long time, until the mosquitoes and chiggers got the best of us or the giraffes decided to sashay back around to the front of the zoo.

One sultry day we arrived panting and sweating to find that the fence had been covered by a dark mesh, and we began to keen and wail. "Don't be such babies," our father said through his teeth. He whipped out his pocketknife, stuck it through a gap in the fence post and began to saw away at the fabric. He made two peepholes, one for each of us so we wouldn't bicker over taking turns. As the years went by and he cut our peepholes higher and higher, the mesh came untethered from the fence and flapped in the occasional breeze. The motion must have interested the giraffes because they began shredding the material with their teeth as though they wanted to watch us as much as we wanted to watch them. Eventually, what was left of the mesh barrier slid to the ground.

The last time we saw the giraffes dance was the day our mother did what she did. The day we were two hours late getting home.

It was November. We woke to a cold rain, but the morning soon turned out crisp and bright, heralding a nice day, a pretty day. The autumn sun had shifted in the sky and the light cut on a slant across the surface of the marsh grasses and the paths of still water that snaked through the swamp like the fingers of a hand. Behind the giraffe enclosure there was a lone sugar maple tree turned to fire among the oaks. June's hair had relaxed, become cloud-like around her face. She wore a cowgirl skirt with fringe I'd outgrown, and her white socks spilled over her loafers. I was twelve and she was ten.

Our parents had been at it late into the night, our mother saying she simply couldn't *do this* anymore and Dad saying she had gone and ruined everything.

She didn't choose this, she said; *she* had wanted to go to Paris, France, and wear a beret and work for an embassy. She had wanted to see the world and be free. Why, I wondered, hadn't he told her he was saving up to take her to the top of the Eiffel Tower, that he had a secret bank account where he deposited thirty-five dollars every month? Why hadn't he said that one day he would wrap up those tickets in the blue beret he'd stashed in a shoe box years ago and holler, *Surprise, Olivia, this is your lucky day*? June and I lived in terror of that day, convinced that if our mother ever made it to gay Paree she'd never come home.

But our mother didn't know any of our father's plots and plans. Last night, she said it was his big you-know-what that had ruined everything for her *again*. She just got stuck cleaning up the mess afterward. As usual. Now here she was, in the middle of nowhere, no job—much less a *career*—and no way to get one, taking care of not one but two ungrateful children, no end in sight. What in god's name had he *expected* her to do, start all over?

Their voices hushed, and there was more talk and then a strange sound, someone crying, not our mother.

The morning after the fight there were two empty bottles of cherry bounce on the kitchen counter. Our father was proud of his bounce, which he made from the wormy cherries off the trees in our side yard and stored in the basement. It was nasty stuff, the taste and consistency of cough syrup, a slimy sludge in the bottom of the bottles, the sludge all that was left in the empty ones on the counter that morning. The house was dead quiet when June and I got up, Mama nowhere in sight.

The two of us sat down at the kitchen table. I could tell by the odd way June held her head that she'd heard what our mother had said. She shivered in her summer pajamas and seemed to be trying to form a word. I kicked the leg of her chair to jar it from her. Normally she would have kicked me back and come out with something ugly, but she just turned and looked out the window at the ill-fated bluebird nest box in the backyard that had been boarded up over two years now.

After a while I got up and went to the icebox. "Want some orange juice?" I asked her.

"I don't care."

That fall June and I had at long last begun to plumb the depth of our mother's unhappiness. In previous years, we'd made what we thought were helpful suggestions to alleviate it. The Christmas before, June, who was the optimist, got the bright idea that Mama would like to learn to sew and talked Dad into buying her a Singer on time. We saved our allowances and bought a pattern for beginners, a pretty lady's sundress for summer, just to give our mother plenty of time to get the knack of sewing. We were careful to buy a pattern for a dress for her rather than ourselves; we didn't want to be perceived as selfish. We managed, after several false starts, to tape together three sheets of Christmas paper, cover the black carrying case, and top the whole thing off with a big red bow. Mama thanked us politely. We suggested she set up the Singer on the dining room table we never used, but she didn't unpack it and Christmas night she took it, still in its case, down to the basement. Every morning from the day after Christmas to New Year's, June and I would peer down the stairs to see whether there were any signs that she'd begun to unpack it, but it remained in its case, still covered with bits of tape and shreds of paper, strangely illuminated by a watery shaft of sunlight from the single ground-level window, looking for all the world like some kind of ticking bomb. Then, a few days after New Year's, it vanished into thin air.

After that we were careful to suggest activities less taxing than sewing. "Pressing Needs" we called them—a leader for our Brownie Scout troop, a mother to go on a field trip to the mill, a church lady to make sloppy joes and hot dogs for Sunday night youth worship, the last a particularly hard sell since our mother never went to church. When we'd present her with one of these opportunities, Mama would smile and roll her eyes and murmur something vaguely indecipherable like "Well, so, I'm . . . well, actually."

So when she took up bird watching, we were all mightily relieved. Dad built her a dozen feeders and nest boxes. June and I got her the binoculars for her birthday, and she wore them like a heavy necklace around the house as she did her chores, pausing every so often to peer at a passing cardinal or thrasher, her eyes bright and watchful. Over the course of the nesting season, her mood rose and fell with the fate of the birds. She still hadn't recovered from the latest disaster. Her bluebirds in one of the nest boxes in the front yard had had a successful spring and were on their second set of eggs, which she checked every morning. When we heard her crying out and came running, we found her out front swatting a swarm of wasps whose nest had fallen from the ceiling of the box onto the bluebirds' nest below. The wasps were stinging Mama all over her arms and face; when we yanked at her dress to pull her away, she hit at us as though we were wasps too.

The wasps finally left, but, alarmed by the commotion, the birds abandoned the nest and over the course of the summer, the eggs, shockingly blue, became weightless and faded.

That Sunday morning after the fight I pushed the empty cherry bounce bottles aside and made up a pitcher of orange juice from a box of frozen concentrate. After a while Dad stumbled in, rubbing his eyes. He hadn't shaved and had on yesterday's shirt. His face had taken on a bluish cast. He got out cheese and bread for cheese toast, then decided it was too much trouble to turn on the oven and just handed us the loaf and the chunk of sharp cheddar and a knife. As we ate, he poured us a spot of his coffee and filled up our cups with scalded milk. He had two cups black with buckets of sugar and a cig. Then he leaned over the table and told us to get dressed, we were going to see the giraffes. He frowned. "Be quiet about it."

I was the last one out the front door, and I shut it without a sound, not knowing what I was leaving behind, not calling out to our mother to say goodbye.

The minute we saw the two of them, we knew they would dance, had already been at it long before we arrived. It was a mother and baby, or so we thought at the time—a big baby, almost as tall as the mother but with an open, unmarked face, lacking the bumps on the forehead of the mother and overall lighter in shade, with a blond background, instead of her reddish brown, for its dark swatches of color. They came to the fence, swaying, in perfect step. They flicked their long gray tongues, looking in that moment more like giant anteaters going for flies. When they batted their foot-long eyelashes at us, we froze in place, mesmerized. Then, together, they bowed once, then again, and began to dance.

Their dance had two parts. First, they threw their necks back and forth and smacked at each other with the sides of their heads. It was an impact that would have knocked my father off his feet, maybe broken a bone or two. Back and forth, back and forth, they went at it, whacking each other on the sides and shoulders, their necks looping out and in, as if moving to a slow song only they could hear. All muscle and animal rhythm. Except for the impact, a soft *woof,* they didn't make a sound. We knew we were seeing something unbearably private, something meant for only the two of them. Watching them dance, I felt as though a bandage had been peeled off my eyes and I could see prettiness everywhere, in everything. The world seemed suddenly large and open, as if I'd stepped through a door into a field of color that stretched out far as the eye could see.

After this long bit of whapping, they walked over to the fence, eyed us, and bowed. Then they stood before us as if waiting for applause, flicking flies with the Fuller Brush tips of their tails. After that, they walked away in perfect step, mother in the lead, the two of them disappearing into the front part of the zoo enclosure.

June turned to me and grabbed my hand. She didn't say anything and I didn't either, but we stood together for a bit, swaying a little from side to side. I could hear Dad inhaling his Camel. In the brush behind me a squirrel was fussing. Then my sister grinned and turned suddenly and whapped me on my shoulder with her head. I hollered and rolled my head around and whapped her back. We started running at each other like little bulls, knocking each other down with our heads. We got up and danced around under the oaks, rolling our heads in circles, emitting strange woofing sounds. Then we collapsed on the grass, flailing about.

Our father coughed. "Grace, pull down your shirt." He mumbled the words, as if he didn't want June to hear them. I felt my face flush, and I tugged at my blouse.

Usually the giraffes cheered our father up, but now he rubbed his eyes and looked out over our heads toward the twisted branches of the live oaks. He seemed to be searching for something in particular, as if he had had another child when we came and momentarily had lost sight of it. After a while he heaved a sigh and said, "All right, time to head back."

The idea of going home to our mother and whatever trouble she was bound to cause stuck in my craw. Something ugly rose in my gorge. "Dad, we want to go to the *real* zoo. We never get to see the animals in the *real* zoo."

The minute I uttered the words they felt freighted with ill intent. An unspoken rule of the trip was that we never talked about the zoo itself; it was as if the giraffes were magically in their natural habitat at the end of Annunciation Street on the edge of the Mississippi River in New Orleans, Louisiana, US of A, a strange savannah of time and space, a gift from our father. I knew I was being a brat; I knew I was spoiling something.

Our father stared down at me, his eyes like the fall light, flicking off the surface of things, making them strange. Then he pulled his wallet out of his back pocket and looked inside. "Yeah, okay," he said, and his voice trailed off. "Yeah, okay, let's get on over to the *real* zoo." He flicked his cigarette butt onto the grass.

June glared at me. "Don't pay any attention to her, Dad, she was just talking."

"No, I wasn't," I said loud and clear. Then I whispered to her, "Do you really want to go back home?"

Of course, she could have said yes, we should get on home to our mother, but she didn't. Maybe I'm not the only one to blame for what happened.

Dad had already taken off around to the front of the zoo, toward the river, his hands in his pockets, not waiting for us, not looking back. There was an oddness to our father's walk, more a flutter than a limp on his right side. He'd lost his big toe in the war and it set him off-kilter. At night, when he walked around the house without his shoes, his sock would flap. We ran after him and when we got to the gate, he bought the tickets and handed them to me. "You've got two hours," he said, "until they start closing down the place."

Neither of us liked the idea of him dumping us there, not coming in with us. June held back, snatched at Dad's hand. He shook her loose.

"Go on. You want the real zoo. There's the real zoo." He flicked his hand at us as if we were flies.

I looked around. Mothers and fathers and grandparents and aunts and uncles were walking in and out of the gates, laughing and cutting up and calling for boys and girls to wait up. "Where are you going? Why aren't you coming in with us?" I asked.

"I'm going to take a look at Old Man River," he said. "I'll see you at five." Then he walked away from us, heading into the sun.

We stood there for a minute, uncertain what to do. We made a move to follow him down the path, but a slant of the light through the dark scramble of live oaks made him suddenly unrecognizable, a stick figure.

"Well, let's go on in," said June, her voice quavering a little. "You wanted to go to the real zoo. What else are we going to do for the next two hours?"

We walked down a long winding path and passed the flamingo pond. It was littered with tickets and cups and popcorn containers. I saw some popcorn in one. My mouth watered and I reached down to pick up the container.

"That's unsanitary," June said. "Come on."

We turned a corner and dead ahead was a polar bear sitting on an outcropping of concrete in a cage barely big enough to turn around in. He had positioned himself under a weak stream of water. It fell down the right side of his cage, so that it ran over that side of his head and shoulder. Where the water had trickled down on him days, years on end, his coat was mossy green. Green on that one side a clotted brown on the other, he looked like he'd been split in half. Shoulders slumped and belly loose, he stared out through the bars of his cage as though he could see something that was invisible to us, his only motion an occasional blink. He looked like an old man on a park bench. He did not seem to be breathing.

June and I leaned into each other and began to hum under our breath. My chest crackled the way it some-times did in the fall. My mother would run hot water and I would kneel beside the tub to breathe in the steam; she would sit on the side of the tub and talk softly to me, running the hot water every so often, calming the flutter of my heart.

I had on shorts and was suddenly cold. (Was this the moment it happened? Was this when we lost our mother?) There were baboons in the next cage. As we backed away from the polar bear and moved in their direction, they seemed to grow unaccountably afraid of us. Their throats ballooned out and they began to make a noise that was something between a laugh and a scream. June put her hands over her ears. I wanted to throw my head back and howl and holler up to the sky too. Instead I started to cry for the poor polar bear, snicking the air, gasping for breath.

"Let's get out of here," June said, taking my arm. As we walked away, I felt the empty stare of the polar bear at my back, pushing me forward as though I were the remains of everything he'd ever wanted, winnowed down to a trickle.

We went out the front entrance and plopped ourselves on a bench, hoping Dad would come back early. We sat there a good long time, not talking, swatting at some yellow jackets that lit on us and moved their stingers up and down, testing us to see whether we were worth stinging.

Then a man came up. He was carrying a life-sized stuffed polar bear that looked like a lumpy rug. It was in a lying-down pose and had a frayed bow around its neck. The man had it slung over his shoulder.

He started talking at us before he ever got to the bench where we were sitting. "Hey, little ladies, want to get your picture took with Bernie the Bear? Make your mama and daddy proud and happy to see they pretty girls having such a fine time at the zoo." He was bow-legged and the late afternoon sun cut a swath between his knees. He pointed at the sign over our heads that read "Audubon Park Zoo. Whites Only. Colored Day Tuesday," and whipped a Polaroid camera out of his back pocket.

June reached for my hand. I shook my head. "No, sir." I was polite, I didn't make a fuss. I'd been taught to respect my elders.

"No obligation at all, little lady girls. You'll make a pretty picture. Just pose for me with Barry here."

June scooted toward me; our thighs were touching. Then the man came right up to us on the bench, so close we could see the splotched veins in his cheeks and nose, and plopped the big old stinking thing across our laps, as if he were a waiter at a fancy restaurant and it was our napkin.

"Wonderful," he said, "wonderful. Smile. No, wait." He grabbed one of June's hands and put it on top of the bear's head. Then he grabbed one of mine and put it on the bear's back, to make it look like I was petting the thing. We both froze under his touch, sitting woodenly with our hands on the animal. I opened my mouth to ask him to take the thing off us, but by that time he had proceeded to take our picture. As he homed in on us with the camera, the bear settled and became warm and heavy against my chest as though it had suddenly become flesh and blood.

The camera pushed out one picture, then he took another. The man studied them, frowned, came closer. "You ain't smiling," he said, with a trace of a threat in his voice. "You got to smile, girls. At least look like you having a good time, for Christ sake." He touched my cheek, pushed up a corner of my mouth. His fingers smelled like fried eggs.

I jerked my face away, and turned to my sister. Her eyes were wide and scared. I whispered, "Just smile. Get this over with."

So, when our father arrived, there we were, the two of us, grinning from ear to ear, our hands posed over the animal as if we were blessing it. The man had just reached up to push my bangs out of my eyes and, in the next moment, snapped his third picture.

Dad leapt like a wild thing out of a clump of oleander bushes, waving and shouting. "Get your hands off her. What the hell you think you're doing?" He grabbed the man by the shoulders and pushed.

"Whoa, buddy," the man hollered out. "Just taking a picture of these pretty little girls for you and the missus. All I was doing was taking a picture, for Christ sake."

"Get your slimy hands off of them." Dad swung, hit the man in the nose.

A lone peacock that had wandered up began to shake itself open and scream.

The man's nose started pumping blood. He stumbled, barely catching himself from falling flat on his back. His hand went up to his face and came away dripping red. He took one look and started hollering and backing up. "Just trying to make a goddamn living, buddy."

Dad rushed him and swung again, this time hitting the man on the chin and knocking him to the dust. Dad snatched the bear off of us and threw it down on top of the man. "Get out of here, you pervert."

The man snatched his camera, grabbed the polar bear, and took off running, hollering that our father was mental. Dad pulled us up off the bench and started feeling around on us as if we might have loose parts. Then he knelt down and gathered us in his arms, and we noticed only then that his khakis were soaked up to the crotch. "Oh my God," he said and his voice trembled. He held us close for a good long time and said it again and again.

We walked back through the brush behind the zoo to the car, Dad between us, his hands on our shoulders. He parted the brush like it was the Red Sea and he was Moses. I looked over my shoulder to see whether the giraffes had come back, but they were long gone.

I asked him why his pants were all wet, and he said it was from the river. His shoes squeaked as he moved through the brambles. I couldn't see why anybody in his right mind would wade into the Mississippi River, with its deep currents and murky water. The banks of the river were steep. He could have slipped and been swept under. Then where would we be?

We were quiet in the car on the way home. No hillbilly. No chitchat. Just the croak of frogs from the swamp around us. Every now and again our father would clear his throat, as though he were getting ready to say something. But then he would just rub his mouth and sigh and light up another cigarette.

My sister and I sat in the middle of the back seat, our shoulders and hips pressed tight. She looked out of the window on her side and I looked out of mine on the other. I wondered how we would find Mama. We were two hours late getting home, thanks to me. What had she done all this long lonesome day? Had she missed us? There was no premonition, no thought of something having given way, of something having been lost. A sparrow in the nest, a commotion. As we drove along, the sun went down across the swampland, and the marsh grasses began to glow with an unearthly light, as if they'd been sown in gold. Although home was just across the Rigolets, it felt as though we were beginning a long journey.

Dad cleared his throat. "You girls need to learn to watch out for yourself. Especially you, Grace. You need to watch out for yourself and your sister."

What he said startled me. I didn't know then what it meant to watch out for myself. I only knew what it meant to watch the giraffes dance, which was to look for what made the heart leap, to see into the blessed motion of things. I wanted to be inside that motion.

I chewed on my nail. June moved away from me and became deeply interested in something outside her window. Neither of us said anything.

Dad coughed. "Do you hear me? You need to watch out, girls. It's like building a fence around yourself."

June stirred. "You mean like a cage?"

"So nobody can hurt you. If somebody tries to reach inside . . ." He made a grabbing motion with his right hand.

"To pet you?" June said, eager to please. Even then she was his favorite.

He coughed again, rubbed his forehead. "Yes, like that. Then you run and scream and get away."

June leaned forward. I wanted to slap her. "Even if he's nice?"

"Yeah, especially then. Just think of yourself in that safe cage and no stranger can touch you. Like at school, when they make you crawl under the tables, in case of the Bomb."

"That's the rule?" June said.

"Yes, that's the rule. Are you listening, Grace?"

The light had finally faded, and a sliver of moon had come up. In the passing dark, the half-green polar bear stared back at me through the window's reflection, his eyes empty of questions, the bare fields swirling behind him in the night.

Dad turned on the radio. The Russians were winning the space race. They were going to launch the Bomb from the moon. They had sent up a little stray dog named Laika to orbit the earth, like one of those lost birds our mother had told us about, the accidentals who'd gotten off track and ended up somewhere they didn't belong. In Laika's case, about as off track as a dog or any other earthly creature could possibly get. Now, Laika was believed dead, though still orbiting in her capsule. The announcer called her Curly the Muttnik, a real sweetheart. She had liked the scientists; she had liked her capsule, which was the size of a country mailbox; she'd thought it was her bed and slept in it. How would it feel, I wondered, to be so cozily at home and find yourself shot into endless space, betrayed by kind hands?

"Remember this day," our father said solemnly, "November 3, 1957."

As it turned out, I didn't know everything there was to know about giraffes. In the years ahead I would learn I wasn't as smart as I'd thought where giraffes were concerned. I would learn that the males hit each other with their necks to decide who is the strongest and who gets to breed with the female. This is called necking, an odd name if you consider the human equivalent. So perhaps it wasn't dancing our giraffes were doing, perhaps it was fighting. But given what I saw, the care the big one, surely a mother, took in hitting the small one, surely her own child, the pretty way it all took place, the tenderness between them, I don't believe they were fighting. And who's to say what is fighting and what is dancing when something you see takes your breath away?

Those giraffes, they opened the world for me, made me crave what the eye loved. What I had yet to learn is how the eye can betray, abandoning us to orbit a vast outer darkness, dazed and alone. Forever too early, forever too late.

The man dropped his camera when he ran from my father. After Dad took us back, I found the third picture, lying facedown in the dust. Now, in the growing dark of my father's Nash Rambler, I pull it out of my shorts pocket and turn it to the light on the dashboard. In the picture my sister and I, we look like we're having the time of our lives.

4

June

Here's how it happened:
When we got home from seeing the giraffes that last time, the house was dark and our mother nowhere in sight. It was almost seven o'clock. We were later getting home than we'd ever been, thanks to Grace's demand to go to the zoo. We hadn't eaten anything since breakfast and were frantic with hunger. I was thinking about eggs, how good a plate of scrambled eggs would taste. When we looked around the empty kitchen, we thought Mama had had her day the way we'd had ours and was now back asleep, without a thought of us. We rolled our eyes at each other. Grace opened the bread box and handed me a slice of Sunbeam. The bread stuck to the roof of my mouth and made me gag.

There was a foreignness about the house, as if we were sneaking into someone else's place in the dead of the night. The leaky faucet at the kitchen sink dripped without a sound. Even the birds, who usually sang well past sunset, had hushed. The house had that silence a place has in the early morning hours when nothing stirs but the cockroaches that scuttle here and there. It was like I'd been struck deaf.

Dad slipped in behind us, turned on some lights, and headed down the little hall to his and Mama's bedroom. The door was closed and there was a note taped to it. He read the note, dropped it on the hall floor, opened the door. We were right behind him and we saw her arm dangling off the bed before he snatched us up and shoved us out the door and shut it in our faces. Not before we caught sight of a dark pool beside our parents' bed. We looked down and saw dark tracks going along the hall to the bathroom and back. I went into the bathroom first. There were red smears on the black-and-white floor tile, as if someone had tried to wipe up. A towel, covered in blood, lay wadded up in the tub. "Grace!" I screamed and she came running and took one look. Then we ran back to the bedroom and turned the doorknob, which was locked. "Go to your rooms," our father said on the other side.

We picked the note up off the floor, took it to Grace's room, spread it out on the bed, and peered at it. *Didn't mean to make a mess of it don't let girls see.* The paper torn jaggedly from my school notebook, a brown smear on it.

We sat on the bed, not looking at each other, picking at the nubs on the spread as if we'd been instructed to groom it. Our father was speaking to someone on the phone, his voice rising and falling as though it were a radio being turned up and then down. He stayed in the bedroom a long time, talking on the phone, then not, then talking again, faster and faster now, his voice like the tear in a fabric.

There was a long silence. Grace took my hand and squeezed it. I pulled away. "We shouldn't have been late, we shouldn't have gone to the zoo," I said. When I saw her face, I wanted to pluck the words from the air and shove them back down my throat.

Then Dad came into Grace's room. His shirt was wet and sweat glistened through his crew cut. His lips had disappeared as if he'd swallowed his own mouth. His eyes were stones.

"Grace," he said. "Take care of your sister. Keep this door closed." Then he shut the door and went back into the bedroom where our mother was.

Grace got her Girl Scout sash from a hook on the

inside of the bedroom door and started telling me what each badge on it stood for. She started with the campfire badge. "You place the twigs first, for kindling," she said. "Then the branches."

After she'd worked her way through to the cooking badge, reciting all the steps in frying a chicken, Dad came back in, his face the color of wet sand. He said, "Go across the street to the Bakers'. Your mother's sick. She needs to go to the hospital."

"No," we said in unison.

Then he put his hands on us, one on each of our shoulders, and herded us out the front door. On the porch he gave us a little push. "Get on over there."

We headed across the street, dragging our feet. We didn't know the Bakers well then and were embarrassed to show up at their door like stray dogs. When Dad went back into the house, we hid in the nandina bushes in the Bakers' side yard and waited. It had begun to drizzle. We started to shiver and wrapped our arms around each other.

"Let's sing 'This Little Light of Mine,'" said Grace. We began to sing in a whisper, each holding a forefinger upright.

It was full dark when the ambulance came and the men in white jackets went inside. The red light on top of the ambulance kept going around and around, making me dizzy. The drizzle turned to rain. We were soaked to the skin by the time they carried our mother out, strapped down. There was a white sheet over her that looked like it had been splattered in brown paint. The rain plastered the sheet over her body so we could see the shape of her high cheekbones. Just as one of them opened the door to the ambulance and they lifted her, the fingers on her left hand edged out from under the sheet a little, then a little more, until we could see her wedding ring glinting under the streetlight. Raindrops rolled off her hand and onto the pavement below.

When the ambulance pulled away, slowly, without a sound, Grace took my hand and we both stood up and came out of the bush.

Dad hadn't gotten into the ambulance but had walked back over to our front porch stoop. He sat down and put his face between his legs, his knees up around his ears, like a giant grasshopper. It had begun to rain hard, splashing the puddles on the sidewalk.

Atop our father's crew cut, drops of water sparkled under the streetlight.

I pulled away from Grace and ran back across the street to my father. For a moment he looked up at me like he'd never seen me before in his life. His face was wet, and the shadows from the ragged leaves of the elm tree in the front yard flickered across it. He snatched me up and held me so tight I could feel his own heart beat inside my ribs, as if it had taken a giant leap through skin and flesh and bone and docked right there inside my own chest.

"Too late," he said.

Then he looked over my shoulder at Grace, and I turned too. She was standing, hunched and forlorn, in the middle of the street, her wet hair plastered to the sides of her face. The streetlight caught her from behind and cast a shadow.

Dad took my hand and led me inside. When I turned, Grace was following us the way a stray dog will follow, a few paces behind, skittish and wary of the stick.

5

Holly

There's a story about the war I used to tell to Olivia the first time I got her pregnant.

I'd start out by saying there are only so many hours a man can stay awake. Nights, I would fall asleep in the foxholes after a day of fighting, my face tucked to the frozen ground. The snow hip deep, deeper in the trenches. My feet would go numb in my boots and the darkness would settle over my face like silk. Then I would dream about having a baby in my belly the way a woman does.

It was always a big one, a boy. It pressed against the hinge on my belt, kicking and turning and reaching for the light. It felt like hunger. In the dream I would laugh and pat my belly and tell the other soldiers they could touch me there if they wanted, feel it kick, listen to its beating heart. *Holly's got one in the oven*, they'd laugh and say. They'd tell me to hurry up and have my boy, give him a Browning so he could shoot some Krauts, help us win this goddamn war.

Olivia didn't think much of my story. She wasn't hot on having children, said there were too many of them in the world already. What she wanted was a place to go in the morning. She missed building boats, she wanted to go back to school. She'd trade places with me in a heartbeat. I could stay home and wipe their noses, change their diapers, figure out something to cook for supper.

I wouldn't have minded staying home. I'd always wanted kids. My own dad was a good man, a good father. Holland McAlister Sr. and me the Junior, called Holly after him. Until the day he died, he was Big Holly and I was Little Holly. One October morning, when he took me duck hunting, he told me a man is judged by his children. If he is a good man, they will be the proof of it, the way a fine coat on a dog or a horse proves it's been well cared for. When he said that, I pictured a little naked child with a fine down all over its body, like the fuzz of a peach. Then my dad's dog, a shiny retriever named Joey, ran into the water and flushed a covey of mallards and we each took two. The wind was coming up from the north. It gathered the falling birds, tossed them around in the air until their wings opened and they looked alive as they fell to earth.

The dreams about my boy started in the middle of the war. I'd met Olivia, but we'd only spent one night together and not in the way you think. It was July of '43. It had just rained late that afternoon, tapping back the New Orleans heat. Steam was rising from the streets and sidewalks. I'd just come into Pascal's Manale with four other wet-behind-the-ears soldiers from the 99th. The bunch of us just setting out, training at Camp Van Dorn over in Centreville, twenty thousand of us, stuck in that red clay mudhole in south Mississippi in the heat of summer. Swampy and crawling with water moccasins the size of tree limbs. That night I first met Olivia, our faces were flecked in blood from the mosquitoes and chiggers. We'd come into the restaurant to try to sober up on spaghetti so we could go out and drink some more before we got on the four o'clock Greyhound back to the swamps.

When I first spotted Olivia, she was sitting at a round table with some other girls, over by a window with a red velvet curtain. She was dark-haired and leggy. Smoking and laughing, leaning on her elbows, both hands flapping like she was some swamp bird about to take off. She was telling a funny story and her girlfriends were laughing and wiping their eyes and hitting the table with their palms.

I eyed her all through my meal. She was eating oysters on the half shell. She ate like she was going to be there all night, mixing her ketchup, horseradish, lemon, and cayenne together, dipping the oyster in the sauce she'd made, then arranging the thing, dripping and alive as a beating heart, on the saltine cracker she held in her hand. She'd pop the whole thing in her mouth, roll her eyes at the other girls like she was in hog heaven, chew for a long time, her cheek bulging. Then she would take the empty shell and tilt it back so the liquid ran into her mouth, her neck white as marble against the curtain behind her, her lips red and wet.

She caught me looking at her and eyed me back. On my way out I stopped at her table. "Don't I know you from somewhere?" I asked. It sounded like a line, but I didn't mean it that way. She looked oddly familiar, like some of the Cajun girls back home.

She winked at her friends. "Maybe. Where are you from?" She took out a cigarette and I lit it.

"Opelika, over in Mississippi, south of Picayune." I was holding my hat in one hand and suddenly realized I had knotted it up. "You from around here?"

"I'm *from* here."

"Opelika's an hour northeast. Guess we're neighbors." It felt like the dumbest thing I'd ever said.

She grinned and winked at her girlfriends. "Never heard of it."

I gave it one more try. "It's just a bump in the road. Hey, wonder if you could give us some directions to Bourbon Street." It was the only street name I could remember.

She rolled her eyes. "You don't want to go there. Seeing as how you're almost a hometown boy, I can show you where there's a little place up on Chartres. You can hear some nice music, dance."

That was the beginning of it. We didn't talk much that night. She liked to sing while she danced, belting out "Stormy Weather" and "That Old Black Magic" as I swung her around. When it was time to go, she walked me to the bus station. After a few blocks I took her hand.

When we stopped to wait for the light to change, she leaned down and pulled a leaf off a scraggly wisp of mint growing on the neutral ground and popped it into her mouth. Then she reached over and took my head and pulled it to her and kissed me on the lips, deep and sweet. She tasted like mint and horseradish. She fished around in her bag, came out with a napkin she'd picked up at the bar, wrote down her address and handed it over. Then she turned and walked away.

The first thing I did when I got back to camp was write and ask for a picture. It came in the mail with just her name, Olivia Grace LaMonde on the back, and the red mark of her lips.

That winter of 1944, I didn't think I was going to make it. We were hayseed doughs in the 99th, farm and small-town boys, mostly from Pennsylvania with a few of us locals sprinkled in. Green as grass, fresh from the swamps of the Mississippi and Texas camps we'd trained in, having never seen a single day of action. So what does the army do but plop us down in the middle of the Ardennes Forest in Belgium, smack-dab up against Hitler's west wall? They threw us out there like bait, spread us out over a twenty-mile front. No reinforcements, no reserves. It snowed day and night, night and day. For a few days after we got there, it was dead quiet. We'd set up camp next to a grove of giant trees, their limbs heavy with snow, touching the ground around us. A mist rose from the snow like steam from a pot. Nothing moved but a few birds. We crossed and recrossed our tracks, trying to find our way among the shrouded trees and hedgerows and rolling hills, trudging through the snowbanks like ghosts in the mist, as though this war was only a dream somebody had conjured up.

It was ten days to Christmas when they came. By then, we'd gotten our bearings and fanned out. Wave after wave of German steel rained down on us. Tanks and infantry and rockets, you name it. Command Post sent in a relief squad of cooks and KPs. Cooks and KPs! They hopped in and out of the snowbanks like scared rabbits, leaping up into the air when they were hit, then vanishing below the snow line. We rushed in to help. My hands shook so, I can't tell you whether I killed anybody, and if I did, whose side they were on. We were pinned down, then one of the cooks hollered, "Hell, no use laying here like dogs." So we all broke into a run, hollering like banshees.

I ran up the middle, not out front where the rocket fire could pick me off, not in the back where they could snag me from the outside or behind. Running through the drifts, hollering at the top of my lungs, I felt heavy and clumsy, tilted into the line of fire. That boy in my belly, he jounced along, not complaining, but not happy either. He wanted to live, he wanted to be Holland McAlister III, Little Holly to my Big Holly. This was his time, this was his only chance.

He was right to worry. Communications were down, it was snowing hard, and men were falling right and left of me. A buddy of mine from Aberdeen, Charlie O'Malley, lost one side of his head and kept on for ten paces, like a chicken after the ax. When he went down, I followed the trail of blood to where he lay, already partly covered in snow. I pulled the letter he'd written to his folks back home from his shirt, the way I'd promised. I had two letters in my shirt, one to my parents and one to Olivia. I'd spent a lot of time on the letter to her, saying I was sorry that I was dead because I'd wanted to come home and have a whole houseful of kids with her. *We would have been so happy. We would have danced our way through life.* That last sentence had taken me a long time to think up.

When we dug into our foxholes at dusk, I took Olivia's picture out of the inside pocket of my shirt, brushed the snow off, looked deep into her eyes. Then I turned the picture over and fitted my mouth to the place her lips had been. I could feel her breath, coming on slow at first, then faster, warming me deep in my belly where my boy was, and I stopped shivering and fell asleep.

In the end, the Germans turned south. We'd stopped them, a miracle really, but enough to turn the tide on the western front.

Somewhere in it all, though, the boy in my belly said he'd had enough, he had a bad feeling. My hands began to shake, my finger twitched at the trigger.

That January I got shot in the right foot and that was the end of it. On the left foot, though I didn't know it then, I'd already lost two toes from frostbite. My regiment went on without me that spring, into Aubel, where the sun was shining, the grass in the apple orchards already green, where the men finally were able to rest. They sent me to Fort Bragg, North Carolina. At the base hospital I piled on the blankets and asked for more. The nurses said there were birds singing outside. I needed to go sit in the sun. But I hated getting out from under those blankets. When I'd get up to stumble to the john, I'd be shivering all over by the time I got back in bed. More times than not, I'd ask for a bedpan.

Then one day someone put a pen and some paper in my hands, and I wrote to Olivia. She wrote back. When I got to New Orleans in late February, it was hot as blue blazes. She met my bus and, from then on, it was Katy bar the door. She changed her schedule at Higgins Boat Yard so we could stay up to all hours dancing and walking the wet streets, taking in the pickle-brine stink of piss and sweet jasmine. In the mornings I'd watch her sleep, her breath coming soft and regular, her mouth parted like a flower.

A month later she was expecting, which put me over the moon. I bought her a pink suit and we went down to the courthouse and sealed the deal. When she started showing, she lost her job at Higgins, which I told her was bound to happen anyway now that the war was over and old man Higgins had shifted to a small operation and hired back the local boys who had come home and needed jobs.

I thought for sure my boy was on his way. That first one was Grace, who was over a month early and came into the world looking like a plucked chicken. Then June came along eighteen months later. I figured my boy was taking his own good time, teasing me a bit. By then we'd moved back to Opelika for me to take the job at the mill. I was set to live a regular life, an ordinary life, all I'd ever hoped for, all I'd ever dreamed of.

The Battle Babies, the Magnificent 99th we were called, was the most decorated regiment in the war. They'd dropped us into hell and we'd torn down Hitler's west wall. Nobody, least of all us, thought we'd kick butt like we did. When the time came, I got my medal along with everybody else. I still walk with a limp: a war wound, my dad used to tell people, and his eyes would glow.

This is the story I would have told my boy, if I'd ever had him. I would have told him that he was a full bowl I carried deep inside without spilling. I would have told him that he got me through. That might have been a lie, it was my shot-up foot that may have saved me in the end. Who's to say? And who's to say where a bullet might come from when a foot steps out ahead, into its path?

I was glad to get Grace and June, you bet I was. But I'd waited a long time for my boy. Waiting for him was like sitting outside a church on Sunday morning. I knew the doors would bust wide open one day, and there he'd be. There he'd be, bright as the sun.

What I didn't tell Olivia: it's easy to tear a rubber, a pinch of a fingernail, that's all it took. I did it for my boy. I couldn't desert him out in that cold outer dark, you see. He was counting on me to bring him home.

Even driving back from the zoo that night, even after sliding into the river and back out again, my two girls waiting at the edge of my mind, even after what Olivia went and did, I still believed my boy would find his way. I thought he'd come home to me, safe and sound. *Better late than never*, I'd say, and we'd both have a good laugh.

So I didn't take her to the hospital when she told me what she'd done. I was so sure my boy would find his way home. Now both of them are gone. My lookout, and the enemy came into the house.

6

Grace

A week after Mama. The backyard mimosa is a skeleton, its branches and a few scraggly birds' nests etched against the winter sky. At supper the three of us sit dazed and bewildered, as if some giant hand has plucked us from distant planets. Bands of late afternoon sun slash our faces so that we look split in two. June and I hunch over our plates, speaking only when we ask for some necessity, no chat, no ease in our talk, our father not asking about our day and we not inquiring after his. *Pass the salt. Bread.* Our words travel great distances, the simplest phrases sounding alien, untranslatable.

We were two hours late and now our mother is forever circling the winter sky. I made us go to the zoo when we should have been home saving her. My father hates me for this.

Dad slumps over the newspaper that hides his plate. Soon he will dump his food into the garbage while June and I silently clear the table. His cigarette smolders in its ashtray; he lights one off the other. A cloud follows him around the house. I'm afraid I will blink and he will have gone up in smoke. He wants to get supper over with so he can go to his room and close the door and open a bottle of cherry bounce.

June and I pick at the food he's prepared: barely warmed jars of Chef Boyardee; runny scrambled eggs and toast; pinkish hot dogs served on Sunbeam bread with frozen French fries, still cold at the center. Afterward, we feel uncomfortably full yet dissatisfied, as if someone has blown air into our bellies.

"If I see another dripping hot dog coming at me, I'm going to upchuck right into my plate," June announces one night after Dad's second hot dog meal of the week.

We're sitting on my bed. I'm brushing her hair. On the radio the Platters are singing "Only You," about love and destiny and the magic they bring to our threadbare lives. Our mother was magic, I see that now.

"Do you remember the time Mama made the rabbit cake for Easter?" June says.

I nod but she tells it to me anyhow: how our mother used one circle pie pan for the face, had cut the second layer into three curved slices for the ears and a bowtie. How she had made the eyes with raisins, the whiskers with licorice sticks. The carrot she'd dug out of the bottom of the icebox and stuck in the rabbit's mouth, an orange cigar.

Whatever our mother's shortcomings as a successful homemaker, she had had a flair for food preparation. You don't grow up in New Orleans and not develop a palate, she'd say. She'd smothered cabbage, boiled artichokes, pickled beets, piled red beans and ham hock on steaming mounds of white rice. She mourned raw oysters and mirliton squash stuffed with shrimp, none of which was available in Opelika, just as she'd mourned her life in what she called *the real world*, as if the four of us, our family, were a dream she was hoping to awaken from.

June throws herself facedown on the bed. After a while she lifts her head and looks up at me, her face pocked from the spread. "Grace, we're going to have to learn to cook or we're going to get gangrene." Her voice is hoarse, her bottom lip trembles. Her hair has become dull as tree bark.

We are both crying a little. Since our mother died, June has been sleeping in my bed, pressed hard against my back, fitting herself to its curve, a parenthesis to the sentence that is me. If we were standing, I would be carrying her on my back.

"Don't you mean scurvy?"

June rolls her eyes, the sadness in them spliced with exasperation. "I'm getting Mama's cookbook, Miss Smarty Britches."

She heads out the bedroom door and shuffles down the hall, the bottoms of her pajama pants, too long because they were mine first, picking up dust balls. I follow, tiptoeing, though not particularly worried about our father catching us up late on a school night. Dad sleeps long hours now, staggering out in the morning, hair flattened and bathrobe inside out, the tie dragging the floor. He fills up the percolator, ignoring us as we glumly make our way through our Rice Krispies. On the weekends, he takes the radio to what's now his bedroom. Through the closed door we hear talk of the 17th Parallel, of satellites and dominoes and more dogs in space. I picture galaxies of tethered dogs, panting and whimpering and spinning through all eternity.

My sister and I don't often go in the room where Dad sleeps. Our mother's blood made a dark lake on the wood floor by the bed. Dad put down a throw rug to hide the stain, but June and I know it's there. Sometimes in the afternoons when he's at work, we will stop at the door and go inside. We understand that our mother's cells are still scattered about, clinging to our fingertips like dust. On the dresser her hairbrush, strands of her living hair still in it; on the bathroom door her robe, her makeup smeared on the collar. These remnants seem airborne, drifting outside the constraints of gravity. Parts of us drift with them like pollen, neither rising nor settling.

We open our mother's drawers and touch her things, drawing them to our faces, then lift up a corner of the rug to look at the stain. It is a secret thing we do together and don't talk about afterward.

Mornings, hurrying past, we glimpse the empty bottle on Dad's nightstand, the overflowing ashtray beside the rumpled bed. We worry about fire.

In the kitchen June pauses to roll up the legs of her/my pajamas, then snatches from a shelf over the stove Mama's *Holy Angels of Mercy Creole Cookbook*, a tattered, grease-splattered hand-me-down from her mother. We skulk our way back to my room, bumping into each other as we glide down the tunnel of a hallway, past our father's closed door.

Our mother had piles of cookbooks but scorned most

of them. She entertained us with passages that summoned homemakers to the art of setting a pretty table, cooking eggs to their husband's tastes, and planning garden parties. Every other recipe called for some form of Jell-O or mayonnaise, both of which she despised. They reminded her of the parish socials she had to go to as a child, where the Jell-O would melt into orange and green and red puddles and the mayonnaise would sprout a sinister yellow crust on top. Instead of following recipes, Mama made up dishes. Our favorite was something she called Chili Mac, a combination of canned chili, slices of white bread, and sharp cheddar, layered like a birthday cake in a casserole dish and baked so that the cheese ran down the sides of the bread like lava.

In the days to come, June heads in from school, drops her books on the kitchen table. In preparation for Dad's suppers, she eats several bowls of Rice Krispies. Then she heads back to our room, plops herself on my bed, and starts thumbing through *Holy Angels of Mercy.* I follow close on her heels, chiding her to do her homework, then setting a good example by pulling out my books and making a show of doing mine. With Dad floating about silently day after day, week after week, letting even his precious boxwoods go without their winter pruning, somebody needs to watch out for my sister, who cares not a whit about school. My natural bossiness rises to the occasion. After all, there's nobody but me, no friendly aunts or uncles in town, no grandparents to call on. Our only living relative is Frances, our old-maid schoolteacher aunt in the City, our mother's sister.

Frances is older than our mother, older than an old wet hen, Mama used to say. Frances the fussbudget, Mama called her, but on weekends when Dad had to balance the books at the mill, our mother would take us on the Greyhound bus to visit our aunt in her little cottage on Louis XIV Street. Mama dressed up for these trips, decking herself out in high heels and rhinestone earclips. Next to the country folk on the bus, she looked like she was stepping on a plane to Paris. As the bus rolled along, past tree farms and dilapidated fishing camps, her hair shone in the morning sun from the previous day's wash-and-set, her bangs curled under like a roll of sausage. Women on the bus would steal glances at her, tuck stray wisps of hair into country buns, straighten their skirts.

Frances met us at the door, her face as open as the sky, her white blouse (she always presented herself in a white blouse and dark skirt) spotless and pressed. The oddities about our mother's face, those features that set her apart and made her, if not pretty, at least what you'd call striking—the way the outer corners of her eyes turned up, the hawkish aspect to the brows, her overly full lips—seemed in Frances to have mutated to a strange excessiveness. Her eyebrows were set so high as to seem perpetually arched; her eyes, behind the specs she wore, stretched to slits, as if she were holding them in that position. Against such a landscape her full lips looked garish, especially when she wore the cherry-red lipstick she always globbed on when we were visiting. The only thing Frances shared in equal proportion was Mama's moon of a face, but on Frances the roundness flattened her head front to back, making her mismatched features look pasted on by an uncoordinated child.

Frances was a do-gooder. She handed out turkey and dressing at the Salvation Army at Thanksgiving and Christmas, marched against nuclear proliferation, tutored children who couldn't read. When the space race heated up, she demonstrated for animal rights. Sending dogs and chimpanzees into space was a crime against nature. How would we like getting tied up in a box and shot into outer darkness? Not much, she bet.

On these visits, Mama wouldn't even bother to sit down and visit. She'd head straight for the bathroom, coming out with a perfect bow of lipstick and sooty eyebrows peeking out from under her bangs. Before our mother hightailed it out the door, Frances would push her specs back on the bridge of her nose and sing out, "Let's all go out for supper on the town, then you can go to your honky-tonk."

Mama would roll her eyes. "Frances, be a pal. Let a poor girl take a break from her dull-as-dishwater life."

Then off she'd go, not to return until the early morning hours, her hair disheveled and her cheeks splotched. Frances had only one extra bedroom, so Mama slept with my sister and me, saying Frances was such a stick-in-the-mud, not to tell our aunt what time she got in. We'd watch Mama undress, cigarette smoke and rotten apples and something curdled we didn't recognize clinging to the clothes she dropped on the floor.

After Mama headed out the door with her two dollars for the taxicab, Frances would bite her lip and then turn to survey us, the booby prizes, standing side by side, June's head tipped sideways so that it touched my shoulder. "Well, now," she'd say brightly, "what do you girls want to do? Can I get you anything?" We would look at each other and raise our eyebrows, sometimes asking for the moon, chocolate cake or lemon meringue pie, just so we could see Frances blink and wince and push her glasses back for the umpteenth time.

But despite her initial nervousness in our presence and our sometimes less than polite demeanor, Frances seemed to view us as objects of study, creatures of another species, younger than her high school students, as yet unformed, full of possibility. She fussed over us, called us "preteens," a term we'd never heard but liked immensely; asked were we afraid of the Bomb, if our parents fought, whether we enjoyed music. We lied with impunity: no, we weren't afraid of old Khrushchev; at school we'd learned how to Duck and Cover, get under our desks, put our arms over our heads; no, our parents didn't fight, they got along like ham and eggs; yes, we adored Benny Goodman and opera, June had seen *Madame Butterfly*.

We kept our distance from our aunt's person. Frances had what June and I referred to as the Lady Schoolteacher Smell, a cross between dust and mold, chalk and cloves, face powder and powdered milk. The smell wasn't unpleasant exactly, but being around her called to mind antique shops and stuffed animals that had once been alive. It brought a vinegary taste to my mouth, like bile.

We haven't seen Frances since our mother's gravesite service when she placed herself between June and me, pressing our heads against her bony hips so that the only sound we could hear was the gurgling of her stomach. So our mouths drop open when, the Friday night after June starts her cookbook research, Frances bustles through our kitchen door with two sacks of groceries and a rectangular overnight case. Saturday morning we find her in the kitchen, wearing our mother's daisy apron, humming "Don't Sit Under the Apple Tree with Anyone Else But Me." She has made leathery biscuits, over which she has dumped a puttyish gravy. That afternoon she takes us for haircuts. She buys us new socks. She lets us get a half gallon of chocolate ripple ice cream at Piggly Wiggly. That night she fries up some chicken. The insides are bloody, the outsides black, all of it smelling like burnt Crisco. June and I wolf it down.

The next Friday she returns, then the next. We settle into a routine. Thanksgiving comes and goes. Frances comes in Wednesday night bearing a turkey, which she cooks to the consistency of cardboard the next day.

By now June has gone back to sleeping in her own room. Despite our protests, Frances insists on alternating sleeping with June one weekend and with me the next, not wanting, she says, "to turn you poor girls out of your own rooms." June worries that the Lady Schoolteacher Smell will cling to us and our schoolmates will laugh at us behind our backs. Already, there have been sneers and whispers, a woman doesn't just up and die of a miscarriage. Dad sat us down and told us a man had been arrested. All I can think about is that two hours at the zoo. All I want to know is when she died, not why, though we know too that our mother was not blameless in her own death; this comes to us not just from words that buzz around us like gnats, but from our father's failure to report for the duty of assuaging our grief, his long trail of silence, which, as time goes on, we understand had already begun that last day at the zoo. He, as much as our mother, is the ghost in the house.

The Sunday after Thanksgiving Frances leaves for what we think will be her regular work week in the City but then she returns late the next afternoon. When we hear her car pull in, Dad and June and I walk out onto the driveway.

Frances gets out of the car and looks at our questioning faces. "School's out for Christmas. Today was the last day." She opens the back door of the car, revealing a monstrous red trunk, the kind you'd take on a sea voyage. As if on cue, a flock of gray pelicans fly over the yard in perfect formation, the flung light of late afternoon turning their wing tips to fire. The four of us look up and Frances gasps *Oh!*, just the way our mother would have done. A wind comes up and some papery elm pods left over from summer swish down the street.

Then Frances stands there and explains to the three of us how much we need her. She's taken leave from her job, she's reporting for full-time duty, now help her get her trunk into the house.

Throughout all this, Dad looks down at the trunk. Then he looks up at June, who's grinning from ear to ear. His shoulders slump. He grabs the trunk and lifts it up and carries it into the house.

Frances comes in, puts down her purse on the kitchen counter. Dad already has some sickly pink weiners boiling on the stove. She pours them out into the sink, runs cold water on them, and dumps them into the garbage. "All right, girls," she says. "Let's get some supper on the table."

June and I jump into action. We love the way Frances keeps us moving along in time. Her favorite command is "sally forth." "Come on, my dears," she'd say, "let's sally forth to the Piggly Wiggly. Quickly now: chop, chop." As the days unfold toward Christmas and the year's end, the weather turning cold and dreary and wet, she worries about the length and tidiness of our hair, the mud on our shoes. She makes dental appointments for us. She shows us how to file our fingernails one way only so they don't break and snag our sweaters. She shops, she cleans, she bleaches our white blouses, she writes thank-you notes for the potato salads and hams and Jell-O molds brought by sly-eyed people after our mother's death.

One afternoon she shows up with a perm and Mango Tango fingernails. She starts wearing rouge at breakfast. She hums under her breath, makes sandwiches for Saturday picnics in the frigid backyard, makes Dad get us a badminton set and put up a net. We need to exercise more, blood flow is important for young girls. She asks for sips of his cherry bounce. She feeds the squirrels vegetable scraps.

The more she bustles about, the more Dad hides behind his newspaper. On weekends he goes to the office.

A week before Christmas she surprises us with a tree. When June and I troop in from school that afternoon, the radio is blaring "Silent Night." She's put on three strands of star lights that twinkle, one red, one green, and one multicolored. She has brought our ornaments up from the basement and tells us to decorate the tree. We cry a little while we do this. Our mother was particular about her tree; she would sit on the sofa squinting and turning her head from side to side to get a better view. Then she would say, "You, Grace, move the star down and to the left. No, not there. *There.*"

While we're decorating the tree, Frances mixes up a batch of sugar cookies, gets out the cutters she's bought in the shapes of Christmas trees and stars, and calls us into the kitchen to roll out the dough, cut our shapes, and sprinkle them with glitter and Red Hots.

That night Dad comes home to a house that smells of sugar and pine. He sniffs the air, glances at the tree, and heads into the kitchen. The cookies, lined up on waxed paper on the kitchen counter, are still warm. Frances pulls Mama's apron over her head and fluffs her hair. "Have a cookie, Holly," she says.

Dad doesn't even take off his coat. "We appreciate your help, Frances, but we need to be on our own now. We need to settle down."

"But, Holly," she says in a happy rush, "I'm just so glad to help out. Maybe I can get a job teaching in Opelika, move down here. You need a woman's touch around this place, someone to watch after these girls. You need a substitute!" It's a dumb schoolteacherish joke.

Dad is in the process of taking off his coat when she says it. He makes an explosive sound in his throat, something between a bark and a growl.

Frances catches her breath, her face flushed and sweaty, the rouge on her cheeks sloughing its way down her cheeks. "Oh, I didn't mean . . . ." She puts a hand to her cheek. She's just put the dumplings into the pot; they haven't floated on the broth the way they're supposed to, the way our mother's would have done, but have belly-upped and drowned, sinking to the bottom of the pot. She begins to scrape them up with a spatula, slimy and flattened and burnt.

Dad clears his throat. "A substitute isn't the real thing."

Frances scrapes harder, her back turned to him. "Sometimes a substitute is better than nothing. Sometimes a person has to think of others."

Dad rubs his mouth. "It's not that, Frances, it's just . . ."

"Don't say it." Frances looks over at June and me, frozen in the task of setting the table, knives and forks in our hands. "Girls, get out the placemats first."

That night it is my turn to sleep with Frances. She always reads before turning out the light, books with titles like *By Love Possessed* and *Compulsion,* but tonight she turns off the light as soon as she returns from the bathroom in her nightgown.

In the night I awake to her tossing and turning. In the moonlight I can see that her face is wet, her nearsighted eyes glazed. "Oh, Grace," she cries out, "whatever is going to become of us?" Her question explodes in the room; pieces of it hover in the cold, still air.

I bury my face in the pillow and start to cry too. Frances puts her hand on my shoulder and I cry harder. "Don't listen to me," she says. "Everything will work out. It will be all right." She moves in closer, her arm pinning me down. I throw off her arm and bolt out of the bed, pulling my pillow with me. "Don't go," she says, but I head down the hall for June's room and crawl into her bed, molding myself to her back as she sleeps.

The next morning when June and I get up, Dad is out in the backyard digging. He has staked out an area the size of our kitchen with sticks and twine and has a determined look on his face. We go out in our pajamas and sidle up beside him. A wind has come up, biting our faces, rattling the mimosa branches. When we ask our father what he's up to, he tells us he's building a bomb shelter. There's a booklet lying on the ground that has a picture on the cover of a mother and father and a boy and girl with smug little smiles on their faces playing cards in a room with shelves and cans and beds that hang from the ceiling. The cover reads: "If You Can Build a Birdhouse, You Can Build a Bomb Shelter. Do-It-Yourself Shelter, Fallout Protection for Four. $150."

Frances calls June and me in for breakfast, scolding us for going out in the cold in our pajamas. She ignores Dad and his pile of dirt. She has set the table for three and placed a stack of hotcakes on each of our plates. The hotcakes are runny inside and burnt outside, but we don't say a word, just eat them with some old sorghum molasses Mama bought from a stand on the side of the road. We carry the dishes to the sink and thank Frances for breakfast, hoping to counter Dad's rudeness with appreciation and obedience. We stand behind her with dish towels to dry as she runs the water for the dishes, her back to us.

"Frances, please stay," I say. "Dad was just talking."

She scrubs hard on the skillet. "I can't, honey. You girls can come into the City on the bus when you get a little older. We can go out to the lake and get some shrimp. Go to the zoo."

The thought of the zoo knocks the breath out of me. When did my mother die? I want to know the hour, the minute, the second. Was it while June and I stood in front of the polar bear exhibit? Was it when that awful man was taking our picture?

Frances finishes the dishes and heads back to my room. June follows her and sits on the bed while our aunt gathers up her things: a pot of cold cream, her nightgown hanging on the hook on the inside of the door, her comb and brush. "Well, girls," she says. She touches first June and then me on the tops of our heads, then picks up her overnight bag and heads out the door. Her red trunk is already on the back seat of the car. We follow at her heels, as if we are one girl rather than two. When she gets in the car, we cluster at her window, as she fumbles with her key. We stand in the driveway as she backs her car out. We wave, but she doesn't look back.

We stand in the driveway a while, as if we are waiting for her to drive around the block and return. June kicks dead leaves and hums like a trapped fly. I start to shiver. A squirrel approaches us from across the yard, then scurries away, disappointed.

"Damn that Frances," says my sister.

"Damn her hide," I say.

7
Holly

In those first weeks after, Olivia would come to me in dreams, the mesh bag she'd used to catch that sparrow hanging loose in her hand. My boy in that bag, his sweet flesh smooth and curved like an egg.

When the police came to the house, I had to tell the girls the truth, what Olivia had gone and done, how there would be an inquest, then a trial. I'd found the address and phone number in her purse. That night I wanted to go out there and kill him myself, butcher him like a hog, the way he'd butchered her and my boy. (It was a boy. I made sure to ask.)

But I had me a mess to clean up. I stayed up all night scrubbing the floor, throwing her gowns, the bloody towels out in the trash. There was so much blood. The next morning I called Routledge's and ordered a new bed, told them to bring it right out and be prepared to dispose of mine. Word had spread, and Jack Routledge had the bed to me by noon. His men turned our marriage bed upside down before carrying it off, so we didn't have to see the blood.

In the days that followed, the girls wouldn't let me out of their sight, following me from room to room. After the burial, I made them go back to school, take up their lives. They were good girls, they did what I said, but it was like they were sleepwalking. June would forget to comb her hair. Grace's socks never matched. At first people brought food, people I'd never seen in my life. When that ran out, I opened cans that Olivia had stockpiled in the pantry, hardly knowing what was in them. At the table I'd pick up my paper and hide behind it, just to shield myself from June's hunched shoulders, Grace's shell-shocked eyes.

I could not bring myself to look at Grace. Those two hours, what difference would they have made? I never asked the time of death, didn't want to know. And, really, the fault is mine: I shouldn't have left that day. I should have stayed home with Olivia. I should have made her go to the hospital, even if I had to drag her by the hair of the head. Not to speak of the other thing I did.

Still, I could not look at my eldest daughter.

Then the teachers started calling. They knew we were going through a terrible time, but I should know that June was sleeping in class, not eating her lunch, failing recent tests in English and geography. Was she bathing regularly? Did I know she was wearing the same outfit every day? Grace had kept up with her studies, but had a bad attitude, refusing to say the Pledge of Allegiance, getting into squabbles in the halls.

One night, Grace left the supper table without eating. June burst into tears and clawed at my newspaper and started raving about hot dogs, how much she hated them. When I got her to bed, I went into my room and called Frances. I just wanted to ask her advice. She was a teacher, she ought to know something about girls. She said she'd come on Friday and stay the weekend and sort things out. It was the last thing I wanted, her in my house, like some strange mutation of Olivia, but I was crawling through a dark tunnel, no end in sight, pulling the girls along behind me, all of us in danger of being buried alive. I choked on the phone trying to say thank you, making a fool of myself.

We went along for a while, me and the girls and Frances. After a while, Frances said Grace and June needed her full time. They needed supervision and structure, they needed haircuts and new shoes. She got them to whispering and giggling again, mostly about her cooking and her bossy ways. She got them dressed properly in the morning and made them sit down and do their homework. She took them to church and the dentist. When Grace started her monthlies, Frances got her set up and told me about it afterward.

Then Frances started drinking my cherry bounce and asking what we were going to do in six months, a year. She started looking at me. Then she brought in that Christmas tree.

The night after I asked her to go and she left in a huff, I put down the newspaper and studied my girls across the table. The skin on their faces was smooth as cream, their fingers long and tapered like Olivia's. I thought back to when they were crawling babies, how they would wait for me to get home at night and scoot across the floor on their hands and knees, crowing to be picked up and tossed in the air.

Now, their eyes looked past mine like they were looking at someone standing behind my chair, a stranger.

June kicked at the table leg while she ate, her hair falling in her face, her shoulders hunched. She reminded me of a picture I'd seen of a Jap kid. He wasn't wearing anything but this torn nightshirt and he was covered in black splotches, radiation burns. He crouched low, peering up into the night sky like he was waiting for the next Bomb to fall.

I forced myself to look at Grace. Her cheek was still round as a little child's, her shoulders bony, her upper arms sticks.

She looked back at me then, her eyes, gray like Olivia's, clouded over, empty and dull as dishwater.

I am an accountant. Two hours is two hours, not an everlasting bill due.

Once I had been a father. Once I had tucked my girls in at night, had taken them to see the giraffes dance.

I had read about the Bomb. What it could do. The fallout they call black rain. I had seen the pictures, eyes staring out from bandages, the open sores.

My dad told me the first thing a man does is take care of his family, protect his family. When he signed me up for Scouts, he gave me the *Handbook for Boys* with the cover I loved. It had an Indian chief in a feathered headdress, naked as a jaybird. He stood over a campfire where boys like me sat cross-legged in their summer uniforms with the red neck scarves. He guarded us boys, teaching us the old ways of the woods. I used to pore over that book, taking good care to read the section on being morally straight. I learned not to steal or lie or abuse my body. When I earned my Eagle, Dad told me I was ready now, ready to take care of a family, be a man.

So I got to digging. It was all I could think to do for them.

Truth is, I was thinking about the war. The comfort of a foxhole at the end of the long lost day, the feel of cold wet dirt on the face.

8
Grace

After our father gets rid of Frances, he perks up. In addition to a bomb shelter, he decides we also need to outfit our basement for tornadoes. The almanac has predicted multiple tornadoes for 1958, you never know when you are going to find yourself in the path of one. It's good to be prepared.

"Don't you think hurricanes are more likely? We're not far from the coast," I point out to him.

"Of *course* I've considered hurricanes, Grace," he says as he lines up candles and flashlights on the kitchen counter. "I've considered *all* disasters. The difference between a hurricane and the Bomb or a tornado is that a hurricane can be predicted well in advance. We can *evacuate.*"

He strides through the house, lists and charts and graphs in his hand, opening cupboards, checking items off his lists, his eyes busy, interested. We'll travel light for the tornado, just some water and canned goods; the bomb shelter is another story, we could be down there for months. Bomb or no bomb, the idea of getting into a hole in the ground gives me the heebie-jeebies. Just last week a bunch of men got buried alive in West Virginia when a mine shaft fell in on them. I eye my father, who is looking downright scrawny these days. Why does he think he can dig a better hole than the Raleigh-Wyoming Coal Company? At night when I lie in bed, my nose fills up with dirt, my hands scratch at the muck, trying to swim underground.

Dad divides his time between digging the monster hole in the backyard and nailing boards across the windows of the basement. He sweeps out the basement, attacking the ancient spider webs on the ceiling beams. He carries armloads of Beanee Weenees, powdered milk, and ten-gallon bottles of water down the steps and stacks them on the basement shelves next to his supply of cherry bounce. He orders three sleeping bags and multiple boxes of candles from Sears, gets blankets and pillows at McCoy's Dry Goods downtown, all of which he totes down to the basement and rolls up neatly in a corner.

"Why don't you just let us stay in the tornado shelter for the Bomb?" June says in her most reasonable voice,

leaning out over the basement stairs. She adds hopefully, "Or we could hop in the bomb shelter when the
tornado comes." June hates basements as much as I hate
the idea of being in a hole in the ground. This is my
fault. Once, when we were little, I told her there was a
puppy in the basement. When she scampered down to
see, I locked the door. I didn't leave her for long, but
when I opened the door, I nearly knocked her down
the steps; she was huddled on the first step. She lunged
past me, trembling and crying. I said I was sorry, I
didn't know she was such a baby.

Now Dad comes to the bottom of the stairs and
glares up at her, a single hanging bulb illuminating
his face, which is pink from exertion. "Because the
radiation from the Bomb can invade concrete, that's
why. The denser the material, the less chance we'll be
contaminated. Plus, the house might collapse on top
of us from the blast, seal us in. We could be buried
alive." His tone is stern.

I'm standing behind June and yell down to him,
"When the siren goes off, how are we going to know
whether it's a tornado or the Bomb?" I punch my sister
in the ribs and giggle. Our town has a siren, but its
mournful foghorn doesn't distinguish among emergencies. It is the first time since our mother died that my
sister and I have laughed.

"We'll have some warning about war, the Bomb coming," he says, frowning. "We are on the brink of annihilation, girls. It's no laughing matter. Go get me the flashlights."

As Dad proceeds in his efforts to save us from an assortment of disasters, June returns to recipe hunting, her books and homework sheets thrown to the floor beside the bed. She scribbles notes on a page of the cookbook. "You're going to get put back," I say. "You're not Miss Brilliant, you know."

She looks up from her scribbling. "You're not the boss of me." Her face is pinched, her eyes glittery as a bird's. "Grace, I'm just trying to get some decent food on the table."

There's an urgency in her tone I appreciate. Between digging one shelter and outfitting another, Dad's questionable interest in cooking has evaporated altogether. My sister and I have been eating more and more Rice Krispies, sometimes with milk, sometimes without when he forgets to buy it. In the afternoons after school, we go down to the basement and steal some of his stash of Beanee Weenees and eat them out of the can since we aren't allowed to use the stove. We mash sugar and flour and Crisco together and use Mama's biscuit cutter to make raw cookies, which we flavor with vanilla. These make us jittery and snappish. Every month I feel woozy when I bleed. The edges of June's mouth crack. In bed at night, I touch and retouch my rib cage.

Now I peer over June's shoulder at a recipe for chess pie. My mouth waters. As she turns the pages, I keep seeing the word *substitution*. The cookbook is a remnant of the war years: margarine may be substituted for butter; potatoes made into pie crusts; dry milk and dry eggs used instead of the real thing, none of it appealing in the least. "What are you going to cook out of this stupid book?" I ask. "Nothing's what it's supposed to be; it's all substitutions."

She lifts her face; she looks calm, serene even. "Coq au vin," she says. It sounds like "coke awe vine."

"What's that?"

"It involves chicken," she says. "A lady from France put it in the book to show how to make old-timey French dishes."

"*Involves* chicken? Why don't you just fry up some chicken? I could sure settle for that."

She looks at me like I'm the fool of the world. "Because this is better."

She hands me a list. "Call Nesbitt's," she commands. "Tell them to send out the stuff. Tell them to charge it to Dad's account."

I look at the list and snicker. First off there's the bottle of red wine, which you can't buy anywhere in Pearl River County.

"Fancy dancy," I say. "Plus, Dad doesn't have an account." Dad never orders from Nesbitt's, says he can't afford it. Mama did on occasion, but only when she was making a special meal and she always paid in cash so Dad would never know the difference. The last time she ordered from Nesbitt's it was a leg of lamb and some mint jelly for Easter.

"Oh, shut up," June says.

She shows me the recipe. Next to the wine she's written, *Substitution: Dad's cherry bounce from the basement*. Next to "few sprigs fresh thyme" she's written, *Forget this: it's just for decoration*, and for "few sprigs parsley," *ditto*. We have the bay leaves, flour, butter, and sugar. For the vegetable oil, she's written, *Substitution: melted Crisco*; beside mushrooms, *ugh*. For something called *beurre manie*, she's scrawled, *What's this? Oh, just forget it!*

The recipe calls for a medium-sized chicken, jointed, cut into eight pieces. This, we know, is important. The back and *carcasse*, whatever that is, need to be reserved for stock. Next to these instructions my sister has written, *What's stock? Look up*. Then there are onions, chopped.

On top of all this, there is, of all things, brandy, a cup of it warmed (*Substitution: more cherry bounce, don't forget to warm it*); two cloves garlic, chopped (*What's a clove? Is it like the little brown sticks Frances chews?*); twenty pearl onions, peeled (*Never mind, plenty of onions already*).

In all, we agree I'll order the chicken ("Ask for a plump hen," June advises), two onions, two clove sticks just in case, two garlics ditto. The recipe calls for four ounces of streaky bacon, cut into strips or lardons. We have no earthly idea what lardons are, so we agree to ask for strips.

When I put in the phone call, Mr. Nesbitt himself answers, which is unusual. When I give him the order, he responds, "All my bacon's streaky. Everybody's bacon's streaky, honey. That's what bacon is, streaky. What you girls up to over there? Your daddy know you're ordering all this stuff?"

"Yes sir." I try to sound cheerful, ambitious. "We're making a special dinner for him. It's his birthday." Being around our mother has turned me into a talented liar. I don't know a delicate way to tell Mr. Nesbitt to put it on our account when we don't have one. "Can we have an account?" I finally ask.

"Don't worry about it, honey," he says. "You better let me cut up that chicken. Y'all don't need to be messing with knives. Likely to cut a finger off."

"We'd appreciate that. But we need the neck and the carc-asse."

"Carc-asse?" He starts to sputter. "You mean the bones? The bones are in the pieces, honey."

I'm about to hang up when June pops up from the bed. "Ask him to send some hamburger and buns and pickles," she calls forth, "and some potatoes and salad dressing and dry pintos and a ham hock."

I ignore her. Clearly she's getting carried away. I don't even know how all this stuff is getting paid for, much less adding on more, like we've got money to burn. The groceries arrive shortly before Dad gets home from work. June and I are standing at the kitchen sink looking out at the doves rooting around under the empty bird feeder when Mr. Nesbitt walks in the kitchen door without knocking. We both jump. The sack of food looks small in his meaty hand.

"All right, little ladies," he says, with a quick look around. "Here's your stuff, but don't start on the cooking until your daddy gets home. Don't want you burning down the place. Tell him happy birthday and this is on the house. We been thinking about you folks." His eyes start to water and he casts his eyes in the direction of the living room. He wants to see into our lives, the private things we do, where we take our rest. "Let us know how we can help out." His velvet words worry my face like mesh. As he looks down at us, big old tears now rolling out of his eyes, I feel like Mama's trapped sparrow, pecking at the bag.

After he heads out the door, wiping his face with a handkerchief, I turn to my sister and see what I haven't seen before. The gold specks in her eyes burn. "Old jackass," she says. "Old horse turd. I could kick his butt. Kick it from here to the moon. Who does he think he is, feeling sorry for us?" She tosses her hair, reminding me of Mama.

"Okay," I say, "let's make it."

"You don't just make it, stupid. It has to *marinate*."

"What?"

She rolls her eyes. "*Soak.*"

"Soak in what?"

"We don't have wine, so we'll substitute cherry bounce." She opens the bloodied wrap, pulls out the chicken pieces, sits them out on the counter, and begins to salt and pepper them. "Go down to the basement and get some of Dad's bounce."

By the time I bring the bottle back up and struggle with the cork, finally managing to poke it down into the bottle, where it bobs like a little boat, she has gotten the chicken nicely laid out in a Pyrex dish. We peer at the directions, which tell us to boil the wine, aka bounce, with thyme and parsley, neither of which we have, and bay leaves, cool for an hour and pour over the chicken and marinate for twelve hours.

"We need to hurry," June says breathlessly. "Forget the bay leaves. I'll put them in later."

I pour the bounce into a cooking pot, noticing with relief that the cork has trapped most of the cherry debris in the bottle. June turns the flame on high and the bounce starts to bubble.

June looks at the kitchen clock. It's already five; Dad will be home in fifteen minutes. "No time for cooling," June says, pouring the boiling bounce over the raw chicken, which sizzles and turns an unnatural shade of hot pink. We put aluminum foil over the steaming Pyrex dish and push it to the back of the icebox, strategically placing milk cartons and leftovers in front of it. The bacon and onion she puts in the vegetable crisper, which is empty since our father never buys vegetables.

That night Dad comes in, hangs up his coat, puts his hat on the rack, heats a jar of Chef Boyardee, and pours it over three slices of white bread. At the table June winks at me over his newspaper.

When we get in from school the next afternoon, we turn on the radio and get to work. June, wearing Mama's apron, props the cookbook on the kitchen counter. She orders me to turn the oven to 350 and gather the rest of our ingredients from their hiding places. The chicken, now the shade of ripe watermelon; the streaky bacon; Crisco as a substitute for the oil; onions, clove sticks, garlics, and more cherry bounce to make up for the brandy. Elvis belts out "Jailhouse Rock" and I dance around the kitchen.

"Do you think we could just leave the rest of the cherry bounce out of it?" I say, eyeing the Pyrex dish of gory chicken. "Don't we have enough bounce in this thing?"

"Nope," she says, throwing the whole pack of bacon into the pan, "we have to flambé it, that's important. You need to get busy. Cut up the onion, remember to peel it first."

I have no earthly idea what flambé is but know better than to ask. I cut up the onion, tears streaming down my face, while June fries the bacon, which is stuck together, causing part to burn and part to stay raw. She pulls out the burnt pieces and we eat them. Then she melts a blob of Crisco in the pan and instructs me to throw in the onions. Wiping my wet face with a cup towel, I'm thinking I'm getting the worst end of this deal. I air my grievances, but my sister is preoccupied. She has the flame up too high and the onions are smoking. She grabs at the skillet handle, which of course is hot, and hollers for me to get her a cup towel. I reach over and turn off the flame, remarking on how much smarter some people are than others.

"Oh shut up. Read me the directions." She scrapes the burnt onions off the bottom of the skillet and dumps a steaming glob of them on the counter.

"'Remove the chicken from the marinade and pat dry.'"

"Do it," she orders.

"We'll turn the cup towel red."

"Who cares?" she growls. "What's next?"

"'Dust the chicken with flour, then add to pan and fry lightly to brown.'"

"Get the flour. It's in the pantry."

I have by now piled the gory chicken pieces on the kitchen counter, which makes it look like a murder scene. I throw the dish towel in the garbage and get out a fresh one. I wash my hands, which are now dyed red, and head for the pantry. When I return with the sack of flour, June snatches it from my hands and dumps most of it on the pile of chicken, giving it the appearance of a series of small bloody hills covered in snow.

"I don't think that's what the French lady meant when she said to dust it," I say.

"To hell with the French lady," June says, adding more Crisco to her pan, firing it back up, and shaking flour from each chicken piece before she throws it into the bubbling grease. The kitchen has begun to look like one of Dad's tornadoes blew through.

The chicken's sizzling along, smelling like heaven, June's turning it with Mama's long fork, and I'm thinking this isn't so bad. I'm still crying, though. The onions have let loose a river. A flood. I shake my head, and my tears splatter my sister. She grins at me. "Maybe if this turns out, we can have it for Christmas," she says.

I look at the next thing to do: "Pour in the warmed brandy and flambé it."

"Did you ever figure out what flambé means?" I ask. I blow my nose on the clean dish towel.

"Don't you know anything? It means burn," she says. "Go down to the basement and get some more bounce." She hasn't been cutting onions, but something is happening with her face. It's red and blotchy and her nose is running too.

I eye the Pyrex dish where the chicken has marinated. It's filled with bounce. Blood too, but who cares? "Let's just substitute this," I said, pointing.

"Okay," she says, "but it's against my better judgment. If it messes up my dish, I'm going to kill you dead. Pour it into a cup. I just need one cup. Forget warming it up." She sounds like she's choking on something. She wipes her eyes on Mama's apron.

"How do I burn it?"

"Get a match, stupid."

I get some kitchen matches from the drawer. I pour the bloody bounce into a cup and pour the rest down the drain. I get a match and try to light it. Nothing happens.

"Wait!" June yells. "You pour it over the chicken first!" She's sweating and her hair is hanging over most of her face. She runs her sleeve under her nose.

"Pull your hair back," I say. "You'll catch yourself on fire if it flames up."

She glares at me. "Can't you see I'm busy?"

I reach over, pull my sister's hair behind her ears. My fingers leave war paint streaks of chicken blood and flour on her cheeks. I make a mental note to tell Dad to take us both in for haircuts.

"Do you think the chicken's done?" she asks, sniffling.

I have to wipe my eyes to see the directions. "It cooks an hour more in the oven, after you put the other stuff in with it, the bacon and onion and all, so it's going to get cooked one way or the other."

She grins, and the grin, along with her war paint, makes her look murderous. Tears are dripping off her chin. "Okay then, bring on the bounce and get a match ready."

The local announcements are on the radio. *Sputnik 2*, with Laika's remains inside, is still orbiting the earth. The town of Opelika will test its warning sirens tomorrow, Saturday, at noon. Next week there will be a display of bomb shelters at the fire hall. *Frankenstein Meets the Wolf Man* is playing at the Lyric, which makes me think of how the movie reel will likely break and flap about like chickens do when they get aggravated, and the boy in the projection booth up in the balcony will do something magical—what I don't know—to fix it. If he takes a while, we'll stir in our seats, murmuring and agitating. But he always splices it somehow. If sometimes parts are skipped where the broken part was, it's a small price to pay.

I pour the cherry bounce over the sizzling chicken, then strike my match.

My sister pauses, searches my face as if she's looking for a crumb she can brush away. The match is burning down. Once we had had a mother. Her pulse had fluttered at the temple. She had put on the daisy apron and cooked food for us in this very kitchen.

June turns up the flame. It flares and the cherry bounce begins to boil.

"Okay," she says. "Light it."

9
Grace

So we went along, the three of us, Dad digging his way to China, June poring over her cookbooks instead of her lessons. I turned outward, joining the band, studying until late into the night, reading the teen magazines so that I could dress myself and my sister in the latest fashions. Along with my perky outfits, I cloaked myself in what you'd call normal teenage girlhood, briskly sweeping aside thoughts of my mother, the way I swept out our carport every Saturday.

Time, which had seemed to stretch out in one endless present tense after Mama died, slowly clicked back into place. The past became past, the future awaited. Monday became Monday, Tuesday Tuesday, each day punctuated by some small activity: a test in social studies, a new dish that June had concocted, a special television program we liked. And so the gears began to grind and we went on, day by day, week by week, month by month, the way people do. Some nights I dreamed I hadn't insisted on going to the zoo that day; instead, we had come home two hours earlier and Mama had made supper. Sometimes gumbo, sometimes just hamburgers and frozen French fries.

Once, in my dream I lifted the lid on a pot and there was a baby inside. It reached out its little arms and said, *Get me out of here.* I popped the lid back on and woke up in a sweat.

Then one bright Sunday morning I woke up and eighteen months had passed. I opened the window. It was April and breezy. The jonquils had turned to paper and folded up for the season. Azalea buds were splitting their green sheaths. Outside my window, at one of Mama's nest boxes, a male bluebird lit all in a flutter, then called for its mate. At the zoo, giraffes were dancing in the morning sun, though my sister and I weren't there to see them.

Although I was not myself beautiful, the giraffes had left me with a fierce attraction to what was. This is how, about this time, I came to fall madly in love with Daniel Baker from across the street. Daniel was two years my senior and quite good-looking in a blond sort of way, and the fact that he sat in the shadows of his parents' screen porch on Sunday afternoons wearing his sister's blouses deterred me not in the least.

"I know he's a bit off the track, but aren't we all?" I said to June, who, along with her best friend, Hilary Lumpkin, was thought by some to be more than a bit off the track herself. It was more of a pronouncement than a question. I swished my ponytail when I uttered it, wishing my own dark hair were the color of my Daniel's, the color of the sun in the sky.

One day I decided to take the bull by the horns and visit Daniel during one of his Sunday afternoon porch sits. And why not? The Bakers had been kind when our mother died, Mrs. Baker sending Daniel over with steaming casseroles and freshly cut mums from her own garden. So it was the natural thing to do, I reasoned, to be friendly, to go across the street to see a friend, a chum, on a glorious spring afternoon.

I went over to my dresser and pulled out my best pair of pedal pushers. They were wrinkled, so I got out the ironing board and iron, thrummed my fingers on the board waiting for it to heat, and then set a nice crease down the middle of each leg. Since the iron was hot, I pressed my best crop top too. Both the shirt and the pedal pushers were purple, my favorite color. They didn't quite match since they'd been bought separately, but they were close enough. I laid them out to cool on the bed and unplugged the iron, which was steaming up the room, making my hair droop and frizz. I took it into the kitchen and set it down on the stove the way Mama had taught me so that it wouldn't burn the house down.

The metallic click of the iron against the stove top stopped me in my tracks. It was at moments like this, when I remembered something my mother had cautioned me about, that I missed her the most. There were dangers in the world I couldn't begin to know—hidden patches of quicksand I wouldn't see until I was up to my waist.

I wolfed down a bowl of leftover chicken potpie, June's latest culinary accomplishment, and went back into my room and brushed my hair. As a final touch I put Vaseline on my lips and eyebrows to make them show up. The house was quiet that morning, Dad having probably overdone it again on the cherry bounce. I tiptoed down the hall and into the bathroom, where I brushed the taste of chicken potpie out of my mouth. I sat down at my desk to finish up my homework and wait for afternoon.

I knew I would find Daniel clean and fresh and pretty, just sitting there, as if he were waiting for something interesting to happen, something new.

Since the weather had turned warm, I'd been spying on him with my mother's bird-watching binoculars, and although I could only make out his shape behind the screen, I had come to think of him as an actual bird, with that kind of lightness and intentionality, as if he'd been washed clean of the world he and I lived in, a world of in or out, you go or you stay. Sitting there on his porch in his splashy getups, he looked temporary, poised for flight.

I knew his Sunday afternoon routine inside and out. Around three, after Sunday dinner and a short nap, the Bakers—including Daniel's sister, Melinda—went for a ride. Sometimes Daniel went with them, but mostly he stayed behind and did his porch sitting. The three other Bakers were usually gone about two hours. Daniel seemed to have a sense of their imminent return and would vanish into the interior of the house about fifteen minutes before the family's gray Chrysler swept majestically up Palm Street and slowed to take the turn into the Baker driveway.

The rest of the week he did ordinary things in ordinary boy clothes. He threw the football with his dad, got the newspaper from the curb each morning, roughhoused with the Bakers' giant collie, Lion. So I thought of Daniel's porch sitting as not so much aberrant as somehow *extra*, a loose end of himself that required expression. He was artistic, that was it; he had imagination, and who could fault a boy for that?

This particular Sunday, about half an hour after the Bakers had pulled out of their driveway, I put on my pedal pushers and crop top, careful not to let them drag the floor, which was as usual dusty, then peered out the dining room window to make sure Daniel had stayed home.

I could only make out his shadow—I knew him most intimately by the tilt of his head—and, yes, there he was.

I stood at the window a while longer, staring across the street while I thought about what to do next, what to say. I was afraid, but felt an irresistible draw, as if I were the tide and Daniel the shore. Was this feeling of inevitability biology or was it love?

I walked out the door casually, as if I were just going out into the front yard where June, ever the struggling student, sat in the old tree swing reciting the countries of western Europe and their capitals, occasionally cheating by peeking at the notecards I'd prepared for her. Dad was listening to her and correcting her mistakes as he clipped his boxwoods.

Neither of them noticed as I made my way across the street, the pavement sending heat waves up through my flip-flops. I lurched toward the Bakers' house on my tiptoes, which gave me the appearance of being about to launch myself into flight. When I reached Daniel's front lawn, I didn't look in his direction as I skirted the piles Lion had deposited and Lion himself, who was lying belly up in the sun, though I knew Daniel would be observing me from behind the screen. In this suddenly miserable moment, I could see myself in his eyes, purple from the neck down, my hair slipping down my back, flat and frizzy from the humidity.

I must have looked a bit shifty, like someone about to commit an act of petty theft.

As I drew closer, I moved more purposefully, as if I were going to borrow some eggs or sugar from Mrs. Baker, as if I didn't know Daniel's mother wasn't at home. Letting my flip-flops flop perceptibly now, I pushed my way through the bee-buzzing nandina bush that partly blocked the Bakers' side porch from the street. I walked up to the screen door and knocked twice. I peered through the screen, but it was rusty and thick with dust. My bottom lip brushed it, leaving the taste of rust in my mouth. I could see only Daniel's shape in the chair, the lankiness of it, his lovely boyishness.

I tapped on the door, softly, as if he might be asleep.

He sat there, still as a post. He reminded me of a blue heron I'd seen on the side of the road in a patch of cattails, hunched and watchful.

I knocked again, louder. "Daniel, let me in. It's hot out here."

He shifted a bit. Instead of letting me in, though, he glided in one smooth motion, partly bent over as if he were suffering from stomach cramps, to the inside doorway and disappeared into the house carrying a pair of lady's pumps in his hand.

I stood there, mule-like, my eyes downcast. It was 3:30 in the afternoon by then. The day was warm for April and I was in direct sun, feeling a bit faint. Sweat collected in my scalp and began to run down the sides of my face and into my eyes.

I waited, but he didn't come back out. What a humbug this was proving to be! I tugged at the screen door, expecting it to be locked, but it wasn't, so I found myself suddenly on the porch and then pushing (I couldn't believe I was doing this, it was almost like breaking in) the door to the inside of the house. The door swung open to a large hall with a living room on the left and a dining room on the right and stairs that led straight up. The house seemed for the first time very grand. The curtains in both front rooms, cut from a heavy reddish fabric, maybe velvet, were drawn. One thin ray of sun spliced the gleaming oak floors.

I peered through the darkness. "Daniel?"

My voice sounded shrill and strange. There was no answer; the house seemed coldly empty. Then suddenly a door upstairs burst open and here he came, bounding down the stairs, in shorts and sneakers and a white undershirt, looking, if you didn't notice the smear of lipstick and pinch marks on each earlobe where his sister's bobs had been, for all the world like a regular boy.

"Hey." He looked at me straight on, full speed ahead, regular boy style. "What's going on?" he asked breezily as if it were not unusual for me to appear, looking, in fact, quite desperately hot, in his front hall.

"Where'd you go?" It was the only thing I could think of to say, so astonished I was, not so much by his change of clothes as by the transformation in his demeanor.

"I was hot," he said, "needed to change from church. You want a Nehi?"

Over time, just a few weeks, we became boyfriend and girlfriend. When I told Dad, he had a fit. It was not as if he hadn't tried to raise me right. Sure, there'd been rough spots after my mother had died. But overall, he'd done all the correct things: firm discipline, a stable home, disaster preparedness. Raising two girls alone was a hard row for a man to hoe, but he'd done his best.

"I'm not Mama's gumbo," I told him. "I'm not going to turn out the way you want just because you put in all the right things and stir the pot."

When I defied my father and took possession of Daniel's class ring, buying a gold chain with my allowance and hanging the ring around my neck for the whole wide world to see, Dad said, "That boy doesn't need a girlfriend. He's his *own* girlfriend." He took to calling Daniel Danielle. He forbade me to wear the ring. I responded by hiding it under my blouse until after I left the house.

Across the street, Mr. Baker was thrilled over our blossoming romance. Over the years, he had become increasingly alarmed at his son's lack of enthusiasm for boyish things, though he did them perfunctorily (Daniel was an obedient, yielding kind of boy). Mr. Baker had long ago signed him up for Boy Scouts, in fact going to the extreme of becoming a troop leader himself. He then cajoled poor Daniel through dozens of badges—everything except cooking, which Mr. Baker said was the *last* thing Daniel needed—and then on to try for Eagle Scout. Daniel finally rebelled when he had to spend a night by himself in the swamp. He staggered out the next morning covered in bug bites and leeches, and politely but firmly told his father, who had taken off work that morning to pick him up at the side of the road where he'd dropped him off, that he was done with scouting, which made Mr. B want to wring his son's neck. When I came into the picture, the Bakers, especially the Mr., rejoiced.

Daniel's sister, Melinda of the stolen outfits, was a senior by then and on her way to Mississippi State College for Women to become a teacher. Melinda collared me one night at a community center dance and led me outside. I gave her a big smile, thinking this was going to be a sisterly chat. Then she started in: She knew more about Daniel than anyone else; she knew, for example, that he read her beauty mags and sometimes tore out the pages, and not for the purposes you'd expect from a boy Daniel's age. She could see some of the hair styles reflected in his ducktail or a stray spit curl that on occasion appeared incongruously on his forehead as if a bird had splattered it there. Personal things had gone missing from her dresser drawers, and over time she learned to look for them in Daniel's room. She knew he used his allowance for hairspray and kept hidden in a shoe box at the back of his closet a wide patent leather belt, a pair of stockings, and a garter belt to hold them up. In sum, I should find someone else to go steady with. Someone more suitable.

Then she put a gentle hand on my shoulder as if she were anointing me in some mysterious way. "It's not you. It's him. He's not what you think."

My shoulder twitched involuntarily under her cloying hand. Inside, Tony Bennett was belting out, "Take my hand, I'm a stranger in paradise," which made my heart swell. Oh, I was no fool; I knew I was tracking my way through a strange land without a map, an island—that was it—just for the two of us, marooned as we were in a sea of dos and don'ts. Poor Daniel!

And now this hand, this busybody hand! I flung it aside in a gesture so vehement that anyone watching from a distance would have thought I'd struck the older girl.

Something in me rose up against Melinda's officiousness. "Mind your own business, Melinda," I said. "Go find your own sweetheart. If you can."

Melinda gasped. She was as plain as her brother was beautiful; finding a sweetheart was not going to be easy. "He's a homo, Grace. He steals my *clothes*," she burst forth. Then she gasped as if this were much more than she'd intended to say, and ran back into the community center.

I stood out under the stars. Tony Bennett was singing the stanza about there being a danger in Paradise, and I took his admonition under advisement and examined

the evidence. I knew very little about homos, and had
no idea where or how I'd acquired the meager bit of
information I had, which was, in a nutshell, men who
liked men and acted like women. But, I reasoned, this
couldn't possibly be true about Daniel because, quite
simply, and why couldn't Melinda see this, he liked *me*.
How then could he be a homo? So what that he dressed
up sometimes? That's why I loved him so, because he
wasn't any old gum-chewing, pimple-faced, stinky
boy. He was something else altogether: he glittered.

As matters progressed, we did the ordinary things
young couples do. When I turned fifteen and went to
high school, we held hands in the hall between classes,
walked home from school together, went to dances
and ball games, parked on dirt roads, went to drive-in
movies, kissed and groped, this latter initiated by me.
I would have gone further, but every time I reached
for him, I was met by an odd twist of the pelvis, a de-
murral, which, in the heat of the moment, I took not
so much as a rejection but a certain shyness on his
part. I walked around in a desperate state; I could
taste him on my tongue. Would you think me odd if
I said I craved his touch in the same way I still craved
my mother's? It was what I missed most: the way she
had of fussing over me and June, examining our nails,

licking her finger and picking the sleep out of our eyes, pulling up our arms and sniffing our armpits before we left for school in the morning.

Dad responded by setting down restrictions: I had to be home *directly* after school unless there was a club meeting or band practice and no visits to the Bakers' house unless an adult was present. Unchaperoned dates were forbidden, I was barely fifteen, for crying out loud. Despite these obstacles, I lurched blindly forward, meeting Daniel at parties, persuading him to sneak out of those parties when all he wanted was to dance.

All of it seemed to exhaust him. Here I was, not drop-dead gorgeous like my mother but sort of pretty (from the side), nice hair and good teeth—what more could a healthy American boy want? But he acted as if there were something both excessive and lacking about me. I suspected he liked me better when he wasn't with me than when he was. He must have felt a certain amount of desperation too; he knew I was the road he needed to travel. His father's anxieties, which played out over everything from the way the poor boy cut his meat to how he walked down the street, must have fueled whatever flickering flame he was capable of mustering in response to my three-alarm blaze. He did have an escape route; after next year he was going to State to be an engineer like his dad. Though engineering wasn't exactly his cup of tea, he was eager to be off, out from under his father's thumb.

Now, as I look back, I think it must have been shame that drove him into my eager arms. Perhaps he loved his garters, the tender, even pressure of the hose on his inner thighs, the tautness of the black patent belt; but he knew they were wrong, wrong, wrong. Maybe he was mortified to feel the sudden heft of his shorts in the locker room in a way he'd never felt it under my ministrations. When it got warm, he went to his afternoon classes smelling like mayonnaise because he never took a shower after track.

Time went on. The week before I turned sixteen, June got it in her head to bake a coconut cake for my birthday. When I came trudging home from school that dark rainy afternoon of my birthday, there June's cake sat like an overblown magnolia on its cut-glass pedestal in the front window. When June opened the door, it seemed to me as if she were the mother and I a child again. The candles were already lit and June and Dad sang to me.

As I gobbled down a piece of cake and quickly opened my gifts, a charm bracelet from my father and a charm in the shape of a star from June, my sister smiled and said, "Don't you love the real coconut? I made Dad drive me all the way to Biloxi to get it at the Piggly Wiggly."

"It's good and moist," I said obligingly.

She leaned over the table, a crumb on her upper lip. "I chopped it open with Dad's ax and grated the whole thing, drippled the juice on the cake. That's why it's so moist."

"Thank you. It's really good," I murmured and then headed for my room to freshen up, eager to get over to Daniel's so he could give me my birthday gift. I was hoping for a necklace, something delicate—a heart would be pretty—to rest in the hollow at the base of my neck.

June followed me to my room. "How about a game of Chinese checkers? Dad's doing the dishes tonight. Then maybe we can watch some TV. Dad will let us watch anything we want tonight."

"Sorry," I said, picking up my hairbrush.

Her face fell. "Daniel."

"Yes."

"I was thinking maybe you'd want to celebrate with us," she said. "Birthdays are for family."

"I'll be back after a while," I said lightly. I was concentrating on my hair, which the rain had flattened. I tried tilting my head down and brushing upward.

"When?"

"Oh, June, lay off, will you? I'll get back when I get back. You've got cake on your mouth."

Her face turned red and she swatted at her lip. "Happy damn birthday, then," she said and stalked out.

The day after my birthday something unexpected happened. A boy came to town. His name was George Genovese and his father was a bigwig at the mill. In Opelika, we'd never seen anybody quite like the Genoveses. They were Italian and from New York, which to us then seemed like the moon. George was just seventeen, a year younger than Daniel, but had skipped the third grade and was therefore placed in all of Daniel's classes. Someone had to catch George up in school, and soon he was walking home with Daniel, crowding the sidewalk so that sometimes I had to walk on the grass, or, worse yet, behind the two of them, as if I were attending royalty. Daniel carried a stack of books in one hand and gestured broadly with the other. The two of them talked Cicero and formulas, tests and diagramming, the possibility of playing tennis at the country club, where George's family had wrangled a membership. Art was their favorite class; they were sketching apples in a bowl on Daniel's dining room table.

"What's the point of drawing a bunch of apples?" I asked them.

"Mastering forms is the first step to becoming a great artist," they answered in unison, then grinned at each other.

George played the piano, and Daniel wanted to learn. Being boys together, they laughed about Miss McDougall's whiskers and Geraldine Ives's big butt. They were in fact a matched set, about the same height, George's deep olive skin with its plum tones the perfect foil to Daniel's blondness.

I tried to be generous; I'd worried that Daniel had few friends, that he seemed to put off other boys.

Soon George was going everywhere with Daniel and me, becoming the chaperone my father had insisted on, Dad as seemingly relieved by George's arrival on the scene as the Bakers had been by my march across the street that fateful Sunday a year ago. Now there was no parking or groping, no privacy. Sometimes, in fact, Daniel and George did things I wasn't included in.

"Where are you going?" I'd ask Daniel.

"Nowhere special, just around, just hanging out," he'd reply.

Once, at a dance, I asked George to get another ride home so I could be alone with Daniel. I never had him to myself anymore, not even on the dance floor. George had an exotic flare, the girls flocked to him. He danced with this one and that, always next to Daniel and me. Sometimes for fast numbers the two boys would encourage us to dance together rather than in pairs; for slow numbers, they positioned me and the other girl so they could look at each other over our shoulders.

George's response to such a reasonable request was to gaze at me like a dog being kicked out of the house in the midst of a blizzard. He bit his top lip, one side of which had a razor-thin white scar that ran straight up to his nostril, resulting in a hint of a sneer. Sometimes I wanted to reach up and trace it with my finger. Once, I'd asked him where he got it and he'd said there was something wrong with his mouth when he was born; they'd had to fix it.

Now he said, "I don't know anybody to ask for a ride."

"Pick a girl, any girl."

He looked down at his feet. "Maybe I could walk home."

Daniel joined us then. "Everybody ready?"

I nodded, and so did George.

On the way home, Daniel glanced over at me. I was sandwiched between the two of them on the front seat,

George having refused to sit in the back. "I'm going to take you home first," Daniel said. "I need to stop at the house and give George a book."

The next morning when I stopped over to get Daniel to walk to school. I was wearing my favorite outfit, a powder blue skirt and blouse. My heart beat faster, the way it always did in anticipation of seeing my Daniel. I went through the screen door and up onto the Bakers' porch, then knocked our special knock. The door opened, and George poked out his head.

"It's just me today," he said. "Daniel's got a stomach-ache."

I took a step back. "I didn't know you were spending the night."

Then he stepped out on the porch and the morning sun hit him full on. His eyes were heavy lidded and had a smudged look. There was a half-smile on his face. He gazed down at me with a look I could only interpret as pitying. He felt sorry for me, the bastard.

I turned and hurried across the Bakers' lawn, stumbling over old Lion, who wagged his tail weakly.

By the time I hit the sidewalk, George had caught up. I stopped short, causing him to stumble. "George," I said sternly, "I'd like to spend more time alone with Daniel. You know what I mean."

Beside me, George stood still, his fingers fast-tapping

his thick science book, as if he were bored by what I was saying.

"Well?" I said.

He cocked his head and eyed me. He appeared, oddly, to be surveying me from a long distance, as if I were a piece of roadside scenery he was passing. "I expect Daniel can decide."

I pulled Daniel's class ring out from under my blouse and dangled it in front of George's nose. "I'm his *girlfriend.*"

"There are other ways to be friends." He muttered this last under his breath, his tone so measured that it sounded a little sinister. Then he shifted the book to his other arm and walked off, leaving me standing there on the sidewalk.

I looked down at the ring; I was by this time not nearly as innocent as I'd been that Sunday afternoon I had walked across the street to pluck Daniel like a prized apple. Unsettled by George's unstated but insistent claim on Daniel, I decided then and there that if ever there were a time for action, it was now.

It was by then April again and mild even during the early morning hours. That night, I climbed out of my window and landed on the ground between my father's two prize camellia bushes. I wore baby-doll pajamas, an older, worn pair you could almost see through.

Across the street, the draping arms of a forsythia in the Bakers' yard, Easter-chick yellow bleached to white in the moonlight, swayed slightly as if to signal some indecipherable message. Overhead, a swath of stars. I tiptoed across the street (how easy it all was!), went around to the back of the Bakers' house, and peeked in Daniel's bedroom window. I'd imagined how thrilled he'd be to see me, the sudden stirring of passion my unexpected appearance in the middle of the night would evoke. I was about to tap on the pane when I looked more closely and saw the two forms in Daniel's bed. The boys were deeply asleep, the dark head next to the blond on the same pillow, Daniel's arm flung over the other boy's chest. Daniel's hair a shock of white. They looked totally at peace. They were naked.

I cupped my hands around my eyes and pressed my face against the windowpane. The moon was shining on them and it was hard to say which of them appeared more glorious. The curve of George's shoulder, the splotches of dark between their legs. Together they were more beautiful, and strangely exotic, than either of them could ever have been separately.

How can I explain what happened next? Something (a bolt?) slid out of place, a hinge creaked in my mind. In that moment, I loved them both.

I made a fist and knocked.

The boys scrambled, George jumping sky high, his eyes rolled back in his head, Daniel sitting straight up and wildly eyeing the door to his room. I had to tap again to make them understand where the sound was coming from, and this I did, quietly, persistently, until Daniel came over and raised the sash.

I held out my arms. "Pull me up," I commanded.

They didn't want me there, but looking at me like that was another thing. They were boys who appreciated beauty, and in the starlight, arms outstretched, hair wild, I could see in their eyes that I shone.

There was also the matter of what I might do if they didn't take me to bed with them. Who I might tell. In that moment, fear of discovery must have buzzed, wasp-like, at the edge of their minds.

Now I know all this. In the moment, though, it didn't occur to me that they wouldn't want me.

It was George who understood and made the first move, taking my outstretched hand, Daniel who grasped my shoulder.

Throughout that spring, the three of us were inseparable. Some afternoons we spent at Daniel's house, some at George's mansion of a place, the only nice house on the mill side of town. Because of June, who, being June, had begun to ask questions, we steered clear of my house.

For the first time since I'd known him, Daniel seemed happy. There was something about me that held the two boys in a kind of fragile suspension. I walked between them to and from school. I sat between them on the front seat of the Bakers' Chrysler. The three of us danced together at school events, startling the chaperones. I was the book to their bookends, the hinge they swung on. For my part, I felt radioactive, fired by the way their hands grazed me as they reached for each other, fired by beauty and destruction, not then understanding the difference between the two, not knowing they weren't one thing. I changed my hairdo to a flip, plucked my eyebrows, lined my eyes so they looked catlike.

How could I have thought this could go on? Mama's douche bag was still hanging in the bathroom, and I used it religiously. It didn't occur to me that if it didn't work for her it might not work for me.

Summer flew by and school started up again. One morning I got out of the tub and my breasts caught my eye in the medicine cabinet mirror. In the morning light, they appeared much larger than I'd remembered them. The tips had turned from pink to a dappled brown. They seemed to have taken on secret lives. Then

I looked down at my belly, also darker, as though a shadow had fallen over it. I began to count.

I'd heard laxatives would get rid of it. I chewed Ex-Lax, drank a bottle of castor oil, and became horribly ill. I sat shivering for hours in a tub of Epsom salts and vinegar. One quiet afternoon, while the boys were playing gin rummy out on Daniel's porch, I went to the top of the stairs in his house and made myself jump, but I landed on my shoulder rather than my stomach. The boys came running: What was I doing on the stairs? Good grief, what was wrong with me these days? That night, I sat on the toilet for hours and beat on my stomach, cursing and crying. Finally, I stopped, hiccupping and dripping with sweat. It was only then that I considered doing what my mother had done, hoping for a better outcome; but I didn't want to die, I wanted to live. So I gave up.

I told only the boys and limited myself to one meal a day. The three of us decided to run away together and raise the child, our child, whose in particular none of us knew but we all three agreed it was better that way. New Orleans was the farthest and most foreign place we could imagine ourselves getting to. The boys took on odd jobs, saved their allowances, and made plans contingent on my ability to elude discovery. We plotted and planned. Mr. Baker flushed with pride when

Daniel started mowing lawns up and down the block. George stole money from his father and cashed out the savings bonds his grandparents had given him every Christmas since he was born. We packed suitcases and hid them under our beds to make a quick getaway when the time came. If the boys considered jumping ship, they never let on. They were troopers, rallying around me. I was by that time feeling like Deborah Kerr in a picture show.

Meanwhile, as fall came on, June spent more and more time staring out the kitchen window as the flocks of finches and a couple of cardinals waited their turns at the dozen or so of our mother's feeders she kept filled. After school, she settled herself at the kitchen table to watch the birds, as if they were children at play, always on the brink of peril. Once or twice I sat down with my sister at her post, wanting to lay my burden at her feet; but when she turned to look at me, something in the intentness of that look, a kind of surveillance, as if I were a bird too, put me off.

One September morning I came up behind her. There was a slight breeze rattling the pods on the mimosa out back. The sun was streaming into the room, showing up the veil of dust and cobwebs over everything.

"Which ones are you looking at?" I asked my sister. It was not the question I wanted to ask.

June quickly lowered the binoculars, as if she'd been caught doing something illicit. "The finches. There's got to be twenty of them out there." She handed me the binoculars.

I put them to my eyes. There seemed to be a film over everything; I could make out only shapes and colors, flashes of yellow. I wondered if this partial blindness were a symptom of pregnancy. I handed the binoculars back to my sister and turned away, not wanting her to see my eyes.

This was the moment June might have looked up and seen that I was crying and asked what was wrong. But she didn't. Instead she said she was sick and tired of me and my shenanigans. Chasing after not one boy but two, leaving her to do all the cooking and cleaning. No wonder the house was a mess, the laundry piled to the sky. No wonder I couldn't see what was right in front of my eyes. She took back the binoculars and put them to her own eyes.

That night she came into my room to borrow an extra pillow, at least so she later said. I was dead asleep on my back, allowing her to make out my little pouch of a belly up against the streetlight outside the window.

I woke up when I felt her touch my midsection and press down hard, as if I were a melon she was testing.

"You haven't had a period in three months," she said.

I just looked at her like a dumb animal.

She fumbled for the light, which blinded me. "Why didn't you tell me?"

"Thought you'd tell Dad."

"You thought right," she said.

The boys were dispatched to boarding schools. Daniel went to McCallie's Academy at the top of Lookout Mountain in Tennessee. George went to a place in northern Virginia, a military school that shipped its students off to West Point or VMI, clipped and empty-eyed, when they graduated.

I was the bigger problem. I wouldn't say who of the two was the father. Shockingly, I said I didn't know. Dad wept at this disclosure; he'd spent his whole life making a reputation in this town and Big Holly before him. How was he ever going to hold up his head again? His shame blew over me like a cold wind. Intent on my plots and plans, I hadn't thought about shame; I hadn't thought about the whispers and sneers, I hadn't thought about my father or sister, especially my sister, what she would have to endure at school.

Dad called Frances, who said, he informed me, that she wasn't the least bit surprised I'd ended up in this fix, but she knew of a place for unwed mothers run by nuns. It was all a matter of money; surely Dad had his pension to draw on. Frances said I could stay with her if I wanted, but Our Lady of Perpetual Sorrows might be a better place for me once I got further along.

So I became one of the girls who *went away*. The previous year it had been Mary Love Bryan. It was October; she'd just been selected homecoming queen and was scheduled to ride in the Azalea Festival the following spring. Unlike me, Mary Love was popular and astonishingly beautiful; she had a father *and* a mother, her life was nothing but golden. It was said she went to live with relatives, but the next fall she was back at Opelika High, her pretty face now etched by the bone underneath, eyes more deeply hinged in their sockets, wisps of shadow underneath. The girls steered clear of Mary Love, the boys tried to date her on the premise she was easy. Teachers approached her with caution. After a while, she stopped washing her hair. One day she disappeared for good. It was a week before anyone noticed.

I gave birth at Charity Hospital, on Tulane Street. I was alone except for the doctor and a nurse who smelled of fried onions. When my baby finally emerged after a day and night of hard labor, after hours of my begging for mercy (*Get it out, get the damn thing out!*), somebody slapped a gas mask over my face, but not before I had the sensation, in that instant, that I was expelling an enormous fish, and with it some unnamed but vital organ. It was then that I was forever lost to the girl I once was, the moment my baby girl landed hard on that cold metal operating table, kicking and squalling, slick with her mother's sin.

When I woke up, the doctor was peering at his watch. He yawned. "February 14, 10:43 A.M."

"Valentine's Day," the nurse said and wrote it down.

Outside, there was a single clap of thunder, then an abrupt downpour, and my baby and I were rinsed in the sweet smell of rain.

10
Frances

After Holly called, I sat down at my kitchen table and worked it all out in my head: Grace could go back home like nothing had happened and I would get to keep it. It would take the place of the lost one, except that *I* would be its mother; it would be mine.

I would tell everyone that it was from far away, Florida maybe. I would say I wasn't getting any younger and there being no husband on the horizon (nor would there ever be, they'd be thinking), I'd decided to give a sweet orphan baby a good and decent home, a child to take care of me in my old age. No one would have to know it was my own flesh and blood, the child of my unfortunate niece.

For her time, I would send Grace to Our Lady of Perpetual Sorrows down on Napoleon, which, despite the inescapable fact that it was a home for unwed mothers, was a good school too, well, not really *good*, but decent, considering it was for delinquent girls. Holly would have to help out, but we would manage.

And what if Grace didn't want to go stay with the nuns, what if she were embarrassed? I'd thought of that too. If she felt that way (as well she should; her behavior was beyond the pale), she could just stay home with me. I could help her keep up her lessons. And why not? I'm a teacher of high school English and social studies. I know my semicolons and branches of government. I can quote you William Shakespeare and Sir Walter Scott from now until doomsday, not to speak of being able to recite in my sleep the number one agricultural export of each and every country in the western hemisphere. For the arithmetic, I can get her tutored and, together, we'll just have to do our best with the science. How hard can tenth-grade science be? Photosynthesis isn't exactly rocket science. She can do her homework during the day while I'm at school; then I'll teach her at night and on the weekends. Nobody drops by anymore but Jehovah's Witnesses or some children looking for spare change for a snowball, but if someone should, I'll just shut her up in the bedroom and nobody will be the wiser.

And yes, of course she'll have her own bedroom, even if I have to move out my school things and out-of-season clothing. She'll have a decent time of it; I wouldn't think of shaming her, though I don't condone what she did for one single minute, and I'm sure I don't know the half of it, Holly being so tight-lipped and all and my poor sister six feet under.

Make no mistake. My niece will have the best of everything. No expense will be spared. I'll take her to the doctor for checkups and make sure she takes her vitamins. I'll cook her my good chicken and dumplings and make her eat her collards for the iron and carrots for the eyes, drink plenty of milk for the bones. She'll be healthy as a horse, and the baby will come out fat, with those scrumptious leg rolls you want to pinch hard, too hard, which I'll of course never ever do.

Afterward, Grace and I will have a special bond. In the summers she can come to visit it, maybe take care of it while I go on vacation to some faraway place. (After all, the world is getting smaller by the day, and I'm not getting any younger.) Maybe one day, after she gets a good job thanks to me, she'll be so grateful she'll want to treat me to a really nice getaway. I'll finally get to go to Greece, the way I've always wanted, and island-hop. I ask you, what could be more perfect?

11

Grace

You see, it never occurred to me I'd have to give up my own child, leave it behind the way people leave a puppy at the side of the road. That came later, after Frances explained to me and Dad how she was going to take it, how I could see it whenever I wanted. How I could babysit it during holidays and summers so she could travel. She spoke like a schoolteacher giving out a lesson, explaining her plan down to the most particular detail. She showed us the room it would sleep in, where she was going to place the crib. The rocking chair would go in the corner next to the window so that she could look out on her bougainvillea while she rocked it to sleep. She'd bought a Dr. Spock book, which she waved in my face.

She told it like you'd tell a good mystery story, scary in the middle but with a happy ending, with her,

Frances the Sainted Aunt, coming to the rescue in the nick of time, saving my Future by swooping up my baby and carrying it off.

I wondered what my mother would think of the plan Dad and Frances had hatched, what my mother would have done. Would she have taken me to that backwoods butcher? Or would she have figured out another way, not wanting to be as careless with my life as she'd been with her own? What a relief it would have been for me to hand her my body's betrayal and say, Here, take this. I liked to think she would have taken my part, made things right somehow. I liked to think she wouldn't have looked at me the way the rest of them did.

Dad's eyes lit up. "If it's a boy, I'll teach it to catch."

"Yes, it will need a male presence in its life," Frances said quietly. "It will need you in its life."

So all was decided. I would give away my baby and keep it too. After all was said and done, I'd go back home to Opelika and have a regular life, go back to being a regular girl, despite the obvious fact I had never been one to begin with. Meanwhile, I would stay with Frances, or, if I'd rather, go lock myself up in a nunnery.

My father rubbed his mouth with one hand, then his whole face with both hands. He hadn't looked at me since the night he had asked me who the father was. He'd kept after me, getting up in my face. Finally I told him the truth: that I didn't actually know, that there were two boys, that I loved them both.

"You slut," he'd said, "you whore." He'd grabbed my arm at the wrist, put his face up next to mine so I could smell the cigarettes on his breath. "Who? Who are they?" His eyes raked my body, his lip curled.

I told him I wouldn't tell, he couldn't make me tell. He twisted my wrist, making me cry out.

June burst into my room. "You let her go. Don't you go hurting her!" Then, as if she hadn't done enough damage, caused me enough grief, she named names.

Dad dropped my wrist. "What? Those two *fags*?" His tone was as thoughtful as it was cold.

The two of them, Dad and June, stood there staring at me, at my stomach, at the place between my legs. I felt like the polar bear at the zoo, bone weary from the dead weight of human eyes.

"Get out," I said to them. "Get out of my room."

"Gladly," Dad said. "And you. You stay in."

That night I tried to figure out how to get to the phone to call the boys so we could hightail it over to New Orleans. George had it all figured out. We'd change our names; New Orleans was huge, they'd never find us. We'd get one of those little shotguns up high off the ground and eat gumbo and oysters.

We'd have a dog that lived under the house. Everything would be coming up roses by now if we'd gone last week. I'd told them I was a ticking time bomb, we couldn't wait forever; but they were just boys, they thought we had all the time in the world.

Fortunately for us, I was taking typing as an elective. All the girls took it (to make a living should we not land husbands) and home ec (which would hold us in good stead if we did, and which June and I had had a crash course in after our mother died). I'd almost failed the latter for being unable to sew a straight seam. Typing, on the other hand, was my true calling. I got up to sixty words a minute in a month. I liked the way my fingers flew across the keyboard, the way the words took shape on the page. What struck me was how many words you could form out of twenty-six letters of the alphabet, how many meanings words could carry, strapped to their sturdy backs. How fleshy and full of possibility they seemed as they took shape on the paper in my carriage.

I pulled my suitcase out from under the bed and added a few last-minute items: underwear, pants with elastic waists, and shirts and flip-flops, some shampoo and cream rinse, my pink brush rollers, and hair spray. I had my Camp Winnatoba sweat shirt hanging on the door to my closet, ready for me to pull on over my pajamas once the moment was right and the boys came to get me. In my purse I kept my makeup bag, a peanut butter and jelly sandwich, three cans of Cherry Coke, and what was left of a bag of stale Fritos. I'd been pilfering the grocery money and had twelve dollars and fourteen cents, plus a coupon for a six-pack of 7 Up, which the boys drank like water.

We were going to push off Dad's old Rambler in the dead of night. We were going to vamoose, abscond, take off like pigeons from the roost, trace the shape of the sleepy Gulf through the swamps and marshes, following the stars in the southern sky. Orion the Hunter, his dog Canis Major, the constellations of Carina, Puppis, and Vela.

Daniel and George talked about getting jobs loading and unloading down at the docks. They thought it'd be exciting and educational to unload goods off of those big ships from exotic places like India and France that brought perfumes and spices and cans of escargot to our shores.

After June and Dad went out the door, I sat on my bed and ate the peanut butter sandwich and Fritos from my getaway bag and drank two of my cans of Cherry Coke. The crumbs rained down and lodged between the nubs on my spread. I picked them out and ate them too.

The phone rang in the hall and I ran for it. Dad got there first. He yelled into the receiver and then slammed it down. He whirled around. "Get out of my sight. And don't even think about leaving the house."

Later June knocked on the door to my room and came in with a plate of spaghetti from supper. She'd piled it high with meatballs. My mouth watered.

I jumped up from the bed and stopped her in her tracks. "Look what you've gone and done. You've just gone and ruined all our lives."

She just stood there with a smear of red sauce on her cheek from supper. She had on Mama's apron, splattered in red. How my fingers itched to slap that cheek of hers!

"Get out and stay out." I snatched the plate from her.

She planted herself in the doorway. "What did you think was going to happen, Grace? Did you think people weren't going to notice when you got big as a house? What were you going to do with it once it came, drop it in a basket on the church steps? At least now you can go stay with Frances, and nobody'll know." She said all that in the most reasonable way possible.

I thought of my aunt's dank house, dark and gloomy from the overhanging trees that scraped the roof on rainy nights. I thought of Daniel and George heading for New Orleans without me. At least we would be in the same city. I could run away from Frances's and meet them there, though of course without me they would have no reason to go; they could just live out their cozy lives here in Opelika. They could go to football games and drink milk shakes; they could lie naked together under the covers and shiver in the crisp night air. I sank to the floor.

June squatted down beside me, her eyes bright, her breath cheesy. "Which one was it, Grace? Which one got you pregnant?"

If I could mark the moment when things turned sour between me and my sister, the way a bottle of milk will curdle overnight in the refrigerator, it was when she asked that question, as if my child, my *child* were a seed spit from the sparrow's beak. Before she asked those questions, before my father had looked at me the way he did, shame was simply a word that required the fingers to strike letters on all three levels of the typewriter, a good word for practicing dexterity. Now I saw myself as she and Dad saw me, as a fool, the one left holding the bag. Daniel and George would still have each other; Frances would have my baby. I'd have nobody.

I reached out and shoved my sister. She tumbled back, onto the floor. How she reminded me of a flipped cockroach. How I wanted to kick her in the soft middle part, stomp her face in. I raised one hand. "Get the hell away from me. Remember this day, remember I said I'd always hate you for as long as I live."

She scrambled to her feet and backed out of the door. When she shut the door, I could hear her rev up to cry. And I was glad.

I wolfed down the spaghetti and meatballs. I knew exactly how June made the sauce, how long she cooked it, the extra oregano she put in because she knew I liked it, the sugar that sweetened it, how she used ground chuck and Progresso breadcrumbs and Worcestershire for the meatballs, sautéed them crisp before dropping them into the sauce at the last minute.

In the end my father told me to stay at Frances's. Why should he give up his pension when Frances would take me for free?

It was still warm when I first got there. My aunt lived in a bustling neighborhood out by the lake. There were a couple of small grocery stores, a barbershop, a po'boy dive called Mimi's, and a constant parade of people eating snowballs from the Harrison Street Snowball Stand a block down. While she was at school, I would sit on her front stoop half hidden by palmetto leaves watching people come and go, laughing and talking together. At night I dreamed of rescue, the boys throwing rocks at my window, the way we'd planned.

Sometimes the crack of the rock against the window seemed so real I'd get up to look out into the dark.

November marked the fourth anniversary of my mother's death. It had turned cold and rainy. The city lights hid the stars. Clouds flew across the face of the moon like huge dark birds.

At night as the salt air blew off Lake Pontchartrain and the fanned leaves from the palmetto scratched at my window, I began to dream that a giant oak was growing inside me, the roots tangled in the rolls of my intestines. The trunk, thick and knobby, rose up between my lungs; the branches curled around my heart.

After I got larger, Frances wouldn't take me out. She said she didn't want anybody to know where *her* baby had come from. She had this way of eyeing my belly sideways, out of the corner of her eye. Dad sent money for my clothes, but she wouldn't take me to the store to buy them. One pink number she'd selected had balloons on the top, which made me look like a clown. I'd grown upward as well as outward, and the outfits were too short. My belly poked out between the tops and the bottoms, and the pants stopped at midcalf. Every night Frances gave me my studies for the next day. Sometimes I did the homework, sometimes I didn't. She didn't own a TV, said they made you stupid. When she came bustling in from school in the afternoons, I'd be so glad to hear the sound of her voice that tears would well up in my eyes. After supper, she'd tell me to clear the table for my lessons. She drilled me on my commas and semicolons, World Wars I and II. She made me conjugate Latin verbs, translate the stories of Caesar's conquests, her Lady Schoolteacher Smell surrounding me like his conquering army. She told me about the early writings, poems and teachings scratched out on something called papyrus, which had been found tucked away in caves. We studied the constellations and galaxies, the nature of gravity, the space race. Now the sky was full of dogs and chimps, each and every one terrified and lonely. Frances's lip quivered when she talked about the animals. In her spare time, she wrote letters, signed petitions. Sometimes she put her elbows on the table and rested her head in her hands and dozed a bit while I translated. I knew I should thank her for keeping me up on my studies, but I began to view the lessons with a dread akin to nausea; after a while, I couldn't tell the difference.

On weekend afternoons, she pored over Dr. Spock, marking passages and taking notes in the margins. "'Trust yourself,'" she intoned. "'You know more than you think you do.'" She looked up from her reading and smiled. "That's reassuring, don't you think?"

I peeked at the book, but it scared me; so many things can happen to a little baby: safety pins and mysterious infections, cripplings and blindings and fevers. You could drop it on the floor, roll over in the bed and smother it, break its floppy little stem of a neck. Pillows and stuffed toys could smother it, don't leave them in the crib. Television would fry a baby's brain.

One morning, just as I was getting out of bed, a little bird fluttered inside me, as panicky as the sparrow Mama had captured. I thought something was wrong, that I was going to lose the baby. I went into the kitchen. "I think the baby's dying," I told Frances. "It feels like it's trying to get its breath." I felt lighter already.

She smiled and said, "Oh honey, that's just the baby kicking, that's just the baby saying hello to you." She walked over to me and reached for my belly.

I backed up. "Don't touch me."

Her hand hovered, then dropped to her side. "Oh Grace, you must be really unhappy. This too will pass."

Dad and June drove in for Christmas afternoon. When they saw me, they stopped dead.

June gave me some Raspberry Bloom lipstick and nail polish to match, wrapped separately. She'd made a new concoction she called Angels' Wings: chunks of angel food cake in a Pyrex dish covered by boiled custard with dollops of meringue on top. All afternoon the three of them sat around and talked about everything but the baby. June complained about how hard Latin was, how the Opelika Gators had finished out the season with only two losses. Dad talked about a new furniture factory, a spin-off from the mill, how it was bringing new jobs to town. I listened for a while, then said I was tired and needed a nap. When I woke up it was the middle of the night and they were gone. I tossed and turned. How was I ever going to go back home when this was over?

But there was no such thing as this being over, my baby wouldn't be gone once I'd given birth. Nor, in that moment, did I want it to be. As Frances and Dad had hatched their schemes, I'd made my own plans. I would graduate from high school, being sure to take shorthand to perfect my secretarial skills. Then it would be Katy bar the door; I'd move to the City and be out in the world making my own living. I'd get myself to a little balcony apartment in the Quarter and acquire the things a baby needs. I'd wait for George and Daniel to find me. Then, one day, we would knock on Frances's door and tell her to give me my baby back. We'd kidnap it if we had to. This was the story I told myself as I tried to get back to sleep.

In New Orleans, winter crawls into your bones. By the first of the year a grim rain had set in and the pumps had stopped working. One late afternoon as I peered through the half dark at the flooded street outside, I gave up on George and Daniel. They hadn't called, hadn't written. As the dank weeks dragged on, I found myself more lonesome for my mother than for the boys. I began to feel hollowed out, preparing to give birth to some strange mutation of emptiness.

One morning in late January I woke up at dawn. The sky was slate gray, and a cold wind was whipping up from the lake. Frances was stirring in the kitchen. I waited until she left for school and went in to get some breakfast. She'd left a grapefruit half with the sections precisely cut, cinnamon toast on a cookie sheet on top of the stove, a boiled egg still in its water. I took the grapefruit in one hand, the toast in the other, and threw them across the kitchen. Then I took the pot of water with the egg in it and turned it upside down. I smashed the egg under my heel.

I enjoyed looking at the mess I'd made of things, then I squatted down and cleaned it up.

Which is when I noticed the paring knife in the dish drain. I took it up and pressed the tip into my palm. It was surprisingly easy to draw blood. I pulled up my gown and touched my belly with the edge of the knife. A welt appeared, then a dot of red, then another dot. I thought about slippage, how easily one thing can lead to another, how bad luck coils and strikes. Two extra hours at the zoo and everything lost.

As the minutes and hours ticked by over the course of the day, the knife became my friend. I played with it, talked to it. I carried it around the house, my palm curled around it. I was holding it in my lap, letting the blade reflect the overhead light, when Frances came in the door. Her mouth fell open and she dropped her books and took it from me.

"Are you blue, honey?" she asked. "Maybe you should be with the other girls in trouble, in your condition? At least you'd have some companionship."

I stared out the window, smeared with rain. "Out of the frying pan into the fire."

"It's not that I don't want you here." She turned her back to me, going to the kitchen sink to wash her hands. "All right. I'll talk to your father. Meanwhile, you should read some books for fun, get your mind off things. I'll pick some up for you tomorrow at the library. Oh dear, I should have thought of that." She turned around and took a deep breath, a shaky breath. Her face resembled a plaster mask, there were dark circles under her eyes. The shoulder seams of her blouse had slipped down over her shoulders, which I noticed for the first time looked like the joints of chicken wings.

Our Lady of Perpetual Sorrows was up on Napoleon. A big house with columns, surrounded by a high brick wall broken only by a wrought-iron gate. The drive up to the building itself was lined in live oaks. Acorns crunched under the wheels of the car.

The gate opened as we approached. At the door, two nuns stood waiting. One took my suitcase and helped me from the car. The other had a few quiet words with Frances, who then turned to me and said she'd see me on Sunday.

I was put in a good-sized room with three other girls, two of whose names I don't remember, our beds lined up against the walls. The other one, Lou Ella, was from a little town in the Delta. She was so skinny she looked like she was hiding a basketball under her dress, playing a joke. She said her uncle did it to her and it wasn't the first time she'd been in this fix. The others she'd managed to get rid of. One was born the size of a chipmunk, scarcely alive and it she'd drowned. Our beds were close by and she whispered her stories to me as I tried to get to sleep. My bed was under the window and I'd watch the moon come up, the North Star and the Milky Way and the Dippers take their places in the night sky. Sometimes I thought I could see capsules filled with dogs and monkeys, dead and alive, alone and together, float silently past my window. I told Lou Ella to shut the hell up, not to fill my head with her ugly stories, but she wouldn't stop. Sometimes I'd take long even breaths so she'd think I'd dozed off, but she kept right on, telling it all over and over, her terrible life.

The four of us in this one room were all due about the same time, but Lou Ella went first. The night her water broke, my first thought was how grateful I was I wouldn't have to listen to her anymore. I knew I'd never see her again because the girls went straight home from the hospital. When the nuns came in to take her to the hospital, she began to cry and say how she didn't want to go home. Please, couldn't she come back to Our Lady? Couldn't they find some work for her to do there? She'd mop floors, clean the bathrooms, cook the food. She'd work seven days a week, Christmas, Easter, and New Year's. The nuns said for her to come along, she needed to get on over to the hospital; for her to get the suitcase she was supposed to have packed for the trip home. They'd had to buy her the suitcase; she'd come in with the clothes on her back.

She hadn't packed her suitcase, that much I knew. So while she sat on the bed, big tears running down her scrawny face, the nuns packed it for her, as efficiently as wrens making a nest. One snapped it shut with a cheerful click and the other took her arm and pulled her up off the bed. "Come along now, dear," they murmured, "the driver's waiting."

Two days later a new girl was in Lou Ella's bed. She was the opposite of Lou Ella, wouldn't say a word, not nice to meet you, not kiss my foot, for which I was grateful.

I went two weeks after Lou Ella, a Tuesday. Nobody had told me what to expect. By the time it happened, I'd begun to worry that the skin on my belly wasn't going to hold, that any minute I was going to pop like a balloon and the baby would come flying out as if it'd been shot from a canon.

I'd seen enough to know about my water breaking, but that wasn't what happened. Instead, a scalding pain in my belly woke me out of a dead sleep. It set me straight up in the bed, gasping and choking.

The new girl was awake. She took one look at me in the moonlight, her eyes dark and mysterious. "You want me to call somebody?" These were her first and last words to me.

I nodded, still trying to catch my breath. She ran out of the room hollering at the top of her lungs, "Somebody! Somebody! Somebody come quick!"

The nun in charge rushed into my room, her habit askew, a red line across her forehead where she'd laid her head on the desk downstairs. Over the past months, Frances had rubbed off on me. I'd planned every detail of this moment. So I was ready, more than ready, the suitcase under my bed packed three weeks ago. Every night after I brushed my teeth, I'd pack my toothbrush so I wouldn't forget it. I'd gathered my favorite things: the ring Daniel had given me, a pretty flower pin from George, a bright orange scarf of my mother's, a bottle of her Forbidden cologne I'd snitched before I left home. I tied the smaller items up in the scarf that I kept under my pillow.

"I've called the ambulance," the nun said. "Let's get you downstairs and ready." She handed me my jacket, which was hanging on the bedpost, and I struggled to get into it while she stood there waiting.

The new girl reached over and took one of my arms and put it in the jacket; then she took the other, as if I were a little girl and she my mother. When she pulled my hair out over the collar of the jacket and smoothed my hair the way my mother used to do, I began to cry.

When I got to the hospital, I realized I'd forgotten the scarf with my things in it. But then another pain hit and I forgot again.

It took me a long time to have my baby. The nurse, whose breath made me gag, leaned over me, hollering to do this and that thing, not do this or that other thing. At the end I fought the mask; I thought they were suffocating me, putting me to sleep like the animal I'd become.

When I surfaced, there was a bright light shining in my eyes. I squinted and caught sight of the nurse as she bent over it.

"What?" I said.

"A girl," the nurse said. "It's a girl." The nurse's voice had an odd catch to it, as if she'd spoken in the middle of a hiccup.

She held my baby under the light, looking down at her with an odd fascination, much, I imagine, as I might have gazed upon her had she been given to me in that moment, had I not been blinded by the light.

Later, when I woke up again, my breasts like molten rocks, I asked for her. She'd been taken away, I was told. Policy in these cases. Never mind, I thought, I'll see her soon enough; she won't have to wait long for me to take her back.

12
Frances

Before you go casting aspersions, put yourself in my shoes. Here I was ready to take Grace's little child, a child not my own: to take it and care for it, give it a decent life. This poor motherless child would have had not only a devoted mother but also an *award-winning* teacher of English grammar, with a plaque from the mayor himself to prove it. Not to put too fine a point on it, but my heart was in the right place; my intentions were, well, noble, downright noble, if I do say so myself.

What happened was most definitely *not* my fault.

First of all, I should have been properly prepared. I went to the hospital expecting a minor problem. Let me emphasize *minor*: "a little something wrong with the upper lip, easily fixed," the nurse said on the phone. Those were her exact words. I pressed her on this point.

"What do you mean by 'a little something wrong'?" I could hear my voice rising as I asked the question. People say I have a high voice; they mean shrill, which in this case it might have been. For one thing, I was exhausted. Grace had been in labor for eighteen hours; I'd gone home to get some rest and had fallen asleep on the sofa in my clothes. The phone had jarred me from a dream about travel, something about Greece: suitcases and a train station, not knowing which train to take, directions in symbols I couldn't make heads or tails of. I had fumbled the phone on the table beside the sofa and almost dropped it.

"Nothing much," the nurse said, "just a bit of minor surgery required." That is a *direct* quotation. She had a voice that made me think of cough syrup. It soothed me, calmed my uneasiness. Grace's baby had finally come, thank the heavenly hosts. Everything was going according to plan, just a little something about the mouth, a bit of minor surgery, which I could well afford. I had been saving up; I had insurance. Babies are not cheap, and I am nothing if not responsible; just between us, the only member of this family who is. Holly promised to do his part, send money every month until it was on its own; but ever since Olivia went and did what she did, and that was *years* ago, he seems like a man bumbling around in the dark. I bet it's all he can do to get out of the bed in the morning and get June off to school and himself to work. (I could have changed all that, made them a home and none of this would have happened. What a fool he was to send me away!)

This same nurse, this woman, told me I would have to wait to pick it up; it would have to stay at the hospital until Grace signed the papers, which she had not yet done since she was still under the gas, would be for hours, the woman said. When we hung up and I went into the kitchen to make a cup of tea, I realized I did not hear her say boy or girl, though surely she must have said one or the other. She must have said that first thing, and I missed it.

I had asked the nurse to call when Grace woke up. I thought she might need something, and I didn't want to make two trips. To pass the time, I went into the baby's room, which I'd painted lime green, a cheerful color, not too loud.

I'd set the crib up against the back wall, the new sheet on it washed twice so it wouldn't be scratchy. Look around this room now, and you will see how prepared I was. I had knitted a blanket and some booties to take to the hospital, and a week ago I'd laid them out on the baby bed so I wouldn't forget them. I'd made sure to get the softest angora, a buttery yellow since I didn't know whether it would be a boy or girl.

I hoped it wasn't a girl. Girls are such a trial.

By late afternoon Grace had bestirred herself enough to send word that she didn't want to see me. She did not feel well. It had been an arduous labor. They were giving her a few days in the hospital for her to collect herself before going home. The nurse told me to stay put; I'd be called when the baby was ready, which would be a day or two. There were legal matters, paperwork to process.

Needless to say, I was disappointed. I thought I'd go to the hospital, sit by Grace's bedside. She'd be happy to see me, her own aunt, blood kin, who'd bailed her out of this mess. Someone in a uniform would roll in the baby. We would look at it together, maybe even get to hold it. We would have that moment to remember always, the two of us seeing it together for the first time, the way a family would.

Having nothing else to do (I'd taken the rest of the school year off so the baby could receive my full-time attention, which only goes to show how good my intentions were), I put my tea down on the changing table in the baby's room and started to count everything, a redundant task, one I'd undertaken many times. In the chest of drawers I'd put six dozen diapers, which I hoped were sufficient to the task, two dozen gowns in varying colors with the drawstring at the bottom for easy access, a dozen white undershirts, pads to put on the bed, rubber pants, socks, everything durable, nothing fancy: babies don't know what they're wearing. No teddy bears. No stuffed toys of any kind. Babies can smother on them.

I sat down in the rocker I'd bought at a secondhand shop. It still smelled of the boiled linseed oil I'd rubbed on it to bring up the wood grain. When I began to rock, it started edging across the floor as though it were making a getaway, which I didn't expect and which was probably why it was given up. As I rocked and the chair scooted toward the front wall, I found myself wondering what it would be like to hold a newborn baby in my arms. I couldn't remember anyone ever giving me one to hold. Would it turn to my useless breasts? What did I know about taking care of a baby? A growing child? How would I manage on my own, alone in the world, Grace having gone back to her life? A strange girl, inscrutable really, though I'd tried to be kind and discreet, never asking the questions other people might have been crass enough to ask.

When I visited her on Sundays at Our Lady, she seemed reluctant to talk about anything but food. She was always asking me to bring her sweets. I would bring them, but not many of them; Twinkies and Moon Pies and Almond Joys are not healthful foods. "Only two?" she would say and then cram them into her mouth, glaring at me, tossing the wrappers on the floor next to the oily-looking sofa she sat on in the living area. In her last month, she would sit with a pillow behind her back for support. I sat in a straight chair beside her and watched her wolf down the sweets as if she were a starving waif on the street. "Don't you get enough to eat here?" I would ask. "No desserts," she would snarl; "they never give us desserts." Her arms and legs were toothpicks; she sat on a slight tilt, as if the bones on one side of her body had mysteriously given way.

I wanted to ask her to come back home with me. Having had her in the house, keeping her up on her lessons, feeding and clothing her, I found that her sheer animal being, the morning sickness, the swelling, the lethargy, had strangely warmed me. I wanted to tell her this, that, after the baby came, I wanted her back—she could live with me and the baby, make a fresh start, go to regular school, have girlfriends, go to slumber parties—but something in her face, a tightness at the mouth, stopped me. I tried to think what might offer her some relief from her predicament. Once I'd suggested we take an outing. It was a beautiful winter day; the exercise would do us both good. "Maybe the zoo," I said. "I read there's a baby giraffe." She gasped as if I'd suggested something so outrageous it shocked even her. I reached over and touched her shoulder, noticing in that moment that her belly had pushed up the maternity top she was wearing, which was a hideous shade of pink and too short. What was I thinking buying the poor thing such an outfit? The baby's roundness had loosened the elastic part of her pants. How I longed to touch it!

For a breath of a moment, she leaned into my touch so that her hair brushed my hand. Then she shuddered and shook her head like a wet dog, tears spraying the air between us. Sunlight poured through the windows, and her tears caught the light in midair before they fell. Then she pushed herself up from the sofa and left me without a word.

I was told I had to wait another day to bring it home. I was told it was a girl. I pictured it wrapped up in the yellow angora blanket. It had taken me three months to knit the blanket and two for the booties, which were much harder. I went to the hospital to see it but they said it was being fed and I should wait for a better time. It was having some issues with feeding; nothing serious, they assured me.

Then they told me Grace hadn't signed the papers. "Why not?" I asked the nurse at the front desk.

She shrugged. "Some of these girls, they like to wait a day or so."

One day melted into the next. The weather was un-seasonably warm for February. When I went out and tried to work in the yard, I found myself soaked to the skin. When I came in, I took a long tepid bath to try to calm myself. I had begun to think the worst: that Grace might have decided to keep the child and ruin her own life, that it might have pneumonia and perish before I had a chance to lay eyes on it. I took to the rocking chair, my lifeboat, rocking endlessly into the night, pushing the rocker from one side of the baby's little room to the other, humming lullabies to myself like a lunatic. In the early morning hours of the second day I fell into bed exhausted, only to toss and turn until dawn.

Finally the nurse called. "Your niece has signed the papers," she said. "The child's been moved to St. Vincent's up on Magazine. You can pick her up there."

I wept with relief. "Thank God."

Then the nurse said, "Oh, and we're assuming Grace is with you. Her father's here to get her, but her bed was empty."

Before I could answer, Holly took over the phone. "Frances, you have Grace there, right?"

"I haven't seen her since before the baby."

"Well, she's disappeared into thin air, then. This is nonsense. I'm going home. June's there by herself, I need to get back. She'll turn up. Call me when she does."

Then I remembered the knife, and I began to tremble. I opened my mouth to tell him he needed to find her; she wasn't in her right mind, hadn't been in months—who knew what she might do—but by the time I began to speak, he'd hung up.

Why hadn't he come by to confer with me, things being in such a state? Which I know is a dangling participle. Which I am aware is a sentence fragment. Why hadn't I been allowed to see my child these three long days; yes, *my* child now, who had now been moved like a piece of furniture to *an orphanage*? I showered and dressed, white hot with fury. How dare they keep me from it! And when it came right down to it—knife or no knife—what an ungrateful wretch my niece had turned out to be! After all I'd done for her!

Despite the heat, I dressed up. I put on my white lace blouse with its nice tie at the neck, my best short-sleeve suit, a navy blue, and black patent pumps. I wanted to make a good impression, let them know they were dealing with a lady of quality and substance. I put my favorite rhinestone pin on my breast pocket, then removed it, thinking it might prick the baby when, at long last, I would be allowed to hold it.

For the child, I took an extra diaper and some rubber pants because you never know what will issue forth from a baby. The blanket was too hot for the weather, I knew, but I decided to take it so those people would know what kind of person they were dealing with, not trashy and irresponsible like my niece but a decent woman, a good mother. Before I left, I mixed the formula the doctor had prescribed (yes, I had located an excellent pediatrician). I boiled the six bottles and nipples I'd purchased a month ago and put all but one in the refrigerator. Just in case it was hungry, I put the one, along with the diaper and rubber pants, into the diaper bag I'd purchased months ago, years ago it seemed. I considered taking the booties but decided against it because of the heat. I just hoped its feet would stay small so it could wear them when the weather turned cool in the fall.

By the time I pulled into the hospital parking lot, the sun was directly overhead and the air was clammy. I dabbed perspiration from my forehead with a handkerchief and snatched up the diaper bag and blanket. As I walked at a clip across the parking lot, my forearm began to itch under the blanket and the heat from the blacktop wafted up my skirt and stung me through my hose.

What happened next is hard to tell. How I came and looked and flew. How what I wanted, my sweet baby girl, had been already defiled. How, when I first caught sight of Grace's little child, all I could see was *it*: that foul breach in the nature of things. Sheer evil is what I saw, the mark of a terrible sin, one I can't even imagine. I knew I'd never be able to look at that child again, operation or no operation. All I'd ever see was that yawning tunnel of a mouth, leading straight to the doors of Hell.

So I sit here rocking, asking you to consider that none of us is without flaw. Think of the mote in your own eye. We all have our empty spaces where something of substance ought to reside, our chasms of moral ineptitude. I lean out over the ledge of mine and see that I am a woman who lacks imagination.

God help me, I could see only what was right before my eyes, right in front of me. What I saw was a creature from another planet.

13
Ed Mae

The child favored water. By the time October rolled around, she'd got big enough to sit up, and I'd put her in the kitchen sink and let her splash around while we bathed the little ones. She had herself one fine old time, whapping the water with her fat little hands, squealing like a stuck pig. Going on eight months and still bald as an egg, not a trace of eyebrows even, nothing to lend her some features, pull the eye up, away from the lip.

My specialty was the newborns, so when the nurse brought her in, less than a week in this world and hollering like somebody'd lit a fire under her, they handed her off to me. Nobody'd warned me, nobody'd said a mumbling word, so when I unwrapped the blanket I near about dropped the child on the floor.

Now I was used to ugly. White girls, they can pop out some peculiar-looking babies, all splotchy and milky-eyed, heads like toadstools. The ones I saw in that place where I worked, St. Vincent's, they were the throwaways. They knew it too, knew they were trash, knew their girl mamas don't want nothing to do with them. They was extra. Extra hung like a caul over their sad little old man faces.

But that one, that Baby Girl, she was the be-all end-all of ugly. Looked like some kind of evil slapped that child upside the head, said, *There, take that, be a big old ugly catfish.* Hooked and brought up hard. All she needed was a set of whiskers and a tail.

No two ways about it, she was God's child and He made her that way, but for what intent and purpose, you tell me. I ask the nurse how come they didn't fix that thing, tuck it in and sew it up the way you do that flap of skin at the rear end of the turkey, and the nurse say let the family what takes her fix it. Whoa horse, I say, who's going to want her, looking like that? All a matter of money, nurse say, which made no sense because this one was eating us out of house and home.

Just to take the cake, she was dark too. Not dark dark, but the color of mayonnaise gone bad. Her skin was actually her best feature to my mind, but she was a white baby and white babies are supposed to be white.

Meantime, Baby Girl, she's growing like gangbusters, getting bigger and fishier-looking by the minute. Folks would come in all gussied up like they're going to their own birthday party, the young ladies with fresh hair, the husbands with their pressed shirts and shiny shoes, all happy and excited. They'd grab each other's hands and tiptoe over to the crib to see their very own baby girl, the one they'd brought the pink blanket and bonnet for. They'd been warned, sure, but nothing prepares the eye. They'd take the first glad look and that would be it. Their eyes would get skittery as mice and out the door they'd head, fast as their two feet could carry them, slowing up just enough to cast their eyes sideways into the other cribs, at the other babies with their sweet faces, nothing wrong with *them,* and wondering why nobody called about that pretty one to their left. Or that other plain but decent-looking one over there in the corner. Back then, there was buckets of babies for white folks, the girls was having them right and left, people could pick and choose, be particular. Why should *they* take a child with a mouth like a tunnel when they could have rosebud lips?

Loud as she was ugly too, carrying on all the time like the world was coming to an end. It was like she *knew.* Even when she was real little, coming to us from Our Lady down on Napoleon, the white girls from families with full pockets but nobody willing to hold them up in their shame and say you are still mine and what comes from you is mine too. She'd root around in her bed like a little pig going for tit. Then she'd get mad as fire and holler like she was saying, *Where's mine? How come I don't get none?* She'd watch you across the room and when she saw you coming at her, she would cry out like somebody'd stuck a pin in her. She wanted petting and talking to, but nobody but me would give her the time of day. The other girls, they fed her and cleaned her up, their hands busy with her business, their eyes always floating up above her, peaceful and uninterested, never looking her in the face. As she got bigger she got more and more watchful, studying those girls for a spark, somebody to look back, be a mirror, other eyes that would say, *Yeah honey, here you be, stuck on this treacherous earth with the rest of us poor dopes. You right here, and us too, we're all in this mess together, Baby Girl. This good earth is your home sweet home.*

I was the one gave her a name. Nurse said we shouldn't name the children because then we'd get attached and that road is paved in sorrow. But when nobody took her and she got to be a permanent fixture, she started studying me like she was asking for her name. She got me to thinking about how a name is like gravity, it holds you down, keeps you from coming apart and flying all over the place. After a while, those little eyes of hers would follow me home. I would see them when I looked at my own pretty children, like they were a window she was pressed up against, peeking into, out of the dark sorrowful night. So I came up with Baby Girl and it stuck, being both personal and not personal at the same time. I said it in a certain way, with the emphasis on the Baby part to set it aside as a proper name, not just any baby girl in the place. I would say, "*Baby* Girl needs a change, I'll be right back," and they'd all know who I was talking about.

The shameful thing was that Baby Girl had a family over in Mississippi. A little town called Opelika. Her mother just a girl herself, whose own mother had passed a few years ago. At first it seemed like everything was going to be just fine. The dead mother had a sister, a teacher lady right here in the City who wanted to adopt the child. The nurse what brought her to me told the story. Teacher Lady had come in to fetch Baby Girl and take her home. The lady had hungry eyes. She brought a yellow blanket she'd knitted herself. "Wool," the nurse said, "and in this weather." A skinny woman with big teeth and a line like a train track between her brows. She'd been warned about the lip. The folks at Charity had explained to her how it needed fixing. But when she saw Baby Girl, her brows shot up under her bangs and the train track disappeared. She said there must be a mistake, this could *not* be her own niece's child—her niece was an *attractive* girl—and when they said there was no mistake, Teacher Lady turned around and hightailed it out the door.

After she left, folks here called the granddaddy down in Opelika, asked him didn't he want Baby Girl. "A girl?" he said. "Adopt it out. I don't ever want to hear about it again. I got enough to deal with." Those were his exact words, folks said.

So me and Baby Girl, we went along, day to day, month to month. She got to be six months old, then seven going on eight. Her eyes turned from blue eggs to hard little coals. She grew two teeth the size of the nail on my little finger and pointed straight out, like tusks.

It was right chilly that morning. Somebody said to get the babies washed early because of Cuba and the Russians and the Bomb. I ran Baby's water a little hotter than usual in the deep sink in the kitchen. I sat her down and she laughed and whapped the water, spattering it up in my face. I soaped her up, trying to stay dry myself. Sometimes when I bathed her, I ended up as wet as her. I was running a little more warm water to keep her from getting cold when one of the white girls hollered at me to do this or that job of work, I can't even recollect what. Those white girls, they gave me the stuff that was too dirty for their taste.

In the tub, Baby Girl was playing hard, splashing around, snorting the way she did because of the hole in her face. She hit the water again with her little pig hand and squealed.

I turned away to do this job of work I was called upon to do. A bad diaper, or some upchuck. How strange it is I can't remember! It wasn't going to take long whatever it was. Baby Girl was doing fine in the sink, she was all right, snorting those soft little breaths the way she did when she was having a good time.

While I was cleaning up whatever mess it was, I got distracted. I got to stewing about my own little Mary. I'd left her with her big brother. My Cleve is named after his daddy, who'd died that past year fighting for his country, holding back the communists over there in the swamps of Vietnam so the dominoes wouldn't fall across the whole wide world and bury us all. Cleveland had gone and got himself blown up in one of the tunnels those communists booby-trap. His lieutenant sent him in to see about another soldier who hadn't come out. How crazy is that? If you crawl into a hole and don't crawl out, isn't that a hint something's wrong in there? Is it good sense for me to crawl in after you? He'd written to me about how they always sent him into the tunnels, told him he was good at it. I think he was proud of that, but I figured they sent him into those death holes because he was a Negro, like those white girls in the place making me to clean up baby upchuck, allowing as how I had such a strong stomach, wasn't I something.

My boy Cleve was twelve. He carried his father's sweetness tucked deep inside him the way the oyster carries the pearl. He was good with Mary, who was a handful, making hay with every kind of mischief she could think up every minute of the day and night. She was six, with just the softest head of hair you ever saw, a dandelion cloud around her face. I worked myself to death over that hair of hers. She liked to take out her braids so it was always wild. She got so she ran off whenever we let her out. We lived in a double shotgun in Black Pearl. Neighbors two blocks over would find her sitting on their porch stoops, hair flying every which way, looking to be let in. At dusk, she'd sneak out while I was fixing supper and go peering into folks' windows like a peeping tom. When they'd open their doors to see about her, she would say she was looking for her daddy, he was hiding from her but she was bound to find him if she kept on looking. They would drag her back home, shaking their heads and muttering about how war widows with pensions should stay home and take care of the preciousness they got left. It's not my nature to talk back to people, I keep my counsel, but one day I told Billie Jones, who lived in the other side of our double, she could have my pension and my children too if *she* could stretch the money Uncle Sam sent to take care of them. Did they think I was working twelve-hour shifts on my feet diapering white throwaways for the pure pleasure of it?

I worked from four in the morning to four in the afternoon so I could have some time with my own children after school. That day, though, they'd canceled school. If the Russians was dead set on bombing us, the young ones ought to be home with their mamas and daddies. What a joke! My babies' daddy blown to smithereens and me pushing a twelve-hour shift. I was worried sick. When I left the house in the dark of that morning, I'd put a note to Cleve on the kitchen table telling him to keep Mary in. I reminded him about getting under the kitchen table if he heard a siren.

As I did that job of cleaning up those white girls had sent me to do, I was thinking Mary would be popping like a firecracker by now. My Cleve would be ready to wring her neck and mine too by the time I dragged myself home on the bus, hanging on to the strap, staring at the empty seats in the front. He'd be waiting at the door like a caged dog. "'Bout time you got home," he'd say and push past me. He'd walk out onto the street and not come back until past dark, doing Lord knows what. "Wait for me," little Mary would holler. "I want to go too." He'd just keep walking, not looking back. Then she would throw a fit while I tried to get supper on. I had a stone setting square on my heart thinking about it all, with no Cleveland in the world, not even a piece of him to bury so I could say, go in peace, my Cleveland, you were a good man, a good husband.

I was in a deep study, thinking as to how it was getting toward Thanksgiving and Christmas, and my children would be running wild in the freezing cold until school started up again in January, if we all lived that long. I had no kin to help me. Both our families had left the City years back and headed for Chicago. My mother would have taken care of Cleve and Mary both if she'd been here. They'd be out playing in the old backyard in Algiers, Daddy pitching the ball, making Cleve believe he was the next Jackie Robinson, Mary playing outfield. But those two, coming back south? Not even in a box, Mother said. She wanted to send us a one-way ticket on the Greyhound to Chicago, but

I couldn't bear the idea of leaving our little double, which was the last place Cleveland and I had lived as man and wife. After I got the children to bed, I'd sit in the dark and think about him like he was one of Mary's jigsaw puzzles, the pieces all crying out to be put back together. I could feel his spirit all around me. Pieces of him fluttered against my face like moths to the light, wanting to hover and touch. This was *our* place. When I dreamed him up in my head, his corded arms and stern legs, his playing eyes, his manhood, it was like I was putting him back together again. If I weren't here, in the place where he was whole, he would fly apart and melt into thin air like he'd never been born.

So I was studying my options, thinking about maybe sending the children north for the holidays, asking Mother and Daddy to send me some money to put them on the bus, though I couldn't stand the idea of my two babies on a bus all by themselves in the dead of winter. Chicago! They could get snatched or lost, freeze to death. I was tied in a knot worrying about my own flesh and blood, the children Cleveland had left me to care for. It was the last thing he said to me, "Take care of the children, Ed Mae." And I'd answered him hard and fast, "They're my children too, Cleveland." Wished now I'd said something softer, wished I'd said, *You know I will, honey.*

So here I was, barely thirty-five years old, stuck like a fly on flypaper to this treacherous earth, two young ones to take care of, no husband and no luck and barely enough money to scrape by. It was a dark tunnel I was in and no light ahead, not even a flicker. That tunnel was about to cave in, right that very minute, and that was nobody's fault but mine, all mine.

When one of those white girls saw Baby Girl's little hand on the edge of the sink and went over, thinking it was a doll got left behind, I was busy planning Cleveland's funeral if ever a trace of him turned up. Then there could be an end to it. Mary would stop her wandering, and we could head for Chicago. In my mind I was hearing everybody singing "Deep River." I was seeing the flag on the coffin, then a triangle in my lap, then tucked away in the bottom drawer of my dresser for Cleve when he got to be a man.

It was like coming out of a dream. There was a commotion and I looked up, across the long cold room of cribs and tables with stacks of diapers and towels, through the open doorway to the kitchen. When I saw the sink and the little hand, something caught in my throat like a grain of pepper.

Somebody pulled Baby Girl out, water pouring off

her. She was shiny and limp on the kitchen counter. Her little head flopped over to the side. I began to run.

We turned her on her stomach. The water came out of the tunnel in her face. It poured out. We hung her head over the edge and pushed on her back. More water poured out but she still didn't stir. I turned her on her back and put my mouth over the bottom part of her face and blew the way we'd been taught, her teeth cutting my lip. I was careful, I had read a piece in a magazine about not blowing too much air into babies, you don't want to explode their little lungs. The white girls turned their heads away like I was doing something shameful.

When the ambulance men came in, they took one step back when they saw the lip. Then the Creole man gathered himself and clamped his lips on the hole in her face and worked on her some more.

But she was gone, her eyes closed, no longer watchful and wanting, her mouth the dynamited tunnel. The other ambulance man stepped forward and rolled her up in the towel I'd left on the counter. He carried her out, not the way you'd carry a baby, but upside down under his arm like this was a fish shop and she was a big old snapper he was taking home for his wife to stew.

After they drove away with her, the nurse came in huffing and puffing. She turned to us all and asked what you'd expect her to ask. And the white girls, each and every one, pointed at me.

Pure and simple. It was me what forgot Baby Girl.

They called the police and the police took me in. I told them I had two little children at home, no family to take care of them. They said they'd call welfare and I begged them to let me put them with a friend, not even knowing then who that might be. When they took me by home, I snatched up my Cleve and Mary and took them over to Billie Jones next door, who was the first person I could think of, the only person in the neighborhood whose full name I knew. I begged her pardon and asked her to watch over them for me until I could straighten things out. She put her arm around me and said she would, we couldn't let them go into the system. She promised me. Then she asked Mary if she liked to color pictures and Mary said yes she did, and then Billie Jones took her by the hand and led her back to the kitchen without even a goodbye for her mother. Cleve hugged me around the waist so hard it took my breath away. I told him I'd be back. I told him not to worry, to be brave and mind Billie Jones.

It's been six years nine months since Baby Girl died. One day, one minute, one mistake, and your whole measly, precious life is dust and ashes.

I was thinking Billie Jones would be a temporary thing, but a week after I was arrested, Mother and Daddy's apartment up in Chicago went up in smoke and them with it. At the jail, they gave me one phone call and I called Billie. "Honey," she said, "I'll keep these babies for you till doomsday if you need me to. They're good children. Just send me some money so I can keep them in clothes and feed them."

"Much obliged," I said, trying to keep from blubbering all over the phone. I barely knew this woman except that she worked at the Tabasco factory down at the river and always smelled like pepper, plus she kept a pot of begonias on her side of our front porch. But anything was better than the system. "I'll send you my army check every month," I said.

"Course you will, baby," she said. "These are your precious children. Don't you worry none. I'll keep them safe as long as you need me to."

Six years nine months is a long time, especially if you spend them in the Louisiana Correctional Institute for Women. Outside things, they change. Today a man landed on the moon. We watched it on TV. Some of the girls clapped when he planted his stiff little flag in that desert of a place, but I didn't clap. A starched handkerchief of a flag up against all that cold emptiness. And for what?

Billie Jones says Cleve is smart in school like I used to be, he's got a scholarship to Xavier next year. Mary isn't the student he is. She's still a pistol, it's all Billie can do to keep that girl out of trouble, away from the boys. For a while, after I got put away, Mary kept up her roaming and started looking for me along with her missing daddy. Then one day she just stopped, Billie wrote, and everybody was grateful those little beady eyes of hers weren't peeking through the slants in their blinds anymore. I expect she finally got it figured out. It's four hours up and back on the bus to St. Gabriel, but Billie brings them to visit every now and then. Then Mary presses up against Billie's side and eyes me like I'm a wreck on the side of the road.

The white men on that jury didn't look at me. I felt like Baby Girl, dirtied in a sin that made the eye skitter and pitch.

I go up for parole in seventeen more years. By then, folks'll probably be living on another planet altogether. Maybe Mary will go looking for her daddy on the moon.

As to Baby Girl, there's not a night I don't get down on my knees and ask her to forgive me for forgetting her.

14
Fred the Ambulance Driver

M y sidekick Joey carried the drowned baby girl out. He opened the back of the ambulance. I stopped him. "Put her up front," I told him. "Don't seem right, putting her back there all by herself. You go ahead and take the streetcar so you can take off early to eat. I'll drive her over to the morgue. No point in both of us having to give up our break, especially when the world's about to get blown to hell in a handbasket down in Cuba."

Joey gave me the stink eye. "Dead's dead," he said.

"Christ sakes, Joey, it's a baby," I said.

It had started as just another day, my Earlie still in bed, smelling to high heaven of sour milk, her face turned to the wall. When I got ready to go to work, I'd leaned over and pulled on her shoulder a little, trying to turn her over to kiss her goodbye, but she didn't budge.

I'd just walked in from the streetcar when the call came. Over at St. Vincent's an orphan baby under water, maybe drowned, maybe not. Me and Joey hustled, sirens screaming. I ran the light at Magazine and Napoleon, almost plowing down a cab. The driver honked and cussed at me. I cussed back, shaking my fist at him.

When me and Joey busted into the kitchen, a naked baby was laying up on the counter. A girl, dark for a white baby, which I knew she had to be, St. Vincent's being for white children. A Negro woman bent over her, puffing air into her mouth, pushing on her chest. The woman was crying big old crocodile tears.

"Lord, woman," I said, "you going to drown the child all over again."

I pushed her aside, then did a double take. The child's mouth looked like a mole hole in the ground, deep and wide and ragged. I looked at the Negro woman and she looked at me, her eyes fairly leaping out of her face. "Do something!" she hollered. I turned the baby over and hit her on the back and some water came out. Then I flipped her back and put my mouth over the hole and pushed air. I pushed and pushed. She didn't stir. Finally, I gave it up.

Joey looked at his watch and said, "Time of death 11:23 A.M."

"Glad you're good for something," I said.

The Negro woman sank down to the floor, put her face in her hands. By then the white girls were pointing fingers at her, telling how she was to blame. Joey took a towel from the counter and wrapped up the baby, and that was that.

Or so I thought.

Truth be told, I'm thinking I'd rather take this dead baby to the morgue than go home to eat, with Earlie so down and out since our own baby came and went like heat lightning. A boy, born blue just six days ago but it seems like a year. In the incubator he'd turned an odd shade of gray, a yellowish gray.

"Oh lord Jesus, what they gone and done to our baby boy?" Earlie cried out when I took her to see him. "Looks like they gone and drained every drop of blood out of him."

The next night, he passed. We never even got to hold him.

If that weren't sorrow and trouble enough, they'd operated on Earlie after our boy was born, for reasons I still can't figure. Now no more babies and she won't get out of the bed, barely pecks at the food I bring. She just lays there like a shriveled-up baby bird in a nest of puddled-up sheets and blankets, bone and more bone, her fingers curled up like claws. And the milk just keeps pouring out of her, like a bad joke. Before all this happened with the dead orphan baby, I was going to run by Piggly Wiggly and bring her some rainbow sherbet, though I didn't have high hopes of interesting her in it.

I settle the baby girl on the seat beside me, the towel a bit looser, the top of her head inching out, a downy fuzz.

I crank up the engine, but then one thing leads to another. I touch the baby's little head. The hair like silk. Been so busy taking care of Earlie, I hadn't had time to cry over my boy. Now here come twin rivers down the sides of my cheeks. I stroke the top of the baby girl's head, studying the fuzz, how it springs to my touch.

Then I can't help myself. I cut the engine and pick her up. I put her in my lap and hold her, just hold her, her little arms falling off to the side, limp and soft. My boy would have gotten to be big like this one. He would have been light-skinned, like Earlie and me, a good-looking Creole boy. We never got to hold him. They took him away, and then he was laying in a coffin the size of a shoe box and that was that. This baby here's big, probably make four or five of him.

Now baby's feet slide out from the towel. Pretty little toes! Plump and firm. I cup them in my hands. I got long fingers. My mother always told me I ought to learn to play the piano, play me some honky-tonk with them fingers, she'd tell me. These fingers, they cup baby's fat toes.

Now I rub her little chest, then pat it. Rub and pat. The waterfalls from my eyes soak her towel around the belly. *Aw, child, aw child.* After a while, the waterfall turns to a slow drip. I give the toes one more squeeze and put baby back down on the seat and mop my eyes. I start up the engine again and pull onto the highway.

We go along a second or two.

Then something tickles at the corner of my eye, like a cockroach scudding across the floor. I wipe my eye again and keep driving. Cars slow down and people look sad as I pass, knowing what an ambulance heading back to town without the lights on might mean.

We're just crossing the next street when the tickle tickles again. I look down at baby's feet. What pink toes for a dead baby! I touch one. Is it warm? Just as I touch it again, the baby girl lets go a little cough and the towel over her face produces a good-sized wet spot.

I jump right out of my skin, landing the ambulance on the shoulder of the road. I rip off the towel, just in time for baby to cough and spew more water. Exactly like a whale surfacing, exactly like that. All I can see now is that dark spout in her face, and water's gushing out of it.

I turn her over, and here comes the rest of the water. After all that, you'd think a baby would cry. Instead, when I turn her back over, she points her two little teeth at me and does her best to smile and doing a damn good job given the equipment she's working with. Ain't no fool, that girl. This ambulance man just held her like a real baby, like she belonged to him, she ain't going nowhere, no sirree bobtail. Now she reaches for my finger. I snatch her up and put her head on my shoulder, hit her hard on the back to make sure all the water's out. She makes contact with my thumb and holds on for dear life. She throws her head back and aims those little teeth at me again. Lord, the one ought to be named Lazarus!

I need somebody to tell me what to do next with this throwaway baby girl.

Then I picture Earlie in that bed, her hand thrumming the covers, her face turned to the wall. I picture our poor little son, wizened as an old man.

So I turn baby girl around and hold her tight in my lap with my right arm. She coos and pats the steering wheel, like she's saying, *Where to, mister?* With my left hand, I pull the ambulance back onto the road. "We going home now," I say, and turn the car in the opposite direction of the morgue or the hospital or the orphanage.

When we get to our little shotgun on Miro Street, I pull the ambulance up to the curb and hustle the baby inside. Thankfully, it's a chilly morning and nobody's sitting out on their porches.

Earlie's still asleep. She's turned onto her back, her chin tilted up to the sky, catching the noonday light coming through the streaked window next to the bed. I lay little Lazarus down beside her, and she looks like she belongs there, their skin the exact same color.

I sit down and put on my thinking cap. Here's a throwaway nobody's going to miss. But her papers say she's white. Even if me and Earlie try to adopt her, this is 1962, somebody'll just think we're being uppity, I could lose my job for even asking, or worse.

Just then, she starts fussing and fidgeting and kicking Earlie in the side. Earlie opens her eyes, then reaches out. Her hand lands on the baby's hand and the baby grabs a finger. Earlie sits straight up in bed.

Then she takes one look and near about jumps up off the bed, then glares up at me. "What you gone and done, you crazy fool man?"

"Looka here, girl," I begin. "I got you a present. This one's a throwaway."

Earlie gives me one long look. Something, a speck of light, flares in her eyes. She picks up the baby girl and looks her over. Then she grins. "Lord, Fred, couldn't you have got me a prettier one?"

"The pretty ones was all taken," I say. "But this one, she's got the Lord's hand on her, this one rose up from the dead. This one here's bound and determined to live. No losing *her*."

Just then the baby girl puts Earlie's finger in her mouth and begins to suck. I hold my breath. Earlie looks at the baby, then at me, then back at the baby. Then her hand finds the buttons on the front of her gown.

And that's the end of the story.

Except that I took back the ambulance that afternoon and filled out the paperwork like I'd taken the dead baby to the morgue. Then I turned in my quitting paper and rode the streetcar home like always. The next day Earlie and me and our baby girl lit out on the Greyhound bus for the furthest place up the line, which was Nashville, Tennessee, and nobody ever said a mumbling word. The first thing I did after I got a job driving ambulances for Baptist Hospital was fix our girl's poor mouth. We're raising her black, and proud of it—what else can we do? She has the happiest of homes, the best me and Earlie have to give, and when it comes time for college, we're going to send her to the best, Fisk University, which, as it happens, is right down the street. She's smart as a whip, says she's going to get a scholarship, not be a burden on us.

Oh, and Earlie wouldn't let me name her Lazarus. Her name's Josephine, after Earlie's grandmother. We call her Josie.

15
June

After my sister went away, I used to think about her little child all the time, wondering what had happened to it. I made up stories in my head. It got adopted by Liz Taylor and swam in a huge backyard pool with its adopted big sister, Maria. It was shipped off to missionaries in the Belgian Congo and is still out there in the jungle handing out bibles to the natives. It got taken by the Amish up north, wears a bonnet or a funny hat, rides around in a carriage.

At night I dreamed of the baby.

It would call to me to come outside to play. It wanted to be found behind the trees and bushes in our backyard. It wanted to laugh and tickle and roll in the grass the way children do. I would tell it no. I would say I was a grown girl, and grown girls don't play like that.

I would touch its fat little bottom, the tuft of hair on the top of its little head. *Are you a girl or a boy?* I'd ask.

After our father took Grace to Frances's, he never spoke of my sister, much less of her little child: what was going to happen to it, where it was going to go in this big wide world. By that time Grace had left Frances's, why I don't know, and had gone to that Catholic home for girls in her kind of trouble. For her birthday, I sent her the Supremes' new album, which I almost wore out listening to before putting it in the mail. To the package I added a pair of red wool socks and a box of Russell Stover chocolate creams. Outside, it was dark and rainy and bone cold. I'd read Dickens the summer before and pictured the girls' home as miserably cold with wet drafty dark hallways, the girls, pasty-faced and wall-eyed, with spindly arms and legs protruding from their pear-shaped trunks, holding up bowls while a nun with a ladle doled out weevily gruel from a monster pot.

I wasn't surprised when my sister didn't write to thank me for the presents. When she'd headed out the door that morning with her one pitiful suitcase, a hand-me-down from Mama's closet, her face was a sheet of ice. I followed the two of them out to the driveway, but she wouldn't even look at me. The few days between the night I told Dad and the morning he took her away, she stayed in her room with the door closed. I slept in the hallway outside her door rolled up in a blanket on the floor, whispering to her through the door. I pointed out that I wasn't a tattletale by nature; I'd done intimate things for her. I'd hidden her underwear, which she'd been careless enough to throw on the bathroom floor after one of her nights out. Once, when there'd been a thunderstorm, I'd tiptoed into her empty room and shut the open window over her desk so her things wouldn't get wet. Didn't I get some credit for keeping her from getting caught up to now?

Secretly I counted her a fool for letting things go along the way she had. Did she think she could just pop out a living, hollering baby one bright sunny day and people wouldn't notice? Not to speak of the fact that she was a spare, lanky girl. Did she think people were blind? Was she going to flush it down the commode at school the way some unknown girl had tried to do last year, giving poor Jackie Simms a heart attack when she went into the stall and saw something grayish coiled up in the toilet, something writhing about, something that looked like it had come up through the pipes?

I regret to say that over time I actually came to think of Grace's little child as a snake, coiled up and ready to strike. What a terrible thing, to think of an innocent baby that way!

There was something about the threeness of Grace's situation that had rubbed off on the baby I dreamed up. A week before the night I first saw the little curve of my sister's belly in the moonlight as she lay sleeping, I happened to be following her as she walked home with Daniel and George. When they stopped to cross a street, George reached across Grace to touch Daniel on the arm, his fingers lingering on the front of her blouse. She arched into his touch, smiling up at him, then over at Daniel, whose hand was, I suddenly saw, on her waist.

Up to that moment, I'd been secretly thrilled by my sister's shenanigans. I actually had a bit of a crush on George, and followed along in hopes she'd turn and then include me in their conversation. My life, unlike Grace's, was dull as dishwater. Her presumed romance with Daniel had all the elements of an ill-fated love story à la Romeo and Juliet. Daniel Baker was just the type to wear one of those tight getups Romeo wore, and willowy Grace would be perfect as Juliet.

But the three of them together bowled me over despite the fact that even at fourteen I fancied myself knowledgeable in the ways of the world. I hadn't gone and done *it*, but I had friends who had. I knew about the boy sticking his you-know into the girl's you-know-what and pictured this activity being performed over a toilet. I couldn't figure out how it would work with two boys and a girl. Before I'd observed the three of them on that street corner, I'd speculated that maybe Grace had been going steady with Daniel *and* George, but separately and secretly. But that wasn't it at all, I now saw; this was something else I didn't have a name for, something that made the hair rise on the back of my neck, like my mother's birdcalls.

When I went into my father's room to tell him Grace was going to have a baby, he was lying on his back on the bed smoking and listening to the radio. There was an empty glass streaked with cherry bounce and an empty bottle on the bedside table. He was on my mother's side, his bedroom slippers on the floor, where she used to keep hers. He didn't look up when I came in.

When I told him about the pregnancy (though not about its obvious complications), he sat up and threw his legs over the side of the bed and proceeded to stare at the wall. The smoke curled up from the cigarette in his hand, the ash growing longer and longer, finally falling onto his lap.

"Dad," I said after a while. "What are we going to do?" The butt was down to the filter now. In another minute it would burn his fingers.

He stood up, crushed the cigarette in the overflowing ashtray on the bedside table, and put his feet into the slippers. He rubbed his face hard with both hands, leaving it red and splotched. "I'm going to kill her," he muttered. "Then I'm going to find out whose it is and kill him too."

In the days and nights that followed, I fixed Grace her favorite foods. Peach cobbler and root beer floats, peanut butter and banana sandwiches. These I put in front of her door, and eventually they disappeared. On the floor outside her door, I woke up every morning with rheumy eyes and a stomach-dropping sense of doom. I stopped doing my homework, and my teachers became alarmed, holding me back after the bell had rung, asking me questions about my "home life" in explosive little bursts, saying I could confide in them if I needed to, looking deep into my eyes.

After Dad came back from taking Grace to New Orleans, he loaded up all his cherry bounce in the car and came back a half hour later without it. In the days and weeks that followed, the two of us tiptoed from room to room, trying to stay out of each other's way. Then he started up with his crossword puzzles. In the mornings he read the *Times-Picayune* from cover to cover. At night he got a pencil, gathered the funny papers page where the crossword puzzle was, and folded it into a neat square. For the rest of the night, he'd sit on the sofa, that little square of newspaper in his hand, his brow furrowed. Sometimes he'd look up and ask me questions like what's another word for *dilute* or what's the name of a desert in Africa? Sometimes I'd know the answer, usually I wouldn't have a clue. He bought a monstrous *Webster's* and a *Roget's Thesaurus*, which he set down on the couch beside him every night, leaving no room for me to sit next to him and watch TV. After he finished the night's puzzle, sometimes leaving a few blank spaces, he'd head for bed, murmuring good night but not kissing the top of my head the way he used to do when Grace was with us.

At school, Grace's abrupt departure, paired with that of the two boys, had started whispers, which irked me no end. Why did I always have to be explaining the strange disappearances of my family members, dead or alive?

"Where's Grace?" my friend Hilary Lumpkin asked after a few days. Hil was my best friend. We were walking from first-year Latin to Home Economics II, where we were making seersucker shorts for the summer ahead. The question shouldn't have startled me, but I was still in such a state over losing my sister, who now hated my guts for ruining her life, that I hadn't prepared a ready comeback.

"She's gone to stay with our aunt Frances. Frances has . . ." I took a breath and considered. "Phlebitis. She has phlebitis in her legs, that's where the veins swell up and get infected. She needs help around the house. So Grace is going to live with her and go to school in the City. She's *so* excited."

Spitting out the lie like that, without forethought, gave me something of a rush. I don't know why I drew phlebitis out of the hat of all the illnesses and diseases and conditions of the world. My grandmother had complained about having it in her legs, so it seemed like something that might immobilize a person. I knew too that it was dangerous; a blot clot could travel, as it had with my grandmother, and strike you down like lightning. One minute our grandmother had been pouring fudge into a Pyrex dish, the next she was dead on the kitchen floor.

Hil nodded, weighing what I'd said. "Sure," she said coolly, linking my arm into hers. "Hope Grace likes it over there."

I especially missed my sister when I was cooking supper. In the afternoons after our mother died, we'd danced around to the radio in the kitchen, me in Mama's daisy apron, Grace with a cup towel tied around her waist. We'd prepared food side by side, singing at the top of our lungs to the Top 40. Creamy Welsh rarebit and stewed chicken in brown gravy and devil's food cake with angel icing had had their way with our father, bringing him back to his senses after we lost our mother. Eventually he'd given up on the bomb shelter, shoveling the dirt back into the cavernous hole he'd dug in our yard, then planted seeds in the loose dirt for an early vegetable garden. He'd sat companionably at the kitchen table reading the paper as Grace and I wrangled skillets and Pyrex pans like we were running a greasy spoon. His inattentive but benign presence gave us a sense of domesticity, a feeling of home.

After my sister left, there was no fun to any of it. In the late afternoon the winter sun cut across the linoleum in the kitchen in one long thin line. At night I sat across the table from Dad, who'd returned to being a ghost.

"Dad," I asked, "what's going to happen to Grace and her little child?" I pictured her bringing it home in a pretty blanket, its little face a tiny replica of my sister's. I had the perfect plan. We'd kill off Frances with phlebitis and say it was her baby, now orphaned and in need of our care. I'd push it around in a stroller, mash it bananas and green beans, give it long baths, first measuring the water temperature with my elbow.

"Frances is going to take it. Grace will come back home and go back to school," he said, not looking up from his paper.

"But Grace will miss it." What I meant was I'd miss it. It would be fun to have a baby around. I could quit school and take care of it.

"No, she won't," Dad said.

With my sister gone, I threw on Mama's now-threadbare apron and made supper as fast as humanly possible, slamming pots and pans around, sighing like an overworked housewife. As my enthusiasm for cooking went down the drain, something else was percolating, something that ebbed and flowed invisibly and whispered wanting and warning in equal parts, stirring me up to boiling and then telling me I'd get burned.

Over the supper table Dad and I would steal looks at each other as though we were strangers eating at side-by-side tables in a restaurant. Then, one night, he looked at me straight on and said, "You know, you look more like your mother every day."

I'd just shoved a hunk of meatloaf into my mouth, so I didn't say anything back, just kept chewing, but how he said it and his strangely famished look made me feel like I was swallowing a rock.

"I shouldn't have said that," he muttered. He pushed his chair back and got up from the table and headed for the TV.

The next afternoon he came in with two TV trays, which he set up in the living room, one in front of the sofa, one in front of a chair on the other side of the room.

"Thought it'd be nice to watch TV while we eat," he said, avoiding my eyes. "You pick."

After that we watched television during supper. Then Dad would clear the trays while I washed the dishes and wiped down the countertops. He would turn off the TV and bury his nose in one of his cross-word puzzles. If I turned the TV back on, he'd peer at me over his reading glasses and ask, "Have you done your homework? Do you need to study for any tests?" I always said yes, I'd done my homework, and no, I didn't need to study, which was no more of a lie than anything else.

Meanwhile, whatever it was that was roiling around inside me was getting more disagreeable by the day. It said, *Watch out, be careful,* at the same time it said, *Go ahead, raise some hell, sister.* Sometimes I pictured it as a bad baby, Grace's baby, kicking and squalling and wanting to get out and boss me around. It came and it went, I noticed with growing alarm, with the full moon, making me worry I might be a vampire. Some nights, it made me toss and turn in bed, touch-ing me with its tiny fingers, almost tickling me but not quite, making things worse, then better, then worse again. I felt tricked, then trapped by a teasing hand.

One Saturday night Hil and I were walking home from the picture show. We'd just seen *Shane*, which was coming back for its third rerun at the Lyric, and I was as usual dreamy-eyed over Alan Ladd. His sky-blue eyes, that lock of hair that fell down over his forehead. It was fall but warm and musky sweet with the smell of fallen leaves. Hil and I passed Alden Park in the center of town. I pictured Alan and me sitting together on the bench under the Temperance Lady statue next to the drooping sycamore, his arm around me, holding me close.

I slowed down. "Do you want to sit down a while?" I walked over to the bench and sat.

Hil came over and sat down too. She sighed. "I love Shane."

"Me too."

I slid over. "Let's do some practice kissing." This was something Hil and I did rather frequently in private. We were practicing for boys, we told each other, each picturing long lines of boys awaiting our favors. Hil was being raised by her mother in an apartment the size of our kitchen and living room. Her mother was a secretary at the mill where Dad worked, and some afternoons after school I'd stop by and we'd pull Hil's Murphy bed down from the living room wall and kiss for a while. In truth, Hil didn't need practice; her kisses were deep and wet as a spring rain and they jolted me all the way down to my toes. Nothing I've felt since has matched them for effect.

After a bit of kissing we would take off our shirts and New Life youth bras so we could also practice rubbing our scrappy little breasts on each other's chest, which we thought would be pleasurable for the boys since it most certainly was for us. Kissing Plus, we called it. It was something we did, like sharing a pack of Nabs or doing our geometry homework on the rickety kitchen table. After we finished Kissing Plus, we would stagger upright and push the bed back up into the wall and put our tops back on and rearrange our pants or skirts, which had inevitably come down or risen up.

On the park bench Hil moved away from me.

Hil never said no to kissing, so her answer took me aback. Boys and girls stopped in the park all the time to kiss on the way home from the picture show. The bad baby in me wanted to grab her face and kiss her hard, make her full lips turn purple with bruising, call out to the world that we were practicing our kissing and getting damn good at it in case any boys were interested, but Hil pulled even farther away. I felt myself flush hot, then cold, a bit like when Mama used to rub my chest with Ben-Gay when I was little and had a cold.

"I think I've practiced enough," she said. "I think I've got it now. I think I'm ready for boys."

I got up from the bench, not looking at her. "Let's go then."

She rose without a word. "For what it's worth," she said, "I think you are too."

The next afternoon, a Sunday, she called and asked if I wanted to go to Calvary Baptist with her and her mother that night. There was a special preacher coming over from Hattiesburg, and tonight's service was going to kick off a week-long revival.

Since Mama had been taken away in that ambulance, I'd vowed never to commune with God because when I did, I worked myself into such a fury at Him for letting my mother die I felt I was going to explode like the Hindenburg blimp. Plus, there was Grace's little child for Him to account for. Last but not least, I was mad at God because Grace was mad at me and, if there were any justice in this world He allegedly created, she shouldn't have been. I also had a secondary list ten miles long of what I was mad at God for: war, famine, the Bomb, tornadoes, starving orphan babies, *Sputnik* dogs dead and alive.

But I jumped at the invitation, said sure, I'd like to go to the revival, sure, I could be ready at six, anything to get out of the house. To this day I don't know what caused me to take up with Jesus, but from the moment I walked up the aisle of the Calvary Baptist Church flanked by Hil and Mrs. Lumpkin, whose tired face flickered like a candle, I felt something strange happen. The preacher was the Reverend Harold P. Chisholm, and though I'd like to say he drew me into the fold with his sermon, I don't remember much of what he said except that the church was the bride of Christ, and that all who were part of the church were brides of Christ.

This idea about being the bride of Jesus hit me like a ton of bricks. Of course! That was what I wanted, what I yearned for, to be somebody's *bride*! To wear a drop-dead gorgeous white dress and carry a bouquet and walk down the aisle (unlike my sinful sister). To have somebody to keep company with, have a decent conversation with, share my innermost thoughts and feelings. *This* was why I tossed and turned at night, *this* was what I'd been missing.

So when Harold P. Chisholm said to come on down and take up with Jesus, I literally floated down the aisle, my shoulders thrown back, graceful as a deer making her way through the deep woods, serene as snow. I vowed to be Jesus's bride, to have and to hold from that day forward and even forever more. I'd been put in a jet rocket by the Holy Ghost and shot up into a beautiful starry sky, full of the spirit, heading straight for my rendezvous with the Prince of Peace.

The music was pretty, something about coming to the Garden alone while the dew is still on the roses, how He walks with me and He talks with me and He tells me I am His own. When the call came, I scrambled like a mountain goat over Hil, who'd nodded off in the pew, to be the first to get down the aisle to the Reverend Harold P. Chisholm and Jesus. Soon there was a flock of us floating down the aisle to the Garden. I would have preferred it had been just me marrying Jesus, but nothing's perfect.

I did get there first, at which point the Reverend asked my name and then whispered to me, "June, receive Grace," which almost spoiled the whole thing.

When everybody got to the front, all of us girls, we dedicated our lives to Him, and then a big curtain in the back of the choir rolled back and there was a swimming pool of water and Harold P. Chisholm shepherded all of us who hadn't received the sacrament of the one true baptism up to it and we walked down into the clear water in our Sunday clothes and he dunked us under and the water was cold as the ice in my sister's eyes.

Grace, I said as I went under, *you don't forgive me, but Jesus does.*

Then I came up, coughing and sputtering, cleansed of my mother's blood and Grace's little child. And my own bad baby, the snake that had roiled within me, it was washed away, forever and eternity, amen.

16
Holly

When I looked up from my crossword puzzle and saw June coming through the door looking like a drowned rat, I thought that Lumpkin woman had run her car into Ponce Creek on the way home from church. I thought my girl was hurt, maybe in shock, the way she was staring and shivering and looking just plain odd. It was the way my buddy Charlie looked that day outside Aubel when he lost half his head. That bug-eyed stare of his, out of the one eye, it scared the life out of me, it was worse than the blood. When I looked into that one eye, my gut heaved and cramped like I'd been kicked in the belly, and that's what it started doing now when June came through the door.

I jumped up from my chair, the puzzle slipping from my lap onto the floor. I said, "What the hell happened to you?"

She just kept on giving me a wall-eyed stare through her wet, matted hair and headed for the bathroom, leaving a trail of water down the hall.

I tailed her. "Wait a minute. What happened? Tell me what happened."

She didn't stop or turn around, just went into the bathroom and shut the door.

I hit the door with the flat of my hand. "Answer me, June. Why are you soaking wet? What happened? Were you in a wreck? Are you hurt?"

I could hear her fumbling around in there. I turned the doorknob but it was locked. And now this, I thought. I kicked the door and hollered to her, "Get out here, June. Get out and tell me what happened. Right now."

A dead silence. Then the door opened. She still had on the wet clothes. Her hair was put up in a towel and she was barefoot, her shoes and socks in her hand. The wet clothes clung to her. She looked like Olivia used to when she stepped out of the bath, fresh and pink. For a second, just a second, I stared at her the way a man stares at a woman. For that second, I forgot this woman, and yes, clearly she was a woman now, was my daughter. It all happened in a flash. My eyes said look and I did.

Then I found myself and backed up fast, slamming into the wall.

She gazed at me, looking absent-minded now, like I was a dish she'd forgotten to put up after supper. Then she smiled a little smile and said she'd been baptized in the spirit. She was saved from her sins. Now she was the bride of Jesus. Wasn't I happy for her?

My mouth dropped open, and, in that one terrible moment, I saw how empty our lives had been since Grace went away, how empty and how full of something I couldn't say. How we'd been trembling on a ledge.

"No," I said. "I am *not* happy for you. This bridge of Christ thing is ridiculous."

She smiled like I was the fool of the world. "It's *bride* of Christ, Dad."

"Bride or bridge, it's crazy. What next? Are you going to come in here tomorrow and tell me you want to become a nun?"

Not that I didn't believe in church. I'd been brought up in one, a little Episcopalian chapel made of stone, with a steeple and a mournful bell, the same church I'd sent our daughters to. Olivia wouldn't set foot in

the door, but our girls needed to learn how to behave
in the world, how to be decent people. I'd gotten them
dressed and taken them to Sunday school. Sometimes I
put on a coat and tie and took them to church too. We
had a deal. If they went without squawking, I'd take
them to see the giraffes. But since Olivia died, I'd had
no truck with religion, most especially not with the
kind that involved getting thrown into a tub of water
or walking into a river with your clothes on. The body
and the blood, it seemed ridiculous, and given what
I'd seen, totally—what's the word for something that's
too much, that's beside the point? Redundant. Where
was God Almighty when Olivia was bleeding to death
in our own bed? What about her blood? It had soaked
all the way through the mattress to the box springs.
I couldn't stop thinking about it, what a mess she'd
left me.

June pushed past me. "I'm tired, Dad, let me go to
sleep." Then she padded down the hall, her dress still
dripping, and went into her room and shut the door.

I looked down at her footprints on the wood floor. I
noticed for the first time that my daughter's feet were
small. They looked like they belonged to a child, someone much younger. They stopped at her door at the
hall's end like she'd sprouted wings, vanished into thin
air, taken off into the wide blue yonder to go live on

the moon. I'd never felt so alone on this earth, not even when Olivia died.

The next morning June came into the kitchen humming "There Is a Fountain Filled with Blood," which set my teeth on edge. A fountain filled with blood. Just what we needed in this damn house. The blood had seeped into the floorboards by our bed, I couldn't get it out. Thanks to my daughter I hadn't slept worth a damn, and when I did fade off, I kept dreaming about the war, people getting blown up in deep banks of snow, splatters of blood everywhere. In the dream I looked down and saw various parts of me gone, not just my toes, which I'd already lost, but a leg here, a hand there. Finally all I had left was my own dripping head. I held it in my hands and stared down into my own dead unseeing eyes.

I put down my morning paper. It was the only pleasure of my daytime hours, and it irritated me no end to have to interrupt my reading. June stood behind the kitchen counter drinking some orange juice from the carton. Since Grace had gone, she'd taken to doing that. Grace used to fuss at her for drinking from the carton, said she was getting spit in the orange juice.

"Tell me what happened last night." I tried to keep my voice level, though the look on her face made me want to slap her. It shocked me the way I wanted to hurt her in that moment.

She turned her back to me, not answering. I sat there, stunned, furious, staring at her back. It was straight as a board, like she was standing up against an invisible wall. What had gotten into her?

When she turned around, she was smiling, more like a smirk. "It's okay, Dad, I was just baptized and rededicated my life to Jesus."

"You never dedicated your life to Jesus in the first place. Plus, you're already baptized. You were baptized as a baby."

She kept on smirking at me. Boy oh boy, did I want to slap that smirk right off her face.

"But that wasn't an *immersion*, Dad. It wasn't a true baptism." She spoke to me like I was the willful, ignorant child and she was the parent.

I couldn't have cared less about who got sprinkled and who got immersed, but I truly detest people who rub religion in your face. I said the nastiest thing I could think of. "Your mother is rolling over in her grave."

"At least I'm going to heaven," she said.

I went for her before I could stop myself. The kitchen counter was between us and she jumped back so my hand couldn't reach her. I wanted to kill her, wipe that smugness off her face forever. Until that moment, I'd never understood why people hurt their children. It felt like I'd been initiated into a secret club I didn't want to join.

"Get out of this house," I roared. "Get out and stay out." I wanted to beat her to a bloody pulp, smash her face into the wall.

She didn't say a word, just gathered her schoolbooks, which were in a neat stack on the counter, took the last gulp of her juice, and walked out the door. She set off on her bike, though the weather was cold and blustery and threatened rain.

When she shut the door with a self-righteous little click, I turned and slammed my fist into the wall, which hurt like hell and didn't make a dent since the wall was plaster. Then I paced the floor, holding my hurt hand in the other one. I paced up and down. I tried to look at things objectively. I was an accountant, and there were numbers. I calculated three gone, two on the way out the door. The way I'd come to think about it, June carried not just her own self but my boy too, the one I'd carried in my belly all through the war, she carried him or the possibility of him into the future.

She'd been my last chance. Now she was the fucking bride of Christ.

When I got to the mill that morning the first thing I did was go storming into the outer office where that Lumpkin woman worked in the typing pool. She took one look at me bearing down on her and her hands froze on the keyboard of her typewriter.

"Don't lay it on me," she blurted out before I could say a word. "She just jumped up and went running down that aisle like the devil hisself was after her, like she was on fire. I tried to snatch at her dress, but she slipped right past me and Hilary both. You could have bowled us over with a feather. Don't blame me. It's hard enough to raise one girl all by myself, much less keep up with them two. I could tell you things."

I noticed then how pointed her face was and how stricken. She looked like a duck my dad had felled once. It was still alive when it went down. We found it lying on its side in the bushes, a whirlwind of ruffled feathers when we went to pick it up, its little chest heaving. Whatever things this duck-faced woman had to tell me, I didn't want to know, then or ever. I turned and stalked off, not even bothering to answer.

That night when I got home, June, who obviously hadn't taken me seriously when I said don't come back, had left some canned soup in a pot on the stove and was in her room with the door shut. I stood at the counter and ate the cold soup right out of the pot, then took some Bufferin for my hand. I started on the day's puzzle but the words wouldn't come; I turned on the news but started to doze off, so I got up and went to bed.

I fell into a deep sleep, but woke up with a start. It was dark as pitch and down the hall June was crying out for me, her voice thin and hopeless.

Was I dreaming? It went on and on, though, and after a while, I realized I was awake. When I got out of the bed and opened the door to my room, I heard her more clearly. *Dad*, she was crying, *Dad*. A trickle of sound, pitched high.

I charged down the hall to her room and threw open the door. She was on the floor on her knees in the dark. I turned on her lamp. She was bent over, holding her arms to her chest like she was hiding some small object from me. Up against the wall, her form cast the shadow of a hunched rabbit, frozen in fear.

"What? What?" I knelt down, pulling at her, trying to pry her arms apart, get her up from there. Then I saw her hands were covered in blood. There was a large stain on the front of her pajamas, which made my heart stop until I saw she'd held her hands to her chest. I was so preoccupied with the blood that I didn't see the manicure scissors at first. I pried them from her fingers, grabbed a blanket from her bed. I put a piece of the blanket between her hands and pressed her hands together with mine, trying to stop the flow. Then I opened one of her hands, wiped it off and saw what she'd done. There was a hole in the palm where she'd stuck the point of the scissors. I opened the other hand, and there was the other hole.

I looked down at her hands, the puncture wounds in both palms. Last week the Sunday puzzle had asked for an eight-letter word for marks resembling the wounds of Jesus Christ, synonym *shame*. I'd had to cheat, look it up in the thesaurus. *Stigmata*, which I'd never heard of, plural of *stigma*, meaning shame, disgrace, dishonor.

"For god's sake, June, stop screaming in my ear," I said.

"Dad," she said, "are you still mad at me?"

"Oh, honey," I said, and gathered her up.

She cried harder, great wrenching sobs that shook her whole body. Then I started up too and was shocked at the sounds that came out of my mouth, sounds a man should never have to make.

It was the first time I'd cried for my wife and son.

We didn't let up for a good long time. When June subsided into sniffles, I pulled the blanket out from between her hands. I wanted to make sure the cuts didn't need stitches. Just needed to get that part of it behind us. The blood had mostly subsided. I noticed how small her hands were, how delicate the fingers. Without thinking, I leaned down and kissed her palms, the way I used to kiss her little hurts when she was a baby. I could taste the metal in her blood.

"Sweetheart," I said, remembering the name Olivia had used to call the girls in from playing on summer nights, "you're still a girl. You and me, we got a long row to hoe before you're anybody's bride." I said it in kindness, but firmly, like a father, like the good father I am.

She looked up at me, her hands still out, palms up. Her eyelids flickered, I could tell she was just plain worn out. Then she lifted her head. "I hate your stupid puzzles," she said.

She was still on the floor. I was still on my knees. I looked down at her, square into her face. What I saw there made me step back. She wasn't Olivia, not anymore. It was me, my own face, my own eyes, desperate and alone, staring back at me in terror and shame, saying the letters don't line up, nothing fits the way it should, there is nothing, not a goddamn thing in this whole wide world that lines up right. June's face, my face, looking back at me like that, made me more afraid than I'd ever been in my life, more afraid than when Charlie looked at me out of that one eye.

Then I saw that one of the puncture spots was beginning to flow again. "Wait a minute," I said to my daughter. "Put the pressure back on that one. I'll be right back."

I went down the hall to the bathroom. I found the peroxide and bandages and tape and brought them back. She was still sitting there on the floor, her head down.

I put my hand under her chin and lifted her head. "Now this is what we're going to do," I said. "I'm going to clean out these wounds and bandage them up and give you some Bufferin, and you're going to go back to bed and get some sleep so tomorrow you can go to school and I can go to work."

Her eyes filled up again and her nose started running. I jumped up and hurried down the hall again and brought back some toilet paper from the bathroom. I held it to her nose and said "blow," like I'd done hundreds of time when she was little. "Now get up," I said. "You need to wash those hands. We need to clean them up and bandage them."

I led her to the bathroom and she came like a dumb animal. I washed and bandaged her poor hands, gave her the aspirin, and then led her back to bed. I sat down on the edge of the bed and covered her and pulled her hair back from her face.

"Tomorrow night we're not sitting in this stuffy old house, we're going to head out to the Dairy Queen for hamburgers and ice cream cones. Then we'll come home and watch *Twilight Zone*," I said. "That'll be something to look forward to."

She nodded. I kissed her forehead and turned out the light.

I left her door open so I'd hear if she cried out again and it brought back what a colicky baby she'd been, how she'd cried all the time those first few weeks, how I was always the one who heard her first.

I headed back to my room, but then I stopped. Earlier that night, before June had come home, I'd been stumped by one whole corner in my puzzle, the upper left. Nothing had worked. I didn't feel like sleeping so I went into the living room and picked up the puzzle I'd let slip to the floor.

I'd gotten into crossword puzzles right after I'd taken Grace to live with Frances and come back with a bellyache that wouldn't go away. I'd gone to the doctor, and somebody had left a book of puzzles in his waiting room. I started one and found it calmed me. I liked the way the words lined up just so. Even if you couldn't think it up, you knew there was the right word out there somewhere. You knew it would fit. Life, it goes every which way and never in a straight line, but a crossword puzzle, it won't go haywire and misbehave, lie to you. You can trust it. Each letter fits into its own little box, snug and tight, and connects to the other boxes just perfect, the way life should but never does. So when the doctor said lay off the booze and get a hobby, I took up crosswords.

As I waited for sunrise, I began to work on those few final words, the ones that would make the puzzle fit. I had folded my puzzle in a square the way I always did. I was racking my brain for the synonym for *an object of worship*. Six letters. It was something I should've known but couldn't for the life of me figure out. I stewed over that word and some others the rest of the night. When dawn came up, I still hadn't squared the box.

Then I heard my daughter stir and I put my puzzle down.

17
Grace

I hadn't planned on disappearing from the face of the earth, I'd planned on going back to high school and learning shorthand, not leaving my baby high and dry but on a temporary visit to Frances, just as my stay with her had been temporary. It happened in a flash, in the single instant when all of a sudden I felt so strangely alien to myself, so utterly removed from *Grace*, that I flung off my hospital gown, my heart pounding, and looked around for my clothes. My suitcase was nowhere to be found, but there was a knapsack they'd given me for the clothes I was wearing when I came in. I put the pants and top back on, even though they were still damp from labor sweat and heaven only knows what else. In the knapsack I stashed a box of Kotex from the bathroom and the pack of Nabs on my bedside table. I pocketed my wallet, which still contained, thank heavens, $120, and headed down the hall for the exit sign. It was late afternoon, around shift change. The nurses were busy exchanging charts so no one stopped me. I saw a sign pointing the way to the nursery and thought about my baby, down the long shiny hall, asleep in a bassinet, maybe sucking her thumb for the first time, hungry for the milk that was already leaking from me.

But I turned instead toward the sign marked *EXIT.*

When I stepped outside, my toes cramped up in shock from the cold. I'd worn my penny loafers to the hospital, but I'd been too flustered to think about socks. I waited a few minutes outside the emergency entrance, stomping my feet to stay warm, uncertain about what to do next. Then a cab pulled up and a man jumped out and ran inside. I got into the cab and asked the driver to take me to the Greyhound station downtown. On the way, my feet, warmed by the car heater, began to spark and burn.

In a bathroom stall at the station, I took off the maternity outfit and put on the faded sweat shirt and jeans I'd bought at a thrift shop next door. When I came out, I stuffed the maternity outfit into the bathroom trash bin, keeping the brown sweater to use as a pillow on the bus. The jeans cut into the loose skin of my belly flab, so I left them unsnapped.

After the clothes and cab, I had $114.12 left, money I'd saved from the allowance Dad sent each month for incidentals. I scanned the board at the ticket counter and decided on Indianapolis, for no good reason except that it was cheap and far. By now my ankles had turned blue, there being no socks in the thrift shop and no heat in the bus terminal waiting room; I wondered whether I might lose my toes to frostbite the way my father had in the war. Waiting for the bus to arrive, I wolfed down my small stash of food, then bought a bag of Fritos and a grape Nehi for the road. I boarded the bus at ten that night, noticing that the "Colored" signs had been removed from the seats since the last time I'd traveled on a bus, the last trip from Opelika to New Orleans I'd made with Mama and June to see Frances, which seemed like a million years ago, another life.

My breasts had begun to throb against the rough fabric of the sweat shirt. My nipples twitched and burned. It was like my whole chest had turned into a living creature, bound and determined to do what it was meant to do.

I climbed onto the bus without as much as a phone call to either my father or Frances. I figured when I got to Indy and got settled, I'd send Dad a postcard to tell him where I was, to say his slut of a daughter was managing just fine, thank you very much.

The bus was only a third filled. I took the first open set of seats, gobbled down the Fritos, drank the grape soda, which I knew would stain my lips a neon purple but who cared? It was cold on the bus, so I used the sweater to cover myself. The bus stopped at each and every country town on its route, letting people on and off to use the facilities or grab a cup of stale coffee. When I finally fell asleep, I slept hard; and when the driver pulled the bus into the station in Darcy, Indiana, about sixty miles south of Indianapolis, and called out the stop, I thought in my grogginess he'd said Indy instead, so I scrambled up and gathered my belongings and got off.

It was only around four in the afternoon, but the sky was dark and close to the ground, as if a giant blanket had been tossed over everything. Banks of grayish sludge had been pushed to the side of the road in dispirited clumps. I'd expected a large, bustling station along the lines of the one in New Orleans, but there was only a ramshackle depot the size of my father's Rambler. The door was locked. A tattered, plaster-covered schedule, dangling from a bulletin board on the door, showed no buses at all until the next day at the same time, late afternoon.

It had begun to drizzle. I was hungry and my stitches stung. I needed a bathroom and a bath. I needed to attend to myself.

I wondered how my baby girl was getting on in the hospital nursery at that very same moment of this cold dark miserable afternoon. Was she hungry and fretful too, wet and dirty? Was she twisting her head back and forth blindly, like a newborn puppy looking for some small comfort, a taste of milk, a gentle hand, a finger to grab on to? Was she wondering where her mother was?

I shivered, drawing my sweater closer and looking up and down the highway for a place to eat. It was mid-February and the winter's snow was still piled high in sad gray hills on the sides of the wet road. The desolation of it took my breath away. At home the azaleas would be ready to pop, birds would be settling into newly built nests.

When I glimpsed a neon light through the fog, I started off walking toward it. I picked my way along the side of the road, next to the snowbanks, my back aching from the jouncing of the bus. Each time a car went by, it sprayed me with dirty water mixed with salt. I was barely visible as I walked along, causing drivers to swerve and stare when I came up in their headlights, as if I were a derelict, a drunk.

I walked slowly, trying not to slip on the ice, bending

forward like an old woman, trying to see the pavement. My belly felt hollow and not just from lack of food. Was my baby girl missing the ebb and flow of my insides, the sloshing of my intestines, the thrum of my heart?

As I walked on, I became deeply thirsty, the way I'd been thirsty afterward at the hospital, my throat one long thin line of sandpaper. Where was the town?

The sign in the distance now seemed to recede and change color as I moved toward it. I figured I'd walked more than a mile, my still sockless feet gone numb in the soaked penny loafers. At one point I thought I saw a city rise up in the far reaches: skyscrapers and church steeples, cathedrals and basilicas, like New Orleans. Maybe I was walking from Darcy to Indy, which, I didn't know then, was impossible. Just as I was posing the question in my mind, the city melted and there were only trees, cedars, spindly and straight, and the outline of a farmhouse and barn in the gray, weary distance. It was oddly tiring not to be able to see the sky. It felt as if I might be walking upside down and not knowing it.

A little stray dog, its wet fur flattened to its scrawny body, appeared out of the fog and drizzle and trotted a few paces behind me. When I stopped to look, it dropped back and disappeared into the gray.

As I drew closer to the neon sign, I saw it said "Best Western." When I finally dragged myself in, I skirted the front desk, where the girl with red spiky hair behind the counter was talking on the phone, and went straight into the lobby bathroom. I cleaned myself as best I could and wiped the salty grime off my shoes. Then I came out and followed my nose into the restaurant, which was empty except for one man. I stood for a while, waiting for someone to come show me a seat, but when no one did, I sat down at the first table I saw and picked up a menu, too pricy, but I was so famished I decided to ask if I could wash dishes for my supper. I'd need all my money to pay for a place to stay and buy a new bus ticket to Indy the next day. I didn't think about what might come next.

In a minute or two, a tall, large-breasted woman with forearms the size of small hams came out from the kitchen to bring the man his check. She apologized for making me wait, saying she was both cooking and serving that night. As she talked, she took in my soaked shoes first, then my hair, which hadn't been washed since the night before I'd gone into labor and was plastered to my head. I tried to say something about doing dishes, but she cut me off with a wave of her hand and told me to go sit in a back booth and she'd bring me something good and hot to eat, not to worry about ordering off the menu. So I dragged myself to the back of the restaurant and sank down in a red booth

with a broken spring and waited, shifting my weight so
the spring didn't hurt so much, trying to stay awake.
In a bit the woman came back with a heaping plate of
creamed corn and mashed potatoes and meatloaf and
two hot rolls and a glass of milk. "Leftovers," she
said.

I thanked her. I was surprised by how much effort it
took to pick up the fork, how leaden my arms felt, how
weary and helpless this unexpected act of generosity
made me feel. My mouth watered, but when I leaned
over the plate to eat, I couldn't eat for crying, big
hiccupping sobs. Over the past months, I'd grown unaccustomed to any form of generosity. The girls at Our
Lady were scrappy and belongings kept tight. Frances
had seen to my basic needs and taught me things I
wouldn't have known otherwise, which, I was beginning to realize, I should be thankful for. But there was
something of a tightness, a reserve, about Frances. I
can understand it now: there she was, a woman in her
early forties; not once had she ever been with a man I
suspected, and there I was, then a mere sixteen, to her
eyes marked for life by one boy and, though she didn't
know it, two. It was a breach, and she approached me
the way you'd approach a stray dog, regardless how
benign and helpless it might seem, with caution and a
certain amount of suspicion. In the long, lonely months

at her house, I'd withered under her downcast eyes, her pursed mouth.

So when the large, kind woman set that plate of food on the table, I wanted to take her meaty hand to my cheek and hold it there. I wanted to kiss her palm. Instead, I mumbled my thanks, then started in on the creamed corn, tears raining down onto the food, making puddles on the plastic tablecloth. I ate everything on my plate, then took the last roll and wiped the plate clean, something Frances had taught me never to do.

When I finished, I pushed my plate to one side and put my head on the table and went dead asleep. I woke to the woman's hand on my shoulder. "Do you have a place to sleep?" she asked in a low voice, and when I looked down and didn't say anything, she told me to lie down in the booth, she'd come get me when it was time to close the restaurant, she didn't want to get in trouble with her boss.

My sweater had fallen open so that, as she leaned over to clear my plate, she saw the wet spots on the front of my sweat shirt. She took a step back. "Where's the baby?" she whispered. Her tone was low but harsh. "What'd you do with it?"

I looked up at her, startled. "How'd you know?"

She pointed at my chest. "Look at yourself."

I looked down, furious with my body, its tears and leaks, its ruptures of privacy. "She's in New Orleans," I said. "At Charity Hospital. My aunt's going to take her."

"When did you have it?"

By then, I was so worn out and turned around I wasn't sure. Was it yesterday? The day before? I looked blankly at the woman.

"You wait right here," she said, sternly. "You lay yourself down and rest. Don't you move a muscle. I need to talk to Nancy the night clerk."

When she turned away, I hopped up, gathering my things, worried they would call the police on me.

The woman hurried out into the lobby. Nancy was still on the phone. She looked like she'd just crawled out of the sack, her orange hair flat and matted. The large woman waved her hand in front of Nancy's face.

Nancy frowned. "I'm talking to Tommy," she said. "Leave me alone, Elsa. Can't a girl talk to her own boyfriend?"

The woman named Elsa didn't budge. Vertically and horizontally, she made two of Nancy.

Again Nancy waved Elsa away, but Elsa reached out and snatched the phone. "Nancy's got to go. Emergency," Elsa said into the receiver and hung up. Then she squeezed herself through the half doorway leading behind the counter and began to whisper in Nancy's ear.

As Elsa whispered, Nancy's eyes widened. She kept turning to Elsa and starting to speak but Elsa shushed her and kept on whispering. Then Nancy nodded. She turned and pulled out a key from one of the slots on the wall and handed it to Elsa. Elsa pocketed it, put her finger to her lips, squeezed back through the half doorway to the lobby, and then headed back into the kitchen. By this time it was 6:30.

Soon after, the elevator binged and a man in a suit strolled out, his hat and coat on, car keys dangling from his hand. "Okay, I'm happy to report that all the rooms have been properly cleaned," he said to Nancy in a pompous sort of way.

She nodded and waved.

When he left, she too hurried back into the kitchen. I went back to my booth and shut my eyes.

When I woke up again, the two of them stood over me. For a minute I thought I'd died on the delivery table; the two of them, their expressions so benevolent, I pegged as angels who'd come to take me up to heaven. I smiled up at them.

"Curled up like a puppy," Elsa said.

"Jail bait," Nancy said.

Elsa pulled at my hands and Nancy took first one foot then the other and placed them on the floor.

"Come on, honey, we got a room ready for you," Elsa said.

When I tried to rise, I banged my head on the underside of the table and started to cry.

Elsa pulled harder. "Come on, now, none of that. We got you a nice bed for the night and a shower for you to clean up."

They walked me out into the lobby and got me on the elevator. "I'm bleeding," I whimpered.

"Of course you are, honey," said Elsa, hitting the button for the third floor. "You just had a baby. You need to clean yourself up and get yourself a good night's sleep."

When the elevator door opened, they positioned themselves on either side and half walked, half dragged me down the hall. Elsa unlocked the door of 312 and gave me a gentle push.

"Get in the shower and clean yourself up. Throw me your clothes," she said.

It was heaven to be taken care of. I didn't question anything the two of them told me to do. I passed them my clothes and got in the shower, made it hot because the room heater was off when we came in and I was shaking with cold. In the shower my feet unthawed, bloomed red, and began to throb.

"Wash your hair," Nancy shouted through the door. "That always makes me feel better."

Elsa hollered, "Do you need some Kotex?"

"No," I said, "but I could use a toothbrush."

"We got that behind the counter," Nancy said.

I heard the door to the hall open, then close, then a few minutes later open again. By then I'd gotten out of the shower.

"What's she doing now? This is the most exciting thing that's happened since that man died of diabetic shock in 229," I heard Nancy say to Elsa.

"She's out of the shower," Elsa answered. Then the door to the bathroom opened a crack and Nancy handed me a toothbrush and paste, some deodorant, a T-shirt that said "Go Boilermakers" on the front, and a pair of men's boxers. "Got these out of the Lost and Found," she said, grinning. "I hope they're clean."

I looked in the mirror. I looked like a drowned girl, washing up by the waves. I came out of the bathroom, my hair still wet. The two of them were sitting on one of the beds in the room waiting. The other they'd turned down neatly. I went straight for it and crawled in. Elsa walked over to the bed and pulled the covers up around me.

"Pitiful," Nancy whispered.

Elsa had my clothes in her hands. "Honey, we're going to run these through the wash, and tomorrow morning Nancy here will bring them up to you. You got to be out of the room by seven o'clock. That'll give us time to get the place cleaned up before the manager comes to work. You can come on downstairs and I'll give you some breakfast and we'll have a talk."

"Nice to meet you," said Nancy.

I tried to smile, but the sheets were too soft, the room too warm and my eyes were closing. I took one fluttery breath, a little bird—for a second I pictured Mama's caught sparrow—set loose inside my chest, and my eyes closed.

The next morning when Nancy knocked, I awoke in the same position I'd fallen asleep in, on my left side, my right hand under my cheek, my left stretched out, touching the bedside table. My fingertips twitched when Nancy knocked the first time, then clinched at the second, louder knock. Where was I? Plastered against my chest a wetness, my breasts again, now hard as rocks and feverish. I thought of my baby girl, maybe at that very moment sucking on a bottle given her by an indifferent nurse, curling her body toward her chest, her little fingers opening and closing, reaching for something more, something she didn't yet have a name for.

A key turned in the lock and Nancy came bustling in, saying she'd stayed on after her shift to get me up. Did I remember her? Nancy? And Elsa from last night? Elsa had given the morning cook the day off and was back in the kitchen, handling the breakfast crowd. She'd told Nancy in no uncertain terms to get me out of the bed, put Dee Ann on the room, she was the fastest of the maids and could keep her trap shut—tell her Elsa will chop her into a million little pieces and serve her for lunch if she tells—and get me down to breakfast.

Nancy passed me my clothes, smelling of bleach and still warm from the dryer. "Get dressed now and get down to the kitchen, or the shit will hit the fan. It's already 7:30. Doug'll be walking through that door any minute now. Take the stairs. What's *your* name, by the way?"

"Grace."

Or Not Grace? I could hardly remember how I got into the room in the first place, but Nancy's face looked familiar and I had a memory of the big woman with kind eyes who smelled like celery. I threw on the clothes and gathered the knapsack and staggered down the stairs, the sleep still in my eyes, my hair a rat's nest.

When I appeared in the kitchen doorway, Elsa frowned and pulled a comb out of her pocket. "Get into that lobby bathroom and comb your hair and wash your face. You need to look *regular*. I can't be seen feeding people off the street. Doug'll have my hide."

Again I did what I was told, and such relief it was to give over responsibility for what to do next to someone so wise and downright practical that my eyes filled up again. When I returned to the kitchen, Elsa told me to sit down at the counter. She set a plate of biscuits and eggs in front of me, along with a glass of orange juice. I gobbled down the food and asked for a cup of coffee. Along with the coffee Elsa brought me an apron, a paring knife, and a bucket of potatoes and told me to start peeling and, if the manager came in, to keep my mouth shut.

After the breakfast rush, Doug came into the kitchen to talk to Elsa about her water usage. When he came in, Elsa wiped her hands on her apron and shot me a warning look.

He had been going over the utility bills and was not in a good mood. One of his best maids had just told him she was quitting to go work at Huddle House, where she could make more in tips. Being in Darcy, the motel didn't draw many visitors unless the John Deere or corn syrup people brought in a group. Traveling salesmen and relatives of Darcy residents were the primary clientele. The motel was usually not even half full.

"I got to worry about staying in business," Doug whined. "I got to make a living."

"I think you do all right," Elsa said. "Better than most."

As Elsa would tell me later that day, she could talk that way to Doug because he appreciated her. He *needed* her. She worked hard and her food was to die for. Customers raved about it. Locals ate in her restaurant all the time; it kept the Best Western in business. Elsa had worked there since before Doug ever took over the franchise. He knew nothing about her, where she came from, the fact that she had two grown children, that her husband had died twenty years before, buried alive from walking down the corn in a silo over at the Farrington place. Buried alive in corn, if you can believe that.

"I'd like to ask you a favor," Elsa said to Doug.

Doug stopped in the doorway. "Elsa, I can't give out any raises right now. I've got to hire a new maid."

"This is my niece," said Elsa, pointing at me. "She's a good girl, a hard worker. She needs a job."

Doug brightened. "Does she clean?"

Elsa grinned at him. "I'll say! She's a real good cleaner. Dee Ann says she'll be glad to train her. She knows she'll just get minimum at first."

"When can she start?"

Elsa hadn't realized this was going to be so easy. She glanced at me, considering my condition. I looked up from my peeling and tried unsuccessfully to manage a smile. "How about next week? She's just getting settled in at my place."

The next eight months passed in the blink of an eye. I quickly graduated from cleaning rooms to cleaning the lobby and the elevators and the restaurant bathroom. I thought about my baby girl, now turning over in the crib, following Frances with her eyes as my aunt moved around the room taking care of her. I thought of her restless little head bobbing on Frances's shoulder as Frances rocked her to sleep. *I'm coming back for you,* I'd say to her. *Don't worry. I haven't forgotten.*

But I wondered if I meant it. I was an accidental in Darcy, but I'd begun to settle in. Elsa clucked over me, and Nancy made me laugh. I'd settled into thinking of myself as Not Grace, a simple girl with a simple job and a simple life. And by simple, I don't mean dumb; I mean a job to do that had a beginning and end each day, good food, a joke or two, maybe a picture show or a good TV show at the end of the day. Dreamless sleep. No dead mother, no lost boys, no baby out of wedlock. No questions asked.

So I hummed hit parade songs—my favorite "Big Girls Don't Cry"—and did my daily chores. The only one I dreaded was the mirror on the left side of the elevator. Every morning it was nothing but smears and smudges. When people's fingers got to tinkering with the floor buttons, they couldn't seem to stop. They pressed, they puttered, they made twirlies on the glass. Some touched and touched again, as if their reflection were a sweetheart they were about to take leave of. The squeegee didn't make a dent on the oil and dirt from their hands. I had to use the rag and that spray stuff without a label that makes me lightheaded when the elevator doors shut. If that didn't work, I'd scrape off stubborn smudges with my fingernails, which over time chipped and cracked.

The mirror was warped on that bad left side. When I polished it, I leapt out at myself, strangely altered, disfigured even, with lumps and bumps in untoward places, manatee-like; I once saw a picture of one on TV, bobbing in a swampy lake in the Everglades. If I moved to the left a step, the manatee's blunt nose would lengthen into a horse's head, and I'd snort softly, flip my ponytail, squinting against the fluorescent glare. Then there'd be a *bing* and the elevator doors would begin to shut and I'd put my foot between the doors, gather my cleaning supplies, and get off, manatee-horse-girl.

Except for that one stubborn panel, I liked cleaning the elevator. Everybody saw those mirrors; they fixed their hair in them, adjusted their clothes, measured the width of their behinds. They thought the sparkle they saw reflected back was their own sparkle, but it was my clean mirrors they were appreciating, even if they didn't know it. Plus, while I rode the elevators, I got to hear traveling people's stories, which were wild things, things I'd never dreamed of. In Darcy, it was always the weather, how the corn and soybeans were doing in the drought, how much snow was expected in the coming winter. The ladies who passed through came from faraway places with their suitcases and pink plastic makeup cases. They came from somewhere else and were on the way to somewhere else; they were there to see a relative or bury one, or do a quick piece of business, seldom staying more than one night. They talked about the latest hemline, death, divorce, and Marlon Brando. They'd seen things and those things clung to them. The funeral was terribly sad or their lives had been wrecked, totally wrecked, by this one or that one. Back then, that was all I wanted, something, anything that had an edge, like the growing crack in the mirror of the right side, a crack that wandered up the whole wall, splitting me in half from top to bottom. It was all I could do to prevent myself from reaching out and testing the fabric of their pressed skirts and jackets, touching the toes of their shiny high heels.

So time went on, each month melting into the next, like a spring snow on warm pavement. On my way into work one morning, the fog swished and bloomed its way across the cornfields and sky, making them indistinguishable. The sight of all that baffling gray reminded me of the day I had walked into town. I clutched the steering wheel so hard my peeling fingertips began to throb and burn. A wreck was all I needed right now after last month's cavities in not one but two teeth, probably from all the Tootsie Pops I sucked as I did my chores at the hotel, so many that one side of my mouth had become permanently discolored.

After a mile or so, the fog thickened and the right line of the road disappeared. When I heard the sound of gravel under the tires, I tried to correct, but the tires spun and I found myself in some kind of hole. I knew what to do. Elsa had taught me to drive. I put on the hazards and opened the car door onto several withered stalks that crackled under my feet as though something wicked was animating them. For the next half hour I stood shivering on the side of the road, my uniform plastered to my skin. I shook from the cold, thinking about how the earth's body spun on a tilt (this is something Frances had taught me), how green and bright it all was from far out, how lovely. How this patch of fog was less than a pinprick on its surface. Then the fog partly lifted and two nice Mormon boys stopped and pushed the car out, getting slung with mud for their trouble. I waved as I drove away, afraid to stop and properly thank them, afraid of sinking down again.

After the mishap, my heart skittered and pitched; it'd been a while since I'd been so scared, so taken by surprise. I'd almost forgotten how anything can happen, anything at all. The thing I liked about cleaning the elevator, the drudgery and boredom of the day-to-day grind—the one thing that made it all okay—was the absence of fear, an absence that continually delighted and astonished me.

As I edged the Ford into the motel parking lot and spotted the blessedly familiar plaid couch and love seat in the lobby, June's coconut cake leapt into my mind, shining in the window as I'd come in from school the afternoon of my sixteenth birthday, the way she'd put the cake on Mama's pedestal cake plate made of crystal, the way my sister (my sister!) had tipped the lamp shade up so the light would make the crystal sparkle.

I hurried through the automatic doors. I'd parked in a far corner of the parking lot to give the customers the good spaces; the one time I was late and parked close, Doug had read me the riot act. "How many times do I have to tell you? Those spaces are for *customers,* not maids!" he'd thundered. After that, I made it a point to park as far away as possible on principle alone.

I waved at Nancy, and she grinned. What a relief to shake off that dismal fog and *see* again, not only lines and shapes but also color, the blessed orange of Nancy's hair, the blue of her sweater. One of the few things I'd come to pride myself on was having learned to take pleasure in things nobody else would think twice about. I had no expectations so I was constantly surprised by small pleasures. A thick peanut butter and jelly sandwich, flocks of blackbirds flashing their red-tipped wings as they swooped down on the corn, Elsa's celery smell at the end of a day in the kitchen. The first snow of winter, which had fallen just the past week and melted the next day.

I grabbed my cleaning supplies out of the laundry room, headed straight for the elevator, and began the day's work by wiping down the mirror.

Then the elevator binged. As it climbed, I quickly sprayed the lower part of the mirror and wiped it down. Then I remained on my knees but didn't spray again. People want mirrors to sparkle, but they don't want to see the labor that goes into it, the filthy rags. They don't want to inhale the cleaner.

When the woman gets on, I try not to stare, which is impossible since the elevator is all glass, nothing but reflection.

This visitor to Darcy is as non-Darcy as you can get. First off, the woman's a shade of burnished copper. She glows. I think she might be Spanish or Greek. Second, she has blond hair, maybe a wig, it's hard to tell. Third, her outfit's to die for: the tiny gold miniskirt, orange blouse, bright green jacket, with a necklace, jade maybe, gold earrings, and a thousand bracelets that tied all those colors together perfectly. A big woman and shapely, her lips candied apples, her nails shockingly chartreuse. She looks like a giant parrot.

And she's singing. Not loud, but definitely singing. And not words, but a kind of backup sound: *ba, ba, ba, boom, baby, baby, baby.*

I'm still kneeling, my heel pressing into my private part, one hand holding my cleaning rag, the other my bottle of cleaning spray, as if I'm about to spray and wipe down the woman's legs. As the elevator descends with a thump, I look up at the woman, up the woman's skirt to her girdle and garters to be precise. My heel shifts as the elevator hits the ground floor, and I feel a throb, strangely familiar. *What's this?*

The woman looks down at me. "Sure wouldn't want your job, girl. People can be pigs." Her voice surprisingly deep.

Suddenly I feel a bit irked, a bit like a country hick. What a nerve! "It's not so bad," I say, "better than cleaning rooms, taking out garbage. What do *you* do for a living?" I'm surprised at myself for asking such a question. It never paid to be pushy with the guests. Doug conducted meetings about what he called employee etiquette. *Pushy* was a word he used often.

The elevator doors open. The woman presses the Hold button, then leans down and stares me in the eye.

In the mirror, I see my face flush. I shrink down. I need this job.

"I'm a *vocalist,*" the woman says. "Used to work at the Blue Note in Chicago till it closed. Now I drive up and down the highway singing wherever there's the moola to pay me. Was heading north to Indy but can't see my hand in front of my face in this bitch of a fog. Now I'm out a gig and stuck in this shithole. Where *are* we, anyhow? Where can a lady go for a good stiff drink?"

"This is Darcy, Indiana," I say. "It's a dry county. You have to go to the bootlegger."

The elevator has begun to buzz angrily. The woman slams her free hand against my clean mirror. "Oh man, this place's all fucked up."

I sit back on my haunches. The elevator buzzes nonstop now. "Shut up," the woman says to the doors. She props her backend up against one, which bumps against her hips. She lifts the pointy toe of her shoe and levels it at me. "Girl, you need to get off your cute little ass. Get yourself out of this godforsaken place."

I remain frozen on my knees before the woman, as if she's some sort of queen who requires homage.

"You got a brain in that head of yours?" she continues. "Don't be a damn fool. Use it."

Then she's gone, clicking across the lobby floor, popping her umbrella open at the exact moment her high heels touch the mud-splattered mat and the automatic doors open onto the fog, then close behind her as if she'd never existed, as if I'd conjured her up.

The doors of the elevator close, though it doesn't move. Inside, I feel suddenly entrapped. I turn in a circle. Everywhere I look I see a drab pigeon where there'd been a parrot; staring back at me from every side an ash-faced, mousy-haired girl in a stained navy-blue uniform. A stringy ponytail. Then, flash forward, and it's as if my whole life has become a reflection of myself in that moment, a reflection of a reflection. In the mirror I can see myself at Nancy's age, then Elsa's, then older than Elsa, my upper arms loose-skinned, swinging as I work, hair dingy as old snow.

That night I write a letter to my father, my first. (Somehow, I'd never gotten around to telling him where I was, that I was doing just fine.) I say I'm ready to come home. *Slut* and *whore* still ring in my ears so I don't say I've missed him. It isn't that I've forgiven him or June. It's just that I see my father as the Open button to my life, a life far away from Darcy's everlasting fog. (Is there a seed of coldness in that calculation?)

Dad wrote back in return mail and sent a one-way plane ticket to New Orleans. He would pick me up the following Thursday, October 25, at 8 P.M. In the letter he said he wanted me back, I had a good mind, I needed to finish high school so I could go to a good college, I needed to come on home. I cried a little over the letter, then straightened my shoulders and started to pack.

The night before I was to leave, Elsa and Nancy and Grace had their own little farewell party at the Best Western. We sneaked up to 312 for old time's sake. Nancy, who'd taken the night off and gone to the bootlegger, came in with a jug of Mogen David and a six-pack of Pabst. We propped ourselves on the beds, put our feet up, and drank until three in the morning. I'd bought a Polaroid for the occasion, and each of us took pictures of the other two and then passed them around, laughing wildly at our images, until all the film was gone. When we finished, first the wine, then the beer, we lay down and went to sleep fully dressed, Nancy and I on one bed, Elsa on the other. We slept well, having not watched television and therefore not knowing that two world leaders were playing chicken with the planet, that the three of us, along with everybody else, were about to be toast.

The next day I gave Elsa the old Ford and my payment book, and Elsa drove me to catch my plane in Indy. When we said goodbye at the airport, Elsa didn't cry but I could tell she felt like it. Her head throbbed, she said, and it wasn't just the wine. She'd never gotten used to children leaving; she'd lost her two to the pleasures of water, one to the Atlantic coast and one to the Pacific. She forced her big motherly smile and tucked a strand of my hair behind my ear. She told me I'd always have a home, all I had to do was show up.

Elsa had saved my life and we both knew it, but she never asked for anything back. In time, she said, my memory of that year would dim and after a while it would seem insignificant in the greater scheme of things. "Just a blip, honey."

Elsa was right. I never wrote or called. We would never talk again, never lay eyes on each other, though I thought of her every single day for the rest of my life.

That last week in October the whole Midwest was ablaze with color. As the plane took off from Indy, the spent soybean fields were a sea of gold in the morning sun. How they glowed as I peered out the window, how full of promise they seemed!

What I found remarkable, though, and what I'll remember my whole life, is the shadow of the plane on the ground. I watched it all the way to New Orleans and it gave me the sensation of somehow watching a trace of myself, something, someone (not me, but somehow tethered to me) *down there*, someone whose predilections, whims, and longings moved surely along with mine, remaining at once remote and intimate. My own baby girl, who might have been but was not sleeping in my arms, at that very instant shooting upward, right past my window, rising from the slosh and trickle of what our story might have been, her little life locked in an endless orbit around mine.

I closed my eyes. There's a smoothness to sleep, an ease in the going under, followed by a terror, a struggle, then a deeper ease. A bubble in the water, a flash of silvery scales, then the long dive into dark.

The attendant woke me, bringing me the Coke I'd ordered. I savored the Coke, not having had one in a while. And as the plane began its descent, the shadow, first against the muddy brown of the lake, then the green Delta land, drew closer and closer until, in the split second before the wheels touched down, it re-attached itself and I took my last sip.

18
June

When Dad brought Grace home from the airport in New Orleans, it was past eleven and
the Russians were camped out down in Cuba about to
blow us all up. I'd been watching TV all night to see
when I would need to go to the basement and shield
myself against nuclear holocaust. Dad had told me
to keep up with the news, he wouldn't be long, three
hours at the most. I pointed out that it wasn't the most
opportune time for my sister to get on an airplane, but
he was intent on getting her home, it was all he could
talk about. He wanted the three of us to be together
again, come what may. He'd even called Frances to see
if she wanted to come down to Opelika. She told him
he was being silly, life had to go on, people couldn't be
running down to their basements at the drop of a hat.

Dad told her she was a fool and an idiot, whistling Dixie while the world was on the brink of annihilation. For days he had been in a frenzy of preparation, grimly lugging a zillion jugs of water and cases of Beanee Weenees and Chef Boyardee and bunches of carrots down the basement stairs. *Carrots?* I'd said (carrots were not my favorite vegetable), but he said raw foods were good for you and carrots were good for the eyes, plus they kept indefinitely. The earth would be poisoned by the Bomb, who knew the next time we were going to get anything fresh. He sent me out to our spent garden to dig potatoes. He'd papered the insides of the window frames with aluminum foil and duct tape so that the basement was black as pitch without the one bare lightbulb, which he said would go off once the Bomb was dropped, leaving us in total darkness. He'd stockpiled candles, matches, flashlights, and batteries galore, plus a Geiger counter so he could measure the radiation outside. I pointed out to him the obvious: that if he stepped outside to measure it, the radiation, if there were any, would kill us all. He looked at me and rolled his eyes as if I'd said something very stupid instead of something very smart. He looked out the kitchen window at our garden plot, the former site of his bomb shelter, and sighed with regret.

When the phone call came, I'd gotten sick of looking at the trench between Walter Cronkite's eyebrows and gone to bed. I'd turned my light out, not because I was sleeping but because I was afraid, and not of the Russians but of my weasel of a sister. I hadn't heard word one from Grace since she'd sashayed out of the hospital and gone on the lam for eight months. The last time I'd seen her, at our pitiful little Christmas gathering in Frances's living room, she'd looked through me like I was a piece of air. I'd hoped she would stop being mad and write me long heartfelt letters with lots of details about being pregnant and giving birth, what it was like, how much it hurt. I imagined pregnancy as a constant state of pain and affliction as you mutated into a human rubber band. I wanted to know what to expect when it came my time so I wouldn't be afraid. I saw my sister as a pioneer in the dark wilderness of reproduction. She'd hack out the thorny path, and I'd glide along behind.

After Dad had taken her to New Orleans to live with Frances, I'd opened the mailbox each afternoon with a flutter of anticipation, hoping for a letter in the familiar loopy handwriting. Over the months the box had for some reason become a gathering place for a colony of tiny black ants. They ran in frenzied circles atop the mail we did get, and I'd have to knock them off every letter and flyer I pulled out. It was almost as if Grace had sent them, a notion I found so deeply disturbing that I gave up on fetching the mail altogether.

Nonetheless I worried when my sister up and disappeared. I'd heard of people kidnapping babies from hospitals but never mothers. Still, the world being what it was, I begged Dad to hire a detective, file a missing person's report, do what people normally did when a girl of sixteen vanished into thin air. I pictured her spread-eagle in some back alley off Bourbon Street, blood pooled beneath her ponytail. But Dad said no, we needed to wait. Grace had walked out under her own steam, that's the way she needed to come back. She had two feet and a brain, though not much of one.

When the phone rang, I about jumped right out of my skin. As I ran down the hall to answer it, I wondered if Grace's plane had been shot down, like that U-2 spy plane, parts of her scattered in a million pieces over several states.

When I answered, a woman asked to speak to Dad. I said he was unavailable. He'd taught me never to say he was gone when I was home alone.

"Is this Grace McAlister?" asked the woman.

I hesitated a second; then, without batting an eye, I up and said yes, it was, yes, I was Grace McAlister.

The woman cleared her throat. "I'm calling from St. Vincent's Infant Asylum in New Orleans. I'm so sorry to inform you there's been a terrible accident." She sounded like she was reading the script from a play.

My head began to swim. Was it Dad? Had there been a wreck?

"The baby, at the orphanage," she said, her voice catching. "The one waiting for adoption. Your baby girl." She faltered, then went on. "She slipped in the bath and, I'm so sorry, but she drowned."

I sank to the floor. Grace's little child still in an orphanage? When Dad told me Frances had reneged on the plan to adopt it, I'd been *glad*. I'd thought maybe it stood a decent chance in life, having been given up to a big beautiful world of possibility. Now I felt like I'd reached into the chicken coop for an egg and come out with a rattlesnake. A little girl! Why hadn't she been adopted? And here she was dead? I flushed with anger, and something else: the shame of it. Here we were, my father and I, her grandfather and aunt, her one and only family, sitting down here in Opelika one hour away going about our ordinary lives and that little baby girl without a home! My father had to have known this, known our own flesh and blood needed us. She must have been eight months old. Now she would always be that age; she would never be anything else.

"Are you all right?" the woman asked.

I said I'd tell my father. I said he would call. I didn't recognize my own voice.

When Dad and Grace got in, I was lying in my bed with the lights off, bug-eyed, on fire with rage. I'd cried a little for Grace's baby girl, but it's hard to cry for someone you don't know. When I heard Dad ask Grace if she was hungry and the familiar voice murmur, *No thanks*, my throat closed and my eyes stung. Earlier that afternoon I'd made an apple cobbler and set it out on the kitchen counter where she'd see it first thing. I hadn't touched a bite so it would stay pretty and fresh, and I'd made sure Dad had picked up some vanilla ice cream on his way home from work that afternoon. I'd left a note saying, *Welcome Home, ice cream in icebox (smile)* and put a big spoon beside the cobbler for her to use when she dished some out for herself.

I listened for the opening of drawers, the clatter of silverware, the squeak of the freezer door, signs that she'd changed her mind and was settling down to some cobbler and ice cream. Before the phone call I had been poised to leap out of bed and throw open the door to my room and go galloping down the hall. I had been prepared to butt into her giraffe-style, the way I used to do, and throw my arms around her and bring her home, back to herself, and to me, her one and only sister.

Instead I heard her go into the bathroom and then a while later into her room. Yesterday morning I'd changed the sheets on her bed, turned it down to look welcoming. I'd put some late blooming mums in a vase on her dresser. I wanted her to know I'd gone to some trouble for her return. Dad would have never in a million years thought of the cobbler or the fresh sheets and most certainly not the flowers. I was hoping she'd come across the hall and open my door a crack the way she used to, to see if I was still up, and when she saw I was, come on into my room and plop herself down on my bed and tell me about the outside world (Indiana of all places, it might as well have been the moon!), what she'd done there, how she'd lived.

But Grace stayed put, quiet as a mouse, a line of light snaking its way under her door and down the hall to my room. I imagined her unpacking, putting her things in the closet next to her old clothes. When she'd left for New Orleans to have her baby, she hadn't taken much in the way of clothes. She'd thrown a few things into Mama's old suitcase, Dad rushing to get her out of town, not being able to stand the sight of that belly of hers. During the time she'd been gone, I'd tried on every single garment in her closet and drawers, some of it several times. I'd look at myself in the full-length mirror on her closet door and squint my eyes so that sometimes I'd look a little like her. Once I wore one of her outfits I particularly liked, a powder-blue skirt and blouse, to school. All day I was a nervous wreck, dreading the moment I'd drop food on it or tear it or otherwise damage it. When I got home that afternoon and hung it nice and neat and unspotted back in her closet, I heaved a sigh of relief.

Dad had stopped at her door and was saying something to her through it. I didn't catch his words but his voice had a different tone than when he spoke to me. Talking to me, his words trudged along a steep, narrow path on the side of a deep canyon; with her they flapped and fluttered, then lifted off. Back in my bride of Christ days, I'd studied the parables. As I lay in bed listening to Dad speak through the door and Grace answer, their exchanges sounding so oddly intimate, what leapt into my mind was the prodigal son, that slouch who threw away his inheritance and then came home and got the fatted calf and the rings and fine robe, et cetera. The *good* son, the one who stayed home and worked hard and helped his father, well, guess where he was left. High and dry, that's where.

When I heard Dad's voice across the hall, all that goodness and light rolling off his tongue like melted butter as he spoke through the door to her, the daughter who'd made such a mess of everything over the past year and a half (and obviously well before that), who'd left without a word, abandoning not only us but her own little child, I wanted to murder them both in cold blood.

After the house got dark and the only sound was the murmur of news on Dad's radio, I went into his room. I went in without knocking. He was sitting up in bed and staring at the wall, a peculiar smile on his face.

When I told him about the baby, he just shook his head, not looking particularly upset or surprised. Then I asked him why. Why hadn't she been adopted? Why was she languishing in an orphanage? I pictured her in a crib in a large room of screaming babies. I didn't know much about babies then, but now I know that at six or seven months, they are sitting up and trying to scoot across the floor. They are old enough to know their people, to recognize a dear face, old enough to know what they're missing.

"It had a deformity," my father said. "Its face. Its mouth."

"It's a she, not an it."

I said the obvious: that we—he and I—should have taken her if nobody else would. That baby girl was our own flesh and blood and he had turned his back on her. That I was ashamed of him and my aunt too.

He looked at me a good long while, not answering. Then he proceeded to tell me there were things I didn't understand. The baby would have ruined my sister's life and possibly mine too. He might have lost his job. We might have all been run out on a rail. Then where would we be? Plus, if the baby were compromised in one way—*compromised* was his exact word—there were probably other things wrong with it. It might not have lived anyway.

"Don't tell your sister, she's been through enough," he said. "It'll just make her feel worse."

"Doesn't she deserve to know?"

He looked thoughtful. "I'm not sure she would want to. Would you?"

That night I tossed and turned and watched the moon cross the sky. I'd taken up talking to the moon, by now having given up for good on Jesus. I'd found over time that the more you talked to Jesus the less he said. Plus, you couldn't see him except in pictures or hanging gruesomely on a cross. Although the moon didn't talk back either, it was something real, it came up and went down, you could count on it to put in an appearance most nights. It seemed to have a face, pocked but kindly; some nights it even looked a bit sympathetic.

The next morning I woke to Dad talking on the phone, a mumble from his bedroom. Grace wasn't up when I got ready for school. I put on a cute pair of navy blue pedal pushers and a nicely ironed (by yours truly, who else?) yellow top with a Peter Pan collar stitched in blue to match. I wanted my sister to know I'd become a snazzy dresser in her absence. For breakfast I ate a good-size piece of the virgin apple cobbler, somebody had to eat it. I made myself a meatloaf sandwich from the meatloaf I'd made two days back and grabbed an apple (against all odds, I try to eat a balanced diet) and headed out the door. Dad was waiting in the Rambler and motioned for me to get in.

"How is she?" I asked as he backed the car out of the driveway.

"She's all right."

"Why isn't she going to school?" Having not been filled in on my sister's educational status, I wondered whether she might have seen fit to finish high school in her time away.

"She's tired. I told her she could start fresh on Monday. If the Cuba thing doesn't blow up on us."

"I don't see why I have to go to school if she doesn't."

Dad slammed on the brakes and the gravel in the driveway flew up under the tires. "June, your sister has been working as a hotel maid for the past eight months. She's worn out. Give her a break, for crying out loud."

The iciness in my father's voice and the way he called me by name, something he never did unless he was correcting me, stopped me cold. I looked out the car window. When I did, I saw the curtains at Grace's bedroom window move.

Dad had begun to back the car up again. I opened the car door on my side and swung my legs out. I could be a bad girl too.

He threw on the brakes again. Before I could jump out, he grabbed my wrist and pulled me back. "For Christ's sake, June. Today of all days you need to do as you're told."

We sat there frozen, Dad holding on to my wrist, me with one foot on the pavement. Grace had opened her curtains several inches wider. I could see the outline of her face behind the pane. Smaller than I remembered and pale for someone so dark-complected. She looked like she hadn't seen the sun in a year.

I raised my foot from the pavement and put it back in the car and shut the door. Dad loosened his grip on my wrist, and I pulled it away. It felt scorched, which in itself was shocking. My father had never hurt me. I rubbed it and glared at him. He started backing up the car again. Then he stopped the car a third time. He put his forehead down on the steering wheel.

I said, "Did you see the baby? Did you look at her?"

"No." He turned off the ignition and looked at me.

"Will we have a funeral? Like we did with Mama?"

"No, the orphanage said everything would be taken care of." He looked down at his hands on the wheel. "You understand you can't tell Grace."

"Why not? Give me one good reason."

"It'll bring nothing but hurt, nothing but heartbreak. Is that good enough?"

We rode to school in a thicket of silence. While I was getting out, he said, "Remember, if anything happens, I'll be right back to pick you up, so be ready."

I grabbed my lunch and books and slammed the car door. I was fighting mad, at my father for not wanting Grace's baby girl, at Kennedy and Khrushchev and Castro for the Bomb, at Grace for not eating my cobbler. I climbed the concrete steps up to the door of the school, which was shadowed by overgrown crepe myrtles, now covered in brown seed balls. Just before I went inside, I looked back. Dad was sitting with his hands on the wheel, staring straight ahead, his jaw set hard. He looked like an old man. I went on in. It only dawned on me later that, given the sad fact that the fate of us all lay in the hands of two stubborn men with fire in their eyes and fingers on red buttons, this might have been the last I ever saw of my father.

In homeroom, half the seats were empty, and our teacher, Miss Whiteside (a particularly egregious example of the Lady Schoolteacher Smell issue; beside her, Frances smelled like a gardenia), didn't say good morning or kiss my foot. She didn't take the roll, which I found thoroughly unfair since I had perfect attendance thus far in the school year. When the bell rang and we settled in our desks, she said we needed to practice our Duck (down to the floor) and Cover (under our desks or a handy table) technique. Just In Case. Having the father I did, I knew all about radiation, what filters it and what doesn't, so I knew this was a patently ridiculous enterprise. I raised my hand and said so. I spoke eloquently on the relative ratio of radiation one might expect from the H-bomb and the A-bomb.

After pronouncing that wooden desks would be of no help whatsoever when the Bomb, A or H, descended upon us, but especially if it was the H, that we were going to be fried oysters despite everyone's good and decent efforts and ought to be at home with our loved ones given the horrendous state of things, I looked around. My classmates looked back at me, slack-jawed. Some of the girls had begun to cry. Miss Whiteside dabbed her handkerchief to her nose and told me to remove myself to the office; perhaps Mr. Spight the principal could arrange for me to return home, given the fact that I seemed a bit anxious. I said fine, hunky-dory, but I wanted to be counted present for the day. I'd come to school, I'd done my part.

I gathered my books from the floor (we'd been told not to put our books below our desks since we needed to be ready to skedaddle under them) and headed for the door.

"Be sure to check out, June," Miss Whiteside said as I walked past her desk. Her voice had a quaver to it as if somebody were shaking her as she spoke. As I left, I heard her tell the class about dog tags, how they were being prepared and would arrive later that after-noon, our full names and addresses and parents' names engraved on them. They would be worn during school hours. She didn't say why we were being bestowed with such martial jewelry, but given my powers of dis-cernment, I figured they were designed to make the identification of our incinerated bodies quick and easy by whatever powers-that-be remained on Planet Earth.

Outside, the morning was sunny and brisk. The sugar maples had turned orange and red and the leaves on the sidewalk made a satisfying crunch as I dodged the bucks and cracks in the sidewalk where the roots of the giant elms had pushed through. The light cut through the leaves and multiplied their colors and shapes. Leftover elm pods rattled down the street.

I welcomed the opportunity to skip school, something I'd never done in an effort to maintain my status as the one decent daughter. Not for lack of wanting to. Since my sister had become one of those girls who went away, the bare handful of friends I had left after Mama's death had peeled off. Hil was keeping herself busy kissing boys as opposed to me. As for the others, nobody was openly cruel, but it was like there was a glass cage around me. People, especially parents, looked at me like I was an exotic creature in a zoo, interesting enough but potentially deadly. There was one older boy who wanted to walk me home from school, but there was something sinister about the way he'd ask that set my teeth on edge. At lunch I sat at the edge of the cafeteria and gobbled my sandwich, then went to the library and pretended to do homework, which of course I'd already done, having nothing but time on my hands. Now that Grace was back, I figured things were just going to go downhill.

When I got home, I dropped my books on the table. Grace had taken her own good share of cobbler, which gave me a spark of hope. The TV was blaring. Down the hall, the door to her room was open, the bed made neatly, no suitcase in sight, no Grace either. I casually strolled through the house, looking here and there. I wanted to call her name like it was a normal morning and we were normal sisters, one of whom had cut school, one of whom had gotten sent home. I opened my mouth twice but nothing came out. It was as though I'd been struck dumb.

I went out into the backyard, expecting her to be out getting some fresh air, but she wasn't there either.

When I came back in, I turned off the TV. Enough is enough, I thought. I was sick to death of doom and gloom. Here I was, *dismissed* from school, nobody to answer to, a pretty October day, maybe my last. My sister clearly on the lam again, wandering off who knew where, same old story. I sat down in Mama's chair at the kitchen table, looked out the window and pondered how to make the most of my limited time on earth. A flock of finches landed in the mimosa tree out back, and I took up the binoculars.

Then I heard a commotion in the basement. From down below Grace yelled, "Damn it the hell," which had been our mother's favorite curse when someone was listening (she said much worse when she thought no one was around).

I opened the basement door and peered down the steps, expecting to see the one lightbulb shining from the fixture. Instead there was only dark. "Grace?" I called out.

"What?" Her voice came from below and behind me.

I took a couple of steps down the stairs, feeling for the string to the light. "What are you doing down here?"

"Waiting for the Bomb."

I found the string and pulled it. I was so blinded by the single bulb that I didn't see her at first. Then I heard her move directly beneath where I was standing and looked down between the open steps. She was crouched in the dark space under the stairs, her arms wrapped around her knees. Her hair in a tangle. Her eyes shone like twin moons, reflecting the light of the bulb. It was as though I'd come upon a wildcat, crouched and ready to spring.

I leaned out over the steps. She looked so wild and strange crouched down there that I wondered if she'd lost her mind in the ordeal of that past year and a half. I couldn't think what to say to her. Finally I opted for the mundane. "How'd you like the cobbler?"

"It was okay."

"Did you have some ice cream on it?"

"Yeah."

"Hey, you know what?" I said. "We've got the whole house to ourselves. I think we ought to raise some hell."

"Aren't you supposed to be at school?"

"All they're doing is making us practice stupid Duck and Cover."

"Like that's going to stop the Bomb."

"Yeah, like that's going to stop anything. Do you remember Miss Whiteside?"

"No."

I wondered if Grace had lost her memory along with everything else. "She's got the Lady Schoolteacher Smell bad."

"Gross," my sister said, and a wave of relief washed over me. I knew I had her now.

"Worse than Frances," I said.

There was a sigh. "I just couldn't deal with Frances. I just had to get out of there."

When she said that, the reality of what she'd been through washed over me like a tidal wave. Here we were, spinning on a planet that was about to become hot as fire, then cold as ice; that was the situation, plain and simple. This is the way Grace must have felt when her life got off track and there was no shelter.

I squatted down and said as much, whispering the words through the openings between steps in the stairs. I told my sister I was sorry she'd had such a devil of a time. I suggested we eat more cobbler and pour on the ice cream and then walk around town. Then I held out my hand, through the opening between two steps. To my surprise, she took it and I hoisted her up. Then she walked around and came up the stairs toward me and took my hand a second time. I backed up, step by step, not letting go.

At one point I teetered and almost lost my balance and tipped forward. I pictured Dad coming home to find us in a heap at the dark bottom of the stairs. Sometimes now, I feel I'm still backing up those stairs, avoiding the spaces between, where the darkness dwells and beckons. Sometimes still, I picture myself pulling my sister up step by step, the precarious world holding its breath, always in danger of tipping.

I'd like to leave us on those stairs, in that one long moment that has stretched out over the years. I would end things right there, with that touch of our girlish hands, my sister's rough and callused from the work she'd done, mine still soft as a baby's.

That day in October, as the world held its breath, Grace and I sat down together and ate the rest of the cobbler and ice cream. After that, she wanted to go over to the Bakers' house, she wanted to ask about Daniel. I had to tell her how Daniel and George had vanished into thin air and how the Bakers had moved one Thursday afternoon last fall; a moving van had come and that was that, they'd gone somewhere in Michigan, where I didn't know. As I told it all, Grace began to cry, saying Dad had told her that Frances hadn't taken the baby. It was a slow, quiet kind of crying, as if she was expecting to cry for a good long time and needed to conserve her tears.

"Everybody's gone," she said. "George and Daniel, and my baby too. Disappeared into thin air."

"I'm here," I said. I went and got some sweaters from my room. We needed to get outside, it was a nice day and might be our last. I pulled Grace to her feet and put my sweater around her shoulders. I grabbed a handful of Kleenexes and divided them between us—you can never tell when you might want to have a good cry yourself—and we set off. We walked through Opelika kicking up fall leaves. She blew her nose, then began to talk about cleaning elevator mirrors, the ghastly fog in Darcy, a friend named Elsa. She didn't talk any more about her little child, and I didn't either, my silence being the one comfort I could give her.

It was years later, after I'd had my boy Noel, that I saw what I'd done. I was only fourteen, please give me that, but still: I'd fed my sister scraps from a dirty table, written her life's story as disaster and shame.

Grace left me without a word. One afternoon that December, she came in from school drenched to the skin and shaking like a leaf. One cheek was skinned and her lips were one big bruise. I ran up to her and took her by the shoulders and asked what had happened. She said she'd taken a shortcut and slipped into a creek.

In the months to come, I would cook and she would clean. Our father would smile as we went about our housekeeping. Only I knew that my sister now lived elsewhere, on a strangely threatening island, distant even from herself.

Grace, I would call out across the water, and there would be no answer. In the end, as the years drifted by, I would choose the familiar shore. I would pull myself out of that murky water and make my way inland.

19
Grace

After I came home from going away and the Russians decided not to bomb us to smithereens, Dad said it was time for me to go back to school. I didn't need urging. My old life, BC, Before Child, my humdrum, what-are-we-going-to-have-for-supper life, had begun to seem like a pair of serviceable shoes that had been stolen by a thief in the night. Now that they had magically reappeared, I was eager to step back into them, not because I was preparing to have a good life, a normal life; I'd long ago lost any hope of that when my mother went and did what she did. But now that I was home and had to stare at what had been Daniel's house across the street every day, I felt even worse than I had when I was cleaning elevators. In Darcy, I'd been lost in a fog, everything gray and indistinct; at home, the sun came out and I saw what I had lost. I needed to get busy, I needed to get moving.

The first day I dressed up. It was early November by then, cold and drizzling, an exquisitely miserable day. I had a bit of a crush on John Kennedy, thinking him very brave for standing up to Khrushchev and saving us from the Bomb, so I decided to wear red, white, and blue to display my patriotism: a blue skirt and white blouse, topped with a red sweater, all a bit tight on me now. I put my hair up in a ponytail and tied it with a red ribbon. I added some blue eye shadow and Electric Red lipstick. June said I looked absolutely smashing. I barely glanced at her. Some days I found my sister hard to look at. I wanted to forgive her for ratting me out to Dad, truly I wanted to let bygones be bygones, but her open, girlish face revolted me in some unfathomable way. Sometimes her grin just seemed to get bigger and bigger, her mouth reaching out to swallow me whole.

We got to school early. I wanted to get settled in my new homeroom before the other students arrived. I wanted my homeroom teacher, Miss Holcomb, to assign me a seat and give me my schedule. I wanted everything to go smoothly. I was confident that Frances's tutoring had kept me up on my studies, that I could take my place with the other seniors. Dad had talked to the principal and arranged everything.

Miss Holcomb wasn't at her desk. I didn't know where to sit so I stood beside her desk at the front of the room, my shoes soaked through and my ponytail drooping. The other students filed in, laughing and chatting, talking about the football game on Friday, the fall dance. When they saw me standing there, up in front of the class, everybody stopped talking and stared. The girls began to snicker and whisper; the boys winked and looked me up and down. One of the boys began to whistle "The Star-Spangled Banner" and some girls broke out laughing. One pretty girl wiggled her little finger at me, sending the others into a fit of giggling. I couldn't remember any of their names.

About that time Miss Holcomb came through the door. She was sporting her blond flip, helmeted down with hairspray, and she had on a hot pink dress that matched the rouge spots on her cheeks. She was carrying an armload of files.

She walked over to her desk and me beside it. "Grace," she said briskly, "welcome back." She glanced at the others. "Everybody, take your seats." She then proceeded to tell me I needed to repeat my junior year. I had not been in any school for *a very long time*, there was no telling what I knew and didn't know. When I'd left town *so suddenly*, my grades had been on the skids.

I did not have The Basics; I was going to be Held Back. I was to go to the principal's office for reassignment.

Miss Holcomb had a booming voice, and by the time I left the room, you could have heard a pin drop. As I closed the door behind me, I heard a hum like a swarm of bees approaching, then a sudden burst of excited chatter, then Miss Holcomb: "Settle down! Get out your books."

After that I wore big sweaters and knee socks and scuffed-up saddle oxfords, threw away my eye shadow and hair ribbons, told June to take my best outfits. I grew my hair long and chewed on the ends. June was a good cook and I ate and ate.

I felt like Methuselah next to my classmates, who were a year younger. I never went anywhere or did anything with them, not that anyone asked me to, except some fast boys who thought I might be easy. Sometimes June and I would go to the picture show, but mostly I stayed home and studied, the way I had when I lived with Frances. Now, though, as the weeks passed, I studied like my life depended on it. Frances had taught me more than I realized, and I became quickly bored with my lessons. I asked to be moved into the hardest classes, the ones everyone except the eggheads avoided: calculus and Latin III, each of which had attracted a

grand total of four students including me. I made all As.
I cleaned house, polishing the furniture so it shone, running the carpet sweeper on weeknights and mopping
the kitchen every weekend. The house, Dad said, had
never looked spiffier.

When I wasn't studying or eating or cleaning, I read.
Every Saturday I headed the half mile to the Pearl River
County Library, loaded up to my chin with take-back
books. I spent hours selecting new ones for the week
ahead, books about the flora and fauna of the Amazon
jungle, books of poems, books about outer space and
ancient Greece and tadpoles and famous murders. I
came upon a book about playing jacks, the best strate-
gies for casting and picking up. I'd rarely played jacks
BC, but now found I was good at the game. Throw
them down, pick them up: there was a rhythm to it, a
neatness. My fingers became little lively animals, capable of almost any contortion. I graduated from onesies
to double bounces, eggs in the basket, pigs in the pen. I
got myself a second set of jacks, practicing with twenty
instead of ten. After a while, June refused to play with
me. Alone with my jacks, I decided to split my talents
and become two players: Grace vs. Not Grace. An even
match.

My father would come into my room and watch as
Grace and Not Grace sat on the floor bouncing the ball

and picking up jacks, their hair tucked behind their ears. Like my sister, Dad seemed to have forgotten the past year and a half; it was as if there had been a time warp and the world had stopped spinning, as if he had never spit *whore* and *slut* at me. Now we were back in time, the past a cemetery with no markers. Now my father looked at me with kind eyes. He asked me if I needed anything, he gave me wads of bills, told me to go downtown and get myself some decent clothes and a haircut. Instead I pocketed the money, thinking if things got worse, I would need a stash.

At night I lay in bed and thought about the boys, what we'd done, how we'd been together. How long ago it all seemed. Light-years. I promised myself I would look for them when I got out from under Dad's thumb. I doubted they would still want me; I was a mess. But they were unfinished business; I wanted to know what had happened to them. I'd come to realize they'd been punished too, they'd lost each other just as I'd lost them.

There is one thing I haven't told.

Behind the school there was a place where a little creek ran. Moles had made their tunnels through the underbrush and their tunneling had left raised paths along the sides of the creek. It was just before Christmas break, the year I returned. One night I'd stayed late to practice Christmas carols with my Latin class. Mrs. McFadden, our teacher, made her students learn the carols in Latin, and on Christmas Eve we were to bundle up and stroll around town and sing all the verses of "Adeste Fideles" and "Silens Nox" and the rest of our repertoire to Opelika's shut-ins. Mrs. Mc-Fadden was serious as death about it; we were to sing each carol solo to her until we had learned every last word by heart. We would be graded also on our decorum around the old sick people of our community. In addition to being prepared, we would be kind and encouraging, or we would fail.

I was starting home, cutting across the football field, when a boy I'd seen once or twice came up behind me. He said he knew my sister. He asked me where I was headed, and I told him. He said he knew a shortcut if I didn't mind a few weeds. I was loaded with books, and he offered to carry them. I thought maybe he liked me.

When we got to the place where the little creek ran, it was just turning dark. There was a flock of little brown birds feeding in the brush. Goldfinches turned brown for the winter, more than likely. My mother would have known. The boy dropped my books, flushing the birds. He took me by the hair. He pulled me along, down to the creek, and pushed me to the ground. My head was half in the water; I could feel the currents passing through my hair. I froze, afraid he was going to drown me.

Why are you doing this? I asked.

What's one more boy? he said.

It lasted just a few seconds, just long enough for the finches to resettle. Then he said, *If you tell, no one will believe you.* Until now I haven't.

He took off, climbing up the creek bank, fighting his way through the underbrush. I lay there a good long time, listening hard, my head wet and cold as ice. After a while I heard an owl call out, then another answer. It was mating season. My coat was soaked and torn, my underwear gone, but I put myself back together as best I could and wrung out my hair. I hardscrabbled my way up the bank and gathered my books and papers from the brush. I pulled my wool cap out of my coat pocket and put it on.

Some people make a mountain out of a molehill. After everything else that had happened, it seemed as small and insignificant as one of those little mole tunnels along the creek bank. I worried, of course, that I'd become pregnant again given my recent history, but when I didn't, I thought I'd had a stroke of luck for a change. Later on, in the halls, I saw the boy on my way from English to calculus, but then one day I didn't anymore. It was like it had never happened. It was like I dreamed the whole thing.

This I do remember: It was a clear night and I walked home under the stars. For a moment I thought I saw something go by, not a shooting star but an object steady and methodical, a machine of some sort, maybe one of those space capsules. After that first little Russian dog burned up in the cold outer dark, the skies were full of living creatures, always circling. I imagined a set of eyes looking down on me. An animal being, brooding over the world.

Good luck, I said. *Be brave.*

20
June

*L*isten, Mama used to say: *there is a crescendo in every aria, a place where everything comes together. You can feel it building.*

Life, she said, *is another story. It heads down back alleys, takes sharp left turns. Then, one fine day it jumps the track and crashes.*

Leap ahead.

The day I know beyond a shadow of a doubt that my life has jumped track is July 21, 1969. Grace is long gone out into the world; I'm out of college over a year and launched into a promising career. On earth it's 4:18 in the afternoon and I'm the unwilling passenger in a car that's at least a hundred and ten degrees despite all the windows being rolled down as far as they'll go. On the moon Neil Armstrong is preparing to walk out and say his little piece about one giant leap for mankind. Jim, my former friend and now brand-new husband, has just that minute turned on the radio. He's driving us due south, from Memphis to New Orleans, and I've sweated through my clothes. No rain in a month and the farmland we're passing through looks more like the moon than the moon itself in the pictures I'll see later that night on TV.

And what am I doing in this blazing hot car barreling down Highway 55 on Planet Earth? I'm peeing in an orange Tupperware bowl and worrying it's going to overflow. The reason I'm peeing in the bowl is that I am pregnant—thank you very much, Jim and Uncle Sam—and the reason we're following the Mississippi River south, a distance of 392 miles, is we've just gotten married at the courthouse in Memphis the day before. I wore an old flowered shift with a Peter Pan collar that made me look like I was singing in a choir of hippies. I needed a haircut. A woman who did the typing for the judge was the witness. Her lipstick had leaked into the corners of her mouth, giving her the appearance of a vampire who'd just had lunch. When Jim tried to give the judge a twenty-dollar bill for his trouble, the judge pushed it away, cocked his head in my direction, and muttered under his breath, "Christ's sakes, boy, buy the little lady a decent meal."

We have company on this loathsome trip. In the back seat, sitting up on her haunches and panting out the window is a sad sack of a dog I found at one of the rest stops we frequented until Jim unearthed the Tupperware bowl in the trunk of the Ford, a remnant from his mother's kitchen. The dog's so covered in ticks she looks like a walking specimen of those speckled melanomas you see in pictures taped up in the doctor's office. All skin and bone and exhausted tits, though there were no puppies in sight when I found her tangled up in the blackberry bush where I'd stopped to take a private puke on my way to the bathroom. (I must admit I didn't for a moment consider mounting a search for the litter; honestly, it never occurred to me.) The poor thing looked like she was trying to decide which truck she should run herself under.

The dog seems vaguely familiar, as if she'd belonged to someone I'd known when I was little, maybe a neighbor down the street. Even without the ticks, she would have looked peculiar, and especially so given her tit situation, which makes her underside resemble a row of sad little balloons the day after the party. The tits are one thing, the ears another. They're the size and shape of beignets. They stand at attention, revealing their pink, oddly private interiors, which are also studded in ticks. A stripe, originally white, runs from the tip of the dog's nose to the top of her head.

"What's this?" Jim says when I lug her, squirming and panting, back to the car. "We can't take that thing with us. We're going to *New Orleans*. Put it back." His voice is uncertain, glazed. Over the miles, the enormity of our misdeed seems to have settled like a fine dust over his face. Behind the wheel he looks even smaller than ordinary, a bit slumped. I notice how slender his wrists are.

I don't answer, just glare at him and throw the dog into the back seat whereupon she turns herself around three times and lies down, puts a paw over her nose, and begins to snore.

Jim glances in the rearview mirror. "What are you going to do with it? How are you going to sneak it into the motel?"

I stare out the window. "It's a she, not an it."

"Man, it's uglier than shit. Why is it speckled?" He peers more closely into the mirror. "Is there *mold* on it?"

"Watch the road. I'll check her when I next have to puke, which I'm sure will be coming right up." What I'm thinking is that it serves him right to get stuck with a tick-studded, half-dead mutt. Maybe along the way I can pick up some more sickly animals to torture him with. Look what I was getting stuck with.

The dog lets out a monster fart.

Jim makes a sound in his throat, which over the years I will come to recognize as an expression of disgust, and turns on the radio. I lift myself off the seat and get on the Tupperware bowl (I have given up on underwear by this point) and begin to pee, which is when the announcer comes on and we hear about the men getting ready to walk on the moon, which chokes up the announcer but does not thrill me in any way whatsoever. After the dogs they fried up there, I never liked the space race. Think of it. Getting strapped in that tiny capsule all alone and shot up into the endless night. I snap the top of the Tupperware bowl shut and put it on the floor, where it commences to slosh with the motion of the car.

The night I found out I was expecting this bundle of joy, a couple of nights before our trip, though it feels like a couple of centuries, we were at the drive-in movie. I wish I could say what was playing. All I remember is that it was about zombies. Zombies leering at pretty blond girls in white nightgowns, who of course screamed when they spotted them, zombies with cataract eyes jumping out from behind every bush, making the girls shriek and run for their lives, losing shreds of their blouses in the process so that the tops of their breasts bounced and shone in the moonlight. Of course, this was years before those pregnancy tests you can buy at every corner drugstore. Jim was friends with a nurse named Sally. Eighteen hours before, he'd delivered my pee to her sealed up in a jelly jar. He'd put it in a brown paper bag as if it were moonshine. He was supposed to call Nurse Sally that night to get the verdict. When he left to go to the concession stand to make the call at the pay phone, I told him to bring me back a bag of popcorn if I were *not*, knowing that if I were, I wouldn't be able to eat a bite. I really and truly didn't think I was, despite definite signs to the contrary. For Christ's sake, here we were a couple of friends who'd never even looked at each other crooked. Jim did my *taxes*, for god's sake—how boring is *that*?

So there I sat, watching the zombies wreak havoc and pinning my entire life's dreams and plans on a bag of stale popcorn. (I would have prayed, but after my kissing friend Hil died sitting at a stoplight minding her own business, I realized that everything is Luck with a capital L, pure and simple. My mother chose the wrong chiropractor, the one who didn't wash his hands.) My current situation is nothing but Bad Luck, which all began with Jim, who, after much changing of majors and other forms of foot dragging, graduated from college against all of his best efforts and, before he could say *rice paddy*, found himself reclassified I-A. Then the worst luck possible. His birthday, September 14, was put into the draft lottery with all the other birthdays, and, lo and behold, it wasn't the hundredth or the fiftieth or the twentieth to be drawn but the *first*. *Numero uno*. With that kind of luck, I figured he'd get shot in basic training.

I advocated for Canada or self-mutilation—maybe cutting off his trigger finger—but his dad's a retired lieutenant colonel, who already found Jim deficient in everything from fly-fishing to football. This military dad was small like Jim, except with bulging biceps and a prominent chin he thrust at you when he talked, giving him the look of a twitchy cock at a cockfight. He'd wanted a manly boy. What he got was a skinny little guy in glasses who sneezed at the slightest change in temperature. Now here was Jim's big moment; knowing he was doomed to be called up any day, he could step up to the plate and finally score points with the old man where it really mattered: jungle combat. What did he have to lose? So Jim hastened himself down to the army recruitment office and *enlisted*. He took his physical, and, sans heart condition, scoliosis, schizophrenia, asthma, or flat feet, was deemed fit as a fiddle, if you didn't count the fact he couldn't see six inches in front of his face without his glasses.

I used to be fond of Jim. We met when I joined the staff of the college newspaper at Southwestern in the foreign city of Memphis in the foreign state of Tennessee, having left home for the first time just a few weeks before. The newspaper office was housed in a ramshackle two-story house from the dark ages. When we were introduced, I immediately noticed the wastebasket that sat front and center on Jim's desk, into which the toilet in the bathroom upstairs dripped from a wet spot in the ceiling above his head. When he left the newsroom for the night, he would take the wastebasket outside and empty it, as if that were part of his job. Being a worrier about diseases like cholera, I found such equanimity impressive and over time discovered myself going to Jim when I needed calming down, which was about every other day. I told him things I'd never told a living soul. What my mother had gone and done about the baby she couldn't imagine, how afterward she'd bled to death one Sunday afternoon in November while our father had taken my sister Grace and me to see the giraffes dance, how Grace had insisted on those extra two hours at the zoo. How Grace had gotten herself pregnant too, how she'd been one of those girls who went away, only to return home still holding her grudge against me for spilling the beans to Dad, how after she went to college up in Chicago she never really came back. How I missed her like a lost limb. The only thing I didn't tell him was that Grace's little child was six feet under because nobody in my family saw fit to take her. It would be years before I'd tell him that shameful story.

Why I chose Jim to tell my secrets to I don't know. Over the years I'd honed the art of making other people talk, laughing and joking and sympathizing with them, putting them at ease. Once I got out into the world, I quickly became known throughout the newsroom as the reporter who could pry open any can of worms, ask the really tough questions and get some answers. *This is a June story*, the managing editor would say, and off I'd go to the penitentiary or the police station or the home of the accused, notepad in hand. But my own story, it was like those giraffes: wild and unwieldy. Who in his right mind would believe it? Jim would, as it turned out. He'd listened to it more times than one, not saying much, just shaking his head and patting my hand and talking about the future: how smart I was, how talented, how I'd just begun to live. My sister would come around and forgive me for ratting her out;

she just needed to grow up and get some perspective. I almost believed him.

When I landed a job at the Memphis *Commercial Appeal* and he stayed at Southwestern in his diligent effort not to graduate, we'd get together every week or so for pizza and beer. Then the night before he's to report for duty I make the monster mistake of taking him out for a drink, a drink for the road, as in *bon voyage, arrivederci, sayonara.* So what does he do but start talking about tunnels. He's heard they send the little guys down into the mud tunnels the Viet Cong build and booby-trap with mines. When one little guy gets blown up, they send in another to drag out what's left of the first one, that is if the tunnel hasn't collapsed on top of him. When Jim tells it, he starts to sweat. He is claustrophobic; he is scared of rats with hot pink eyes that glow in the dark; roaches and spiders give him the fantods. His eyes tear up and his glasses start to slip down on his nose. "Just a mud hole," he says. "They make you crawl in like some kind of animal. It's dark and there are *things* crawling around. What if I lose my glasses? What if I'm buried alive?"

I don't have the answers to those questions, so one drink leads to another. One minute we're sipping our Seven and Sevens and grooving to "Light My Fire," and the next thing I know we're back at my place and he's holding on to me like he's in sniper fire and I'm the last tree in the jungle. So I open my branches and give him shelter, it was the only decent thing to do. After that, we pass out. I hardly remember *it*, except it was over like heat lightning and I was left sizzling.

He's gone at the crack of dawn to report for duty. He leaves me a note saying how beautiful and sensitive I am and how he *loves* me and always has, which is why he hopes he doesn't get killed so he can come back home and *marry* me. I am the only one for him. He will never forget last night.

I throw the note in the trash, embarrassed by the whole thing. I'm a Mississippi girl with a neat bob who manages to talk herself into falling in love with somebody before I jump into bed with him. Plus: nothing has ever gotten my attention like practice-kissing with Hil.

I drag myself off to the newspaper office at eleven the next morning. I don't let myself think about tunnels and rats. I finish up a story on a reunion between an eighty-five-year-old black woman and her seventy-year-old daughter, who was born out of wedlock, the mother having been raped when she was fourteen by a gang of white boys, though she wouldn't let me put that in the story, which was supposed to be an upbeat feature. She'd been sent to the store by her grandmother for a box of Tide. She was just walking through the woods on her way home when the boys jumped her. She told me she remembers how the box broke when she tried to fight them off with it. *It snowed soap powder*, she said, *they were covered in white, it was pasted on their faces.* She tried everything to get rid of the baby, including jumping out the window of a three-story schoolhouse and breaking her collarbone. When it was born, she refused to have it in the house. She threatened to strangle it. A girl, the baby was first taken to an orphanage and then, when she was older, taken for a worker by some white people in Minnesota who had a farm out in the middle of nowhere.

It was her daughter's son who had made the connection and then called the newspaper to try to find the mother. Turned out the mother didn't much want to be found. When I interviewed her and the daughter the day before, I got the distinct impression that, now that they'd been thrown together by this busybody son/grandson and this busybody reporter, the mother and daughter didn't much like each other, in fact were downright furious at each other. Between them was that little light-skinned child that the daughter thought the mother should have held on to and the mother looked at and saw soap flakes. During the interview the mother gazed at the floor and whapped her Japanese fan on her knee while her daughter talked on and on in a singsong monotone about how lonely she'd felt all these years, how hard *her* life had been. Then the mother looked up at her daughter and slapped her knee and began to laugh, like she'd just been told a good joke.

What I know now is how there are always stories behind the stories people tell. They're stacked like crackers in a box behind the ones they do tell. You could listen for the rest of your days and never get to the end of that box, never know the one true thing. This story I'm telling about Jim and me, it's stacked on top of another story, the one about Grace and those boys and me telling on her and her little dead child; and then there's the one behind that, of our own mother and why she did what she did, which is and will always be a mystery, and on and on, back to the beginning of time.

But that morning, all the news about those two that was fit to print amounted to less than a page and I was on deadline, so we called it quits and they departed, hastily, the son/grandson holding the door for them both, mother first, then daughter. They moved quickly for women their age, careful not to touch each other on the way out.

I wrote up the interview and headed out to get some Bufferin and a Coke. I popped three Bufferin into the bottle, my stomach doing bellyflops off the high board. The motion of the elevator made me break out in a sweat. (How did my sister manage to ride up and down cleaning one of those things every day of the week?) When I walked into the newsroom, Carl, who had the desk across from mine, said, "A skinny little guy with glasses was in here looking for you. He left you a note. Seemed all worked up."

I sat down at my desk and there was a typed note in the carriage of my typewriter. It said: *Hi. I'm back. Pulled off bus and sent to eye doctor. Glasses lens too thick for gas mask. Call you later.*

Six weeks later, the zombies on the screen are lurking and leering and reaching here, there, and everywhere. Jim is talking to Nurse Sally on the pay phone in the projection booth. When I see his shadowy form coming toward me across the blacktop of the drive-in parking lot without so much as a kernel of popcorn in either hand, I think maybe they're out of popcorn; sometimes they run out of popcorn, it's not unheard of. But then, as he opens the car door, I see the half smile on his face in the flicker of the picture and a giant zombie hand reaches down from the screen and snatches the heart right out of my chest. I want Jim dead in the rice paddies.

I need to find somebody who will get rid of it but I have exactly seventy-six dollars and some change in the bank and know better than to ask Jim, who's already acting fatherly; plus, the only people who do such things where I come from are chiropractors like the one who went to Parchment Penitentiary for butchering my mother. I've heard they use ordinary kitchen utensils like stirring spoons and tongs, sometimes coat hangers wrapped in duct tape, and just the idea of a man coming at my softest place with something like that in his hand makes me want to run for the hills. (Where's Grace when I really need her? She's around the world in Alexandria, Egypt, studying chicken scratches on papyrus. A graduate student with a big fat grant. I don't even have a phone number.) A Lysol douche is supposed to work, but when I try it, lying in the cold bathtub, the first few drops set my insides on fire and I lose my nerve. The next day I drink a bottle of castor oil and promptly vomit it back up, almost asphyxiating myself. For half a day I consider suicide, picturing myself all laid out propped and pretty on my bed when they find me, but I haven't a clue about a method that will produce an attractive and relaxed-looking dead person. I'd heard OD-ing on aspirin only half does it, turning you into a moron and forcing you to puke your brains out in the meantime. There's also the unfortunate side effect of me being dead like Mama.

So, here we are, on the way to New Orleans for a one-night honeymoon (ha!), courtesy of the *Times-Picayune*, whose editor called Jim the day after we found out about the baby and asked him to come interview to be a sports reporter. Footnote: *I* am the bona fide reporter, hardcore police beat and such, first woman in my paper's history to work the news desk. No shrinking violet either. I'd covered the sanitation workers' strike last year, getting gassed right along with the demonstrators. For that gig I wrote the straight news story and a sidebar, interviewing the widows of the two men who got crushed by an old garbage truck that malfunctioned. While King lay in a pool of blood outside the Lorraine Motel, I was the first reporter to get to the one phone booth on Mulberry Street and dictate the story off the top of my head as I scraped away a piece of bubble gum on the glass with my fingernail. It was my first job out of college and I was immensely proud of myself for talking my way into it. But this is 1969; there are no pregnant women news reporters. There are no married women news reporters, except in the society section. Plus, you can't interview someone and puke in their face at the same time. So I call my managing editor and tell him I'm married, and he says congratulations, he just wishes I'd given him more notice before quitting; he'd really gone out on a limb hiring me in the first place.

I turn around and check the back seat. The dog opens her eyes and gazes at me wearily. The tips of her ears wobble with the motion of the car. That's when I see it. Ears, almond eyes lined in black, a flare of white down the muzzle. She's the spitting image of Laika, the little mutt they shot into space the day Dad took us to see the giraffes, the day our mother died. The Russians shaved her to attach the electrodes like she was a criminal about to be executed, then led her into a capsule the size of a rural mailbox and strapped her down. She was chosen out of forty others who'd been trained by being put in smaller and smaller cages to see how little wiggle room they could tolerate; she freaked out the least of all, sweetly yielding more and more space until she could barely turn around. She lasted only a revolution or two before she boiled in the hundred-and-twenty-degree heat.

As I ponder little Laika's miserable fate, my ankle starts to itch. I reach down to scratch and come up with the flea, which I squash and throw out the window.

"Was that a *flea*?" Jim asks.

"No," I say.

When Jim pulls the Ford into the motel parking lot and checks us in, I run into the room, to pee, of course, and do a bit of obligatory dry heaving. Then I rinse my mouth and call my only friend in the city to get the name of a vet who'd give the dog a flea-and-tick dip. I'd met Anne when my editor sent me down to cover an anti-Vietnam rally at Tulane and Loyola. Back then she was a photographer for AP. Now she has a husband and a set of triplets and sundry animals; she is accustomed to emergencies. She is thrilled I've gotten married. She thinks everybody should be married.

"Girl or boy?" she asks as she looks up the vet's number.

The question throws me. Then I realize she's talking about the dog.

When I tell her, she asks what I'm going to name my "new little friend."

The question takes me aback. "I'm going to take her to the pound once I get her cleaned up, let them find her a home. The last thing we need right now is a dog." I form the words *I'm pregnant* but they don't come out. Where I come from, people say you're *expecting*, as if it's a package coming in the mail or the plumber. I shudder when I think of telling my poor father I'm *expecting.* What will he say? What are the odds? How many females in one family can get knocked up? We're obviously fertile as turtles and reproductively challenged; in my case, this new thing called the pill being nearly impossible to come by if you're a nice unmarried girl in Tennessee. Plus, who knew Jim was going to lose his starch and go all tunnelly on me? With Dad, I intend to bring up the marriage first, the other later, much much later. Then I will hold this baby in until I pop; I will set the world record for the longest pregnancy in the history of the planet.

When I express my intention of taking this down-and-out mutt to the pound once I get her cleaned up, there's a shocked silence on the other end of the line, then a rush of breath. "No, June," Anne says ever so patiently, as if I'm one of the triplets. "You can't take that poor baby girl to those dog killers. They'll gas her. Do you know how many animals they *euthanize* every day? Do you know how those poor things suffer? It's a holocaust. Plus, that dog will save your life one day."

I open my mouth to laugh and it comes out sounding like a hiccup. "Save *my* life! And for your information, she's a mother, not a baby girl."

Anne says, "You mark my word, June; this is your lucky day."

When I make the call to the vet's office, the receptionist says there are no appointments available until
next week, so I tell her it's an emergency. When she asks
what's wrong with my animal, I'm suddenly tongue-
tied, recognizing that a pressing need for a flea-and-
tick dip might not be considered an emergency by most
people's standards. The first thing that comes to mind
is constipation, which is heavy on my mind because I
myself am suffering acutely from it, one of the many
unsavory aspects of being pregnant, I'm fast discover-
ing. I'm peeing like a leaky faucet but wouldn't have
been able to have a decent bowel movement if a train
ran over me.

So I tell the receptionist we've just arrived in the
City and this dog is experiencing severe constipation.
How long? Four days' worth, insofar as I can tell. Yes,
she seems extremely uncomfortable and I do indeed
consider this an emergency.

When I get back into the Ford, the dog is sitting on
the front seat behind the wheel as if she's about to make
off with the car. I slide her over and get in, whereupon
I'm bit on the butt by something. I have on a skirt (all
the better to pee in) and can feel the biter high-tailing
it around to that area Frances used to call Between the
Legs, where my underwear normally resided—*Did*

you remember to wash Between the Legs? she would call out to Grace and me after Mama died and she took care of us before Dad ran her off. I head back into the motel room and pull up my skirt, noting in the dresser mirror that, for the first time in my life, there is a perky line of dark hair growing straight down from my navel into my pubic hair. I think, *Great, what's next—a beard?* I bend over and ask Jim to check for fleas. He's been following my strip act with interest, having never actually seen me naked, partly or otherwise, in broad daylight. He looks for a good long time.

"Well, what do you see? It itches right here, right here." I put my finger on the place.

"Yeah, I see a welt right there, but no flea," he says. "Maybe it hopped onto the floor."

I look down at the gold shag carpet and lose hope. I shake out my skirt and head back to the car. Behind the wheel the dog is panting. I realize suddenly I haven't given her a drop of water since I picked her up hours ago. I run back into the room and get a plastic cup and fill it up. When I get back, she's looking downright desperate. It's at least a hundred degrees out there, and I've left the windows down only a little for fear she'll jump out. I get in and roll them down a bit more and shove the cup of water at her. She leaps at it, sticking her long nose to the bottom to get every drop. I make a mental note to take better care of the poor thing and we head out for the vet's.

His office is at a tire-screeching intersection—motorcycles, trucks, cars, all honking and pushing on the gas. The exhaust stings my eyes. As I drive up, I realize I don't have a leash. Sensing trouble, the dog tries to crawl under my feet as I brake. I drag her out and carry her inside the vet's office, holding her away from my body. Her beignet ears are directing themselves sideways now so she looks like the Flying Nun. At the front desk they take one look and hustle us into an examining room. When the vet comes in, he looks me over like I'm the one with fleas. He says this is going to cost, this animal I've brought in is a mess. I ask if they have a payment plan and he says only for locals. I say okay, I'll pay, and the vet's assistant whisks her off. Ears back and down, she casts one last desperate look my way, her back legs bicycling for footing.

I go around front and sit down in the waiting room, where I'm now allowed and where there are a bunch of prissy foo-foos in ribbons waiting for their toenail trims. The radio is on loud and everybody is all excited about the men getting geared up to walk on the moon. I check my arms and legs and find a tick settling in for the long haul in the crook of my elbow. I pull it off and slice it in half with my fingernail. When it squishes and blood squirts out, I feel the urge to puke, so I head for the bathroom and gag a while until the feeling passes. I've long since thrown up the saltines I managed to get down for breakfast. I come out and read a magazine article about Jackie Kennedy's new life as a widow and get all choked up. My belly feels like it's filling up with blood, as if *I'm* a tick. I am so hungry I'm salivating over a bowl of dog biscuits on the counter.

I wait a good long time. Long enough to read three magazines from cover to cover, find out about how to make a Thanksgiving centerpiece and cook a turkey, how to build a sandbox for your little ones, how to updo your own French twist with four hairpins and a pick. When I get tired of reading, I entertain myself by imagining the people around me as having various types of tails, which has always been a favorite pastime of mine.

There is an old woman sitting next to me holding on her lap a cage enclosing some form of animal life that's curled into a tight ball. The woman has spread out a *Life* magazine on top of the cage. As she turns the pages, tears are rolling down her cheeks onto the magazine. She makes no effort to sop up the tears, just keeps turning pages; each one she looks at for several minutes. When she is called in, I take up the magazine she has put down. It's the June 27 issue, and it has a boy named William C. Gearing Jr. on the cover, next to the headline "One Week's Dead." William Jr. is frowning into the camera as if the sun is in his eyes. His mouth is pursed. He has a broad nose and freckles. There is a lock of red hair across his forehead. William Jr. is twenty, three years younger than Jim. He is from Rochester, New York. I open the magazine and there they are: 242 of them marching across twelve pages. Crew-cut, lop-eared, snaggle-toothed, newly dead boys. They sport an impressive assortment of hats. Helmets with numbers and chin straps, pointy cloth hats, square white hats with bills. Graduation caps, straw hats, what appears to be a fishing cap, an airman's cap with goggles, a wide-brim that looks like it might belong to a Canadian Mountie. I wonder what kind of hat Jim might have worn, how it would have fit his forehead where the bone rides so close to the surface. These dead boys look uneasy, as if they'd strayed onto a movie set. Under the hats are the eyes, which, different as they are, seem to bear the same cast of light. They gaze at something just over my left shoulder but far out into space.

Do I see the name first? Or is it the set of his jaw, familiar yet strange: square now, trap-like?

Daniel Baker. Number 197, top left, page 28.

Something (a feather? a cobweb?) touches my cheek, then rolls down. I taste salt. *Did I do this?*

A moment later, I'm called back, and here's the dog, wet and trembling. She has little red welts all over her but she's lost the melanoma look. She smells like the insecticide Dad uses on crabgrass. When she spots me, her face lights up and her tired eyes glow. She starts to smile and pant.

"We have some questions about . . . What's its name?" the vet's assistant says. She has black curly hair and a long nose. I imagine her with a poodle's tail.

I hesitate. "Laika," I say, finally.

"How do you spell that?" the poodle asks.

"L-a-i-k-a, like the *Sputnik* dog."

The vet glares at me. "You're naming your dog after a *communist*?"

"Yes." I let the *s* sizzle.

The vet shuffles his papers. He's a large man with enormous hands, mottled in freckles and little black hairs that look remarkably like the flea-tick combo formerly on my dog. "How long has the animal been constipated?"

"A while," I lie. "Several days."

"Exactly how many days?"

"Four."

"Has the animal been vaccinated for rabies?"

I don't like the way his lip curls around the word *animal.* "I don't know. Maybe."

He comes to attention; his eyebrows look like helicopters about to take off. "*Maybe* isn't good enough. We can't let you take this dog out of here without a rabies shot." He sniffs.

"And how much is that going to cost? This is a stray dog."

"You're going to have to get it vaccinated before we will release it. Otherwise it will go to the pound. We have a responsibility here."

At that point, as if she can understand he's talking about a needle in her near future, Laika, who is not as trusting as her namesake, starts struggling to get off the table. I pick her up and put her on the floor. She sniffs around a bit, like she's looking for a particular bite of food. Then she positions herself like a comma and begins to toss back a trail of turds the size and color of new potatoes. She inches along in a half circle around the examining table, barely missing the vet's shoe. She just keeps humping along and leaving her trail behind. She looks as purposeful as a flower girl throwing rose petals at a wedding.

The vet looks down. "Well, she's sure not constipated *anymore*."

Without a word the assistant hands me a roll of paper towels, so I start picking up what the dog's laid down, trying not to go into the dry heaves. Meanwhile, a much-relieved Laika kicks up her heels and scampers over to the door leading out.

"She needs to be spayed," the vet says. "We can do it on Monday."

When I open my mouth to say, *No thank you, we're just passing through*, I begin to gag uncontrollably. I grab a garbage can and vomit clear fluid into it. I have become the world's leading expert in throwing up, so I do it neatly, without much ado, wiping the saliva off my mouth with the back of my hand.

"Oh dear," the assistant says and turns white around the gills.

"Sorry," I say, "got to go, hope it's not contagious." I grab my dog and get us both out the door. I carry her straight through the waiting room at a fast trot. When the receptionist stands up and says, "You. Just a moment, please," I call out, "I've got a really terrible stomach flu, please send me a bill." Then we're sprung, out the front door, into the parking lot and the roar of the traffic.

Just as I'm opening the car door, a truck backfires

and Laika jackknifes from my arms. I make a pass for her little rat tail as she hits the ground, but she's the slippery fish.

For some reason, maybe because I have the dead soldiers on my mind, I holler: "Halt!" I'm the General with a capital G and my dog's in the minefield, two seconds from being blown to smithereens. She stops short at the curb, four lanes of wheels clattering by, dump trucks and cement mixers, fancy cars and beat-up wrecks. She sniffs the air, suspicious of any of the choices she needs to make.

Then, after what seems like a year, she crouches down on the curb and looks back at me slyly, as though she wants to plan a party.

I stalk her as stealthily as any enemy. As the cars whizz by, I tell her there is hamburger in her future. We will plan the best of all parties. I'll never fly her to the moon.

She crouches there on the curb, inches from a gruesome death, still planning her party—would it be steak or chicken, hamburger or hot dogs? I creep up to her, barely touch her tensed back. She sits for my touch, wanting it. I gather her up and she lets herself be gathered, whimpering a little. I hold her tight and feel her heart clattering about in her chest.

That night in the motel Jim and I lie in bed and watch the first man walk on the moon, plant his little flag, and salute it. Against the pocked surface, it looks like a postage stamp.

Jim takes my hand and holds it to his cheek. "At least everybody's still alive," he says. He doesn't look at me when he says it, just turns his face into my palm as if to smell it.

"No," I say, "everybody isn't."

He raises his head and looks at me. I tell him about Daniel. "Would have been me," he says. He sighs and his head falls back onto the pillow. He takes one long exhausted breath and is asleep.

As the TV flickered, time seemed to flow out before me like a vast canopy of galaxies, millions of light-years into the future. My heart pounded, and I was deeply afraid. I had seen how all the light had gone out of my sister's eyes. I had seen my mother's blood on the bed sheets. Since my bride of Christ days, I'd feared that what happened to them would happen to me, and now it had.

Then, I didn't know that when my child emerged from the dark tunnel I'd become, he would come in peace. He would fasten on, as if we were the only ones living on this cold moon of a planet, as if love were as strange and unfathomable and vast as all of outer space. I didn't know that one night our boy would be crying with a fever and I would walk into his room and find Jim standing in front of the window with him in his arms, naming the stars: that my heart would flare and burn with a dark energy, streak across the sky like a comet.

What I didn't know would fill up that black, black sky. I didn't know our boy, our Noel, would be born six weeks early, on Christmas Eve. I didn't know he would turn out to be a difficult child, would call one teacher a woolly mammoth, tell another she had lovely acne, get suspended from *second grade* for refusing to draw pictures of flowers, instead covering his pages with numbers ten miles long. I didn't know I'd need to give up everything and teach him at home until one day, when he multiplied 1,285,009 times 15,897,121 in his head and came up with the right answer, it would become clear that he was not only difficult but also outrageously brilliant. And what would I have done had I known those things? What would you have done?

That night when the first man walked on the moon, I turned out the light and Laika crawled into bed between us. She brought the only flea in the room with her. It hopped back and forth among the three of us. All night we fought it, itching and scratching and, in the case of Jim and me, cursing.

The next morning I found it sitting on the tip of my dog's nose, as if it had landed there from somewhere far far away: another country, a distant planet.

21
Holly

When Jim called, he told me the baby was early.

"Sorry, sir," Jim said. "We'd hoped it'd be late so you wouldn't know."

"Boy or girl?" I said and he said boy.

Early or late, I didn't give a flip. All I heard was *boy*.

I jumped in the car and headed for New Orleans. It was Christmas Eve and the City looked like a crown of diamonds in the dark water of the Rigolets. To tell the truth, I'd been pretty down that night, half concentrating on my crossword, thinking of Christmases past, wishing for Olivia and my boy, and my girls too of course, wanting my family whole. But now my boy had finally come into the world, and I sped across the bridge into the City, my heart pumping.

When I walked into the hospital room, all smiles, June was sitting up in bed with the baby in her arms. He was boohooing and so was she. She handed him off to me. "Take him, Dad. I don't know what to do with him. I don't know what to do with a baby." Then she sank down under the covers and turned her back to us both.

My boy didn't look a single day early. He looked right on time, his face fat as a chipmunk's, his hair all grown in. I walked with him around the room once, then twice, and, bingo, he stopped crying. *Well, I'll be dogged,* I thought. *Here you are, come back to me. You sure took your own sweet time.*

Oddly, he favored Grace.

That night my crossword asked for a synonym for *regret,* three letters: *rue.* Words, I'd discovered over the years, took on color. *Rue* was gray, the color of the sky the day Grace's baby died and the world almost went up in smoke. That baby I never saw. I wonder who she favored.

On the weekends now, I drive over and stay with my boy so June can get out a bit, do some errands, get her hair done. I bring stuffed animals and candy and books and a little telescope. I take him for rides in the car. Last week I got the notion to go by and get Frances over on Louis XIV and drive over to the lake just a few blocks from her house.

I hadn't seen Frances since the Christmas Grace was pregnant. She was planting begonias in the bed outside her front door. "Want to take a ride with two fellows?" I asked.

She looked up from her digging and squinted at me. "Look what the dog dragged in."

Her hair was gray now. There was a lock in her eyes and her face was flushed and a little sweaty. She looked softer somehow.

"It's not a good time," she said, pointing at the flowers.

Then Noel popped up out of the seat and patted the dash and she said, "Good heavens, Holly, a baby shouldn't be bouncing around in a car like that."

"Well, he won't be if you'll get in and hold him," I said.

At the lake we sat on a bench looking out. Noel went to sleep in Frances's lap. The tide was coming in and lapping at the breakwater. Some pelicans cruised the waves. We sat there a good long time, just being quiet together. I didn't ask why she hadn't taken Grace's baby girl, and she didn't say. I reached over and patted Noel's head, then left my hand there in her lap.

Now that Noel's older, I sit him on the sofa between me and Frances and read him the girls' old Uncle Wiggily books. The other day he pulled the book away from me and began to read out loud, the words coming out all wrong: backward and haywire. *Said alligator scalery-skillery the now you got I have.* He looked at me and grinned from ear to ear. He's only three. Sometimes he scares me a little.

When I was a boy and my granddad would come to visit, he'd take me on his knee and tell me about a little fellow down in the low country who'd been born with an upside-down brain. The stories made me laugh. This little fellow tried to ride a bicycle backward, ate the rind of the watermelon instead of the red inside part, hugged a fish, and caught a snake. If there was an oddball, topsy-turvy way to do something, he'd find it.

"Our boy's going to be a pistol," I say to Frances.

She looks up from her book and frowns. "It's time to teach that boy to read from left to right, Holly," she says and pulls him into her lap.

22
Grace

I did what I needed to do. I made what happened on that creek bank into a Sappho poem, a fragment of a fragment, so jaggedly torn you couldn't even tell what the letters had been. But sometimes, out of the corner of my eye, I saw dark water and that flock of little finches feeding in the brush. Some nights when I shut my eyes to sleep, the scene flared like a distant star against the black underside of my eyelids: stunned girl half in/half out of the water, wet hair sticking to her cheek, bruises opening on her thighs like dark roses: Not Grace.

One day I called Frances and asked why she hadn't taken the baby.

"I just changed my mind is all. I just couldn't do it," she said breezily, as if she'd decided against getting an ice cream cone or going to the picture show. "It's better," she added, "for the child to have younger parents, a mother *and* a father, not some old maid schoolteacher like me. Better to make a clean break."

Chicago was the farthest I'd ever been from home. I might as well have been on the North Pole. Gone were the scrub pines and alligator-still water, the blanketed breathless heat, and for that I was grateful. At college I stayed as far away from boys as I could get. My second semester I fell head over heels in love with Greek, the letters reminding me of the shapes my jacks formed when I'd throw them across the floor, all piled up and askew, a puzzle to be deciphered with a flick of the wrist. I signed up for a course in Greek culture and history because it sounded exotic enough to transport me from my small shameful life. Over those first weeks, I tunneled into the distant past the way my father had tunneled into our backyard after Mama died. I moved seamlessly from undergrad to grad school; and somehow, as the years passed and the grants and fellowships poured in, I was visiting the world's collections of papyrus, bending over the cloudy tangled texts with my magnifying glass, trying to decipher meaning from fragments, trying not to sneeze from all that ancient dust. I felt like a spider who had cast a looping thread out into the unknown, and it had caught on another life, another world.

When Dad went to New Orleans to live with Frances, he called me to come get my few belongings left in the little house with its fenced corner yard. St. Augustine grass had covered the trail Mama had made pacing our fence line; our old swing set was rusted orange, with one of the two swings hanging listlessly by one chain. Dad's precisely pruned boxwoods had shot up into unruly trees. The house was hard to sell. Dad hired a man to replace the stained boards on the bedroom floor, but he did a shoddy job and the oak planks he inserted turned out a lighter shade than the rest of the floor, causing potential buyers to ask questions.

After grad school, Chicago kept me on, and between research trips I endured a frigid fourth-floor apartment near campus where I kept my single bed and desk. Against all odds, I still waited for that tap on the window, the letter or phone call coming when least expected, the unannounced appearance at my door, the two of them full of news. What would they be like now? Would I even recognize them? Sometimes they got muddled in my head. Daniel's blue eyes imbedded in George's olive skin, George's thick fingers at the ends of Daniel's slender wrists. I would tell them what I knew: that we had had a baby girl and now she was almost a teenager. I would ask them to help me find her.

When the job offer came from Vanderbilt, I jumped at it; my first thought was Daniel and George and how they'd have a better chance of finding me in Nashville, closer to home. The three of us would set out to find our daughter. It wasn't that I hadn't tried to find her once I discovered that Frances hadn't taken her. In New Orleans I'd gone first to the orphanage, only to find it gone and in its place a posh set of condos. There were no records of her adoption in the city or parish offices. Neither Frances nor my father was any help, saying only that they felt sure she was fine, best to let sleeping dogs lie. There was something odd about how they said it, as if my baby girl were a figment of my imagination, as if they were humoring me in acknowledging her existence.

As the years rolled by and Daniel and George didn't come and I'd not found my daughter, it occurred to me that I needed help. It was 1981 by then, and hiring a private eye was all I knew to do. There was no Google or ancestry.com, only Dick Tracy of the funny papers and Jim Rockford on TV. People could get lost if they wanted to.

I picked my private eye out of the Yellow Pages. His name was Landon Higginsworth. He had a tasteful ad promising immediate results and a money-back guarantee. Detective work seemed to me a shady business, all guns and drugs and nasty divorces accompanied by compromising photos, but Landon Higginsworth sounded like a trustworthy name.

The location of his office was reassuring: downtown, on the fourth floor of the old National Life building, which seemed like a reasonable place, not sleazy. His name was on the door. I walked right in, expecting an office and a receptionist, perhaps a scattering of shady characters sitting in the waiting room reading *Field & Stream.* Instead, there was Landon Higginsworth himself sitting behind a card table in the middle of a tiny office with one window, covered over inside and out by cobwebs strewn with the carcasses of moths. On the floor were stacks of boxes. Dust particles floated in the air.

He looked at me apologetically. "Sorry things are such a mess, I've just moved in." His voice was mild-mannered, reasonable.

Still, I didn't believe him; the dust looked and smelled old and so did he. When he rose and shook my hand, I got a whiff of him that reminded me of Frances, but with a touch of vinegar, something with a bite.

He was a small man, with skin weathered and ancient, and arms that hung longer than you'd expect, giving him the appearance of a monkey. His eyes were gold nuggets and lively.

In the corner, on a grimy pillow, lay a large dog of no discernable breed. It lifted its head and gazed in my direction briefly, then put its head back down, sighed, and put one paw over its eyes, as if it couldn't bear the sight of me.

I sat down in a metal folding chair across from Landon Higginsworth and told him about Daniel and George, gave him what little information I had. June had told me about the military schools they'd been banished to. Both the families had left Opelika, the Bakers almost immediately and George's parents the year after. That was all I knew.

"Usually the ladies come in looking for one man, not two," he said.

"The three of us were friends."

"Friends?"

"Yes."

He twirled his pencil and raised an eyebrow.

So I told Landon Higginsworth everything. I told him about the baby too, how I was sure it had been adopted. Some nice family had the baby, who of course wasn't even a baby anymore, but hopefully a happy,

well-adjusted young person, on the brink of a brilliant career, maybe as a fledgling astronaut—the first
woman in space, sturdy and brave and adventuresome,
blasting off into the great unknown.

Landon Higginsworth didn't even look up while I
told it all, just kept on twirling the pencil. You could
tell he'd heard worse.

"Five up front," he said.

"Five?"

"Hundred. Five hundred. I'll throw in the child."

I wrote out the check and shoved it across the dusty
desk.

"I'll call you," he said.

Ten days later the phone rang as I was heading out
the door to teach. He asked me when I could come in. I
said that afternoon.

He was standing behind his table, in front of the
window, his long arms dangling. The window faced
west and the late afternoon sun poured through the
cobwebs and cast his frame in deep shadow. He came
around and pulled out my chair and hovered as I sat
down. He patted me once on the shoulder and walked
around his card table, his fingertip on the surface,
tracing a line in the dust as he made his way to his
seat. There was a stack of papers on his table.

When he sat down and looked across at me, I could tell by his eyes the news was not good. It was May and warm outside but the metal folding chair beneath me felt like a block of ice. I began to shiver.

First he told me about George, how he'd traced him to Seattle where he'd worked on a fishing vessel for a while, then over the border to Vancouver, where he'd spent the Vietnam War taking tourists out whale watching; how he'd gone from there to Herendeen Bay, Alaska, where he'd worked at the Bering Sea Packing Company, and then, two years ago, he had packed his things in one duffle bag and paid the outstanding rent on his single room above the Voodoo Bar, and vanished into thin air. "Off radar," said Landon Higginsworth.

I digested this information, wondering whether my five hundred dollars had bought me anything but more questions.

Then he stood up, cleared his throat. "You need to prepare yourself," he said.

He picked up one of the pieces of paper on his desk and began to read. Second Lieutenant Daniel Baker, fresh out of ROTC at Virginia Military Academy, had fought bravely. He had led his platoon into the village of Cà Mau in the southern tip of South Vietnam, June 7, 1969. After receiving an order to level the village, he had run out in front of his men, by all accounts leaping into the air and flapping his arms like a wounded bird, thereby calling attention to himself, thereby taking the heavy artillery fire, thereby saving the four men directly behind him.

My ears seemed to fill with water; there was a roaring in my head, as if I were swimming in the deepest ocean. This despicable little man, taking my five hundred dollars and telling me Daniel and George were gone, vanished like my daughter into thin air! What a joke! What a rip-off! How I wanted to slap his impassive face! His lips—tight, thin lips—pinched together now, his words drifting here and there about the room like dust, in all the languages of the world.

Landon Higginsworth started to speak again. I told him to shut up, I didn't want to hear anymore.

The dog in the corner lifted its lip and began to growl.

"I'm sorry." He said the words tiredly, as if he were disgusted by the slick sound they made on his tongue.

I put my hands over my ears and backed up, feeling for the doorknob behind me. "I don't hear you," I shouted at him. "I can't hear you."

The dog rose from its pillow and barked once. Landon Higginsworth pointed at it and it sat back down.

He came around the desk and reached out to take my arm, to touch my arm, to comfort me. I smelled his vinegary sweat, old sweat pressed into soiled fabric, new sweat pressed into old. What a *smelly* little man, telling such lies.

I said, "Don't you dare touch me! Don't you dare get near me!"

He took one neat step backward, those quick gold eyes of his glittering in the late afternoon sun.

I thought: *June. This is your doing.*

"The baby," he said, tiredly, soberly. But I was out the door by then, I was running down the gray and silent hall into the rest of my life. Only later would I wonder why he'd called my almost grown daughter a baby.

When I got home from that despicable man's office, I didn't even take off my coat before calling my sister. June answered on the first ring.

"You killed my Daniel," I said, without preamble. "You as much as killed him."

"I know," she said, her voice a filament of sound, threaded through a needle. "I know I did."

"How can you live with yourself? How can you get up in the morning and look in the mirror?"

A long silence. I could hear her breathe, her inhalations ragged as wind in straw. Then a click—gentle, final—as if she'd put her finger on the button just to let it rest there.

Later, I wanted to call her back. But I wasn't ready to admit the truth: that I, not my sister, was the one who had launched George and Daniel into outer darkness. Without me, the two of them could have carried on indefinitely, they might have even gotten away with it, gotten off scot-free, perhaps gone south to New Orleans or north to New York, lived out their lives happily, quietly.

That was a decade ago. Since then, I've had my compensations: Alexandria and Vienna and Copenhagen, the thrill of bending over the ancient texts. I show my slides to yawning sophomores and write the occasional article. I've been praised and promoted. I've bought a house in a neighborhood with old trees. I've made friends with my neighbors next door. I tutor their sons in Latin; in turn the boys shovel my driveway in winter and their mother invites me over for Christmas dinner. I joined the Audubon Society of Davidson County and go out birding. My life hasn't been so bad.

Men I've stayed away from, except a casual encounter every now and again, and after a while, even those came to an end. The heart is, after all, only a muscle.

Later, much later, I regretted not letting Landon Higginsworth tell me what had happened to my daughter. Over the years I'd watched girls her age— the young women in my classes—to see how they acted, what they wore, how they fixed their hair. I imagined her beautiful like Mama, but braver, brave enough to live a large life in this flawed and treacherous world. Once, I even called the number I had for Landon Higginsworth, but it had been disconnected. That's when I knew she would live out her own precious life without me, that's when I let her go.

On summer nights now, I sit on an old splintered bench under the dogwood tree in my backyard, sipping gin and tonics and swatting mosquitoes while the Johnson boys next door shoot hoops in the steamy dark, calling back and forth. I think about my sister and me, how, when we were little, our mother would summon us in from our night play and sit us down to supper. At the table, Dad would ask us about our day, how it had been, had we run into any giraffes out back? We would giggle and say yes, we had. Several, in fact, had galloped through and said to tell him hello.

Some nights the clouds pass over and block the moon and stars, but sometimes, when it's clear overhead and you can see far out into space, I think of Daniel flying, forever flying into the gunfire, George silently wandering a world of ice. My baby girl too, always loud in my thoughts, forging ahead in her distant life like a bird in winter, her eyes glittering, seizing on dark berries amid the snow.

I finally called June to say I was sorry I'd blamed her for what happened to Daniel and George. That's how we'd always patched things up; I would call and mutter a halfhearted apology and then we'd talk about something mundane, the more boring the better, as if the humdrum details of our lives would somehow anesthetize the slice left by my knife. June, who'd been mostly homebound with Noel, would go on and on about extremes in weather. In the summers she talked about how hot she was, how her air conditioner was on the blink again, the latest tropical storm or hurricane in the Gulf; in winters, it was the rare freeze and worries that her water pipes would burst. The more extreme the weather, the quicker the call would come.

This time, though, she didn't pick up the phone. I called again, morning, afternoon, evening; I wrote her a short letter of apology, but she didn't write back. I was hopeful when it snowed briefly in New Orleans that winter. But nothing. The weeks melted into months and the months into a year; then in a breath, one year became ten.

And so time rattled along like Dad's old Rambler in its last days. When the 17th Street levee broke the Monday after Katrina and all of Lakeview went under, Dad and Frances made their way up into the windowless attic of her little house, not thinking they should take an ax to chop their way through the roof. I was in Cairo, so June had to make all the arrangements. They were cremated and once we were all able to get back into the City, we took the two boxes of ashes over to the lake and scattered them onto the breakwater as the sun set over the water.

As we sat on the bench Noel had pointed out as Dad and Frances's favorite place, I turned to June. She glanced over at me. Her pupils had grown cataracts of ice.

"You don't mind if I handle their financial affairs, do you?" she said. "I'll send you your half of whatever's left."

"I can help."

"That's not necessary. Jim can help me."

"What about their things?"

"There's nothing left, Grace. Everything was under-water for three weeks."

Noel, who'd grown up to be an astrophysicist, buried his face in his hands and began to cry.

June put her arm around him. "It's time to go."

"I think I'll stay a little longer," I said.

"Suit yourself," said June.

"You're welcome to stop by our room," Jim said. Their house had been lost too; they were rebuilding it from the ground up. We were all staying in a Hampton Inn up on St. Charles.

June shook her head. "I need to get to bed."

"Well, I guess this is it," I said, but she had already gathered the two empty boxes and headed toward the car.

Time went on. My bones began to ache on long flights, and I cut back on my travels, fieldwork now out of the question. Homebound, I became every bit as enamored of birds as my mother had been, my yard sprouting a profusion of feeders, birdbaths, and nest boxes. I began to settle.

Then one night, the phone rang, and it was Jim. June, damn her hide, had gone and gotten cancer. She was at Zumba with her friend Helen and had fainted dead away. Jim explained what stage four meant. He said they were trying to stay positive.

The morning after he called, a gorgeous sunny fall morning, I awoke with a weight on my chest so heavy it took my breath away. I lay there all day, barely moving, not even bothering to call in to cancel my office hours and a committee meeting. At dusk I finally got up, moving like an old woman, which I suppose I am (unbelievable, all those years gone!), and went outside to put out corn for the deer, already clustered in the deep bowl of my front yard, having missed their morning feeding. I stood under the canopy of towering trees and listened to the sounds of their shuffling and soft breathing. The bats that lived under one of the shutters out front were emerging into the darkening sky, swooping here and there to feed. The air was sweet and crisp; the trees sighed and swayed. There was smoke in the air; someone was burning leaves.

Unthinkable, the idea of losing my sister.

I sent cards and flowers, then made that first visit and, before I knew it (*why* did I do it?), opened my big mouth at the table, over June's nice meal, and the words, old and crippling, swarmed out like yellow jackets, and for no good reason; nobody had poked a hole into that nest. I said something sarcastic and underhanded, something about how my sister couldn't keep a secret. It was meant as a joke but June flinched like she'd been slapped. When I left the next day, she stood, bald and gaunt, by the front door. The house was full of stray dogs, and my nose was stopped up from dander and no small amount of crying. My throat felt like a sandpapery tunnel. When I turned my swollen face to my sister, she scanned my eyes as if she were looking for a lost fleck of color.

I took one long ragged breath and my throat collapsed under the weight of the words I wanted to say. I tried to say them, but they wouldn't come, they didn't come.

23
June

I hadn't wanted to go but I'd gone because my good friend Helen had asked me to. She said she wanted company, didn't want to go by herself. She said to bring Jim. Jim said he didn't want to go either, it was his night off, but he would because it was Helen.

Whatever Helen asked us to do, we did. She was like a sister to me, better than a sister, or at least better than mine. Grace sent cheerful Hallmark greetings that, as the cancer was making progress in its valiant effort to put me six feet under, had gone from "Get well soon" to "Thinking of you." She wrote perky little notes in the cards, saying how busy she was at the university, where she'd become a big muckety-muck professor, deciphering chicken scratches on papyrus.

Grace, I wrote to her over email, *don't worry about coming, I'm fine. I'm tip-top.*

There was also the fact that Grace still hadn't let me off the hook for ratting her out. After the cancer, though, I had bigger fish to fry than asking my sister for the millionth time to forgive me, to get over the fact that I'd told Dad on her a lifetime ago, that I had told him the truth: that my sixteen-year-old sister who, as it turned out, had a teenage *menage à trois* going strong in hicktown Opelika, was pregnant. When I got the diagnosis, I didn't want Jim to call her. He waved me aside and picked up the phone.

You killed him, you killed my Daniel. Her words still rang in my ears. She hadn't needed to say it. Ever since I'd seen his picture in *Life* the day the first man walked on the moon, I'd come to understand that I had set something in motion that could never be undone. My actions had propelled that boy into outer darkness. Through the years he had circled and circled my small life. It was as if I'd given birth to him; the face in the picture had become my second son.

Grace came to visit a few weeks after Jim called. She stayed the weekend. She took me to the grocery store and helped feed the dogs. I thought it was finally going to be all right between us. I thought at least I'd leave this world knowing she'd finally forgiven me even if I hadn't forgiven myself. The last night, as we sat at the dinner table, something Jim and I had stopped doing years ago, Jim began to rant about all the backroom shenanigans in Washington, one of his favorite topics. One of hers too, as it turned out. Grace, to my surprise, had gotten political; she was working for John Kerry; she agreed with Jim that the Iraq War was a crime and things were going to hell in a handbasket in Washington. Earlier in the day I'd asked Grace what she wanted me to cook and she'd grinned and said *coq au vin* if I felt up to it, and I'd grinned back and our eyes had met and I could tell she remembered how I'd cooked our way back into the world after Mama died. "You'll be surprised at how much my *coq au vin* has improved," I said with a wink. Between Jim's ravings and my sister's murmured assent, punctuated by the clink of ice cubes in their third gin and tonics, things were going swimmingly at the meal until I said, "Maybe we should all run for office. Any one of us could do a better job." Grace got a gleam in her eye. She leaned toward me, over the congealing plate of what was left of the *coq au vin*, and said, "You'd never make it as a politician, June. You can't keep a secret."

Which of course wasn't true. I've never breathed a whisper about her baby girl being dead, the biggest secret of all.

After the words popped out of her mouth, she looked confused and rattled by them. She started chewing on her thumbnail the way she used to do as a girl.

What she said felt like a grain of sand in my eye. I wanted to say: get out of my house, get out of my life. I can't abide that blaming look; it burns a hole in my heart. I wanted to say: I don't have the energy for all of this, for any of it, really. The past: Mama and what she did, Grace's little child now decades-ago dead, Daniel and George. Everybody's old stale stories: just lay them down, sister, I wanted to say, let them rest in peace, just as I'd soon be doing, just as we'd all be doing before long. I wanted to say all that and tell Grace to go fuck herself. I pushed my plate aside and opened my mouth, but Jim glared at me and launched back into his rant on Halliburton and needless bloodshed and political scheming, and we got through the dinner.

"Why does she do it?" I asked Jim while we were doing the dishes. "Why does she keep holding my feet to the fire? Haven't we all suffered enough?"

"You're her memory," he said. "You remind her."

Grace left the next morning and she hasn't been back, though the cards continue like clockwork, one per week, usually arriving on Tuesdays, as if they have become a routine weekend chore. These days it's all I can do to drag myself out of bed and get to the grocery store for Christ's sake, much less get worked up over something I'd done when I was fourteen years old. Under normal circumstances, I'd ask Grace for help. I'd ask her to take some time off. But after that dinner, I gave up on my sister the way you'd give up on a hopeless alcoholic or drug addict. I said enough already, I quit.

But Helen, our Helen, was a jewel, a queen. She was Jim's friend first, since she worked at the paper, but over the years, she'd gotten to be my friend too. Stuck at home with Noel when he was little and so wildly brilliant that a whole complicated assortment of tutors was the only way to teach him anything, I did freelance work to help pay the bills, but other than that, I had no outside contacts beyond nodding acquaintances with the neighbors, who viewed me with suspicion for keeping my son home from school. I'd latched on to Helen like I was drowning. For years we'd had a regular date for coffee every Monday, and then, after coffee, we were off to the Jazzercise class she'd made me sign up for with her, saying I needed to sweat, let it all hang out for an hour once a week. How else was I going keep from losing my mind staying at home every day? When Noel turned fifteen, she and Jim told me it was time for him to go to college. She helped him fill out application forms for Harvard and MIT and Caltech. When he got into all three, she kept me company while Jim and Noel went on campus visits, and when the day came for Noel to go for good, she drove the two of them to the airport and afterward brought over chicken soup and homemade bread and a bottle of Jim Beam.

When I was diagnosed with cancer of the ovaries—a cosmic joke if there ever was one—it was Helen who drove me to postsurgical appointments and chemo while, as always, Jim worked nights and slept days. It was Helen who put a pillow under my head and a blanket over my legs while I lay on the bathroom floor, too weak to move after hours of kneeling at the toilet. When things were at their worst, she washed our clothes and got the plumber over when the sink clogged, made me up a fresh bed every time I soaked the sheets with hot flashes from the attack of the fiend called sudden-onset menopause.

So here Jim and I were, dragging our reluctant butts twenty miles out to the suburbs, to the Jefferson Parish Cooperative Arts Center for a concert we didn't want to go to, meeting our friend Helen, who was waving at us from her seat. The interior of the place was all black. Black walls, black stage curtains, floors painted black. I felt as if I'd been sucked into a giant black hole in space. In a dark corner, an enterprising traveling masseuse worked on a man's neck and shoulders as he sat on her stool with his face splayed out in the head support.

Helen stood up as we approached our seats. She had on a red skirt and peasant blouse, gold-hooped earrings and a bangle of bracelets on her slim wrist. Against all that black, she glowed like the setting sun.

Jim and I got to the aisle and I went in first. As I leaned over to sit down I felt my wig slip and reached up to right it. The thing was hot as blue blazes. The reason it had slipped was that I'd snipped the lining at the edges in the back to let in some air. Still, the top of my head felt like I was being torched, like I was some unfortunate saint tied to a burning stake.

The main reason I hadn't wanted to go to the concert had been the wig, having to wear it in July. A dull brown, woven thick as a blanket, it reminded me of an osprey nest. How I'd wanted to be one of those Audrey Hepburn types in chemo whose head had a lovely shape, who had high cheekbones and gazelle eyes that were only enhanced by a head bald as a post. As it turned out, my skull was cloddish and lumpy, as pocked as the moon (I told myself lots of people must have pocked heads; you just don't know their secret unless they have the bad luck to go bald). Though my eyes, my mother's eyes, were my best feature, without brows or lashes they looked watery and insipid. I was a walking toadstool. If ever anybody needed a thatch on top it was me.

As I approached her on the aisle, Helen reached out and pushed me back. She grinned, her earrings sparkling in the stage lights. She said, "Let Jim sit in the middle. Give me half a man." Helen had been married to a Toyota salesman named Fred, who complained of plantar fasciitis and made a beeline to his La-Z-Boy the minute he walked in the door. She'd left him a year ago and never looked back.

Jim grinned and said, "I'm enough man for the two of you," and scooted by me. Jim perked up in Helen's presence, I'd noticed lately, even when he was worn out, even when he was sad.

"I'll say." Helen winked at him, patting his hand as he sat down beside her.

The program promised music that was a mix of Hindu songs and bluegrass. Hindigrass, it was called, a combination I couldn't imagine. Clangy and shrill, it was like listening to an itch that couldn't be scratched. There were three men and three women. Two of the men sat cross-legged on platforms covered in colorful tapestries, holding their instruments in their laps. One played drum, another some string instrument I'd never seen before, but which I would learn from Helen at intermission was called a sitar. It had a brass bell on one end, which the man clanged at odd moments, in no discernible pattern, as if to add some exotic accent to the piece.

The violinist was a woman with long blond hair, which she tossed and flipped before and after each number. She wore stiletto pumps and the slit in her skirt showed off her very long, very white legs, which, I noticed, Jim was eyeing. A piano was shoved to one side of the stage, its wood glowing a burnished chestnut against the black wall.

About two-thirds of the way through the performance the man with the sitar introduced a piece he said was about sundown, which in India, he said, is called "The Meeting of the Light."

To start, it was as clanky as the other songs, but when the blond violinist bowed her head over her instrument and began to play, her long white arm (to match those perfect legs) bending and straightening, the other players muted their music and the piece seemed suddenly to flutter and then soar.

It was about midway through the Meeting of the Light number that I saw the cat. It was sitting under the bench of the unused piano, seemingly unbothered by the cacophony of sound coming from the players around it. It was a small tabby, thin, with a head the size of a child's fist and ears twice that size. It was mostly white with swaths of gray and brown on its legs and tail as if it had just walked through a pile of dust.

I wasn't surprised to see it. Animals had a way of popping up in my life in untoward places and at inopportune moments. Over the years I'd come to respect their sudden appearances. It was as though they came to punctuate something, and without the space in time their intervention created, certain significant moments would have passed me by altogether. Laika, our *Sputnik* dog, was the apostrophe, right at the beginning with Jim and me, when I was so wrapped in fear I felt like a thousand-year-old mummy. What Laika taught me was you don't always get to choose who belongs to you, or what condition they come to you in; you don't get to decide the ones you're responsible for, the ones you end up loving. When Noel was little, he would get unaccountably angry at me when I took him away from his numbers. For hours on end, Laika was the only sentient being he would allow to touch him. I'd find the two of them curled up in the back of Noel's closet. Laika was just the right size; like her namesake, she didn't mind tight spaces. Noel liked her to lick his fingers. He would dip them in peanut butter and sugar. When he spent hours in the back of the closet multiplying and dividing numbers that were three miles long, she would squeeze around him so that she was between him and the wall. She would wag her tail vigorously, making Noel's strange numerical chantings into a private game. When I'd look into the closet, she would look back at me over my son's shoulder and her eyes would glow.

By the time I got sick, I had taken on too many animals. Laika was long gone, and over the years, I'd found that bringing as many animals as Jim could tolerate into the house made me happy in a way nothing else did. At first I'd fostered dogs for Orleans Parish Humane. One year I was named Foster Mom of the Year, having taken in and acclimated thirty-five dogs to human handling. All but one had gotten adopted after being in my care. The one, a little shepherd pup named Nanny because she looked a bit like a goat, I'd nursed from a wormy puppy. She'd turned up at six months old to have hip dysplasia and had begun hopping like a bunny on her stiff back legs. Her I kept.

Those dogs of mine, they weren't pretty to look at, and after Noel left, I made a point to choose the ones I knew didn't have a rat's chance of getting taken.

Schnauzer mixes with buck teeth, Chihuahuas with ratty puffs of hair around their backsides (I took on two of those, a brother and sister), min-pin crosses with comically tufted tails. The dogs that roamed my yard were accidental freaks of nature, the ones nobody in their right mind wanted. Without me, they'd have been rotting in plastic bags in the landfill. Now that Noel was down in Florida working at Cape Canaveral, they were what I lived for. Every few weeks, I'd get a call from one of a dozen shelters (none of which knew I was taking dogs from the other eleven) and I'd sneak a particularly sad case into the house. (There were so many by that point Jim couldn't tell when another arrived.)

We had a sizable yard, which had gotten as bald as I was, especially in prime places: under the trees for the resters, on the fence line for the pacers. I wasn't irresponsible; when I got sick, I hired a high school kid down the street to clean up every afternoon. The dogs milled about out there, coming and going into the house through the dog door in the back, bringing in everything from dead birds to small tree limbs. I admit the debris had piled up. Actually, at the present moment, I had so many dogs that I'd lost count. As I listened to the music, in fact, I was wondering if they were all right, if anybody was fighting.

Jim was long-suffering about the dogs, though now he'd taken to sleeping in Noel's room with the door closed. He'd moved his clothes into Noel's closet. The dog hair, he said. No room for him in the bed.

"Aren't you going a bit overboard?" he'd asked a few weeks before, looking out at our living room covered in dogs, peacefully lying about on the floor and furniture, their toys and other debris strewn across the floor. "We can't even let anybody in the house anymore. It's embarrassing." He turned to face me, in the process stepping into a food dish. He hopped about, hitting the dish on a chair to dislodge it.

"I'll get somebody in to clean, I know it's messy today. It's my fault, I let it go too long. I haven't felt well the past couple of days," I said, craftily shifting the subject to the state of the house, then pulling out the cancer card for a double whammy.

"Okay," he said, "but, really, June, this is getting ridiculous. Some people would say you're hoarding animals. I'm surprised we haven't gotten complaints." What he wanted to say, I knew, was what the hell was he going to do with a house full of ugly-as-sin canines when I passed on to my eternal rest. He was, in fact, peering at me as if I were already half gone.

I patted him on the shoulder, then kneeled down and pulled the dish off his foot. "I promise. Sorry."

His face melted and he smiled at me one of those I know you're dying and I don't want to upset you smiles. One of the good things about cancer, aside from the fact that it gets you out of the house, is that people don't say no to you.

After Jim left our bed, I began to dream about Hil. It was always the same dream. She would visit me as I lay there alone and tell me dying wasn't so bad. Then she would crawl in under the covers and practice-kiss me over and over.

Now everyone was looking at the cat under the piano. Actually, now it had moved out in front of the piano, left stage. A woman behind me started to giggle. It was stalking something, given the look of the place most likely a cockroach (who could tell, since the stage floor, like everything else, was painted black). The cat crouched down, began to twitch its bottom and back legs, its tail flicking back and forth, oblivious to its surroundings. Then, after a while, it lost interest and walked over and rubbed the violinist's leg. She jumped and lost her place in the music, causing the crowd to titter. Startled, the cat glared out at the audience, its green eyes flashing neon in the stage lights.

Then it leapt into the air and ran across the stage in

front of the players, hopped down from the stage, and disappeared. The audience gasped. The players faltered briefly, then began to play more frantically. The sitar guy dinged his bell.

I glanced over at Jim, who was elbowing Helen. They were enjoying the moment together, Helen covering her mouth to keep from laughing out loud, her long thick hair, threaded with a few well-placed blond streaks, brushing my husband's shoulder. I smiled, leaned forward to catch their eyes, join in the joke, but they were leaning in the other direction, following the cat's progress as it began to make its way up the aisle like a bride going the wrong way.

The violinist started up again and the music began to swell. I turned back to the stage, for the first time enjoying the concert. Then I felt something touch my leg ever so lightly in the dark, a feather of a touch. In our heyday Jim and I had been known to engage in public leg rubbing. I darted a look at him but he too had turned back to the stage, caught up in the music. The place seemed rattish; I shivered and quickly lifted my legs. Just then, another touch, lighter than the first, higher up, a tickle.

Suddenly I smiled. Without even looking down, I knew the cat had found me. I let my hand drop down and felt warm breath. *Of course*, I thought.

With all the dogs, I'd never had a cat, which struck me in that moment as a chasm in my life. Did this one need a home? Would it take to the dogs and, more to the point, they to it? It arched under my hand, its backbone disturbingly prominent. I reached underneath and lifted; no more than six pounds, I judged, fur over skin and bone, not much else. When was the last time it ate or drank? Would it get locked in this dreadful black auditorium and starve to death? I poured some water out of the bottle I keep in my purse (chemo makes me dehydrated) into my palm and lowered it. I felt the cat's rough tongue lap the water. It was thirsty! By accident I touched its throat. It was purring!

Just as I was pondering what to do, the cat looked at me and then glided to my left, its white body a cloud floating across the black floor. I followed its progress and was about to elbow Jim and point to the cat now skirting his legs, heading for Helen's.

Then the cat froze and, after a moment, looked back at me. It was now between Jim and Helen. I leaned forward to see what its next move might be. Wouldn't it be fun if it jumped right up in Jim's lap? Jim was wearing Birkenstocks. Maybe it would lick his toes!

It moved forward a couple of paces and stopped again, still looking back at me, its eyes glowing as if lit from a hearth somewhere deep inside its skull. Then it lowered its head.

I followed its motion, down to the floor between Helen and Jim.

And what did I see there when I looked down, amused, ready to poke Jim in the ribs and point? I saw my husband's left foot, in its weathered Birkenstock, dear and familiar, and Helen's right foot, in its stylish red thong, pressed up against each other, two peas in a pod, ankle to ankle, calf to calf.

The cat looked down at this roadblock in its progress down the aisle and gazed back at me, its eyes half closed. Then, in one tidy motion, it leapt over Helen and Jim's feet (easy since they were pressed so tightly together) and disappeared into the black. Helen and Jim never knew it was there, never suspected a thing.

I don't have all the time in the world, so let me cut to the chase. If you find these scraps of writing after I'm gone, don't tell Helen and Jim I saw their future in the face of a cat. They'll think I was crazy as a loon at the end, that the cancer had eaten holes in my brain, that I'd gone back to being the bride of Christ (which I admit has its appeal at the present moment). Or worse yet, they'll think this was sour grapes. After all, Helen and Jim both pride themselves on being good people, kind people.

Don't tell them what I predict: that a year from now, maybe sooner, they'll be living the life I wanted, the life I should have had. They'll return the dogs (I've kept impeccable records of who goes where), hire a landscaping outfit to roll patches of overfertilized neon-green sod across the backyard, and throw lawn parties with Japanese lanterns and margaritas in Mexican glasses with blue rims, crusty with salt. They'll have the same work schedules and carpool; Helen will get promoted to editor of the "Living" section. They'll go on a belated honeymoon to Paris and will not see my mother's ghost strolling the streets, not see her sitting in a sidewalk café sipping espresso, not hear her cursing the plundering house sparrows under her breath as they play in the puddles and eat crumbs. They'll congratulate themselves on having found such a good college for my son, a place where he can *thrive*. Jim will tell Helen he couldn't have managed without her.

Then one day Helen will stand in front of the mirror and see a thickening (she's fifteen years younger than me after all) and she and Jim will have a perfect child, a lovely child, who will grow up and go to regular schools and have friends and birthday parties and sleepovers and learn to drive and go to college and have little children the two of them can dote on in their old age and not be in any way unusual or difficult.

Don't tell them any of this. Don't tell them how faithful I will be to them, tracking their every move, night and day, day and night, as long as they live, as ordinary and constant as weather.

At their tastefully small wedding, say congratulations to the groom and best wishes to the bride, say June would be pleased. Say June would be happy for you.

24
Grace

There's a commotion in the yard, a flutter, then a splash of color.

I catch it out of the corner of my eye but don't look up from my desk; there's a piece of a sentence in my head (something about regret) and who knows where it'll fly off to if I don't write it down. Here it is Sunday afternoon, the article's due tomorrow, and it's a big fat mess. "Sites of Memory in Classical Poetics": what was I *thinking*? And such a pretty spring day outside!

My neck hurts (what I'd give for someone to come up behind me and massage it!). I need to sit up straight, get an ergonomic chair, go to physical therapy. My shoulders fold like the flaps of a box over my computer; there's a hump at the base of my skull.

I'm old now, no time to waste.

Back in the day, I was quick on the page, my mind a busy runway of sentences taking off *zoom, zoom, zoom* like clockwork. Sometimes now, like this afternoon, I have the sensation of stumbling through a dark woods, lost and alone. Some days I simply stop cold in my tracks, and the words don't arrive, upright and reliable, to lead me out of these thickets. Lately, when I'm teaching a class, I'll stop in midsentence, having lost the word I need, no idea of what I've been talking about. At a dinner I hosted one night I couldn't think of the word *container.* "Put the potatoes in the plastic . . ." I said to my younger colleague, who looked at me quizzically. After a moment or two, with her standing there with the bowl of potatoes waiting, not looking squarely at me but eyeing the floor, a hint of a smirk playing at her lips (how I wanted to slap her!), I got up from the table and pulled the Tupperware container out of the kitchen cabinet, an ugly orange bowl, one June had lent me a zillion years ago and I'd never returned.

Last week I went to the Harvard-educated neurologist at the university hospital memory clinic, a Dr. Roe, a young woman who looked about fourteen. Dr. Roe's first name was Heidi, and she looked so much like the blond girl in pigtails on the cover of the book June and I had shared when we were girls that I half expected her to start yodeling.

When I told Dr. Roe that my brain had gone on the lam, she looked at me oddly, then started talking so fast I could only understand every third or fourth word. She gave me some oral tests, quickly stated lists of things (she talked so terribly fast): something like elephant, cat, woman, house, elevator, profession, zebra, money, lion, desk, capsule, giraffe, and a zillion others. Then she asked me to repeat them. Good grief, I could only remember giraffe and capsule, which Dr. Roe said, with a Heidi-like lilt to her voice, was a surprisingly poor result for such a high-functioning person as myself.

I wondered whether the doctor had talked too fast on purpose. I suspected Dr. Roe needed research subjects.

Given my dismal failure with the list, I was remanded to the basement of the hospital for an MRI. "Just think of it as going back into the womb," said the technician as he got me up onto the platform that would slide me into what appeared to be a plastic tunnel.

I chewed my bottom lip as the platform gave a lurch and then began to glide. The way the whole device slid me in, its silent resolve, made me think, unfortunately, of how a funeral home would slide a body into the crematorium. June says she wants to be cremated. After that time I'd locked her in the basement when we were girls, she hated the idea of rotting away underground; she said she'd rather go in one glorious blinding flash, she'd rather explode in flames. June had been in Florida the day the *Challenger* had exploded. Noel had been in college by then, so she'd taken a special assignment to cover the space launch. She'd called me that night, sobbing. *The terrible thing,* she'd said, her voice muffled by a bad connection, *was that it was so beautiful. It was the prettiest thing I ever saw, like fireworks on the Fourth of July.*

The platform shifted slightly and something grazed my cheek. A quickening, a folding and unfolding of wings. I jumped.

June? I wondered, but then rejected the idea. Of course it wouldn't be June. When I was a girl, especially after Mama died, I used to feel my sister's touch even when June wasn't nearby, as if each of us were one half of a whole person. Even when I went on the lam after the baby, she'd stayed close. I'd be cleaning the mirror in the elevator or lying in my single bed at Elsa's, and there'd be that brush of something soft against the face or arm, velvety and friendly. Over the years, though, since I had walked out of Landon Higginsworth's office and picked up the first phone I could find and told my sister she'd killed Daniel Baker, I'd lost the feeling of June's *thereness*. It was as if part of myself had gone up in smoke.

And yet, I still have a strange feeling of someone peering over my shoulder, watching and waiting and wanting. *Who?*

Now, the platform stopped silently, and I halfway opened one eye. There it was: the ceiling of the tunnel, two, three inches from my nose. *Little Laika in her space capsule.* I began to gasp for breath and squeezed the panic ball without thinking.

"Are you okay?" the technician asked from the glass booth across the room. His voice crashed and boomed all around me, despite the earplugs. I shuddered, clenched my teeth.

"Get me out of here."

I'd traveled the whole world. I'd wanted to have such a large life.

"Are you sure? It's going to mess up the pictures."

"Out! Get me out!" I bit the side of my mouth, tasted blood. Then I couldn't help it, I started kicking my feet, my knees banging against the top of the tunnel, squeezing the panic ball on and off, on and off.

Just when I opened my mouth to scream, the platform shuddered and began its glide.

The next day I was back, limp with Valium and terror. This time I had a technician who'd been instructed as to my claustrophobia. She handed me not one but two washcloths and told me to put them over my eyes. "Open them before you go in to make sure you can't see," she said. "Take deep breaths and think about something nice. Think about the best meal you ever ate."

June's first effort at cooking, that bloody chicken drenched in Dad's awful cherry bounce: what a joke and how it melted in our mouths like manna from heaven. The thought of it brought tears to my eyes, which, despite the washcloths, ran down the sides of my face into the folds of my ears.

A week later Dr. Heidi Roe came into the examining room bearing a laptop and a box of Kleenex. When she showed me the picture of my own skull, I gasped. Olivia! My own mother, long gone: yet there she was, in the curve of my skull, in the shape of the jaw and teeth, in the laps and folds of my brain. I saw suddenly how my mother had just parked herself there, inside my own head, like she owned the place. How odd, how disconcerting, to be so inhabited and not know it.

Then Dr. Roe reached over and touched my arm. "Do you have any family nearby, Grace? Anyone you'd like to call? We could do Skype, if you'd like." She moved closer as she spoke, and I shrank, gripping the cold metallic edges of the examining table where I was perched.

"Just tell me," I said.

Dr. Roe moved closer still. Her breath smelled like curry. "I'm sorry but it appears you're in the early stages of Alzheimer's. We can't be a hundred percent sure of this, but I'm ninety-nine percent sure in your case." She spoke so softly and quickly that I could barely make out the words.

"How can you be sure?" I asked.

She looked down at her feet. "Only an autopsy would allow a definitive diagnosis." She slurred the word *autopsy* so that it sounded innocuous, like the *topsy* in topsy-turvy. "The good news is that there are new treatments coming out that can help. This is a research hospital; we have several trials ongoing. You'd be a good subject for one I'm doing if you want to be included."

My scalp tingled.

"Show me. I want to see." I'd read somewhere that the brain has the consistency of hard Jell-O.

The doctor gave me the laptop, and I looked closer at Olivia's skull. How beautiful it was! How alive!

The doctor pointed to the base of my brain. "See that area with the different texture? Those are the plaques in the neuron forest. They're sticky protein fragments that come from tangles within the cells. They interfere with the neuron impulses. Then the neurons don't function anymore and the neuron forest begins to decline."

"Neuron forest?"

"We call it that because the neurons develop in clusters. See?"

I peered at the shaded area. The blob of plaques floated right above the place where my mother used to put up her hair in a quick bun when she cleaned house. I had read my AARP magazine. I knew the plaques and tangles would reach out like kudzu and take hold here, there, and, eventually, everywhere. I was reminded of that little dog of June's, the one she found at that truck stop in the middle of nowhere, how it liked to shred toilet paper, loved to carry an unraveling roll around the house. My Jell-O brain would soon be littered like that.

As I stepped from the doctor's office out into the cold cloudy March afternoon, I had a sudden vision of myself becoming lost and disoriented in a forest covered in kudzu. I pictured it hungry and greedy, slithering up the towering oaks through the delicate underbrush of my neuron forest, covering everything in its path. What should I do now? Retire? I couldn't quite imagine it, the endless days without form or structure, that stretch of brittle sun on winter afternoons. In the winter, I always made sure to hold office hours around four until dark, for the company. What if there were no classes, no office hours, nowhere to go at four o'clock? What if all I had to do was watch the sun's rays snake across the floor?

Back in my car, I pulled down the sun visor and looked in the mirror. My face was lined and—how to say it?—colorless? no, *pallid*, that's it; *colorless* won't suffice. I reached into my purse and took out my lipstick and put it on. My lips were shriveled; I looked closer and noticed for the first time that the left side of my upper lip was higher than the right, giving me a bit of a—what's the opposite of smile?— *sneer*. I tried to erase it by wiping a bit of color off the top. I ran my fingers through my hair to fluff it and it stood straight out from my head, wiry and wild the way the boys used to like it. Now I looked better, now I could think straight. I decided not to tell anyone, not even June. If I told, it would take shape, it would be real.

I remembered I needed bread and decaf from the grocery, a good sign! I cranked the car, turned on the radio, and headed in the direction of the store, whose name I'd suddenly forgotten.

Now, a month later, here I am, drudging along at my desk this Sunday afternoon, the tangles and plaques running amuck in my neuron forest, still mired in this infernal essay. (Honestly, who gives a rat's ass about the site of memory in classical poetics?) Now, as I turn back to my work, a piece of color snags my eye, then another. Red? Green, maybe blue? A fleck of yellow? I lift my head. Have the finches molted already? It's only early April. I peer out the window at my thistle stocking, but no, the birds are still winter brown, not a single yellow one among the four clinging to the sides of the stocking, pecking away companionably. I turn back to the computer screen, start a new paragraph, and am reminded of some lines from Sappho. They seem important to the project, something about the moon and the salt sea and fields deep in flowers, something about memory and beauty and regret. It's a passage I know like the back of my hand, but it eludes me. I get up and go over to the bookshelf.

I'm picking my way back across the room, book in hand, when I see him out of the corner of my eye. He's sitting on a branch in the big water oak out front, fooling around with an acorn in his curved beak, taking it in and out of his mouth (I can actually see his tongue, which is the color of ash), knocking it against a branch. When I turn to look at him head-on, my eyes widen. This one's a brilliant mishmash, certainly a male: orange head, yellow neck, green body, his face strangely reminding me of my sister's. Some sort of parrot, the size and shape of a large dove, except longer tail feathers, much longer, really quite remarkable tail feathers, green with slivers of blue that glisten in the sun. Maybe he hitched a ride on a freighter from Brazil? Maybe he's an escaped macaw from somebody's house or a zoo? You have to keep their wings clipped.

I head into the kitchen where I keep—what do you call them? Bio-specs? Goggles? No, that's not right—the glasses that let you watch birds? *Damn!* I have my mother's, which are good as new, and I snatch them up, and tiptoe back. But now the bird is gone, vanished into thin air. I wonder at this point whether I dreamed this exotic creature. Are visual apparitions a characteristic of Alzheimer's? The day, this ordinary Sunday afternoon in early spring, has turned strange.

When I walk out into the front yard, the finches flit away. I'm still in my pajamas, haven't combed my hair today or washed it since Thursday morning when I last went in to teach. I look up and down the street. Nobody's around to see me in this state of despair, I mean *disrepair*. I don't worry about the Purvises across the street from my house; they're in their late eighties, nearsighted and sometimes not all there (though I'm not one to throw stones). Mrs. Purvis's outdoor activity involves hanging Mr. Purvis's socks and yellowed boxer shorts on a rickety clothesline in their side yard. His project, which he pursues year round, is to rake the needles from his towering pine trees to the street, scraping his sloping yard to bare dirt, which erodes with every rain and runs over the curb and into the street in muddy gullies. Except for the weeds and that magnificent stand of giant pines, his lot reminds me of the bare yards of country women, who use brooms to sweep them clean and make designs in the dirt, except their designs are pretty, artful. Once I suggested to Mr. Purvis that people pay good money for pine mulch, just leave it where it fell, it was good for his trees. "Damn them trees," he'd said, then peered at me suspiciously through his cockeyed glasses and kept on raking.

I put my bio-specs to my eyes and scan the branches of the water oak and overlapping trees. Nothing there now, nothing at all except a squirrel who peeks out from behind a tree and eyes me hopefully, awaiting its share of the deer's corn. I know I shouldn't feed the deer, my very nice neighbors who have gardens have asked me not to. The neighborhood association has sent out carefully phrased notices about "some of our kindhearted neighbors who are contributing to the serious overpopulation problem, which in turn leads to tick-borne disease." So now I do my feedings on the sly, before dawn and after dusk so no one will see, dropping the kernels surreptitiously from a pocket in Mama's old apron, now frayed and faded and stained beyond recognition. I rather enjoy the secrecy of it, my own sneakiness. There's a thrill to it that reminds me of how I'd hop out my bedroom window on those hot summer nights and run across the street to the boys through thickets of honeysuckle and night jasmine. How I brushed my hair a hundred strokes and put Vaseline on my lips and eyelids so I'd shine for them.

I scan the water oak again, just to make sure I haven't missed anything, though the bright stranger would be impossible to miss. Still the bare branch. The yard had come alive as it did every spring, the early-bird dogwoods now opening their greenish white blossoms alongside the nandinas' red berries from winter, bare branches of my forsythia flecked in yellow. A flock of about fifty robins lands and starts pecking away in the moss. Looking out over it all, I vow to make myself happy and content in the time remaining: blissful even.

I'd travel to exotic places. Take a plunge, call June and try to talk her into going on a safari to Africa. Africa, that was the ticket! I had savings, I'd foot the bill. I could just see it: the two of us spotting lions and elephants and giraffes, *galloping* giraffes; paddling a canoe down the Nile, well maybe something a bit more substantial than a canoe, something with a motor; sitting around a blazing fire, *camping*. I'd never been camping in my life but I'd heard the really nice safaris were like staying in a luxury hotel, just outdoors in tents with bathrooms attached—and no walking after dark! The idea of prowling lions right outside my tent gave me a delicious shiver. June would love it.

It was only when I got into the house that I remembered my sister's cancer. It was as if a ghost had laid a cold hand on my back and pushed. I walked through the door from the carport and fell, slam-bam, face forward, to the kitchen floor.

It was cooler inside than out; the tile on the floor icy. I shivered, then pulled myself up on the kitchen table. I'd cushioned my fall with my right hand and my wrist throbbed. But nothing seemed broken. I looked at the clock on the microwave. A few minutes before four. The house was in semidarkness from the surrounding trees, my corner lot crowded with them: towering oaks and sweet gum and pines, smaller dogwood and redbud and a tree that bloomed pink puffy flowers in the spring, nut trees of all sorts. Each spring, before the copperheads woke up and the mosquitoes hatched, I would walk around the yard and check my trees for rot and dead branches. Most of them grew to astonishing heights, their trunks grown spindly in their stretch to meet the light. I spent a fortune on removing dead branches, though I winced when the electric saws sprang into action and insisted on supervising even the smallest prunings. I always called in a registered— what do you call a tree person? Starts with an *a*. When a storm came and the wind whipped up, I'd sit on the porch steps, folded up like a grasshopper, and watch the Purvises' queenly pines gyrate across the street. Sometimes a limb would come crashing down. I thrilled to that cracking sound, then the boom. Once, in a storm, a whole tree fell from my yard across the street, taking out the Purvises' electric line. They'd come running out into the rain, quaking and crying with fright. I took them into the house, the first company I'd had in months, and gave them towels to dry themselves and some hot tea.

When we were little, June and I would have loved this forest of a neighborhood with its overarching canopies. We would have played hide-and-seek until we dropped, one of us tweaking the branches to confuse the other, giggling and touching. On long summer evenings, our mother would have her drinks on the porch, clinking the ice in her glass and chewing on her lime, not calling us in until after nine. Sometimes I imagined us out there shrieking with delight and confusion as the giant trees murmured in one voice, like another child, a wild forest creature, invisible and mischievous.

Then my mother would call her perfect children, my sister and me, in from the growing dark.

Now, so many years later, it's already Monday morning and I still haven't finished that infernal essay. The sky is pinking up and I'm out in the yard feeding the deer when I hear a squawk from high up in the trees, then a full-throated chatter. I drop the corn in a pile and race back into the house to get my bio-specs. I scan the trees. Nothing there. I have only a couple of hours before heading off to teach my graduate seminar, so I run upstairs and jump in the shower and throw on my school clothes, the serviceable dark slacks, white blouse, and jacket (unlike my mother, I've never had a shred of fashion sense). I glance at myself in the mirror and am reminded of Frances, which stops me dead in my tracks and makes me reach for the Gap Fresh Scent that I bought myself on my last birthday. Even when I'm showered and presentable, I worry I've acquired the Lady Schoolteacher Smell.

Now, this Monday morning, when I go to the bedroom window and peer out again, my wet hair whipped up in peaks all over my head, the dawn's come up watermelon pink. I have a good view of the yard through the tree branches, but again I see nothing remarkable. A flock of pine siskins swoops in and feeds on the cones of the Purvises' trees. A wren throws its voice here and there from a camellia next to my window and two cardinals flit from limb to limb, calling out *cheat, cheat, cheat,* as if each is accusing the other of infidelity. No orange or green flashes, no squawking. I head back into the bathroom, comb out the tangles in my hair, blow it dry, fluff it up, and go downstairs. I grab a cup of coffee, head back outdoors, and sit down on the front porch step. I pick up the goggles, I mean bio-specs—no, *binoculars!*—where I left them and scan the trees.

Then I see him. See his head actually. A dollop of orange and yellow the size and shape of one of those stick-on Christmas bows, poking out of a hole in the trunk of a dilapidated water oak, one I know I'll have to have taken out soon. The tree's a zillion feet tall, now with just a tip of green left at the top, its trunk deeply creviced. The bird (what *is* he?) perches on the edge of the hole, his head now cocked. One fierce raisin eye, lined in white, looks directly back at me.

How I yearn to pick up the phone and tell my sister about this remarkable creature living in a hole in my very own water oak! I'm dying to take this crazy bird story and offer it as a peace offering. I wonder whether June has been able to set out feeders and nest boxes this year. What would she do if I just pick up the phone and say, *Hi, just called to tell you about this strange and wondrous bird in my yard?* After all these years of blame and silence? Might she laugh and say, *Come on, a parrot in a tree? Sure it's not a partridge in a pear tree? Are you getting senile on me, Grace?* Then, after I send her a picture on my phone, might she instruct me to call Wildlife Rescue? Might I tell her that, as a matter of fact, I am indeed growing more senile by the moment, that even as we speak, kudzu, green and vigorous and deadly, slithers through my neuron forest?

Suddenly the bird squawks again, then begins to chatter and cackle. I jump, and, damn, slosh coffee on my good pants. Now, oh my, he's coming out, sitting on the edge of the crevice, gazing straight at me like I'm the wild one, the pretty one. As I watch, open-mouthed, the bird hops from his perch to a long branch of the oak and begins to strut—that's the exact word, *strut*—back and forth as if to say, *Here I am, look at me.*

Who are you? I ask. Too small for a macaw, with a curved beak the color of bone, which is odd too because all the macaws I've seen have had dark beaks. I participate in the Audubon Society annual bird count every year, get respectable tallies. But this one has me stumped. Now he adjusts his head, ruffles his feathers, then raises a three-fingered claw as if in greeting. His eye seems to know me in some uncanny way, in some way I don't know myself.

I glance down at my watch. It's 8:15 and I haven't done the last-minute prep for my ten o'clock class. Still, I run to my bird book and quickly scan it. I find absolutely nothing in the book that has the coloring of my bird. Maybe it's an odd mutation of one of those South American parrots down on the Gulf coast, an accidental. Could he have migrated all the way up to Tennessee? I know next to nothing about parrots. June and I used to see them around the zoo in New Orleans, clustering in the tops of the date palms, eating the fruit and shrieking at the tops of their lungs. But they're mostly green and much smaller than this bird. I'll have to go online and look at exotic birds, the kind in zoos that come from the Amazon jungle. This is clearly an escapee who likes to live in tree hollows and eat acorns. Was he drawn to the deer's corn?

It's a brisk morning; I worry he's cold.

When class is over, I head back to my office and start looking up parrots and macaws on my computer, quickly scanning the pictures and descriptions. No matches. Then I look up exotic birds and rainforest birds. Still nothing. I consider calling the president of the Nashville Audubon Society, Natalie Somebody. By now, though, I'm—how do you say it? *Intrigued*, I'm intrigued by this bird. Enlisting outside expertise would be cheating. And although I hesitate to say this for fear of sounding somehow like my mother (which I am most definitely not!), I pride myself on *understanding* birds. I bend my days to their habits, hurrying home in winter to put out seed for the last flurry of feeding before dark. I enter their privacy like a peeping Tom, watching them mate in spring. In late spring I peek into their nests and count the eggs.

I hurry out across campus to take an overdue book back to the library. At the library entrance there's a poster advertising an art exhibit inside. My mouth drops open. The subject of the exhibit is the Carolina Parakeet, a splashy thing. Extraordinary. A dead ringer, stem to stern, for my bird: the orange head, yellow neck, green and blue plumage.

How could I have missed it? Why wasn't the Carolina Parakeet in my bird book? As the question flits from one side of my brain to the other, hopscotching over and under thickets of kudzu, the hair on the back of my neck rises. Of course. It wouldn't be in my book. What a fool I am! The Carolina Parakeet has been extinct for almost a century. Had I spotted an accidental lost in time rather than in space?

I gallop up the steps of the library (I catch myself mirrored in the glass door, loose-limbed, wild-haired, a glorious blur of motion!), and drop my library book into the slot without paying up. Inside the exhibit, everywhere I look there's my bird (I think of him as mine now) in all his glory, there and there and there, in the exquisite drawings, oils, and watercolors. Gorgeous cavity nesters, their range in the swamps and river bottoms of the Midwest and southeast, noisy chatterers, victims of farmers who shot them for eating the corn, of feather traders for the outlandish hats women wore back then, finally of the honeybees who stole their tree cavities and set up shop. Sociable, always flying in flocks, large murmurations (how I adore that word *murmuration*, taught me by my own mother!) that rose and fell together, always together, like massive families.

Never shot for food because their favorite seed came from the poisonous cocklebur and made their flesh deadly. Gone from the Carolinas by the Civil War, last confirmed sighting in a Florida swamp in 1904. Declared extinct in 1918!

Reading all this, I know there has to be an explanation; my bird can't possibly be a Carolina Parakeet. But what a lark (though not one) to think it might be!

I dash home around midafternoon, neglecting my office hours. I'm so distracted I almost don't notice the hullabaloo going on across the street. Two huge flatbed trucks have pulled up in front of the Purvises' house and a third is unloading a giant water bird—I mean *crane*, a giant crane. Four pickup trucks and a sedan are parked up and down the street. The Purvises, Mrs. P in her apron and Mr. P with that infernal rake in his hand, the two of them American Gothic personifications, are standing out in their yard talking to some workmen clustered around them. Mr. Purvis is pointing at the sky: that, that, and that, he points.

Above him those gorgeous pines swish in a whisper of a breeze. And those delicious pine cone seeds. I've read how the Carolina Parakeet loves them. How wise of mine to roost in a tree cavity directly across the street from an endless supply! The perfect habitat!

The leader of the men nods, a pact sealed.

I pull my car into the driveway. I get out and walk up the driveway toward the street, ostensibly to get my mail but actually to get a sense of what the Purvises are up to. By now a man has driven the crane to the center of the Purvises' large yard and parked it. I pull my mail from the box and make a show of sorting it, looking up every now and then at the Purvises, who are continuing to point upward and talk with the men. After a few minutes, I walk back down my driveway and into the house. I'm hoping the men are there to shore up the dilapidated carport next to the Purvises' house. It looks like it's going to fall in any minute and crush the couple's rusty Oldsmobile.

Whatever they do, I worry their work will disturb my Carolina Parakeet (yes, *mine*), scare him away if he's thinking of nesting for the season, and what a thrill that would be! Is it possible he has a mate I haven't seen? I consider calling the Audubons to come see, but hesitate. Something about all this feels deliciously private.

By the time I drop my briefcase and purse on the kitchen table, change and dump my school clothes on the bed, and head out the door with my binoculars, the men have departed in their cars and pickups, leaving the crane and flatbed trucks parked across the way. The Purvises have disappeared inside. I scan the cavity in the water oak, and, happy day, there's that orange and yellow bow of a head, right on the edge. Is it possible he's sitting on a nest of eggs? Where is his mate?

There is something about a bird on its nest that is reserved and secretive, and so the hungry eye seizes upon it, yearns for it. A grin plays at my mouth; there's a strange *knock-knock* in my chest, as if my heart is trying to break through my rib cage. *Who's there?* The last time I had this sensation was a half century ago, a *half century, think of it,* when Dad used to take me and June to watch the giraffes dance at the back of the zoo.

The next morning I sleep through to dawn, the first good night's sleep I've gotten in weeks. Then something loud (a crash? a bomb?) jars me awake. Then I hear a high-pitched mechanical sound, then a booming crash that sets me bolt upright in bed. I leap up, cross the bedroom, look out the window. Across the street, the men are back. One is up in one of the Purvises' pines looking like a monkey clinging to the trunk; he has a rope around his waist and blades on the inside of his boots, like sideways ice skates. At that moment, as I pull back the curtain and focus my eyes, he lops off the top of the tree, one of the Purvises' largest and greenest.

That's no way to prune a tree! I throw on some clothes and bolt down the steps, reminding myself to keep a firm grip on the banister. Over the past few months I've gotten a bit clumsy, one foot drags a bit, I drop things. I'm terrified of falling again and not being found, of lying there for days. I should get one of those medical alert devices. At the bottom of the stairs I throw open the front door and race across the street, twigs and pebbles scraping my bare feet, threading my way between the trucks and the men standing around watching the man in the tree.

In that instant of running toward the Purvises', I feel suddenly leaden, as if I'm swimming a belabored breaststroke to my destination, the man in the tree. Am I moving at all? Hell yes, I'm moving. Not just moving but running. Not just running but shot out of a cannon, damn the pebbles, damn these men. By now I'm close enough for them to see the fire in my eyes, my fisted hands, mottled with age spots. My hair, long and silver and ratty, standing out from my face as if I'm running into a high wind. Their eyes widen, their mouths drop open. One of them shouts, "*La Llorona!*" and makes the sign of the cross. They approach me with their hands in the air. "*Cuidado!*" they shout, pointing upward. *Watch out.*

"Stop," I scream at the man in the tree. I come to a screeching halt in the middle of the Purvises' yard. "Stop it right now. You can't prune a tree like this. This tree's . . ." I can't think of the word, something about jewelry, stones, diamonds; something beginning with *p*. Instead I say, "*protected*, this tree's protected." I stop a moment, realizing suddenly that the men don't speak English, realizing that even if they did, I haven't conveyed what I mean. Meanwhile the man above, who hasn't even seen me standing below, has moved down a few notches and is applying the chainsaw to a large uppermost branch.

"*No, no!*" the men shout up at him and point at me. "*Abuela loca!*"

The man doesn't hear them. He continues to cut, oblivious to the commotion below. He loops one of his ropes around the tree limb, pulls it taut, glances down to check below, then thankfully sees me, the crazy grandmother, waving my arms, saying something. He stops and gapes. I run for the Purvises' front door and go straight in.

The Purvises are sitting at their kitchen table with their heads bowed and eyes closed, holding hands. They are praying the trees won't fall on the house. When I stride in, they leap to their feet, their faces

splotched with alarm. "What are you doing letting
that man hack away at that beautiful old tree?" I
demand. "It's healthy as a horse." The word comes to
me: *precious. That tree is precious.* I wave my arms
in the air, point out the door, which I've left ajar. The
men have stopped their work now and collected on
the front porch.

Mrs. Purvis glares at me. "They're our trees, we
can do whatever we please with them."

"What do you mean, them? You're going to prune
more than one?"

"Getting rid of them," she says with satisfaction.
"Every last one of them. Thirty-two in all."

"Sick of the needles," Mr. Purvis says. "Sick to
death of them. Spent my whole life raking them, about
drove me crazy."

"One of them's going to fall on the house and kill
us both," Mrs. Purvis says, her lips in a grim line.
"You going to save us then, dig us out? Pay for our
funeral?"

My mouth drops open. "You can't do that. It's got
to be against the law, the zoning ordinances, to cut
down that many trees. These are . . ." I want the word
about the past, how the past is precious too, a simple
word but I can't find it. (What a bother Alzheimer's is
in an emergency!) Surely, though, there are ordinances

prohibiting the removal of thirty-two mature trees on one lot! We live in a university area that's downright prissy about preservation, prissy about *everything*. Men in kelly green outfits resembling overgrown leprechauns collect the recycling in matching green trucks with trees painted on the sides. The cardboard, corrugated only, has to be presented at the curb tied neatly in twine or it won't get taken. In my neighborhood, the city plants and mulches and prunes trees here, there, and everywhere; *vacuums* the streets.

Mr. Purvis says, "I planted them fifty years ago. Stupid fool thing to do, plant pines. We got them for free." He whips out a piece of paper.

"What's that?" I ask.

"It's my permission letter. The trees are endangering my house."

I snatch the piece of paper from him. It's a form stamped "Tree Removal Approved."

"We'll just see about this," I say, and head for the door, the letter in my hand. Then a light bulb goes off in my neuron forest. I stop and take a good look at the logging trucks outside. I turn back to Mr. Purvis. I'm pretty sure I have an unattractive sneer on my face. "How much are these trees worth in timber?"

He glares at me. "None of your damn business."

"That's the real reason you're cutting them down. You're *selling* them." My heart flutters and flaps in my bag of a chest. What a wild unruly heart I still have!

The men give me wide berth as I sweep through the Purvises' yard, head back across the street to my own house.

Once inside, I go straight to the phone and call the mayor's office. The chainsaw starts up again. On the phone I'm directed to zoning. The man I talk to looks up the Purvises and says yes, they have permission for tree removal.

"These are healthy pine trees, huge trees, magnificent trees," I say. I'm proud of myself, foraging among the kudzu and coming up with the adjective *magnificent*. I try to keep my voice low and firm, though I desperately want to scream. "This is outrageous. This is a beautiful neighborhood. They have a logging operation going on over there, right across the street, and there's an extinct bird roosting in my water oak." I bite my thumbnail so hard it splits halfway down.

"Do you want me to connect you to Wildlife Control?" the man asks.

"No, you idiot," I say. "I want you to make them stop cutting down perfectly good trees." Finally the *h* word comes to me: "*Historic* trees."

"It says on their petition here that the trees are a hazard to the house," the man says. He sounds as if he's in a hurry, has something more important to take care of. "He's obligated to provide new landscaping once the trees are down."

I snort. "He's never planted anything but those pines. It's going to be a wasteland over there. And think of the birds, the wildlife he's disturbing. Can't you do something?"

"Ma'am, he's gone through the process."

I can feel the pulse pounding in my neck. Maybe I'll have a stroke and that will solve everything. "Who do you think you are, letting these old fools cut down a beautiful forest? You . . . you *jack-donkey*!" I slam down the phone and run to the window. The noise is deafening. There is that familiar taste of bile in my mouth.

How I wish for my sister in this moment! June would know what to do, something wildly improbable, a wreck, a fire, a demonstration. Do I dare call her?

I know the number by heart: (504) 228-2554.

To my surprise, she answers on the first ring. "Well, if it isn't my long-lost sister."

"June," I gasp, "they're cutting down all the trees across the street, and I don't know how to stop them.

I've got a Carolina Parakeet nesting in my yard, and they're going to ruin everything."

"Have you lost your mind? Those things are extinct. It's April. Are you sure it's not a painted bunting? An accidental? They're migrating now."

"Not this one."

There is silence on the other end of the phone. Then she says, "Maybe you should chain yourself to one of those trees."

I think she's just being sarcastic, but then she says, "Seriously. At least you'll stop them for now. It'll buy us time to figure out the next step." She sounds excited; actually she sounds thrilled to death.

"Okay," I say. "Okay!" We are in league. Later we will plan and plot. She's not dead yet.

"Call me back," she orders. "And send me a picture of that bird of yours. Put my number in your pocket in case you get arrested."

"I don't need to. I know it by heart."

"Go!" she commands.

The man is back up in the tree working on that one big limb. It crashes down, raising a cloud of dust when it falls. Some agitated bluebirds dip and swoop overhead. Four squirrels hightail it across the street from the Purvises' yard to the sanctuary of mine.

I pull a light jacket from the closet, tie it around my waist, and get a bottle of water and the can of Mace I carry in my purse when I teach at night. I go into the bathroom and pee. I snatch some Kleenex from the box on the back of the toilet, why I don't know. Having no chain, I cut a section of twine. Then I race out the door.

When I get back across the street, the men do not look at me. I do not take this personally. I am spoiling this job; this job is all they have.

I walk up to the trunk of the tree the man is cutting and sit down. I know I'm supposed to do something else, but I can't think what it is. I can't figure out why I'm holding the twine.

The men turn to me in horror. What's the *abuela loca* doing now? They shout at the man above to stop. He makes a gesture of disgust and lets the chainsaw go slack on its rope. It dangles directly over my head. One of the men, the foreman, wipes his forehead with the back of his arm, walks up to me, and delivers a long row of syllables I don't understand. Here I am, fluent in Greek and Latin and Arabic. I can examine a piece of papyrus and give you its age within twenty years, but, idiot that I am, I've never learned Spanish. I assume he is telling me to move. I shake my head no, I won't, I absolutely will not move an inch. I flap my hand at the men to go away, *por favor,* leave me alone.

The foreman then goes and knocks on the Purvises' door and when they open it, he points at me. I sit with my legs crossed, leaning slightly forward. I now wish I'd brought a pillow to put between me and the sharp shingles of the tree trunk. Pine has the roughest bark of almost any tree; plus, these trees are so massive there are deep crevasses between the shingles. Sitting here, I don't know what's going to happen next; I just feel something has turned, something is just beginning.

How do I describe my wildness, the enraged coil of my body against the tree? I can only say it's beautiful, like something thrown away by accident, then found against all odds, a piece of water in the sea.

My sister has returned to me.

Mr. Purvis comes out and tells me to get off his property, but I don't, I won't. I just stare straight ahead, don't even turn my head to look at him. Nobody's taking out *this* tree! He talks at me for a while; he even approaches, puts his withered hand on my shoulder. I shrug him off, point my can of Mace at him, and raise my eyebrows. He backs away, heads back to the house, shouting over his shoulder, "You're crazy, lady, you've gone plumb crazy." It strikes me that, after all these years, he doesn't even know my name.

In a while a police car rolls up, and two policemen wearing creased uniforms get out. They come up into the yard slowly, as if they're ashamed of what they are about to do, as well they should be. "Ma'am, you're trespassing on this property," one says. By this time, some neighbors from down the street, a young couple whose names I can't recall, are drifting by, walking their dog. They stop just after they pass the Purvises' yard and stand quietly, watching.

"Do you see these beautiful pine trees?" I shout in their direction. "They're going to cut down every last one of them." They look sympathetic and worried until I add, "and here I have an extinct bird nesting across the street." Then they jerk on their dog's leash to move her along. The dog, bless her, wants to get in on the action and pulls them in my direction. But they walk away, eyes lowered, dragging the dog. The dog gags, barks once, then twice, as if to say she's on my side, goodbye and good luck.

"Ma'am, we're going to have to remove you from this property," the policeman says, moving in. "You can't be here."

"Well, I *am* here," I say.

Picture this: The workers clustered together in a semicircle in a corner of the yard. The Purvises framed in their picture window, the paint peeling around the edges, two pigeons on a roost.

Now I point my can of Mace at the policemen. I say, "You'll have to come through *this* first, you fucking bastards."

Their eyes widen. They move to either side of me and take me from behind, by the arms, pulling them back and hurting me, really hurting me. I tell them I am a member of the Audubon Society, there is an extinct bird to consider. I accuse them of police brutality. One pries the Mace from my fingers, the other pulls the handcuffs from his belt. Him I kick.

As they drag me toward the police car, an old woman bursts out the front door of my nice neighbors' house next door. I know who she is, though her name escapes me; she's Cleveland Johnson's mother. She came to live with him and his wife, Alita, years ago. Cleveland's in the biology department; I've known him and Alita and their two sons for years now, though their sons are now men out in the world, carrying with them (I hope!) that smattering of Latin I taught them. Every winter I miss those sweet little boys who shoveled my driveway. In the summers I miss sitting outside and listening to them shoot hoops. Now, I only see them on holidays.

"Hold up, now!" Cleveland's mother calls out, bustling down the street in her fuzzy blue bedroom slippers. "Hold up!"

The police and the men in the yard turn their attention from me to her. She's limping a bit in her slippers, but she's coming fast.

"Listen here," she says, huffing and puffing. "Nobody needs to take a person to jail for trying to save a tree. That's silly."

One of the policemen opens the car door and tries to push down my head. "She was threatening a police officer."

"She most certainly was not," Cleveland's mother says. "I've been watching the whole thing. Look at her. She's a *professor* at *Vanderbilt*. She's not threatening nobody. If it comes to it, I'll testify to that. Fact is, I think it may just be the other way around. Um-hum. Yes sir."

The policeman loosens his hold on me.

"I'm her neighbor, let me take her home," says Cleveland's mother, moving in to take my arm. "My Lord, she's almost as old as me. There's such a thing as senior abuse, you know."

"You'll be responsible for her?"

"Course I will. I've been knowing this sweet lady for years. Come on, honey, let's go."

Cleveland's mother leads me back across the street, and I ask her to come in. She pushes me down on the sofa and asks if I want her to fix me a cup of tea. I say

I'd rather have a bourbon. Will she join me? She says she believes that under the circumstances she will. Do I have any Coke to mix with it? While I'm fixing the drinks, she draws the living room drapes so we won't have to look at the trees coming down.

Boom, they go. *Boom, boom, boom.* They shake the house, rattle the dishes in the sink.

Cleveland's mother settles on my sofa with a sigh and I tell her to put her feet up, make herself at home.

She sheds her blue slippers and puts her swollen, knobby feet on the coffee table. "These feet. Sometimes they hurt so bad I'd like to cut them right off."

I hand her the drink. "Thank you for saving me from jail."

"Jail's no place for you," she declares. "No place for much of anybody except the most no-count of the no-count. I could tell you stories."

When June calls later that night and I tell her what happened, she sighs and says, "At least you tried. At least you have a friend. That's one more than I've got right now."

In a week, all that remains of the Purvises' pines are jagged three-foot stumps. In the place of the trees, a giant aluminum sculpture of a deer has sprung up in the middle of their denuded yard. It has sharp points where the joints come together, the points where it was assembled. It's so blinding that when the sun strikes it in late afternoon I have to draw my drapes as I continue to write on this infernal essay, whose subject has come to elude me.

The Carolina Parakeet is long gone. But who knows? Maybe it will return next spring, maybe the remnants of a cracked egg remain right there in my very yard inside the old water oak or scattered among its tangled roots.

And really, the bird's the lucky one, balanced on the farthest ledge of time, splendidly aloft, proof positive of the universe's capacity for . . . what am I trying to say? Surprise? Joy? Because anything can happen, you know, anything at all. There is a living world underneath the one we see: the giraffes' dance, the voice underwater.

Later, I will walk down to Cleveland and Alita's. Cleveland's mother called this morning. She's fixing a pot of red beans and rice. Sometimes, often really, I imagine June and I making *coq au vin* the way we did that first time, making a bloody mess of it with Dad's cherry bounce, that god-awful stuff. The three of us at the kitchen table. How beautiful we appear, like a picture. Our father behind his paper, my sister and I, girls together, setting the table, putting the dish on, sitting down to eat the good hot food.

How I'd cracked the glass, put the plates away dirty! It is a treacherous thing, to turn away from one's own sister.

Now, as I labor on with this infernal essay, it is hard for me to remember how June looks as a grown woman. But her girl face, it still perches as clear and bright in my mind as a strange and unexpected bird, a blaze of feathers.

25
June

Okay, so here's how it went: the doctor put his hand on my shoulder and shook his head. The latest chemo hadn't worked: there'd been no remission, we'd just have to wait and see. In the elevator on the way down to the parking garage, Jim put his arm around me, told me he didn't know what to say, but then he went on to say the regular things: he loved me, he was sorry. I reached over and pulled a long dark hair from his jacket, blew it into the air.

So there I was, doing my dead-level best (pun intended) to enjoy my final days on earth. I'd gathered my neck pillow and comforter and built myself a nest on the living room couch. I only asked for one thing: a fifty-one-inch smart TV to replace the dinosaur box that just wouldn't die. I wanted Netflix and HBO and

Amazon and Pandora. I wanted high-def, surround sound.

In the mornings I turned on the Cooking Channel, salivating over apple and potato hash, salmon slathered in miso and maple syrup, almond pound cake with raspberry glacé. It was December and dark came early with the cold New Orleans drizzle. In the afternoons, I dozed. Jim drifted in and out, working nights, sleeping until ten, paying the bills, feeding the dogs, fucking Helen behind my back. She came by every other afternoon, bearing one of three monstrous mutations of cream of mushroom soup casseroles (French green bean with fried onion rings, tuna and English pea with fried onion rings, corn and bacon with fried onion rings), all of which I thanked her for and deposited in the fridge for Jim to eat. For me, I instructed him to buy only vegetables, which I threw into a big pot with some water every few days and let bubble until they made a reddish brown broth, which I sipped from the time I woke up until the time I got into bed at night. It wasn't that I had hopes of being healed by a vegan diet or anything that silly; it was just that the soup was the only thing I could stand the taste of.

Jim and Helen waited, moving in and out of the house like cats with lizard tails hanging out of their mouths. Their eyes took on an identical cast, a slight smokiness that made them look like they had simultaneously developed cataracts.

The dogs drifted in and out too, whining, putting their heads under my limp hand, sensing something under the limpness, not sure whether it was decay or the remote possibility of a romp.

So we waited. We all waited, day after day, week after week, locked in an endless orbit of hospice nurses and supervised showers and pajama changes. The nurses kept asking me to tell them about the pain on a scale of one to ten. They kept trying to give me pills of many colors—deep crimson, twilight pink, yellow rose of Texas—but when I pushed myself up from the couch to use the bathroom or make my soup, my body seemed to slosh with too many poisons already. I could smell them in my oily urine, in my night sweats. I could taste them on my tongue, feel them burn ulcers in my mouth. They eroded my ashy fingers, which itched, oddly, underneath the nails.

The weeks turned into a month, then two months. During chemo, I'd stayed busy. I'd gotten out of the house and made friends. I'd been driven back and forth to the clinic by cheerful volunteers, chatted with my bald, eyelashless chemo chums on the phone about nausea and marijuana. I'd spent whole days vomiting.

I'd gone to Tupperware-like parties to select wigs and scarves and, for those who needed them, breasts, giggling with my new friends when a wig looked particularly hideous, trying them on backward, sipping sparkling cider in wineglasses. Now I was back at home, alone for all intents and purposes, drooping like a cut mimosa leaf, too weak to even visit Noel down at Cape Canaveral or play ball with my dogs. Dying was boring me to tears.

Jim insisted on calling Grace. He told her the latest, then handed the phone to me. She was crying on the phone, crying hard, as if something had broken open. I said it was okay, I was resigned; maybe there were some wild adventures ahead on the other side, maybe I'd come back to haunt her. I laughed when I said it, but she just cried harder.

"June," she said, "something is happening to me too."

"What? What do you mean? Are you sick?"

She took a shaky breath. "There's a black hole between what I want to say and the words. A gap. My brain. It's like the night sky: cold and dark and empty. I can't think what to say in class, I can barely write a sentence."

I began to laugh. What a runt of a problem! A touch of memory loss. What a humbug!

I said, "The sky's not empty. It's full of stars and satellites and space trash."

"To me it is."

I said, "You been hugging any trees lately?"

Two days later Grace called back. Before I could say hello, she blurted out that she had Alzheimer's. The tree episode had been her first such incident; the second had occurred just yesterday when she set fire to a poster of an aborted fetus during a demonstration by an anti-abortion group on campus. "I was sick to death of looking at those things," she said. My professor sister now had a police record! Plus, she'd started seeing whole flocks of Carolina Parakeets in her yard. They were everywhere she looked. When I laughed and said good for her, good for the trees and the birds and the burned poster, she began to cry. She was a basket case, her brain had gone on the lam, she couldn't even write a simple essay, she was going to have to retire and spend long winter afternoons by herself. She would have to go to one of those awful Alzheimer's places, which would bankrupt her because she hadn't had the good sense to buy long-term care insurance.

The night Grace called, I dreamed I was floating farther and farther out, past the pocked moon, past our speck of a solar system, out past the whole night sky, seen and unseen, until I teetered on the ledge of the blue-black darkness beyond, almost tipping over, almost letting go. Grace was right, I thought, it *is* empty. This is how we leave our home, blindly and alone. Laika in her space capsule.

But no sooner than the thought of the little dog popped into my head (do you know she *barked* for five hours up there before dying in that thing?), I felt something move against my body: a persistent tickle, making me squirm and thrash about in my sleep. (Was it one of the dogs, just then drawing closer in the cool night?) After a while, though, it became something more than a tickle. It became an irresistible pull, a suction, as if I were a piece of lint being vacuumed up off the floor.

And then, how can I explain it? I just turned, from there to here, from the ledge overlooking the hungry dark back to the green world of you come and you go, you laugh and you cry, you get what you want and you don't get shit. The turn was smooth but sudden, as though I'd been caught in midflight by an invisible thread and spun back into some vast fabric.

When I landed, it was in a tree. A messy *kerplop* of a landing. A flap and a flutter, a bit of a squawk escaping my lips.

When I woke up the next morning, I felt clear for the first time in two years. I got up and made myself a cup of coffee and it tasted right. I walked out into the backyard and was surprised that it was warm. My dogs' ears went up and they came running. They jumped up on me and I didn't fall down.

Holy cow, I thought, maybe I'm going to live. What a hoot! What a kick!

I waited a month. I felt better and better. My tongue stopped burning. My nails turned pink. I could smell again: coffee and cheese and burned onions and dog farts, cherries and soap and orange marmalade. I went back to the doctor, and he ran the tests and said yes, something had happened, he didn't know what, he didn't know why. He didn't know how long it would last. I should be cautiously optimistic. Miracles happen.

That afternoon I told Jim the gig was up. He needed to move out and leave me to live or die in peace. He could have Helen and her miserable casseroles. All I wanted from him was the house and a sizable amount of money.

Jim, who had gotten pudgy and pasty-faced from his nonstop diet of additive-laden, high-sodium casseroles, cried and told me how sorry he was. He didn't know how it had happened, his falling in love with Helen while I was dying. He couldn't believe it himself.

Over the next week, he left in bits and pieces, forgetting the most essential items, like his shoes, almost as if he didn't really want to go. When he and a friend from the newspaper came for the last things, the heavy things, and were carrying his desk out the front door, Jim missed the one step down, a step he'd taken up or down thousands, maybe millions of times. He broke his ankle in two places, threw up in the azalea bush next to the door. After taking Jim to the hospital, the friend, grim-faced and apologetic, came back and loaded the rest by himself. I held the door and warned him about the step.

After the last load was out, I drove to the store and got some chicken and wine and garlic. Then I came home and poured myself a glass of cabernet and made myself some *coq au vin*, which I hadn't done in a zillion years.

There were weevils in the flour, but nothing's perfect. I sifted them out.

The next morning I opened the heavy front door to let some light in through the glass storm door. Where had the New Orleans winter gone? The azalea out front was blooming to beat the band, waving in the breeze. My caladium was unfurling pink and green and white. A male bluebird was flitting in and out of the yard, calling out the words our mother made up: *where, where, where are you?* (Where indeed? How the body drives us!) He was scouting my nest boxes, which I suddenly realized hadn't been cleaned in two years. I headed out into the yard and opened them up and scooped out the nesting debris. Leaves and twigs and a tiny pile of twig-like bones. Had the house sparrows visited last year? Would they return?

I was tired after all that, but it was a satisfied sort of tired, not an I'm-dying sort of tired. I slept hard that night. The next morning, when I looked in the mirror, my bald head, which normally shone like a piece of rounded glass in the morning light, wasn't shining. I found this worrisome. I'd gotten used to the shininess, had come to think of it as somehow festive, despite the moon craters in my skull. I peered into the mirror more closely. Then I saw the down. It was coming in unevenly, patches of it here and there, as if my head were growing one of those wild feathery hats women used to wear. It was coming in white. I would be an old woman now.

I went outside and fed the dogs. One of my favorites, a little gray pit bull named Silly because she often was, licked my hands, sensing some excitement beyond the chow, her pink jowls loose and wet. After they finished breakfast, Silly and the others cavorted, tossed some bedraggled toys in the air, making me understand they had missed me. I came back in, and they all rushed in behind me, dragging their toys, shaking them enthusiastically. As they milled around my legs, I made coffee. I made it extra strong, then stood at the kitchen counter and drank the first cup with milk and sugar, lots of sugar. Then I ate a bowl of cereal, chockfull of vitamins and fiber. Sugar on it too. After that, I had another cup of coffee and, with it, a banana.

Then, without giving it a second thought, I picked up the phone and called Grace. She was crying when she answered. She thought it was Jim, she thought he was calling to say I'd died. I told her I hadn't and wasn't going to in the foreseeable future.

I said things had taken an odd turn, a surprising turn.

I said I needed her to do one thing for me, a favor. I told her to build a fence around her backyard, a tall fence. Also to stock up on antihistamine. I was coming and I was bringing the dogs. I was coming to stay.

26
Ed Mae

I recollect it now, what it was I was doing that morning. It came to me last night right after I took out my teeth. I was just standing there, holding them in my hand, waiting for the Polident to stop fizzing in the dish. I looked out the window at the lightning bugs playing in the first dark. A little sliver of moon was cresting over the dark line of trees in the field behind the house. And then here comes Baby Girl, riding that moon like a rocking horse, saying, saying, saying my name.

I say, *Baby Girl, ain't you taken enough skin off my hide?* And she just laughs that little laugh of hers and keeps on saying it, saying my name. And that's when it came to me, rolling like thunder over flat land.

There was this one child at St. Vincent's didn't have good sense. He was big, four or five years old, but he still wore a diaper and stayed in this old playpen parked in the corner. He played there all day and slept there all night, not causing anybody any trouble. It was like he knew he was too big a baby and needed to be specially good or he'd get shipped up to Baton Rouge and end up in one of those places for the feeble-minded.

Then one day he got to fooling around in his dirty diaper. After that, every morning I'd put these big old rubber britches on him, but somehow or other—you could count on it—he'd get into his pants and get to fooling around. It gave him a truckload of pleasure. Always had a big smile on his face when we caught him at it, gave new meaning to the expression shit-eating grin.

So that was the job of work I'd set out to do, been *told* to do by those white girls. That's why it took me so long to get back to Baby Girl. This other one had gone and dirtied up his pants and smeared it all over his face, looked like one of those blackface minstrel singers back in the day. The fix he was in! I had to scrub him up with a wet cloth and change the diapers, the clothes, wipe down the playpen. Then take all his mess to the laundry to boot. He kicked and carried on while I cleaned him up. I had to grab his legs and wrestle him down. Not one of those white girls helped me. I remember wondering what was going to happen when he got bigger and stronger. I hoped I'd be history at that place by then, which in fact turned out to be true since that was the very moment Baby Girl went under and drowned herself.

I got out of jail finally, on February 1 of 1986, just a few days after that spaceship exploded in the sky down in Florida and that teacher lady and the others got blown to bits and all the pieces fell into the deep blue sea. That morning us girls who'd stayed clean got to watch the launch on TV, which was a special privilege. I'd studied up best I could on space and galaxies and stars while I was getting ready for my GED. My schoolbooks were old castoffs my Cleve had sent me, but I learned about time and space and how the light we see from the stars is billions of years old by the time it gets to us. How it's time we're looking at when we watch the stars, time and light and deep space.

I was so worked up over getting to watch the *Challenger* I got up at four in the morning just to be wide awake before the dawning of that new day. That night I dreamed my cell was one of those capsules they seal you up in and I was the schoolteacher lady getting blasted up into the great beyond. I was the one seeing our pretty little planet turning, turning from way up there, relaxing in my capsule like it was my easy chair back home, taking it all in. I stood behind the other girls while we watched, too thrilled to sit. When the whole thing blew up like a firecracker on the Fourth of July and made those two terrible plumes of fire, I felt like I was seeing my own life, starting off with Cleveland and the children, so happy and proud and hopeful, and then busting up right before my very eyes. *I* was the one whose pieces went every which way, a blasted duck over the cold dark pond of the world, all my loved ones watching.

By the time I got out of jail, I felt old as Methuselah. A thousand years old and just plain tuckered out. All those years they had me working the kitchen, cooking up grits and stews and beans in big pots, nasty stuff some of it. I would give myself little pep talks. I would say, *Ed Mae, girl, better to be peeling potatoes and picking weevils out of the flour than mopping floors and going from cell to cell, all kinds of meanness locked up inside, all kinds of ugly words troubling the air, mopping up other folks' filth.* Still and all, day in day out all those long slow years, the cooking wore me plumb out. You didn't get done with breakfast before you had to turn right around and start on the dinner and then the supper. I was on my feet from five in the morning till six at night, seven days a week. My legs swelled and my feet, they about killed me, burning and stinging like I'd been walking on hot coals. At night I had to hang my feet over the edge of my bunk, couldn't bear to touch my heels to the hard mattress. I had to bunch up my extra uniform under my ankles to get relief, turn my socks inside out to get the softest part. Over the years my hands and arms got all covered in scars from the burns. It's a hard thing, handling big pots, ladling and pouring. Stirring grits when they're boiling and splattering all over the stove. Folks hollering at you to hurry up and get the food on the table. Folks talking ugly about your cooking. Try it sometime.

I was the only one the guards trusted with a knife, why I don't know, I'd have liked to have chopped them all to bits some days. It was mainly because of the onions that I needed the knife, them and the gristly meat we got every now and again. I chopped every last onion served in that place, rivers of tears rolling down my cheeks. I got good at math. If you count the years I was in that kitchen (23) and then say 365 days to each year (8,395) and multiple that by 10 onions a day, why, that's 83,950 onions I chopped! Sometimes the knife wanted my hand to slip and slice the soft inside of my wrist. It whispered in my ear, *Why not? Why the hell not?* But I held the knife firm and steady. Top and bottom off first. Peel the skin and cut in half. Then chop into small bits, prison onions being tough and stringy. I wanted to live to see my Cleve and Mary outside that place. My story wasn't over, I'd say to myself, my story was just dragging its feet, poking along behind me, like Mary used to do in the grocery store. One day it would catch up, huffing and puffing, and tap me on the shoulder and say, *Here I am finally, live me! Hurry, before it's too late.*

Truth is, you live on the edge of the knife, then one day you slip and fall. When Baby Girl went down in that tub, I went down too. That blade sliced me in half. One half said, *Sorry, guilty, oh so guilty.* The other half said, *Those white girls, they made me do it, they made it happen.*

So the years crawled by and I paid out Baby Girl with every single one of those onions I chopped just right and, after a while, it wasn't about her, it was about people pointing fingers, saying this is black and white, guilty is black, guilty is forgetting. But I tell you, Baby Girl, it was complicated. You and me, we're on the same side of this. You and me, we're sisters.

When I finally got out, I was good for nothing. Shaky and creaky and looking for a good soft easy chair, an

RC Cola, and reruns of *The Jeffersons*. That was my idea of hog heaven.

When my Cleve came to pick me up, I fell into his arms like an old dog who'd been left on the side of the road to die and managed to find its way home. And here I'd been feeling right proud of myself. Here I'd gone and done my time and gotten my GED to boot, studied hard for it, memorizing the grammar part: *those* shoes, not *them shoes*; I *am*, you *are*, he she it *is*. If I could've shucked twenty years off my time, I'd have tried to go to college, better myself in the world. I would have studied the stars, got myself some science, maybe some job of work with those space people.

So it shamed me, the way I wilted and folded up like a box when Cleve's good strong arms snatched me up and held me tight, so tight I could hardly draw air. I'd used some of the money he sent to order myself a decent dress from the Sears & Roebuck catalog to wear that day. I wasn't going to look like trash. I'd studied holding my head high when I walked out that gate with the barbwire on top. I had a picture of myself in my head, brave and strong, coming out of the pit of hell, scarred and crippled, with a mouthful of rotten teeth and a pair of broken-down feet, but still alive and kicking. Still a woman.

But there he was, with his pretty Alita and their two twin boys, Joel and Jerome, and it was like Christmas except that I'd missed so many Christmases and those boys were too big. Billie Jones had been their real granny. Over the years she'd doted on them, bought them presents at Christmas, made them these good fruitcakes. She'd written me about the boys, how much they reminded her of Cleve. She sent me baby pictures, kindergarten graduation pictures, pictures of pretty picnics in the woods, everybody laughing and smiling. When I went to hug Cleve's boys, an extra granny all beat up by time, they looked sideways at me like I just flew in on a broomstick. But they let me hug them, run my hands over their precious faces, their wiry arms. They stood for it, but I could feel them pull back, fight the urge to run.

Time, that's what I saw when I looked at the four of them, the years and years I'd missed. Here I was coming at them from millions, billions of light-years in the past. All of them as strange to me as I was to them, even my Cleve, who didn't look like himself anymore. He'd turned into the spitting image of Cleveland, which made the hair stand up on the back of my neck. *Lord, Cleveland,* I thought, *here you are, landed back on this earth, a full-blooded man, all your pieces put back together, and here I am a dried-up old fool.*

"Don't want to be trouble," I said right off as we started our trip back to Nashville, where they lived.

"No trouble at all, ma'am." Alita was the first to say it. She was sitting in the back seat with the boys, had made a fuss about me sitting in the front so I could see the view. She leaned up next to me and giggled in my ear. "You can help me keep these three in line. We need another woman in this family. I'm tired of being the only one around here who can boil an egg."

Cleve looked over at me. "We're happy to have you, Mama, we've waited a long time. Right, boys?"

"Yes, sir," the boys said, which caused me to tear up.

So here we went, catty-cornering it out of Louisiana and then Mississippi. We traveled through swampland and then, spread out before me like a tabletop, was the pretty, pretty world. The cotton and soybeans rumpled and brown in the fields, farmland flat and rowed up as far as the eye could see. I'd looked at things close up for such a long time my eyes felt stretched like rubber bands to look out over that everlasting land. I looked and looked, but it was like I was seeing the world through smoky glass. I could make out shapes, though: the curve of the earth, the tilt down where the brown land met the gray sky.

The closer we got to Nashville the more excited I got. My Cleve, he's at a highfalutin college named after some rich white folks called Vanderbilt. He studies, of all things, lice. What you want to go studying lice for, I asked him when he visited me one time. He said they carry typhus and some fevers, they're nasty little bloodsuckers, people in poor countries die from them. I don't ask him if he remembers when he was in second grade and got sent home from school with lice. He cried and cried. *Mama, how'd I get lice? Negroes don't get lice.* Which is exactly what I'd said to the principal when he called for me to come get Cleve. *This little Negro does,* he'd replied, *and three more in his class.* I'd always kept Cleve clean as a whistle, so I was mortified and took the day off to get the medicine. While I washed that head of his, he was hollering, *Wash it harder, Mama, scrub with your fingernails.* After I rinsed it, he told me to wash it again, so I did. Then I combed and combed until every last one of those nasty nits was gone. I washed his sheets and towels in scalding water and then grabbed Mary, hollering and carrying on, and treated her too. Now Cleve's working on a vaccine to prevent the diseases lice cause, has a whole lab full of microscopes. His Alita is a foot doctor, which couldn't have been more perfect since my feet are a cross to bear. They live in a pretty two-story house with trees in front and back, and they have white neighbors, which I had trouble believing until I saw them going about their business, nodding to me and being friendly and nice, asking how I was doing, saying how nice it was to meet me.

Cleve and Alita had finished off one side of their garage for me. I had my own room and bathroom, and my own little color TV, so I could have my privacy and they could have theirs. At first I felt shy about going into the main part of the house when they were home. I slipped from room to room during the day when the boys were in school and Cleve and Alita were at work. After my cell, the place seemed like a palace. I would walk around and count my steps. From the guest bathroom to the kitchen was thirty-eight steps! From the kitchen to Joel's room upstairs was fifty-one! At first I never touched a single thing except *Jet* magazine, which I couldn't resist. I didn't turn on the big TV, afraid I'd break it. I didn't want to get in their way, you see, didn't want to end up being the creaky old ma'am who casts a dark cloud, makes everybody feel like they can't have a good time, can't be natural with each other.

So the weeks flew by. (Time is a strange thing. On the inside, one week had seemed like a year, one minute an afternoon.) I got used to the four of them and they got used to me, or at least I hope they did. Alita bought me a nice tweed coat and some warm sweat pants and sweaters. When I told them things looked blurry, they took me to the eye doctor and got me some specs. The doctor said nearsightedness was common in inmates. You get used to seeing only what's right in front of your face and the part of the eyes that makes you see far away gets lazy. One Saturday Alita took me to her pretty office downtown and made a mold of my knobby old feet and ordered me some orthotics for my shoes, which gave me a whole new lease on life. All of a sudden I was cooking supper for everybody, which I was happy to do to earn my keep, and soon I was going to Kroger with Alita and sometimes Cleve. I hadn't eaten a single fresh vegetable, unless you count onions, all those years in jail, and the mountains of carrots and collards and beet greens just about knocked my socks off. I loved the way the spray came showering down on them every now and again. It was like being in my own mother's little side-yard garden when I was a girl, snipping collards and mustards in the rain. Alita and Cleve and I gathered up the vegetables, and I cooked them in those little fold-up wire things and a deep pot called a wok. It was the joy of my life to put those pretty colors down on the table for the four of them.

Alita and me got into a little fuss just once, and it was about a mess of green beans. Green beans! She wanted me to steam them. She wouldn't let me snap them, wanted them whole, wanted them *crisp*. The fight happened right after I'd got there and was just starting up cooking for them.

I ask her why she was carrying on so about a mess of beans.

"It's clean eating," she says. "Cleve likes to eat clean food."

"All my food is clean," I say, which is a lie given what nasty stuff I had to cook up in prison. I add, "I've always washed my food," which is true.

Alita's standing in the kitchen holding the sack of beans in her hand. She looks down at the floor, a little smile playing at her mouth. "That's not what I mean. Clean food means there's no lard, no red meat, no butter, not much salt. You season with onions and garlic and spices to make it good, maybe a little olive oil."

"No red meat!" I say before I can stop myself. Here I'd been in jail for all these years thinking about ham and pork roast and meatloaf until my mouth watered. "What you talking about, child? I wouldn't be alive today, and Cleve wouldn't be neither without red meat! You put pork in green beans. Beans ain't beans without a piece of ham, a bit of bacon, a piece of pickled pork."

Alita sighs. "Miss Ed Mae, please." (She hadn't started calling me Mama yet.) "Cleve can't eat that kind of stuff. His cholesterol is up to 230. There's too much fat in his blood already. He could have a heart attack." Now she looks out the window and sighs again. "You got to promise me you won't go putting any of that stuff in his food."

I shake my head and stare her down. I'm thinking about how good a hambone is in beans, how, if you cook it long enough, the marrow will float to the top.

Alita doesn't say anything but she doesn't give me the beans either. I reach for them. She's taller than me and holds them high.

"No, ma'am," she says and now her voice turns. "Do you want your son to have a heart attack? Do you want him to die?"

There's only one answer to that question, so I say okay, all right, no ham, no pickled pork, no bacon, no nothing that makes beans beans, and she gives me the beans. "Slice an onion on top of them," she says. "That'll give them flavor."

The business about clean food cramped my style in the kitchen. I longed to fry up some chicken, make a nice brown chuck roast with carrots and potatoes, but I wanted more than anything to please Cleve and Alita, for them not ever to sit me down and say there was a "nice place" across town and they'd already put in a deposit.

Sometimes, though, I'd sneak into the kitchen before they got home from work and make the boys some cinnamon cookies the way I used to do for Cleve and Mary. I had to use olive oil instead of butter. (In that house, butter was scarce as snow in July!) The olive oil made the cookies swampy so I put in more sugar and vanilla to cover it. Those boys, they loved my cookies. Poor things, they never got any sweets at home. We'd hide a plate of them in the back of my closet so their mama and daddy weren't the wiser. As time went on, I'd have them cut out and ready on the cookie sheet when Jerome and Joel got home from school, tired and hungry the way boys get in the late afternoon. They'd sit down at the kitchen table while we waited for the cookies to bake. They'd chat me up about basketball or how this one or that one saw another one doing something, and some afternoons we'd get the plate of hot cookies and head out into my garage room and watch reruns of *The Jeffersons*, which are a hoot.

Those sweet boys never once asked me what I'd gone and done to get myself thrown in jail. Maybe Cleve told them, I don't know. I never did because the words for it never came to me. I was wool-gathering and forgot to remember Baby Girl, that's what it boiled down to. But the words, they stuck in my craw like gristle. And shame on me for not spitting them out, not owning my crime. I wanted those boys to know how life can turn on a dime, on one second, one mistake the size of an ant, as simple a thing as forgetting to brush your teeth in the morning. I wanted them to be careful, be watchful. I wanted to tell them it can be light-years from forgetting to remembering, they needed to remember everything. But what kind of thing would that have been to say to two black boys? They had double, triple the trouble coming down the pike at them, I don't care what decade it was or what fancy schools they went to. All they had to do to get into Trouble with a capital T was walk down the street. I'd heard Cleve talk to them about being black men. I'd seen Alita go through their drawers and throw away their sweat shirts with hoods.

So the five of us, we went along like that, and it got better and better. Alita and me, we get along just fine now. She's a sweet thing, finally started calling me Mama Ed Mae. She told me she'd lost her own mother when she was five and living in Atlanta. She didn't say how, but Cleve told me her mother had left her and her little brother with an aunt one Friday morning in October and headed for the Piggly Wiggly, then never came back to get them, which made no sense; Alita's mother would have cut off her arm for the two of them, she'd never in a million years have left her babies. What was left of her was found in the next county a month later, out in the woods under a pile of leaves. When Cleve told me the story of Alita's mother, I thought, *And now this too, what a mess of a world this is.* Even if nobody forgets anybody, even if you're doing everything right as rain, even if you're just going to the Piggly Wiggly, you're still not safe. Tunnels collapse, good people die, nobody pays, and the planet goes on its merry way, turning and turning through the night sky.

Every now and again, Alita will get tight-lipped. She'll snap at me, tell me *she* wants to cook, why doesn't *she* ever get to cook. When she acts that way I know she's talking to me the way she'd talk to her own mother, with no fear or worry that I wouldn't love her if she acted up. I'm gentle with her, just say, sure thing, honey. I slip off my apron and head for the hills, maybe take a little walk, maybe go sit in the backyard and read the evening paper or just go back into my little apartment and watch the news. After a while, she'll call us in to supper (not as good as mine would have been) and be all smiles, like nothing ever happened.

The first Christmas after I got out, Billie Jones and my Mary and her girl, Kenyatta, named after this African freedom fighter, came in from Atlanta. Sad to say, I wouldn't have known my own girl if I'd tripped over her in the street. Dressed to kill in one of those

African wraparound getups, fresh braids and hoops the size of oranges in her ears. She hugged me over and over again, and little Kenyatta grabbed me around my hips and held on like I was a tree she was getting ready to climb.

Billie Jones bunked in with me and that first night in bed we lay there in the dark and talked old times. Billie was fit as a fiddle, and thanked me for leaving her my children. "They made my life worth living," she said, a catch in her voice. "I can't think what I would have done without them."

When Billie Jones said what she said, I couldn't find my tongue. Is that why Baby Girl had to die? So Billie Jones could be happy? Why couldn't Baby Girl have been happy too, got her lip fixed, got taken by some good people? Have her life too? Then I could have had mine and my babies could have had their very own flesh-and-blood mother, not some Billie-come-lately substitute. And Baby Girl's playful spirit, the pleasure she took in her little life, splashing water, giggling, where did all that go? Poor Cleveland, doing what he'd been told, following orders like a good soldier, then getting blown up in that tunnel, no point to it, no rhyme or reason, no gathering up of the pieces, nothing left to remember him by but a stinking flag. Where is he now? I have my doubts about heaven or hell, but one thing I know for sure: the departed don't just up and vanish like smoke. They can't. They got to stay until they get sick and tired of watching the living having all their fine times. They got to stay as long as somebody remembers them, as long as somebody won't stop thinking them up. Cleve and Mary will always remember Cleveland, he was their daddy and they knew him deep in the blood. But Baby Girl, who will remember her once I'm gone? I was the one what named her, which is something a mother does, but I wasn't her mother, wasn't even a good nursemaid. I named her, then I clear forgot her. Which got me thrown in jail, which made Billie Jones's life worth living. What a joke!

I throw a look to kill in Billie's direction, wanting to slap her face for taking her happiness from me and Baby Girl. But I don't say a mumbling word. I'm in Billie Jones's debt for life. You won't hear a word against her coming out of this mouth.

I'd been dying to see my Mary. Cleve had told me she was divorced and delivering the U.S. mail. Billie Jones, who just had to be taking care of somebody else's children, had moved to Atlanta to take care of Kenyatta. "You know how I used to love looking into people's windows?" Mary said. "Well, delivering the mail, it's kind of like that. I make up stories about people's lives by their mail. When I put the letters in the box, I say to myself, 'Here's some good news about that college he wants to go to' or 'This one says a sister or brother is sorry to ask but needs fifty dollars.'" She grinned. My Mary was doing all right, and little Kenyatta said she wants to be a doctor of all things. I told her when she got out, she could doctor all of me except for my feet, which I'd reserved for Alita, I still owed her for my orthotics, and this made everybody laugh like crazy.

So the years have rolled on by. Kenyatta's a doctor now, a heart doctor who puts in stents. Joel and Jerome acted up in high school, both of them did, and about drove us all crazy doing dumb stuff, but they got into the University of Tennessee and have done all right. Better than all right. Joel's in real estate and Jerome is a science teacher in Wilmington, North Carolina, right on the coast. We all visited him in his condo on the beach and I got to see the Atlantic Ocean for the first time and walk along the sand at night and look up at the stars. There was a full moon the last night I was there. I couldn't get enough of that moon. I sat on Jerome's deck till dawn, watching it move across the sky. He loves the ocean and thinks he may go back to school so he can study starfish, of all things. He calls them by their Latin name, *Asterias rubens,* says he loves their musculature, the way they wrap themselves around rocks and shells. I call Mary every Saturday. She tells me she's getting carpel tunnel from putting people's mail in their boxes and is applying to work inside the post office. She can pick her poison, I say, she's got her mother's feet and if she stands on them eight hours a day, they are going to end up looking like roadkill and feeling worse.

I have a hobby now, stargazing. There are some folks, like my Cleve and his Jerome, who like to look close up, who like to see into the life of things. I'm one for looking far out. On the inside, I used to read about the planets and solar systems and galaxies. I followed the charts and graphs in the science books they gave us to study for the GED. I know Saturn has sixty-two moons and rings. I know the difference between a planet and a star. I know about the Big Bang and black holes. Our cell didn't have a window, but I drew the planets of our solar system on the wall over my bunk. The constellations Ursa Major, the Great Bear, and Ursa Minor, the Little Bear with his long tail, pointing the way home. Sometimes I dreamed I was traveling in my little space capsule from star to star, galaxy to galaxy, making light-years seem like minutes, like seconds. I drew charts and graphs from the books I read. Jupiter to the west, ringed Saturn in the east, Polaris the great North Star, Leo the Lion, explosions and collisions and comets galore. Our puny galaxy, the Milky Way, a few grains of sand.

I talked stars so much that Cleve gave me a telescope with a stand I can set up in the backyard. So at night now, I toddle out and stargaze like nobody's business. I love the way the sky wraps around me like a blanket. If I had another life, and who knows, maybe I do, I'd want to be an astronaut. Just imagine it, being up there and looking back on our measly little planet, then, oh, outward to the great mystery!

It's November right now, and I can't take my eyes off Andromeda in the northern sky. Rings of fire! A giant spiral spinning its way through the universe, busy and pretty, over two million light-years away. Andromeda, poor thing, she was stripped naked and chained to a rock by the sea, rescued in the nick of time by her husband-to-be, just before the sea came crashing in over her. How scared she must have been! What if he hadn't come?

I'm moving slow now, but Cleve and Alita and me, we're doing all right, eating our clean food, all thrilled to the teeth about Barack Obama. Now that it's election season, we watch the news every night. We have our schedule. At six they hurry in. I have supper on, and we watch the first thirty minutes of *PBS News-Hour with Jim Lehrer* while the supper heats up and we have our wine. (Cleve says a glass or two is good for you, so I've developed a taste for it, look forward to my two glasses of pinot noir, maybe three if there's something to celebrate.) Then we switch to Anderson Cooper on CNN. Around nine o'clock we wrap things up with Rachel Maddow, who's new on TV but already my all-time favorite and who I can tell loves Barack as much as we do. Somewhere in there we eat our supper in our laps, not wanting to miss a second about Barack doing this or that.

Cleve had to go through a whole bunch of rigmarole to get me a voting card because I'm a convicted felon. Convicted felon! What an ugly sound it has! How did he say, *My mother is a convicted felon*? Did he say she isn't a bad person, just forgetful? Just an old lady who wants to vote for Barack Obama?

We're all three on pins and needles. Cleve and Alita and me, we plan to vote the Saturday before Election Day, but when I wake up that Saturday morning, I have to run to the bathroom and upchuck and then I'm too dizzy to do anything but get back under the covers.

They've got to go to work on Election Day and want to run home right afterward to catch the first of the returns, so I tell them I'll get a ride to the polls. The Democrats will send somebody to drive an old black lady like me, somebody who remembers Rosa on the bus and Martin on the balcony and Colored Day at Audubon Park Zoo.

The next morning, Sunday, I'm feeling fine, just a little weak in the knees. Alita and Cleve head down to Democratic headquarters to call folks to remind them to vote. When they come home, they've got me a ride to the polls. The lady what's going to fetch me will call Monday to get directions. On her way out the door Monday morning Alita hands me a piece of paper with a name and phone number and says, "If she doesn't call by early afternoon, you call her."

On Monday morning, just when I'm starting in on my second cup of coffee, which I make strong enough to walk out the door after pouring out that watery stuff of Alita's, the phone rings and a woman asks to speak to me.

"Speaking," I say.

"Are you the lady who needs a ride to the polls to-morrow?" I can tell by her voice she's a white woman, or at least I think she's white. Her voice has an odd way about it, like it's fighting with itself.

"Yes, I am, much obliged," I say. Here I am, I think, getting driven to the polls by a white woman (I think) to vote for a black president! What a world!

"Would afternoon be okay? I have to be in court in the morning."

A white lady lawyer! "Sure," I say. "What time should I be ready?"

"Around three? Is that too late?"

"No, ma'am," I say, and then I'm mad at myself for calling her ma'am. It's a hard thing to stop doing. On the inside the guards made us do it, even the white girls at St. Vincent's made us do it. When I was thirteen, I'd started cleaning houses after school. My mother had taught me to always say ma'am to white women, but to always cross my fingers when I said it. Much as I hated myself for doing it, every now and then a *ma'am* would pop out of my mouth like a sneeze you can't hold back. Cleve fussed at me whenever it slipped, said those days were long gone, I was a *senior*, folks should be ma'aming me, not the other way around.

The woman made it right by saying it back to me. "All right, then, ma'am. I've got your address and the people down at the Democratic headquarters gave me directions from the house to your polling place. I'll see you around three tomorrow."

"Much obliged," I said.

"My pleasure."

When we hung up, I went back into my room and started looking over my clothes. I wanted to wear something special, a nice outfit. These days I spend my life in sweat pants, which just wouldn't do. I pulled out the navy blue pants suit Alita got me on sale at Dillard's. She'd hemmed it once, and then, after I spread out a few years later, hemmed it again. It was nothing to jump up and down about. (I sincerely hope they don't bury me in it. I'd hate to think of going through eternity in navy blue, which is about my least favorite color in the world.) Then I went looking in my closet for that watermelon pink blouse Kenyatta had given me a couple of Christmases back. She'd said she thought it would brighten up my wardrobe. What a hoot, somebody wanting to brighten up my wardrobe! It seemed too loud for an old lady, and, between you and me, I'd never worn it. But it hit me that it would be the perfect thing to put some kick into that dull-as-dishwater navy suit. I sat down on the bed and pulled off my sweat shirt and sweat pants. I looked down at my old legs, veiny and spotted and ashy with dryness. They looked so worn out I wondered how they even held me up anymore. And my bosoms under my undershirt! They bagged and sagged like last week's balloons.

I put on the navy pants first, wanting to get those legs out of sight as quick as I could. When I pulled them up, I wished Alita had gotten an elastic waist. I hated anything binding my middle, which had gotten bigger as the years had rolled by. The waist was okay when I stood up but it about cut me in half when I sat down. I unbuttoned the button above the zipper and that helped some.

Next I put on the pink shirt, which had a nice bow tie, and fitted just fine. Then the suit coat. The arms were long, so I rolled them up, showing the striped lining, which I thought looked stylish.

When I had the whole getup on, I pulled my black New Balances out of the closet. They looked like overgrown roaches, but there was no getting around in anything else, though I'd have liked to wear a nice pair of shoes, some low-heel pumps, but those days were long gone. I put my inserts into the New Balances and put them on.

I went back through the living room into Alita and Cleve's bedroom where there was a full-length mirror. I didn't look half bad. In fact, with rouge and lipstick and some hair mayo, I thought I'd be getting toward passable.

The bow tie on the blouse was wrinkled so I took the iron out from the pantry, set it on the stove, and plugged it in. I took off the blouse, put a cup towel on the kitchen counter and stretched the tie out on it, holding the blouse while the iron heated up. Then I pressed the tie, real light so it didn't scorch, and turned off the iron, unplugged it, and put it back on the stove. I was always real careful with that iron.

By the time I'd hung everything back up in my closet and changed back into my sweat pants, it was four o'clock, time to start fixing supper. I'd forgotten to eat my turkey sandwich or watch National Geographic or do any of the little things I do during the day. I'd planned a special supper, a good spaghetti sauce, but that took time to simmer and here I'd gone and I'd frittered away the day. So I decided to pull out a pan of leftover whole wheat, vegetarian, soy cheese (what else?) lasagna from the freezer and start warming it up in the oven. I'd make a little salad and that would be that. Save the sauce for tomorrow morning. Tomorrow night we were having company to watch the election returns. My friend Grace next door and her sister June. Cleve and Alita and me had been mighty glad when June showed up to take care of Grace, even if she did bring a pack of barking dogs with her. By the time June got here, Grace's arms and legs were sticks and there were train tracks in her face. Something sad there, something hard.

She'd started walking up and down the street in her nightgown. Said she was looking for a bird, some kind of parrot.

Yesterday June took her for a walk by our house. I was outside getting the mail, enjoying the crisp fall air, the pretty leaves under my feet. "Cleveland's mother," Grace called, pulling her sweater down at the shoulder. "Look how my sister is patching me up." Sure enough she had a little patch on her shoulder, some medicine for the Alzheimer's. It looked like a square Band-Aid.

Grace scratched at the patch. "It bites," she declared and started to pull it off.

June took hold of her hand and pulled her sweater back up.

"See the nubs, all fuzzy like antlers," she said to June, pointing at her shoulders. "They're coming out now. Look!"

"I'm looking," said June and turned her around to go back home.

"Cleveland's mother," she called back to me, "have I grown wings?"

"Sure do look like it, honey," I called back to her.

Alzheimer's has got to be the meanest joke God ever thought up.

The morning of the election I woke up early so I could take a shower before Cleve and Alita left for work. They don't like me bathing when they aren't in the house, say I might fall and break a hip and lay there all day, cold and naked as a jaybird. Alita bought me a pair of Crocs to wear in the shower so I won't slip.

That girl, she watches over me like I'm her own mother. Sometimes she'll sit by me on the couch and hold my hand. I'll look down and see my wrinkled old fingers with the knuckles like walnuts peeking out from her soft-as-velvet fingers, and I think about my little Mary, how she used to want me to hold her hand while she nodded off. How sometimes I'd be so tuckered out I'd fall dead asleep, sitting straight up on her bed, my head drooping over like a sunflower. Some nights I'd just slide down right next to her, in that twin bed of hers, still holding that little hand. I'd wake up in the morning feeling her heat next to me, thinking my Cleveland had finally come on home.

Election morning I spent in my brunch coat so as not to get my going-to-vote clothes messed up. I started the sauce, canned tomatoes and onions and garlic and peppers and black olives and carrots (I don't much like carrots but Cleve insists on them, says they're good for my eyes). My secret ingredient was anchovies, which Alita approved of because they were full of good fish oil. The trick to the sauce was cooking it all day. After I got it going, I started in on myself. I oiled my hair and pulled it back and put some bobby pins in it to make it lay down flat on the sides. I put on my pearl bobs that pinched and creamed my face good so the rouge wouldn't cake. After the rouge, I drew myself some perky eyebrows. I held back on the lipstick, for worry it'd stain the blouse.

By this time it was two and I still hadn't put a bite in my mouth. I was so excited that I wasn't a bit peckish, but I didn't want to get light-headed so I went into the kitchen and put on an apron so as not to mess up my outfit and made a peanut butter sandwich, no jelly, which has a tendency to drip. I ate it standing up so I wouldn't get crumbs on myself. I drank some water, sloshed it around in my mouth, and went back to the bathroom to check my teeth, which looked all right, and used the toilet one last time.

I got out my purse and my wallet. I made sure my voter card was right there on top. My heart was galloping along like a wild horse, so I sat down and collected myself for a minute. Lipstick! I went back to the bathroom and put it on, a nice shade of peach that went with my coloring.

But the hair, it still wasn't behaving. In the past year, it had thinned out and now it was coming out of the pins, and I could see that all the hair mayo in the world wasn't going to amount to a hill of beans. So I thought about my most prized possession except for my wedding ring—my mother's hat, which was in a nice box at the top of my closet. Billie Jones saved it for me, I'll give her that. I got the stool from the kitchen and put it in the closet and fumbled for the hat in the box and popped it on my head. It was a loud thing, green and orange feathers on the top and soft brown wraparound feathers that cupped the sides of my head. Mama had bought it off a lady who was down on her luck. It clashed with my Kenyatta blouse, but beggars can't be choosers.

It's a quarter to three by this time, and suddenly I remember the sauce. Here I am about to go and forget it and burn the house down! So I hobble back into the kitchen, open the top to stir it one last time, lift the lid, and damnation! It boils up and splatters the lapel on my navy blue jacket! I go to the sink, get the dishcloth, and try to scrub it off but the anchovy oil leaves a big shiny stain, right there in front where you can see it. What a mess! I hurry back to my room and look around in my top drawer for something to cover it, a scarf, anything. I look among some of the small boxes I keep my jewelry in and come up with a brooch Mary gave me a while back. It's got rhinestones galore and she gave it to me because it's in the shape of a star. I hurry to the bathroom (by now I need to go again) and sit down on the commode and put on the brooch. (Alita would say I'm multitasking.) The brooch almost covers the stain. It's the best I can do. When I get up, I check my teeth one last time and pin the hat to my head with the long hat pin Mama kept on the inside band.

Just then the doorbell rings. When I open the door, I'm blinded by the afternoon sun behind the woman standing there. In that light, I can't see her features, in fact she looks like she lost her face. I take a step back, squint up at her.

"Mrs. Johnson?" she says. "I'm Josie." She takes a step forward, has one foot inside the front door, pushy in my opinion. Now that she's out of the light I can see she's no spring chicken, looks at least forty-five. Her hair is long, dark, and wavy, her mouth pinched a little on one side, like a drawstring purse. She reminds me of somebody, but I can't place who.

Then she smiles a big toothy smile. "Are we ready to go vote for the next President of the United States, Barack Obama?"

"I been ready ever since I was born," I say. "Let me get my bag and cane." I use a cane when I go out now, Cleve's orders.

She stands in the foyer looking around at the house. Is she surprised I live in a nice house like this, not some dump? Was she expecting to pick up some old sad-sack black lady in sweat pants? Ha! She's probably wondering why my own people aren't taking me to vote, maybe she's thinking I'm the maid.

"Much obliged for getting me," I say. "My son's teaching at the university and my daughter-in-law's a doctor, and they're working. I was going to go with them to vote on Saturday but I got sick." I want her to know what quality of folk she's dealing with.

She nods. "Happy to do it. We need every vote we can get, right?"

So we get into the car and head out.

"Josie. That's a pretty name. An old-fashioned name." I feel obliged to make conversation. This lady's come all the way across town to take me to the polls. The least I can do is be polite.

"Short for Josephine. I was named for my mother's grandmother."

"Where your people come from?"

"New Orleans. My mama and daddy grew up in the City," she says, taking a corner too fast in my opinion.

Oh Lord, I think. And here's one who saw the light. I say, "Where in New Orleans?"

"Over on Prieur. Near Charity Hospital. My daddy was an ambulance driver." She glances over at me.

Charity Hospital. All of a sudden I feel light-headed. That Baby Girl! She's got her nerve, coming back on me just when I'm having such a nice day. *Don't forget me*, she always says when she pops in, *don't leave me behind*. She was born at Charity, the nurse what brought her had told me. *When's your story going to be over, Baby Girl?* I say back, though I know the answer to that question. Baby Girl's story will be over when I'm six feet under, and not a minute before.

We're pulling into the school parking lot when this Josie turns and looks at my hat like it's an animal that snuck its way into her car. "Are those feathers real?"

"What feathers?" I say.

"The ones on your hat."

I touch my head. I'd forgotten about the hat. "I think they're real feathers."

She frowns. "Using feathers from exotic birds is against the law."

"It was my mother's. She got it secondhand. I think these are old crow feathers that got dyed." I pat the sides of the hat where the feathers cup my head.

Josie nods like that explains everything. She's making up a story in her head about a black lady working for a white lady with a fancy hat. The white lady gets tired of the thing, says here, Emma or Essie or whoever, you can have my old hat with the stained headband. The feathers, they're the white lady's doing, not mine, not my mother's.

"My mama paid good money for this hat," I blurt out. "It's the only thing of hers I got left."

She looks over at me and something shifts in her face. "It must be nice to have something pretty of your mother's. It's just that I love birds."

Then we see the voting signs, and she pulls into the parking lot of Jacobs Elementary. She parks the car, then looks around. There's a big sign over in a corner that says: "Handicapped voting this way." She starts the car up again, backs up.

"What are you doing?" I ask. I'd been working the door handle, fixing to get out.

"I'll take you over there, to the handicapped voting." She points. "They'll bring the ballot to you. You won't even have to get out of the car."

I raise myself up in my seat and turn around to glare at her. "I'm not *handicapped*."

She throws a look at my cane, which I've got firm in my hand.

"Just because somebody uses a cane doesn't mean they're handicapped," I say, trying not to sound aggravated. "I want to go inside the voting place to vote."

Josie glances at her watch. "But look at that line. Don't you think it'd be a lot easier not to have to stand in line?"

"Easier isn't better," I say. "This one's walking in on her own two feet. I got dressed proper for this and I'm not sitting in your car or anybody else's to vote. I bet they don't even count the handicapped votes."

Josie snorts. "I'd like to see that. I'm a lawyer. I work for the ACLU, and I'd be after them like white on rice." Something in the way she says it makes me look at her again.

"A lawyer? Where'd you go to school?"

"I got my undergrad degree from Fisk. Went to Howard for the law."

"Howard?"

"My mama and daddy were Creole. Everybody thinks I'm white." She throws the words over her shoulder as she gets out of the car, like the difference between black and white doesn't amount to a hill of beans.

She comes around to my door and opens it. She puts out her hand. I ignore it, put my cane down on the cement, and push myself up on the door handle.

We head for the line. It parts like the Sea of Galilee, everybody stepping aside and nodding and smiling. I don't want special treatment, but by this point I'm glad to get a little of it.

I get pushed up to the front of the line and show my card to the white man behind the table. He looks at it and gets a funny look in his eye, like he knows something the rest of us don't. He looks down at his book and finds my name. Then he gets up and walks over to another white man who's standing under a sign that says "Poll Watchers." That man goes to a table and types something into a computer. We wait. After a while the man at the computer gets up and walks over to the man behind the table. The two of them whisper to each other.

Josie slides her hand under my elbow. She watches their every move. "What's the problem?" she says, loud enough for everybody to hear. "We don't have all day."

The second man, the poll watcher, comes back over. "I'm sorry, ma'am," he says, "you'll have to cast a provisional ballot since you're a *convicted felon,* and we'll have to verify your card."

He says the words loud. Real loud. I'm mad now. I think, *Baby Girl, get on out of here, just let me have this one measly day of my life.* People around me are sucking their teeth and looking at the floor.

Josie grabs my hand and about squeezes the life out of it. "She has a bona fide voter's card. You can't keep her from voting and you can't give her a provisional ballot." She whips out her phone, her hair flying. "I'm calling Democratic headquarters right now, and we'll get a lawyer out here quicker than you can say Obama. Meanwhile, since I'm a lawyer myself, I'll hold the fort." She grins this evil grin, and with that wild head of hair, she looks exactly like a witch.

I say, "I got this card fair and square. My son is *Dr.* Cleveland Johnson, and he got it for me. I may be a convicted felon but I didn't mean to forget Baby Girl."

Josie says, "It doesn't matter what she did or didn't do. She has a card and it's good for this election and we're going to vote in this election unless you're going to wrestle down two very nice women, one of them a disabled senior citizen, right here in front of everybody, in which case we'll sue you and win." Her eyes are slits, she looks like she's grown half a foot.

So the white man stood down and we got my ballot, a regular one, not a provisional one, and Josie came into my little box to help me vote. It was the first time in my life I'd voted so I figured I could use some help. She said why not vote the straight Democratic ticket, but I said no, I wanted to put my mark on the line by

Barack Obama, and then I'd consider the other can-
didates. So that's what I did, and then she voted the
straight ticket, which took no time at all, and finally
we swept out of there like Cleopatra and the Queen of
Sheba, past the white man poll watcher and his bud-
dies, past the check-in line on the inside and the line
that had formed on the outside. Past it all, Josie and
me, and by then we were tight as ticks. I was Andromeda and I'd been near drowning and she'd come
to rescue me, and I'd sure enough have done the same
for her, and who knows, if what goes around comes
around, maybe someday I will. Now Barack was going
to win, not in Tennessee, but in lots of other places,
and he was going to be our President with a capital
P, and, Baby Girl or no Baby Girl, it wasn't going
to happen out there in the future, but now, right this
very minute, while I was still alive and kicking.

Josie and I make our way home in the five o'clock
traffic. We don't say much, but there is something
between us, an afterlife of all that's past, a mystery.
It's perched on the seat between us, like a little child.
I don't know this white black girl from a hole in the
wall, but something about the tilt of her head, the
pucker around her mouth, makes me want to tell her
about how what happened with Baby Girl was about

time, how me and Baby Girl, we were two fiery comets flashing through the great night sky. Heat lightning, that's what we looked like from here below. We collided, and Baby Girl, she went down in a blaze so pretty it's made me hold my breath for the rest of my days. A falling star, that's what she was.

I look in the side mirror and see old sun dropping in the sky like an egg yolk to the skillet. I'm thinking I like this Josie. I'm thinking it would be nice if she came inside for some pinot noir and a plate of my good spaghetti and sat down and watched the election returns on CNN with me and Cleve and Alita and Grace and June. And who knows, maybe she'll say yes to my invitation, maybe the six of us will stay up all night and get tipsy when Barack wins.

I think now in terms of light-years. How our puny little lives take hold of time and hitch a ride out to the farthest ledges of the universe. How what we did today—our puny little business on this sweet earth— won't be seen for billions of years by the folks on those planets in the Andromeda spiral, and maybe not then if they don't remember to look out for us. How what happened with Baby Girl hasn't even happened yet.

There's a dark energy pushing things along, stellar explosions and supernovae, black holes, dormant and active. We all burn, shapely and bright, in space and time.

I'm thinking that even if we all drop stone-cold dead tonight, there'll always be a tomorrow somewhere, flying out there ahead of us.

Acknowledgments

No book is written in a vacuum, and for *The Accidentals*, this has been particularly true. The support I've received in the making of this book has been nothing short of phenomenal.

There aren't many editors—or anyone else—who will stand shivering in the frosty air of a busy New York street corner at nine o'clock the Saturday morning before Christmas to discuss anything with anyone, much less book revisions. Heartfelt thanks to Carrie Feron for her beyond-the-pale commitment to my writing. And before *The Accidentals* flew Carrie's way, Jane von Mehren made this book possible by agreeing to represent it and offered wise and invaluable suggestions in helping me shape an early draft.

Some very talented individuals have generously given extensive time and energy to this book. My deepest appreciation to George Bishop, Rebecca Mark, Julie Mars, Anne Raeff, Margaret Randall, and Linda Wagner-Martin.

As always, I owe a mountain of gratitude to Jill Mc-Corkle for her unwavering support of my writing from the very first. I also thank Elizabeth Spencer, whose no-nonsense enthusiasm for my work has been a shot in the arm on days when I needed it most.

Some of my most important moments in the conceptualization of this book came at the University of New Mexico Writers' Conference in Taos and Santa Fe. I appreciate the encouragement and comradery from that writing community, especially Jonis Agee, Pam Houston, Jesse Lee Kercheval, Debra Monroe, Sharon Warner, and Summer Wood. I owe a special debt of gratitude to Sharon for inviting me over the years to lead a variety of writing workshops, whose talented participants taught me at least as much as I taught them.

My thanks also for encouragement and commentary go to my colleagues and friends in the writing, scholarly, and teaching community at UNC: Bill Andrews, Gaby Calvocoressi, James Coleman, Pam Durban, Karen Booth, Elyse Crystall, María DeGuzmán, Stephanie

Elizondo Griest, Ed Fisher, Rebecka Rutledge Fisher, Marianne Gingher, Laura Halperin, Fred Hobson, Jennifer Ho, Heidi Kim, Randall Kenan, Susan Irons, Lori Ostlund (at UNC for an all-too-brief two years), Ariana Vigil, Alan Shapiro, and Linda Wagner-Martin. I appreciate too the encouragement from my graduate students past and present at UNC, particularly Jameela Dallis, Gale Greenlee, Mary Alice Kirkpatrick, and Harry Thomas.

Thank you also to *Southern Cultures* for publishing "The Girl Who Went Away," taken from one of Grace's chapters.

Far-flung friends and family members too numerous to name have been cheering me on these past nine years. Thanks especially to my cousins Jane and Linda Jane Barnette and to the remarkable Salvaggio clan. As always, my daughter and son-in-law, Carol Gwin and Shaun Leverton, top this very long list.

Thanks to the incredible production staff at William Morrow/HarperCollins, especially copy editor Kim Lewis, whose scrutiny of the novel's half-century time line saved me from more missteps than I'd care to admit.

Animals abound in *The Accidentals*, so it seems appropriate to thank my cats Violet and Pumpkin, who prostrated themselves on either sides of my laptop, providing the most comfortable of armrests, while hoping against hope that an accidental would fly off the screen and into their clutches.

Finally, this book is dedicated to Ruth Salvaggio, who showed me the giraffes one beautiful morning in New Orleans and who later read and commented on more pieces more times than either of us can count, bringing an intelligence and attentiveness to nuance that shine through what is best in these pages.

THE NEW LUXURY IN READING

We hope you enjoyed reading
our new, comfortable print size and found it
an experience you would like to repeat.

Well – you're in luck!

HarperLuxe offers the finest in fiction and
nonfiction books in this same larger print size and
paperback format. Light and easy to read, HarperLuxe
paperbacks are for book lovers who want to see
what they are reading without the strain.

For a full listing of titles and
new releases to come, please visit our website:

www.HarperLuxe.com

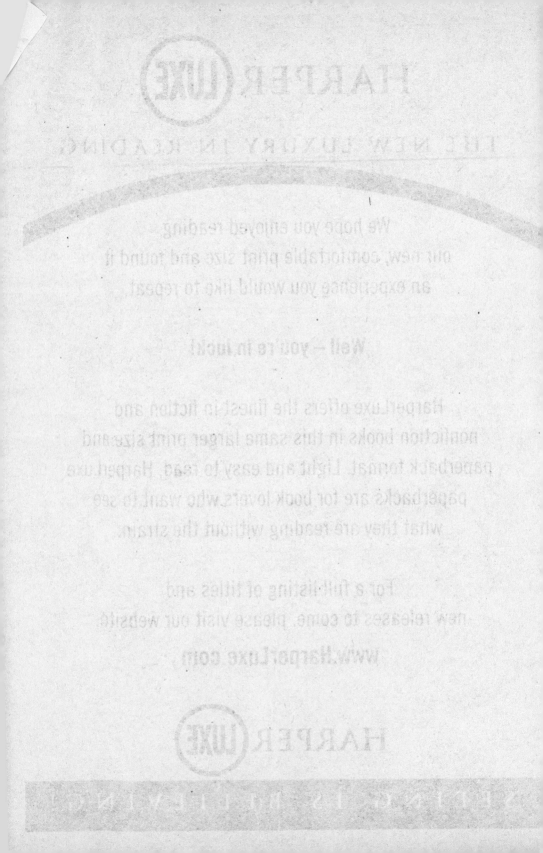